AF581980

TITLES BY OX DEVERE

Rage of the Jinn

The Devil's Eye

GORGONS

A THRILLER

OX DEVERE

This is a work of fiction. Unless otherwise indicated, all the names, characters, businesses, places, events and incidents in this book are either the product of the author's imagination or used in a fictitious manner.

ISBN: 979-8-9895424-4-4

for

Woman, Life, Freedom

Even if the night lingers long and late,

Even its darkness cannot endure for long.

Day will come, like a spring blazing bright,

And the world will glow like a gem.

FERDOWSI

CHAPTER ONE

SERIFOS, GREECE

On a sweltering Tuesday morning, they found the engravings of a man who never existed.

Dr. Nasrin Aslani had been up before dawn that day. She'd tied back her tawny mane, donned her lightweight pants, hiking shoes, and linen shirt, then taken her coffee out on the patio of the rental house.

The whitewashed homes of Kato Chora lay scattered to the outer banks of the island, where the Aegean Sea lapped at a crescent beach. As the sun swelled up over the horizon and the water began to glitter, Nas felt a prickle in her stomach.

Something was going to happen, soon. They would find *something* on this dig that would make all these months worth it. She thought it might not be today, or even tomorrow, but it would happen before they had to leave this island.

She had just finished her coffee as her father emerged with

a bowl of yogurt and fruit. Dr. Jamshid Aslani was sixty-four years old, a sultan of a man with thick black brows and a graying beard. He stood at her side and drew in a deep breath.

"The breeze at dawn has secrets to tell you—"

"Don't go back to sleep," she said, finishing the poem.

"I think today we find a treasure chest."

"No, a dragon's lair."

"Excalibur," he said.

"We maybe need to switch islands."

Whenever her father was starting to feel discouraged about a dig, he would offer up a list of fantastical ambitions for the day. He had done this even when she and her siblings were playing make-believe in their small home in Tehran. It had been a way of escaping the mundane during their life there.

A warm wind riffled her hair against her cheek.

Nas didn't offer her own feeling. For some reason she didn't know, she wanted to keep this one to herself.

Together, they packed their lunches and water bottles and drove to the dig site, winding north through the hills in their white Jeep Renegade.

Jamshid, casually known as "Jimmy," prided himself on being the first one on site each day. He was the Lead Archaeologist and the most senior member on the dig. On this team, however, there was one young excavator from Thessaloniki named Nik who seemed determined to beat father and daughter to it each morning.

He was there already that day when they reached the site, laying out his tools on a table. He always lined them up meticulously before beginning his work. His fussiness sometimes irritated the other excavators, but Nas found him brilliant to work with. He had exactly the type of painstaking fastidiousness that one would want in a coworker who was digging out and brushing off ancient ruins.

"Good morning, good morning," Nik greeted them in his thick Greek accent.

"Good morning it is," said Jimmy, setting their bags beneath the tent.

Nas touched his arm in greeting as she passed. "Morning, Nik. Take care of your babies there."

She looked out over their site.

It was the kind of wondrous mess of stone and dust that she lived for. There were pillars jutting up from deep beneath the earth, crumbling walls and toppled columns. Months before, they had realized that the strange settlement was in fact a palace.

As they uncovered a complex of workshops and storage rooms, shattered pottery and faded frescoes, Nas and Jimmy had become more and more excited. This could be the discovery of their lives.

Yet there was no record at all of this place ever existing. They had found nothing yet to indicate who had reigned here millennia ago. The style of architecture and art looked like a mix between Minoan and Mycenaean. They had been able to date some of the material to between 1500 and 2000 BC. Almost certainly, the palace had collapsed due to an earthquake, and been slowly buried over time by the winds and soil.

But they had yet to find the name of a single ruler who had once lived there.

For their team of thirty-two, the work had thrilling potential. They estimated the palace complex to be two or three times the size of what they had dug out so far. This discovery would take years to fully expose.

That morning, the sun seemed to rise with a vengeance. It grew hotter than any day that Nas could remember on the island. Her sweat mixed with dust as she bent over shattered urns and climbed up stone walls and assigned shifts for each of the team members throughout the grid.

She had just pulled off her boonie hat to wipe her brow when she heard Nik's voice—sharp and urgent—across the complex.

And that funny feeling in her stomach surged up again—Nik was working in the throne room today.

She scampered through the site as fast as she could, dancing over the rope grid and around excavation pits.

When she reached Nik, he was on his knees, digging furiously in front of a large stone slab that was just emerging from the earth.

"It's a stele!" he exclaimed.

Nas crouched down beside him as a few other members of the team began to gather around. Nik had already brushed clear the top of the stone piece, where parts of a few letters were visible. Ninety percent of it was surely still buried.

Nas glanced back at a few of the team members standing behind them.

"You have a trowel?" she asked, extending her hand to a young woman in capris.

The excavator fumbled it to her. Nas knelt in the dirt and began to dig alongside Nik.

The buzz rippled through the entire dig site. Nik and Nas were soon joined by two other excavators to hurry it along. Jimmy came to oversee, to marvel at the day's discovery. It was excruciatingly tempting to try to start reading the inscriptions with every level they uncovered, but Nas would not let them stop to do it. She wanted the entire thing at once.

They scraped and dug and brushed for two hours, until the entire five foot length of the stele was uncovered, until their clothes were damp with sweat.

Nas sat back on her heels, her eyes roving the ancient stone slab. Her father stepped up beside her, and bent over to peer at it.

"It's Linear B, I think..." said Jimmy.

"Please, B," said Nas.

Linear B was the script of the Mycenaeans. It had not been deciphered until 1952, when two British men, one an architect and one a self-taught linguist, had cracked the code.

Linear A was the older script of the Minoans. It had never been deciphered.

Jimmy squinted at the stele.

"Ah, it is Linear B!"

Nas grinned in relief. She beamed at her father, whose face had lit up.

He traced the carvings with a light hand. "This is—this is the stele of a king."

"Who?"

Jimmy scanned, reread, and mouthed quietly to himself for a moment.

"King Polydectes."

There was a silence of pure shock amongst the archaeologists.

Nik spoke first. "But Polydectes wasn't real."

Nas leaned toward the stele. "Baba, show me the name."

Jimmy pointed to a line at the top, a series of strange ancient letters.

"It is King Polydectes of Serifos."

Nas stood up and looked at her father, nearly gaping.

"He was a myth," said Jimmy, "only a myth..."

She put her hands on her head in disbelief. "We found our Excalibur, baba."

Jimmy had not taken his eyes off the stele, still murmuring to himself.

Then he froze, and in a strange, tight voice, said, "This is not just a traditional royal stele."

He looked up at Nas.

"Here—this word is 'Medusa.'"

CHAPTER TWO

WASHINGTON, D.C.

Booker Douglas shifted in a chair, tugging at the collar of his dress shirt. He didn't often wear ties. They made him feel like he was being choked by his own clothing.

As he sat now in one of the reception areas in the State Department building, the CIA Division Director appeared formidable. He was in his fifties with tight, close-cropped gray hair and the build of an aging linebacker.

When he'd joined the agency decades ago, he was warned that a black man wouldn't find nearly as many undercover postings internationally. It would be hard to establish his bona fides. His father was white, though, giving him a lighter complexion that meant he could blend in better than a white man in certain Middle Eastern countries.

He had sometimes hated himself for being grateful for that.

In the end, their warnings had come to nothing. Now he sat in one of the most important buildings in the nation's capital, the director of a clandestine division known as Osprey, ready to meet with a State Division Chief as equals. It was a far cry from his meager upbringing.

"Director Douglas," came the secretary's voice, "Mr. Lasch is ready for you."

"Thank you," he said, rising from his seat.

With a leather portfolio in hand, Booker entered through a pair of grand wooden doors.

The office was high-ceilinged and paneled with mahogany. An Oriental rug sprawled all the way to a stately desk, where a trim man of fifty was getting to his feet.

"Director Douglas," he said, straightening his three-piece suit and reaching out to shake hands. "Joe Lasch. Welcome to State."

"Thanks, pleasure to meet you. You can call me Booker." His magnificent basso voice could make people feel like they were in the presence of James Earl Jones.

Joe Lasch was clearly balding, so kept his hair buzzed short. He had a gravelly voice and looked enough like Humphrey Bogart's cousin that he could have fit right into a black-and-white film noir.

"Booker...that's an unusual one," said Lasch, gesturing to the dual brocaded couches facing each other over a coffee table.

"Black boy growing up in St. Louis, your last name is Douglas and your white father's proud—you get named after a man like Booker T. Washington."

They both sat by a marble fireplace. Above the mantel hung a portrait of a battle from the American Revolution.

Much of the State Department still proudly displayed colonial-era ornateness. There were embroidered rugs everywhere, chandeliers, paintings of the American founders, furniture pieces of Thomas Jefferson, and even some silver crafted by Paul Revere.

The fine drawing rooms and reception halls were a far cry from the drab offices at Langley.

"Is he still alive? Your dad."

"No, he, uh...passed eleven years ago. Lung cancer."

Lasch shook his head. "Cancer. One day we'll get it right and kill off that plague like we did smallpox. Anyhow, it's not often I get in-person visits from the agency, and I'm not familiar with your division. But you must already know that, given your designation."

Lasch was the Division Chief of Overseas Operations in the Diplomatic Security Service of the Department of State. It was his job to manage security for all American diplomatic missions, facilities, and personnel overseas. This was a mammoth responsibility that encompassed everything from budget and resource management to developing emergency action plans to coordinating with other federal agencies.

It was for this last reason that Booker Douglas sat across from him today.

"I do know that. Our operations are limited, and our people don't get to write any bestselling memoirs after they leave the agency."

There was a canny glint in Lasch's eyes. "But Jerusalem... that was your people on the ground, wasn't it?"

What had happened in Jerusalem had been beyond the capabilities of the Osprey division to keep under wraps. Billions of people had watched the camera phone footage that had been almost instantly uploaded to the worldwide web.

Booker had been in the city that day. Two of his operatives had been at the center of the spectacle. Afterward, they were called to account by the Director of the CIA, who told them essentially two things: you failed your prime directive to work in the shadows, and also good job on saving the world.

A few murmurs had rippled through the federal agencies

about the involvement of a clandestine unit, so secretive that they wouldn't even know where to hide it on the hierarchy. Whenever Booker had to pop his head up and coordinate with another agency, it was a tightrope of disclosure.

"There's no way I can confirm that," said Booker.

"Sure, of course. So how can I help you? Where do our interests align?"

Booker shifted forward and laid his folder on the coffee table.

"The Islamic Republic of Iran," he said. "A story broke in the news today of an incredible historical find in the Cyclades, some palace belonging to a king."

Opening the folder, he pulled out two photos and slid them over to Lasch.

"My red alert went off, and I'm sure yours did, too, when I realized who the lead archaeologists were."

The division chief leaned in to scan the photos.

Booker went on, "Jamshid Aslani and his daughter, Nasrin Aslani. Iranian dissidents. She was forced to flee the country in 2012 after the uprisings, since she had become one of the most prominent young critics of the regime. He followed her here to the States in 2013 after his wife died of cancer.

"They've both lived in Chicago for years, but Nasrin never quit speaking out against the Iranian government, especially with the death of Mahsa Amini and the Woman, Life, Freedom uprising that followed it...I'm sure you know all this already."

A wry look of appreciation passed over Lasch, but he was taking in Booker's words with intense focus.

"We know," said Lasch. "Transnational repression. One of the biggest threats we've been dealing with over the last few years. Mostly Chinese agents going after refugees on our shores, but Iran is active, too. They've assassinated dozens of dissidents abroad."

"Are the Aslanis under protection right now? 'Cause they just put up a landing flare to the Islamic Republic, bein' out there in Greece. Dangerously high exposure."

Lasch cocked a brow at him. "What do you have to do with them, Director?"

Booker drew in a deep breath and exhaled slowly. "Nothin' yet, but I intend to."

"Tell me a story, then. You want a drink first?" asked Lasch, gesturing to the decanter of amber liquid at the end of the couch.

"Just a couple hours too early for me, thanks."

"Mind if I?"

Booker nodded and Lasch was on his feet, pouring himself some whiskey, neat in a lowball glass.

"Joe, my interest is about what the Aslanis found. I have a professional investment in the contents of this dig, now, and I'd like to put an operative on their detail, if they've already got one. If they don't yet, they're gonna need one, so..." Booker lifted his hands, "let's work together."

Lasch sat back down on the couch and took a sip of his whiskey. "I don't suppose it would change much about this interaction if you knew the level of my security clearance."

Booker offered up a conciliatory hand. "You're right. It wouldn't."

"We don't have a security detail on the Aslanis right now. There have been some rumblings around the daughter for a few years. The FBI keeps track of that. One of the Islamic cultural centers in Chicago is almost certainly running surveillance on her, but she never wanted a protective detail. The father isn't so public about his criticisms of the regime, but he's probably still at risk given his relation to her.

"But you're right, Director Douglas. This story popped on our radar early this morning. I wouldn't say the Aslanis are dumb as shit for going out to the Mediterranean and making headlines, but maybe dumb as a panda in a zoo. We've got people assessing that threat level right now."

"Are the Greek authorities aware?" asked Booker.

"They will be by this afternoon. They're friendly enough, and they don't want an assassination on their shores. That would be inhospitable. Now, you want an operative embedded but you can't even tell me for what objective? That's not really *co*-operation."

"What I *can* tell you is that if our division comes around, there's somethin' in play you haven't seen before."

Lasch looked at him for several seconds. He was unhappy with the answer, but it wasn't his first go-around with the CIA. The agency coordinated overseas protective work with him often enough, but every now and then a division came around that kept just about every single one of their cards flat against their chest. And he had to work with those, too.

"We'll work this out," said Lasch finally. "I'll send over our threat analysis and plan of action today, soon as we have them."

Booker collected his folder and got to his feet. He extended a meaty hand to the division chief.

"I appreciate your time," he said. "Lookin' forward to working with your department."

Though he nodded, Lasch had the sense that he had just encountered something that he would not—even in the end—be able to understand.

After a long pause, Lasch gave a nod. "Okay. I'll send a man with yours. You better have a top operative in mind, though, to keep up."

Booker smiled.

"Won't be a problem. I have the one."

CHAPTER THREE

DALTON, NEW HAMPSHIRE

Ridley Samaras stood in a dusty patch of field, her torso tilted forward, poised at the ready.

She wore a weighted vest over a black tank top. Her bare arms, grimed with sweat and dirt, hung loose by a thick belt that bristled with ammo magazines. A pistol was tucked into a side holster. She wore tactical black leggings that looked like they'd been rolled in ash. Thick mahogany hair was braided down her back. On her head, she wore a purple cloth headband, foam earplugs, and a pair of UV-tinted shades.

"Three..." came a shout from behind her, "two...one...go!"

She and five other women in tactical gear launched into action. They began throwing weighted bags onto a wheelbarrow.

Once they were loaded, Ridley grabbed the handles of hers and bolted off the starting line.

Out of the corner of her eye, she saw the redhead two lanes down keeping pace.

They both plowed ahead to a wooden obstacle wall, dropped the wheelbarrow handles, and heaved each of the heavy bags over the wall.

Finishing with the last bag, Ridley reached for the top and hauled herself over. With her five feet and eleven inches, she knew this would be where she could get ahead of her opponents.

Also by being better.

As soon as they landed with a thud on the other side, the women had to instantly reverse course, hurling the sandbags back over the wall, climbing up and over, reloading the bags into the wheelbarrows, and racing back to the start.

As Ridley hit the line, she dropped the wheelbarrow, unloaded the bags, and sprinted to a line laid out in the dirt a dozen yards away. She snatched her CZ Shadow 2 pistol from the holster, jammed in a magazine, and aimed downrange. She tried to control her breathing, tried to hold her arms steady, gripping the pistol while her forearms felt like they'd been pumped full of acid.

Two dozen feet away, a carousel of small steel plates rotated slowly. Ridley squeezed off a round—a loud *ping* echoed—

She fired again and again and again—until all eight of the steel plates had swung back.

The redhead was just stepping up to fire when Ridley sprinted back to the starting line and threw herself across it.

The timekeeper nearby hit the stopwatch.

Ridley strode off with her hands propped on her hips. Her lungs heaved like bellows. Her muscles were scorching.

As the other competitors raced to the shooting line, she ambled off for a bottle of water. She guzzled it as the cacophony of gunshots filled the muggy New England air.

She glanced back at the gathered spectators at the other end, and her eyes found the man she could never miss. He stood with his arms wrapped around his thick chest, his gray hair glinting in the late afternoon sun, a faint grin of pride hovering on his face.

Booker Douglas had rolled into town.

Ridley flopped down to sit in the open trunk of an SUV. She'd rented the Land Rover Defender for the weekend to haul around the amount of gear she needed to compete in The Tactical Games. Right now, everything behind her was a mess of Pelican cases, empty magazines, and various items of clothing.

"How'd you do earlier today?" asked Booker as he wiped his glistening brow.

Ridley grabbed a tupperware and a fork from her cooler. She ripped off the top and began devouring a beef and sweet potato scramble.

"On prone rifle, the targets dodged my bullets," she said through a mouthful. "They're so crafty."

All of the vehicles and tents were set up in a giant field. Everyone was tailgating with their gear, grills, and coolers full of sports drinks. As a group of the men's competitors strolled by, one of them—a stocky, cheerful guy with a buzz cut named Jacob—grinned at Ridley.

"Did you bring any extra Pop-tarts for me this year?" he called.

She reached back into the Land Rover and pulled out the distinct silver packaging to waggle in the air.

"Strawberry, you strange boy," she said and tossed it to him.

He caught it, ran over, and kissed the top of her head. She laughed and stabbed him away with her fork.

"All that dust," he said, backing away and smacking his lips. "Just an appetizer. Thank you for my splendid treats."

He began to devour the Pop-tarts as he walked away.

Ridley turned back to Booker. "But then we had a six-mile ruck run with increasing weights in the backpack every two miles. Second place, so I'm in good standing for tomorrow."

Booker squinted off into the distance.

"Oh, come on," she said, seeing his expression.

The boss showing up to yank me out of my real life and into realer life.

She pulled off her sunglasses. Ridley's eyes often surprised people. Despite her strong build, they were soft, the color of amber, with dark gull-wing brows slashing above them. Though she wasn't beautiful, her arrow-straight nose, full lips, and the slightest overbite made for a strikingly attractive picture. Now, it was streaked with dirt and sweat.

"You're gonna like this one, though, Rid," said Booker.

"Enough to lose Nationals by dropping out?"

The redhead passed by just then, carrying a Bravo Company rifle on a sling, loaded up with all the modifications that were legal in New Hampshire.

"Feed the beast!" she yelled.

Ridley inclined her left ear. "You mean feed the *best?*"

"You mean you're asking me out to dinner, Samaras?"

"And Pop-tarts for breakfast, babe!"

"See you in the dust tonight!" The woman gave a grin and a wink as she sauntered off.

With a shake of her head, Ridley watched her go, then looked back at Booker. "I can finish out today, right?"

"Go ahead. Sounds like a date."

"One more event tonight. I'm gonna smoke her."

Booker chuckled. "Down, girl. You're gonna need some sleep."

She took a swig from her water bottle. "What's the story?"

"*Mysterious ancient palace discovered in Greek islands. A* father-daughter archaeology team found evidence of a king everyone believed was fictional...until now."

"Who's that?"

"King Polydectes. It's the myth of Medusa."

Ridley gave a smile. "I've heard of it, yeah."

That Greek mythology is in my DNA.

"Right, humor me for a minute so I can keep it all straight, Artemis. Now, Perseus went and retrieved the head of Medusa the gorgon to bring it back, tryin' to impress the king. But when he got back to the island, he realized that Polydectes had been abusing his mom. So he pulled out the head of Medusa in front of the king and turned *him* to stone."

"She had that effect on men. Women were never dumb enough to go looking for her."

Ridley took another bite of her scramble and regarded him for a moment.

"Yeah, mythology...but you're saying Polydectes was actually a real king?"

Booker nodded.

"Seems so. They found a stele in the site that confirms his name."

"Okay," she said, processing, "and you got excited because..."

His dark eyes lit up. "What's written on the rest of that stele."

Ridley lowered her fork.

"Medusa," she said.

He smiled. "Medusa's dead—slain—but she had two other sisters. Both gorgons. Medusa was mortal, but the *sisters* were immortal. I got no idea why...unfortunate family dynamic there."

"Are they mentioned on the stele?"

"Well, it's more of a guide...to each of the magical items that Perseus used to slay Medusa—the ones given to him by the gods."

There it is. There's the Booker hook.

"Is someone else already after the stuff?" she asked.

"Not as far as we've been able to tell. Don't doubt someone will be soon. But there's a bit of a...a complicating factor."

"Booker, you tell these stories like ancient epics. What's the catch?"

"The archaeologists are Iranian, and they're dissidents, and the biggest discovery of their lives just made them a clear target of the Islamic Republic. Right now they're sittin' out there in the open in the middle of the Mediterranean."

Ridley finished her meal and put down the empty tupperware. Her lower back had been rubbed raw by the rucksack that morning. Her forearms still burned from the wheelbarrow hold. Her muscles felt like demolition sites.

However desperately she wanted to finish and win these Games, it was the uncharted challenge of an Osprey mission that most excited her. She'd come back to finish off the redhead next year.

"So who's my partner on this one?" she asked.

Osprey pairing was unique to the mission at hand. Operative skill sets were matched to complement each other's, though most of them were equipped with the talents and training of Special Ops. It was a small division overall, and still Ridley probably only knew a third of the operatives. They were never gathered together for "team meetings" or anything like it. Their briefings and debriefings were specific, not broad.

Whatever the needs of a mission, Booker would find the perfect partners to work together, even if—in the rarest of cases—that meant himself.

"This is where we'll be playin' a little different," he replied. "These Iranians are naturalized citizens, which means they're under the protection of the United States government. Which means your new partner is gonna be a State Department officer."

"Oh, no, come on, Book—"

His voice grew steely. "I don't want to hear it. We gotta work together and play nice on this one."

"Who is he? Or she?"

"You'll meet him tomorrow. And don't look like I just robbed your playpen. After all this time, you're finally goin' back to Greece."

CHAPTER FOUR

WASHINGTON, D.C.

Booker was grabbing himself a coffee in the agency cafeteria the next day when his phone rang.

The Secretary of State would like to see him. Today, if possible.

This was *unusual.*

He tried to keep his mind from brewing too hot as he drove himself from Langley to another giant federal building.

A young man with pink cheeks and a sharp suit—clearly an aide—spotted him the moment he entered the lobby, and hurried right up to him with an oddly cordial greeting.

Booker followed the aide to the office of the Secretary of State.

The CIA man had been there twice before in his career. The office was somehow less grandiose than Lasch's, but this was the same one where everyone from John Foster Dulles to Henry Kissinger to Condoleezza Rice had conducted some of the most consequential business in an American century.

Now, it was the domain of Neal Rhodes.

As Booker entered, the Secretary of State rose from his desk chair with a smile.

"Director Douglas, thanks for comin' last minute," he said in a mild drawl.

They shook hands. Booker was not accustomed to being outsized, but this man towered over him.

"I've got a few minutes," said Booker as they moved to sit on the couches.

"Joe Lasch just told me about this new coordinated mission with your agency," said Rhodes, "and I thought we should meet to discuss it."

Booker thought that must have been the fastest he'd ever seen the federal government move.

"Well, I haven't been in here in a while," said Booker. "I like what you've done with your version."

He nodded to a large portrait of a chestnut Thoroughbred that hung by a window.

"Oh," said Rhodes, "that's Prospero. What a specimen—best side of horseflesh east of the Mississippi! We're retirin' him this year, turning him out to stud. He'll sire the next generation of great racing offspring."

"Looks like Secretariat himself," said Booker.

Rhodes grinned like a proud father. "A like comparison. My wife is an exceptional woman, and her eye for horses? I wouldn't trade for any man's. Now, I don't want to waste any more of your time, but I'd like to help you out, if you could fill me in a bit more on your objectives with this. I'd have to be sure that our missions aren't conflicting."

This was the fishing expedition.

The Kentucky man was a seasoned diplomat. His soft, bland

face looked kindly enough, but his stature was commanding. Those sleepy blue eyes could turn to ice when negotiating with the worst heads of state in the world.

In contrast to the thin-skinned president, Rhodes was broadly respected. However, he'd gotten tired of his boss' volatile petulance. The word was that he would be leaving the office toward the end of the year and heading back to his farm in Kentucky where his real passion lay: breeding and racing horses.

He wouldn't want to go out with any mission failures to his name in the last few months.

"It may sound strange that my division has any place in the CIA," said Booker, "but we're interested in all kinds of strange findings around the world. I follow a lot of archaeology. A lotta people put stock in 'ancient findings' and start to act *extreme* to get to them, ya know?"

"I've heard of this." Rhodes nodded.

"We're the ones who track those things down, before the extremists can get a hold of 'em."

The Secretary of State almost smirked. "You're doin' a lot more than that. You've got just about the highest level of classification in the National Clandestine Service of the Central Intelligence Agency and you tell me you're chasin' around some old dusty tablets?"

He wasn't dumb.

The Osprey Division had been formed during World War II to counter Heinrich Himmler's obsession with the occult. Roosevelt had been convinced by the founding father of the CIA, William J. Donovan, that whatever his own beliefs about the supernatural were, they needed to stymie the Nazis' pursuit. It was a "just in case" operation unit that had become a "thank God" shadow unit, time after time.

They were small enough to be adaptable, and strange

enough that they needed the utmost secrecy. Their budget was negligible when lost in the swirl of national defense spending, and their success rate was high.

That was something for which the world should have been grateful a hundred times over, but it was vital they didn't know. The chaos would be unbearable, as it had almost been after what happened in Jerusalem...the mission's end that could not be concealed from the public.

Of course, Booker couldn't tell Rhodes much of this, even if he was the Secretary of State.

"Unlike some of the other divisions out there," said Booker, "our missions remain classified for good, but I'll tell you what we're interested in. It's open-ended, like a lot of our starting points."

Rhodes nodded for him to continue.

"This archaeological team—father and daughter, Iranian dissidents—discovered the ruins of a palace in the Greek islands."

"I read about that."

Booker was surprised, but went on. "Well, they found a stele there—that's a huge stone tablet—indicating it belonged to a king that we thought never existed. So on that stele, there was some writing about items that are hidden around the Mediterranean. Like a scavenger hunt for archaeologists."

Rhodes furrowed his brow, but looked intrigued.

"What kinds of items?"

This is where it was time to lie.

"This part isn't exciting," he said. "Sandals. A sword. A helmet. Nothin' worth much on the market, but I'm interested because that's what I do, and I know these archaeologists are gonna be interested because this is like catnip to them."

"So you think the father and daughter are goin' after these

items, and you want an officer with them, and you want one of *our* agents to go with them, too. I have that right?"

Booker gestured a hand toward him.

"That's about right."

"Have you been in touch with these archaeologists yet?" asked Rhodes.

"Not yet."

"How do you know they're goin' on this treasure hunt?"

"Oh," said Booker with a glint in his eye, "I can promise you. They're goin'."

Later, he would muse as he walked out into the sullen summer afternoon. The Secretary of State himself was going to be keeping an eye on this joint mission.

This needed to be clean, smooth, and successful.

Booker slipped on his shades. He admitted to himself that it would likely only be the last of those three.

Ridley Samaras was never clean and smooth.

CHAPTER FIVE

WASHINGTON, D.C.

Sometimes Ridley felt like the only place she ever saw inside of Dulles Airport was the international terminal.

She'd arrived early enough to sit at the wine bar with a glass of Etna Rosso and surveil the throngs of travelers going to and fro. Her muscles still ached, and her lower back was tender from the grueling events of yesterday. A ten-hour flight wasn't about to help with the stiffness, but wine could surely do a job.

Ridley had gotten back to D.C. from New Hampshire in the early hours of the morning and collapsed into sleep. She tumbled out of bed only a few hours later, grabbed a few everything bagels at the nearby bakery, and went to her neighbor's place.

When Ana opened the door, she laughed at Ridley's dusty, disheveled appearance.

"You're early."

"Thank you, from my best morning self," said Ridley.

Ana was a brunette in her twenties who walked straight on her toes like a dancer and was always wearing something flowy and bohemian.

Ridley handed over the bag of bagels, but her eyes had already found what she was really there for: Maddie.

A little mutt came scrambling across the wood floor, squeaking wildly. Ridley crouched down as the pup collided against her legs.

The scruffy dog with the big doe eyes was the only thing she ever truly cared about coming home to. Maddie wriggled into her hands and lapped at her face. She leaned hard into Ridley's chest.

"Turns out she doesn't like avocado ice cream," said Ana.

"No," said Ridley. "She has very Italian tastes—prefers gelato."

"I'll do better next time, which is..."

Ridley grimaced a smile at her. "A few hours from now?"

Ana lifted her eyebrows. "So *that's* why you're back early from New Hampshire. Emergency translations."

As far as anyone in Ridley's life knew, she was a translator for a high-ranking diplomat who traveled the world meeting foreign dignitaries. It covered all her bases and made perfect sense for a professional skill set that included eight languages.

She was endlessly grateful for Ana, who ran an online business that allowed her to work from home, who adored her neighbor's dog, and was generous to a fault.

"Go on, then," she told Ridley. "Take your time. I'll be here this evening whenever you want to bring her back."

So Ridley had taken the afternoon with Maddie to play fetch outside, explore the riverbank for the promising scent of ducks, and even eat a bit of gelato. Then she showered and packed while the little mutt watched quietly from the bed, never lifting her head, already resigned to being left behind again.

As Ridley was rolling up a linen shirt, her eyes drifted to the small safe in her closet. She knew she shouldn't get sidetracked, but she couldn't resist. She punched in her code and opened it up.

She pulled out a black PC laptop and sprawled onto the bed. Maddie snuggled closer to her shoulder.

The head technician at Osprey had given the laptop to her off the record. It was a dark web ghost of a machine that required a retinal scan as well as a combination of passcode responses to access. It might have all been an illusion of security, but she wanted no trace of her activities being linked to the CIA.

She had spent too much time hunting down this shadow villain.

Andreas Colby.

He was a billionaire real estate developer with a diverse portfolio, including ownership of the Miami Dolphins and a football team in England called Leeds United. He was on his third wife now, with four children of indulgent wealth who occasionally made for juicy news items of their own.

Ridley cared for nothing of that tabloid nonsense, because Colby was a commanding member of a much more terrible thing: the Order of Raphael.

They were the kudzu of nefarious clandestine groups, with vines that could wrap themselves around seemingly anything. They were radical remnants of the more glamorous Templars.

Yet unlike the Templars, who had faded into little more than relics themselves, handing out honorary medals to each other in quaint European towns, the Raphaels had gone a different direction. They had accrued real power in the quieter, more elite circles, and so endured for nearly a millennia. Their strength and influence could not be underestimated.

Ridley had run into them before, to near catastrophic consequence. In the end, she'd walked away with a victory and the name of the next commander in line. She had hunted him ever since, on her own time. Though she could do nothing to move against him, she was sure their paths would cross one day.

The Order always wanted the kinds of things that Osprey sought.

Whenever they finally met face to face, she would not be caught off guard.

It's becoming more of an addiction than real research...

She knew it herself, but couldn't let it go.

Ridley scoured the file she'd built on him for any sign that he might be interested in the discovery of a Greek palace. He was a donor at an archaeological foundation, but they did most of their work in Turkey, Egypt, and Peru. No mention of Greece.

After nearly twenty minutes on the laptop, she finally slammed it shut and slid it back into the safe.

Maddie picked up her head, hopeful about what this meant for their next activity.

"Sorry, girl," said Ridley. "You'd love Greece."

A few hours later, Maddie was back with Ana, and Ridley was sitting in the airport, swirling her third glass of Etna Rosso.

Then she caught sight of him.

Strolling across the terminal like a man on vacation was a tall guy in his thirties. He had golden hair and blue eyes. He wore dark jeans and a periwinkle T-shirt, and carried a tightly packed bag that looked more like a satchel than a suitcase.

Like Adonis just rolled out of Abercrombie.

His gaze landed on her at the bar. She raised her glass but didn't smile. He walked over.

"Hi," she said flatly.

He looked at her with an expression that read more like sizing up a potential rival than trying to pick up an attractive woman in a bar.

"You're taller than I thought you'd be," he said finally, and his voice was richer than it should have been for his gleaming appearance.

"I'm sitting."

He clutched his bag in front of him with two hands and cocked his head with a faint smirk, as if saying, "I'm still right."

Those are Paul Newman-level blue eyes—shit.

He was going to draw attention everywhere he went. It was everything wrong for spy work.

She hated this already.

Ridley looked away and gestured to the bar. "You want a drink?"

He slid onto the stool next to her and caught the attention of the bartender. "Negroni."

The bartender nodded and got to work.

"Gin," said Ridley. "That fits."

"I try not to ask for the Bond cocktail when I first meet someone. They can find it intimidating."

She twisted around to look full at him. "You can drive an Aston Martin and screw Honey Ryder and drink all the martinis in New York and also go to hell if you think you're intimidating anyone sitting in this seat."

He leaned back to take her in.

She shrugged, not quite apologetic.

"I'd be mad if I had to tag along on a detail, too," he said.

"*You're* tagging along. I've actually got a mission."

"To play Indiana Jones with some archaeologists? The mission is keeping the principals alive," he said.

"You don't even have the clearance to *know* the mission."

He chuckled. "I'm sure you got the bullet points from my file. Like I got yours."

The bartender slid the Negroni toward him on a napkin. He grinned a *thank you* and picked it up for a sip. Once the bartender was out of earshot again, he went on.

"You're a spooky chick—"

Spooky—short for "spook." Slang for spy. Thanks for not blurting it out in an airport, asshole.

"—almost became a Navy SEAL but your ear got fucked up. Not your fault. You work hard, find your way to one of the alphabets, make a new career for yourself. It's respectable. I respect it."

"One can almost smell the respect," she said. "Whereas you grew up outside of Des Moines, got a degree in criminal justice but didn't join the police, went into bodyguarding, and eventually got a job with State. And, despite your prep boy appearance, you're seriously into Dungeons and Dragons."

At this, he looked genuinely surprised. "That was in my file?"

"It was a big bullet point. Someone has a sense of humor in DSS."

He nodded for a moment, then asked, "You speak Greek?"

"Natively. I spent my summers on Paros growing up. You speak anything helpful?"

"Danger."

"I'm gonna need to go pick up my eyes that just rolled out of my head to the next gate."

"I took Italian in college to talk to women, and I know enough Spanish to know when people are talking shit," he said.

"Well, be on the lookout for Spanish troublemakers, then. All the ones that come from Iran."

"Look," he said, "I'm not happy having a partner from a

different agency with a different mission. From your charming disposition, seems like you're not either."

She drained the last of her wine from the glass.

"Or I'm just not happy having a partner who seems like an asshole," she said.

He cocked his head in thought. "Maybe we're both assholes."

And that was how she met Special Agent Gabe Tolkin.

CHAPTER SIX

ATHENS, GREECE

Athens in the deep summer was *hot*, even for Ridley.

The moment she and Gabe stepped out of the airport into the morning sun, the heat on her skin felt like stepping into life. A dry breeze riffled her dark blue V-neck.

Almost home.

"This is the surface of the sun," said Gabe, sliding on a pair of mirrored aviators.

"It would be so sad if you melted."

The liaison assigned to their transportation had met them at the gate, but they'd both insisted on carrying their own bags and simply asked him to pull the car around to the pickup area. They quickly spotted the gray Mercedes in the churn of vehicles.

Gabe opened the back door and stood away like a gentleman. Ridley just looked at him as she opened the passenger side and slid into the front seat.

"Your point was deafening," he muttered as he climbed into the back by himself.

Lawrence, their puffy-faced liaison-chauffeur in a white polo shirt, shifted the car into gear and started off.

"You can adjust the air to whatever you'd like," he told them. "It will take us about an hour."

"To get to the embassy?" said Ridley, puzzled.

"No, we're going to the Alimos marina, near Piraeus."

She glanced back at Gabe, who was looking down at a message on his phone.

"Yeah," he said without looking up, "seems like the RSO doesn't want to waste any more time here on the mainland and thinks we can just get our briefing on the way to the island."

"Good timing on relaying that message," she said.

The tension was clearly making their driver uncomfortable.

"And they'll have food for us on the boat," he said. "No need to stop for that breakfast, Lawrence."

This is gonna be the longest mission of my life.

"Lawrence," she said, "could you take us the southern route? I need the scenery."

"Yes, ma'am."

And Ridley lost herself in the world beyond her window.

They wound through a quiet suburban neighborhood with shaded balconies on every story, ripe oranges hanging off trees like ornaments, and cafés where people sat in the shade, lounging over their coffee and *bougatsa*.

Within a few minutes the ocean appeared in the distance, a slash of blue that glittered in the Mediterranean sun.

Lawrence asked if they'd mind some music. Neither did. He turned up the volume on an upbeat synth pop. The woman's voice serenaded them into the Greek Riviera, where palm trees fluttered, trams slid by, and street vendors had already begun hawking their goods. The real early risers had already set up their umbrellas on the beach, where children scampered about in the surf.

Ridley didn't even want to count the years it had been since she'd set foot in Athens. It had never been her home, but it was the place she'd passed through dozens of times on her way to her grandmother's. It was this ancient city—the city that created democracy, the city of Plato and Socrates and Maria Callas—that was really the beacon of her heritage.

Since her Icelandic mother had died when Ridley was only three years old, it was the land of her Greek father that had taken up her childhood.

She could hardly remember her mother—the mother who had saved her from drowning, who had pushed her little toddler up onto the boat before being sucked down into the waters by an undertow.

The mother who never made it back to the surface.

Sometimes Ridley thought she could piece together enough of the fleeting images, the impressions that slipped by too quickly, the sounds of a voice lost to her...that she might be able to form real memories. The rest was filled in by photos and videos of a woman who was gone before her daughter even knew her.

It had ruined her father, who didn't know what to do with himself. He towed his son and daughter around the world while he worked as a project manager for an international construction company. There was nowhere they could call home for more than a year, and most of their time in European cities was spent getting into scrapes, sneaking around with trouble, and picking up the local languages.

Fortunately, their grandmother knew they needed something more.

Charis lived on the Greek island of Paros, running a company that offered tours on horseback. She wouldn't host her grandkids through the schoolyear, but every summer, Ridley and her older brother Alexios would go live with her. They helped with the business, and by the time Ridley was a teenager, she was leading clumsy tourists around the island on her favorite chestnut mare.

Her grandmother was as salty as the seas around them, a magnificent and proud Greek woman of the islands. She was generous, and expected her grandkids to be the same. She also worked herself to the bone, and expected them to do likewise.

Ridley was seventeen when her grandmother died. She had been in Milan when her father got word. He put his fist through a table. She wandered outside, pacing the city in a catatonic state, unable to cry.

She had only been back to Paros twice since that day: once to help clear out her grandmother's estate and attend her funeral, then again for a cousin's wedding.

Now as the car glided along the coastline, they saw the Alimos marina open ahead of them. Hundreds of bobbing white masts bristled up from the sparkling bay.

Lawrence pulled into the parking lot. Ridley and Gabe got out, once more into the mid-August heat. They took their bags, thanked him, and headed for the docks.

"She'll recognize us," said Gabe. "Obviously she has our pictures."

Ridley scanned the parking lot as they went. Tourists going on charter rides towed their noisy luggage, and seasoned sailors trekked from the nearby grocery store with their bulging bags. She couldn't help but surveil everything within sight. To her satisfaction, she noticed Gabe doing the same, his head on a swivel as they walked.

A life in protective services would really require that of someone. He was discreet but vigilant.

Throw a couple bonus points his way, even if he wastes them later.

Ridley was notorious for holding the highest standards for her partners. She worked ferociously hard in her off time to sharpen every one of her professional skills. She demanded perfection from herself. That she expected only excellence from a teammate was practically gracious.

She had established enough trust with Booker to know that he wouldn't pair her with any Osprey partner who wasn't up to standard, but this guy—who knew?

They passed yachts and catamarans and sailboats, their white hulls gleaming in the sunlight, their pennants fluttering overhead, their rigging clanking with the breeze.

Ridley stopped at the end of one of the docks. No one seemed to be registering them, aside from the awed looks that Gabe was getting in passing.

How does he get assigned to any *discreet guard detail looking like Brad Pitt? Who picked this guy?*

"You sail?" he asked.

"Whenever the sails are there. You?"

"I know how to crank a winch."

"Don't worry. There's no way we're taking a sailboat between islands," she said, glancing hopefully at the larger yachts.

A woman's husky voice came from the nearest dock. "You're right. Even though I'd love to see you two crew a vessel."

CHAPTER SEVEN

ATHENS, GREECE

Ridley and Gabe turned to see a woman rising up from the cooler she'd been sitting on.

Though she didn't rise very far. She was barely five-foot-four. In her early thirties, she was tan with blonde hair, dark eyebrows, and a pretty but pugnacious look.

"We're taking a real boat that gets you places," she said as she approached them. "Laura Melden, RSO."

Regional Security Officer. A State Department employee posted abroad, the RSO always worked at consulates or embassies, overseeing all regional security issues and risk assessments. It was their job to advise the ambassador on relevant matters, work with local law enforcement, and supervise all operational matters in their area.

It was surprising to both the partners that someone so young held that posting here.

She's either incredibly good at her job or a vanity pick who's terrible. No in between.

She extended her hand. Ridley shook it.

"Ridley Samaras."

"You're the Greek."

"Half, but yeah."

"Well, that's the half we need."

Melden turned to Gabe. "And you're one of ours."

"Yeah," he said, shaking her hand. "Gabe."

"Okay, kids, let's go for a ride."

She grabbed her cooler and headed down the dock. The partners followed her almost to the end, where a motorboat that looked like a mini-yacht was moored. There was an older man climbing about onboard who had the leathery look of a seaman.

"Everybody, meet Clark," said Melden, handing her cooler across to him.

"Hi everybody," he said, with no smile.

They leapt aboard.

"This is a Primatist G57," he said proudly. "We'll be cruisin' at thirty-five knots so we should be gettin' into port in about two and a half hours. Make yourselves comfortable. You can put your bags in these compartments right here."

Clark slipped the line off their mooring and climbed up to the wheel.

Ridley and Gabe stashed their bags as Melden settled down into the white banquette. She opened the cooler and gestured for them to help themselves.

"No beers, sorry. Can't have any agents showing up plastered to meet the island cops."

"All you have to do is offer them one," said Ridley.

She grabbed a can of *portokalada* and sat across the table

from Melden. Gabe took a seltzer and sat with his legs propped off the end of the cushions.

As Clark motored out of the marina, each of them reveled in the breeze. Ridley twisted the cap off her orange soda. The first sip felt like a burst of glory on her tongue.

"God, this is so much better than the ferry," said Melden. "How did people do this before motorized water travel?"

"Slaves in the galley?" said Gabe.

"Slavery: like pressing the 'easy' button, but evil!"

Clark pressed styrofoam plugs into his ears and then opened the throttle. The boat surged forward into the open ocean.

Over the roar of the engine, Melden had to raise that throaty voice.

"I know you both got briefings separately and together," she said, "but here's the setup on the ground. Who could have predicted, but after Jamshid and Nasrin Aslani made global headlines with their big dig, Iranian channels lit up with talk of the bounty that the Islamic regime would obviously be putting on their heads. Killing is good but capturing would get you better pay, and welllll—that bounty was taken up. We don't know by who or how many or if they're even Iranian. We're workin' on that. We'll know soon."

"How long ago was that?" asked Gabe.

Melden looked at her watch. "Two days and thirteen hours ago. The Aslanis were living and working at the dig site on Serifos, but we moved them to Paros so we could actually get them some police protection. Cops were probably psyched to get something other than 'goat watch' for a few days at least."

There are a lot of goats on Paros.

"So they're in Parikia right now?" said Ridley.

"No. Naoussa. A lot quieter, and not the main port of entry."

"Yeah, I...spent a lot of time there as a kid."

"Oh, great. Perfect. Well, maybe you can talk some sense into this pair. They don't want to go back to the States. Something about a 'historical discovery' but they won't tell anyone else shit about it. We advised them against meeting in person with any reporters who want to interview them. I want them at least back on the mainland. They *are* naturalized citizens, so this *is* our problem."

"What's their attitude about a protective detail?" asked Gabe.

"They're good with it. They're grateful. They just won't return to the US until they've accomplished—" Melden waved a hand about with a roll of her eyes, "whatever it is they want to do out here. *As archaeologists.*"

She looked straight at Ridley.

"I guess that's what you're doing here."

Ridley sipped on her soda. "I won't know 'til I've met them. Why are they such priority targets for the regime?"

Since finding out about her latest assignment, Ridley had done her customary prep, finding out all she could from both public channels and intelligence reports. But the State Department would no doubt have a more complete profile.

"It's really Nasrin they hate. She became popular on social media back in Iran when she was a student, posting all kinds of videos that 'made archaeology cool' for younger people. I've seen some of them—translated, obviously—I don't speak Farsi —and they're pretty fun."

Ridley had seen them, too. They *were* pretty fun.

"But then, the Day of Rage protests went down in Tehran. She got so into it, posting videos, being out in the streets, documenting all the violence against civilians. Nasrin was on fire and got thousands more followers...finally the regime noticed and thought she'd become enough of an annoyance or a *threat* to their brutality that she had to go on the run in 2012. She left behind the rest of her family, came to the States as a refugee, eventually got her green card and became a citizen."

"She's a teacher now." said Gabe.

He did do his homework.

Melden nodded, pawing back the hair that kept whipping against her face.

"University of Chicago. Made an actual life for herself. Her dad came over and joined her two years after she left. He's an archaeologist, too. Weird family business...but the regime sort of lost interest in them until a few years ago."

Squinting against the seaspray, Ridley leaned forward and propped her elbows on the table. "Until 2022, right? Woman, Life, Freedom. The Mahsa Amini protests."

Mahsa Amini.

It was a name that every Iranian had come to know after she died in police custody. She was only twenty-two when she was arrested on the streets of Tehran for wearing tight pants and not wearing her hijab correctly, according to the police chief. The police beat her to death for it.

Authorities announced that natural causes alone were to blame for her death. The Iranian regime had doctors forge fake medical records.

Her family denied all of it. The public didn't believe it.

Within hours of Amini's death, demonstrations began to inflame across the city and the nearby provinces. They flooded social media. The hashtag #MahsaAmini was seen by tens of millions of people around the world. The Islamic Republic was so afraid of the power of their message that an internet blackout was implemented.

The authorities unleashed live fire on the protestors. The demonstrations became bloody and often deadly. In the end, nearly two hundred people were killed.

Yet the protests had become a movement. The name of

"Mahsa Amini" rippled through the world, with murals of her appearing in Toronto, Sydney, Dublin, Jerusalem, Buenos Aires, and cities across America. Images spread of the brave young people of Iran. Women and girls began to remove their hijabs in the streets. And "Woman, Life, Freedom" became the rallying call for justice and freedom.

But justice did not come. Nor did freedom. The Islamic Republic retained their power. They continued to arrest and torture women for not wearing the hijab. They executed critics of the regime.

And halfway across the world, Nasrin Aslani grew louder and louder about all of it.

"She's a fuckin' thorn demon in their side," said Melden with a grin, "and I love every single thing I've ever heard her say."

"How long has she known the regime's been after her, with bounties and all?" asked Ridley.

"She knew it even before it happened. No mystery what happens to the dissidents abroad who won't keep their mouth shut about the horrors going down in that country. She did all this with eyes wide open."

"And then went abroad," said Gabe. "So she's brave but not smart, huh?"

Melden looked at him. "Oh, there's some shit in the bottom of the cooler that you could eat."

He lifted a toast to the RSO.

Stifling a laugh, Ridley asked, "How are the Greeks taking it? Iranian assassins descending on their country...the Persians invading again..."

"They're happy to help us defend their guests, but they want us to get them out—back to the States," said Melden. "So I'd like you two to join that pressure campaign. Can't force them, but can't stay here on protective detail forever."

"Loud and clear," said Gabe.

That's not my assignment. Not my style.

Nearly two hours later, through small chat and sun-basking, Melden pulled the cooler up next to her. She detached a compartment from the bottom and out slid two trays.

On each lay a Glock 19, a slim inside-the-waistband holster, and two extra magazines. She pushed them across to Ridley and Gabe.

"You're licensed to carry them, of course, through the DSS, through State—diplomatic immunity and all that," she told them.

Ridley had been issued a diplomatic ID by the State Department before she flew. It felt strange, like being exposed. None of her prior missions had been conducted in any sort of declared official capacity. She had always needed to move like a ghost through other countries, evading and finagling her way past law enforcement and authorities rather than declaring herself a foreign agent. For Gabe, though, bureaucratic credentials were standard operating procedure.

They each picked up a Glock and gave it a quick weapons check. Fully loaded. Ridley switched off the safety and secured the holster inside her belt.

Printing all over the place, I'm sure. At least I'm wearing a dark color.

It was hard to pull off total concealment of a handgun in the summer. The outline of the gun "printed" through thin material like a T-shirt and gave away the game for anyone looking closely.

"And which one of you asked for this nasty-lookin' death claw?" asked Melden.

She pulled a folded knife from the back of her waistband. Ridley's expression spread into a grin.

"That's for me."

She took the piece from Melden and hefted it for a moment. Dark titanium handle with a sleek clip on it. She flipped it open. A curved blade of black steel. Just what she had asked for: an Underwater Demolition Teams M390 folding karambit. The knife that looked like a mini raptor claw was her pet weapon. She had used it for convenience, and used it for death. This little version would serve her well for concealment.

Ridley clipped the folded blade onto her belt loop.

Then she saw the *Portos*.

Rising from the ocean were two huge, craggy rocks that formed a narrow gateway. Her grandmother used to tell stories of how they were ancient guardians set by the gods to protect the island.

Ridley leaned on the edge of the boat.

There beyond the rocky gates lay the island of Paros.

She was almost home.

CHAPTER EIGHT

PAROS, GREECE

THE CLUSTERS of limestone buildings glowed white under the high sun. Hills covered in scrub brush rose behind them. Turquoise waters lapped at the shore.

As Ridley stepped onto the dock, she felt a surge of emotion so strong that it almost took her breath away. That saltwater smell, the island breeze that ruffled the palm fronds and rippled the blue and white flags atop their poles.

Get a grip, Samaras. This is a mission, not a homecoming.

She gripped her bag tighter.

Next to her, Gabe popped an Altoid. He looked at her for a second, then offered the tin. She shook her head.

"We've got a car ready," said Melden, swiping aside a message on her phone. "Let's go meet your principals."

The gray Honda CR-V was waiting for them in the marina parking lot. Melden pulled the key out from the back wheel well and unlocked it for them.

Greek security.

The drive was barely fifteen minutes north, cutting through the middle of the island. Gabe wanted to crank the air conditioning, as he fussed with his hair that was starting to dampen with sweat. Ridley put her window down and reveled in the dry, hot wind.

They passed groves of olive trees and thick bushels of oleander and hibiscus that seemed to spill from their gardens. They drove by ancient ruins crumbling on the roadside, and every vehicle they passed seemed to be covered with the dust of summer.

When they arrived on the northern coast, Melden propped up her GPS. They wound through the narrow outer streets until they finally had to park and continue on foot. The RSO grumbled about the setup, with the safehouse not having a quick escape route.

As they passed outdoor cafés and boutique shops with brightly painted doors, Ridley had to sidle up and mutter to both of them.

"Slow down," she said.

No one else was striding toward a destination like they were. The tourists, shoppers, and locals *strolled*. They ambled and meandered along the stone streets.

Melden and Gabe slowed their pace, suddenly self-conscious.

State Department doesn't do "undercover" like the CIA.

They stopped finally at a two-story house, gleaming white as all the others. Melden knocked on the blue door and called out in her throaty voice.

IN GREEK: *"Good afternoon. I'm here to pick up a package."*

There was silence for a few seconds. Then a man's muffled voice came from the other side, and the door swung open.

A paunchy man in his forties stood there, looking at them as if he was bored.

"Hello," he said in a thick Greek accent, "please come in."

They entered and he shut the door behind them.

The house was sparse and bright, with moderate furnishings. Ridley thought it looked like a mid-range Airbnb, not a place where anyone actually lived. It was also entirely quiet apart from this one officer.

Melden frowned. "Where are they?"

"At lunch."

Her eyes nearly popped out of her head. "With *one* officer? You knew we were coming!"

He shrugged. "It's okay. Andritsos is with them. We can't keep them here like prisoners—they want to go out! Especially the woman."

"What's your name?"

"Kostas."

"Okay, Kostas, great, thanks so much for your help. Now take us to where they're having lunch."

He hesitated.

"You don't *know?!*" she exclaimed.

"No, I remember," he mumbled.

"Okay," she said, sweeping her hands toward the door. "Take us there. Please."

He wasn't sheepish at all, but seemed annoyed by her annoyance. Nonetheless, he led them outside, locked the door behind, and headed toward the water.

It wasn't surprising that this plainclothes cop wasn't ready for a protective detail that actually moved about and had opinions. The biggest thing the island police ever guarded were the icons in churches, where pious villagers laid all their family wealth in jewels as they pleaded to the saints in prayer.

They made their way through the narrow streets, and Ridley could see Gabe taking it all in like he'd stepped into a fairytale.

He was right to be impressed. It was like something out of a Mediterranean dream, the dizzying colors and salty hot breeze and fragrance of flowers everywhere. Cats sauntered and sprawled about, tails curling, their eyes squinting as they settled under nearby flowerpots for their afternoon naps.

There were always steady streams of tourists in Naoussa during the summer, but in the last decade, it had gotten even worse. They were relatively harmless—shopping, taking in lunch, and snapping photos of the bougainvillea vines that exploded in fuchsia against the white limestone.

Ridley could practically hear her brother Alexios' voice in her head: *Don't resent. Be grateful. Yaya made a living from their money.*

The crowds may have swelled, but the streets and shops and bakeries had remained the same as ever. Memories flitted and scampered across her vision...*racing through the streets toward the beach after church, their Sunday clothes be damned...late nights at the bars trying to skim vodka off distracted adults...fetching warm, flaky bougatsa pastries at the nearby bakery for Charis, and always grabbing an extra piece of baklava for herself...*

Ridley inhaled the scent of jasmine as they wound their way to a little plaza decked with blue and white chairs. The surf was sloshing up along the rocks, delighting some of the tourists nearby.

At the far end of the little square, seated at a high-top table, was an older man and a younger woman. Ridley recognized them instantly.

Nasrin Aslani looked like a lioness in linen. Her tawny mane was billowing about in the sea breeze, but somehow the hibiscus blossom tucked behind her ear remained in place.

Jamshid Aslani looked severe, with dark brows and an

aquiline nose, but the way he looked at his daughter was anything but.

The two of them glanced up from their lunch when they saw Kostas arriving. His partner Andritsos, who had been sitting across the plaza, jumped up to greet them as well. Before he could reach them, Nasrin smiled at the newcomers.

"Hello!" she said with a faint Iranian accent. "You must be our new friends."

She really isn't afraid.

Melden was clearly uncomfortable with the open-air interaction, but she stepped forward to greet the father and daughter.

"Hi, my name's Laura. I've been communicating with these two men here—" she glanced at the Greek officers, "—to move you from their protection to ours."

Jamshid had stood up as she was speaking, and wiped his mouth with a napkin.

"I'm Jimmy," he said, extending a hand to shake hers. "We're very grateful for your help."

His daughter grinned at Melden. "Nas," she said, shaking hands.

Automatically, Ridley and Gabe had positioned themselves at complementary angles. Their eyes scanned every person in the small plaza.

"Nice to meet you both, great," said Melden. "We have some things we need to talk about—someplace *not* in the middle of a tourist alley."

"But it's such a beautiful day out," said Nas. "Can we maybe just move into the taverna?"

Ridley appreciated that she called it a *taverna*, not a café. The woman knew her setting.

The taverna had too many people in it to speak freely, but the restaurant next door hadn't opened for business yet, so it was ideal. Kostas persuaded the bewildered owner to let them into the dining room to talk. For another few dozen euros, he even put away the octopus he was carving up and vacated the premises.

Kostas and Andritsos stationed themselves outside.

When they were finally alone at a table with the Iranian father and daughter, the two American operatives introduced themselves.

As any person with eyes would be, Nas was dazzled by Gabe's appearance, though to her credit she at least tried to act like she didn't notice. His eyes had seemed irritatingly more blue since they'd landed on the island.

Like goddamn Adonis just returned to Greece.

"We're here to provide for your safety until we can get you back to the States," Gabe told them.

"Oh, we cannot go back to the States right now," said Nas. "We're working."

Melden leaned forward. Ridley could practically hear the sigh of exasperation brewing in her.

"We understand—anticipated—that you'd feel that way," said the RSO, "and we respect that you want to continue with this incredible dig you've...dug up. But we can't seriously safeguard you both unless you're on American territory."

Nas gave her a puzzled look. Every expression on the woman's face felt amplified. Her eyes were dark pools beneath angular brows, and when she looked straight at someone, they radiated intensity.

"We don't want to run back to 'safety,'" she went on, getting more animated. "We're grateful for your help, but we can't just give up everything about our lives to cower in fear in some safehouse in the United States."

Jimmy leaned forward, touching his daughter's arm.

"We're not afraid," he said to the Americans, "and we want

to cooperate as much as we can to make your jobs easier...but we have made the most important discovery of our lives. Can you see that?"

He looked to each of them.

Nas went on, "We love America! It's our home, the country that saved us. And we know the risks that we're taking—we know better than anyone what the Islamic Republic of Iran would do to us. But we're not done on this dig. We've just begun our discovery process!"

Melden held up a hand. "Dr. Aslani! Dr. Aslani. We're not taking you away right now. We're giving you a protective detail and monitoring the threat, but as we expressed to you when we first had the Greek police pick you up, there is an active bounty out there *right now* for both of you. Both."

What passed behind Jimmy Aslani's gaze at that moment, Ridley would probably never be able to grasp. He said nothing.

Though she'd been letting Melden run this operation so far out of the official mouth of the State Department, Ridley finally sat forward and spoke.

"Jimmy. Nas. You found something most archaeologists would give at *least* one limb for. You've changed history already. Gabe and I are here to protect you—but also to make sure you can follow up on whatever loose ends you have to before you make your way back to the States."

I'm not here to drag you back home. I'm here to go on your adventure.

Nas looked at Ridley so intently that she wondered if the woman had heard her very thoughts.

"We're both so, so grateful," she said.

"Yes," said Jimmy, "and you're right. We have some things we need to follow on before we return home."

Gabe gave Ridley a sideways glance. She knew his mission plainly: protect the principals. He did not know hers, but he'd be trying to guess it with every step they took. She'd wait as long as humanly possible before letting him in on the classified side.

Jimmy looked out the glass doors, at the bright waters of the Aegean Sea spilling against the building. He murmured to his daughter, as if they were the only two in the room.

IN FARSI: *"Last night I passed by the ruins of Tus, And saw that the owl had taken the place of the peacock. I asked, 'What news from these ruins?'"*

Nas reached up to touch the hibiscus blossom behind her ear, and finished the poem in a soft voice.

IN FARSI: *"It answered, 'The news is—Alas, Alas.'"*

The Americans couldn't understand a word, but they could see the look that passed between father and daughter, like they'd just taken some solemn oath.

"We'll take you there this afternoon," said Nas. "To the dig site. We'll show you—you can see for yourself what we've found and why we have to keep going."

CHAPTER NINE

PAROS, GREECE

Two hours later, Laura Melden declared her work here done. As much as she wanted to spend the night on fairytale island, her official duties would not allow it.

They all piled into the Honda CRV with the Aslanis and drove back to Parikia, to the port. They bought four ferry tickets to Serifos, then they bid goodbye to Melden.

"I'm in touch with your boss," she had told Ridley just before heading down the dock to where Clark was loitering on the mini power yacht. "State's running point, but I'm not an asshole. Usually. It's a joint operation."

The division chief at the CIA will be so thrilled to hear that from a Regional Security Officer sitting in an embassy office that probably doesn't even have air conditioning.

"What a relief," said Ridley with a smile.

On the ride to the ferry, Agent Gabe Tolkin had communicated to Nas and Jimmy Aslani what this protection detail would be like.

"Your safety is *my* entire objective."

It's sort-of-not-really mine.

"I'm not here to cramp your style or prevent you from doing what you're here to do," he'd said, "but I'm gonna need your cooperation to help me keep you safe."

Nas and Jimmy both listened attentively.

"That includes no social media posting. Keep your cell phones turned off, or on airplane mode, unless you clear it with me for a specific use. I'll tell you what to expect in each hotel, traveling through cities, on ferries—all that."

He gestured at Ridley.

"She's helping you get all you need out here—your own objectives. But if things ever go sideways, I make the call. You can't find shit if you're dead, so..."

It was true, but Ridley hated the thought of having to give up operational command.

Nas and Jimmy had nodded, saying they understood and would cooperate with whatever they had to do.

A few minutes later, as Ridley and Gabe boarded the ferry, each of them had become a discreet head on a swivel. Only a handful of other people were aboard the ferry at this hour, a couple Greeks and the rest tourists. No one showed the slightest interest in the Aslanis for the hour-and-a-half trip.

They sat two and two facing each other across a table, Ridley next to Jimmy, Gabe next to Nas. Eyes in both directions. The four of them played rummy to pass the time.

Ridley had gathered information on the Aslanis, but it was something else to watch it all come alive in front of her.

Jimmy was the quiet one, a thoughtful man who took time choosing his words, but was soon possessed of some whipping trash talk.

Nasrin was a self-proclaimed "loud woman." She was animated as if by rocket fuel, her voice lifting, her hands gesturing about, her eyes flashing when she spoke. What had made her such a beacon for the women of Iran—even as she resided half a world away—were so many of the things that had also made her a lightning rod for the wrath of the Iranian regime.

Can't keep her hidden...

She was also wretched at cards, but nonetheless somehow delighted in playing every hand.

"Baba," she laughed as Jimmy laid down his fourth run of cards, "have mercy on your new friends!"

Gabe had to keep pushing her hand up to avoid seeing the fan of cards she was holding.

"I have no friends in cards," he said as he put down a discard. "I see only losers."

Ridley leaned forward, picked up from the deck, and laid out three kings.

"I don't lose at cards," she said with a Cheshire cat grin, "or any other game."

Nas gave a gasping laugh. "Oh no, you're going to kill each other. He is only a terrible man when he plays cards, I promise."

"And you wanted us to play cards?" said Gabe dryly.

"I didn't think you would beat him."

Jimmy sniffed. "Nobody has beat me. Keep playing."

Gabe put down a jack, building on Jimmy's run. "Maybe everyone will."

"No weapons," chuckled Ridley as the Iranian man gaped.

"Did you two know each other before?" asked Nas, glancing between the Americans.

With a bemused look, Gabe gave a little shake of his head. Ridley pulled an expression of, *definitely not.*

"Well, I'm glad you're both here. And about to lose to me."

Nas laid down the rest of her hand, slapped a discard face down onto the pile, and grinned at them.

Ridley blinked in surprise, trying to mentally tally up her cards. Gabe snickered, shaking his head, and Jimmy muttered something under his breath in Farsi.

"It was my hair that blinded you, wasn't it?" said Nas. "It's very powerful. It scares the ayatollahs."

SERIFOS, GREECE

The island of Serifos looked much like Paros, with the same scrubby hills, sparkling waters, and stacks of bone-white buildings, though it was barely a third the size of the other island. There were just about 1,200 inhabitants here, with tourists comprising the rest of the throngs that milled through the port and lolled along the beaches.

Ridley, Gabe, and the Aslanis stepped off the ferry onto a broad concrete dock. A heavy wind tore at their clothes as they headed toward land in a swarm of people wheeling suitcases and lugging their bags.

Expect trouble here. This is the Aslanis' base, the island that made the headlines with their discovery.

She and Gabe had instinctively taken up flanking positions with their protectees. They might clash in every other way, but she felt a brush of relief that they could operate together without friction.

So far.

As they approached the small parking lot at the end of the dock, Ridley caught sight of a young man standing beside a white Jeep Renegade. He had close-cropped dark hair, olive skin, and the look of a curious otter. He was searching the crowd, and when he spotted Nas and Jimmy, his gaze locked in.

Ridley muttered to Gabe, "Unknown person, one o'clock, white Jeep."

"I spot him."

Though she generally found protective work achingly boring, the threat alert still cranked up the voltage in her.

They were closing on the end of the long dock—twenty yards...fifteen...

Then the man shifted his weight forward, about to move toward them—

Ridley pulled Nas back, stepping in front, hand hovering at her waistband. Gabe did the same with Jimmy, fingers grazing the hem of his T-shirt, at any second ready to yank it upward for the draw.

"What—" said Nas, but quickly saw where they were both looking. "Oh, that's Nik! That's our ride. I know, he may look like an assassin, but he's just an archeologist."

Ridley and Gabe both relaxed.

"He's an excavator," explained Jimmy, which meant nothing to either of them. "Very fussy."

As they walked toward the Jeep, Nik greeted them with quick smiles.

"Welcome back," he said to the Aslanis.

"Ah, I can't wait to get back to our dig!" exclaimed Nas, giving him a hug. Then she turned to introduce the newcomers. "Nik, this is Ridley, and this is Gabe. They're our new protectors!"

"Oh," said Nik, his eyes going wide.

Ridley decided to use the second of her eight languages to break the ice.

IN GREEK: *"Don't worry. We're not here to interfere with the dig."*

Flawless. The excavator nearly took a full step back. Then he broke out into a full smile of delight.

IN GREEK: *"You're Greek?!"*

IN GREEK: *"I only spent summers here."*

IN GREEK: *"Oh, but you are still Greek! Welcome back!"*

Gabe leaned in. "How 'bout we just stick to some corn-fed English, as long as we all speak it?"

Her irritation at him trickled back.

"Come on," said Nas, waving a hand and heading to the Jeep. "I want to drive."

They all climbed into the Jeep. Gabe sat in the center in the back, mashed up snug against Ridley and Jimmy, while Nas took them on a ride.

They wove up into the hills beyond Chora, past the whitewashed village and blue domes and rickety windmills.

Somehow, Ridley had never been to Serifos before. Anytime she had left Paros, she preferred the quiet beaches of Naxos and its temple ruins, or the rugged azure glory of Zakynthos, or the White Mountains of Crete.

This place was a plucky little sibling of the more popular Cycladic destinations of Santorini and Mykonos. It had earned the reputation from antiquity, when it was one of the few islands that warded off the titanic invasion of Xerxes and his Persian legions, who had overwhelmed the three hundred Spartans at the Hot Gates of Thermopylae.

The Romans later used it as a place of exile, a pitiful place for their outcasts. Later it was the Byzantines, and then the Venetians, who exploited its mines for iron and copper.

Yet it had just gained a new shine. Thanks to a pair of Persians, it would forever be known as the island that reordered

Greek history—that hauled mythology into archaeology, and once-fictional heroes into the textbooks.

The dig site that had changed all of this looked like a sprawling rocky pit at the top of a remote hill.

As Ridley and the others climbed out, she marveled at it.

All the wonders of history still buried beneath the earth...and Osprey's here ready to clean them all up.

"This has been our work," Jimmy said to her, "every day for two years."

"Finally worth it?"

"You have to enjoy every day of the work. Even if it comes to nothing. You have *done* the work. That is good."

He gave her an encouraging, fatherly nod and headed toward the tents.

Gabe drifted toward Ridley's right side as they followed the others. He muttered something under his breath but it was muffled by her bad ear.

"Say again?" she said, turning her head.

"I said, are we gonna stand around here for weeks and watch them dig out coins?"

She let him hang in the pause for a moment, then spoke as if she knew something he didn't. "I think not."

The sight ahead of them was a tangle of gridded strings, scaffolding, towels and brushes and buckets and sieves. In the late afternoon sun, it seemed labor had slowed. A dozen dusty workers remained, some delicately brushing a wall, some organizing artifacts on tables.

Nik went over to a tablet screen setup under the tent. Nas made a beeline for a man who was just emerging from the palace ruins.

"Nasrin," called the man with a quick wave, "we're finishing for the day."

"Hi, Yannis. We're just here to show my new friends around—and don't worry, they have diplomatic immunity."

She grinned, beckoning the Americans to join her in the excavation.

"This is Yannis Kimoulis," said Nas. "He is the Senior Archaeologist of the Ephorate of Antiquities. The Greek government sent him to babysit us, when they realized that we really had discovered something *so important.*"

Yannis Kimoulis eyed the newcomers like they were intruders. He was an oak of a man in his forties who looked like the kind of archaeologist that a hermetic romance novelist would want on their cover. His button-up shirt was weathered and dusty, his thick chestnut hair pulled back in a tousled ponytail. He spoke with a mild Greek accent.

"Who are you with diplomatic immunity?" he said.

"Bodyguards," said Jimmy, passing by Yannis with such calm authority that the topic was immediately closed.

"Don't touch anything," said Yannis. "This is the property of the Greek government. You cannot take anything. That would be a crime and I don't care if you're a diplomat. A crime against our history."

Gabe flashed a sardonic two-finger salute.

Ridley gave him a smile and spoke.

IN GREEK: *"We don't want your stuff."*

His brows rose in surprise as she passed.

Nas and Jimmy wound their way through the grid, gesturing to each part of the site and rattling off all of the fascinating things they'd found, from stucco snakes painted on the walls to the shape of the ovens in the bakery.

They really love digging stuff up.

Then the two of them stopped in front of a large stone slab. Nas stared at it in wonder, as though seeing it again for the first time.

"This is it," she said.

To Ridley's eyes, it was just a mass of bizarre characters and foreign letters. She could read modern Greek, but not this jumble of shapes.

"You have it translated," she said, less a question than an acknowledgment.

"It's Linear B script," said Jimmy, hovering a sun-wrinkled hand over the stone. "We had it translated."

"You know what it says?" Nas turned to them in delight, her eyes aglow.

Obviously not—

"That Medusa really existed, and that Perseus brought back her head, and that King Polydectes died when he looked at it."

She drew a quick breath, and almost laughed out her next words—

"The gorgons were real."

CHAPTER TEN

SERIFOS, GREECE

There it is.

Ridley had known what was coming, but the archaeologist's words landed on Gabe as if he'd just been told that dragons were sighted over New Jersey.

Nas didn't wait for his response. She had no time for that, so swept straight into the story.

"A construction team discovered this place," she told them, leading them back out of the dig itself, up to the tents. "And it was so incredible but we had no idea whose palace this could be when we started to dig."

Gabe glanced at Ridley, looking for some affirmation of his own bewilderment. She only smirked and gave him a wink.

It had the intended effect to irk him—as he realized that none of this was a surprise to his new partner.

Nas stopped at a table in the shade, gesturing to a series of hand drawn diagrams and a cluster of computer tablets nearby.

"We think that we've uncovered forty percent of the whole palace so far."

"In two years?" said Gabe.

From a few yards away, Nik spoke up, coming in like a bull in a ring. "Two years of work? This is amazing."

Ridley couldn't help but peer over the maps of the complex. The sketchings were mundane enough, but then she caught sight of another piece of paper. On it was a small printed copy of an etching containing a strange alphabet...

"So, the stele," she said. "Let's talk about that."

Nas looked at Ridley, a grin blooming across her face. She snatched a book from the table and held it up.

The Greek Myths, by Robert Graves.

"Yes, let's talk about it."

Moments later, Nas and Jimmy sat in fold-out camping chairs across from Ridley and Gabe. The winds atop this hill swept at their hair and billowed their clothes.

Nas had lit up recounting the story of Medusa, Perseus, and King Polydectes. While Ridley had let Booker tell her the tale, she was more than a little familiar with it, having spent so much of her time on the islands with a proud Greek grandmother.

She was now mostly watching Gabe discreetly. He was hard to gauge as he listened to these rather fantastical claims, though his bright blue gaze never left the eyes of whichever Aslani was speaking.

"Perseus did not want to become king," said Jimmy. "He gave up the throne to the brother of Polydectes."

"But he still had all of these gifts that the gods had given him to slay Medusa," said Nas. "He was the most powerful man on the island! Nobody ever told about what he did with all of those items. But this stele," said Nas, leaning forward and holding up the paper copy, "it does."

Jimmy was watching his daughter intently as excitement rippled off her. He seemed to be reserved about all this.

"What were they?" asked Ridley.

She already knew, having done her traditional meticulous preparation on the plane ride from D.C., but this was Nas' story to tell, and Gabe needed the primer.

Walk him through it.

"A polished shield that Athena gave to Perseus so he could see Medusa in the reflection—not look at her directly.

"He got a pair of winged sandals from Hermes so he could get near her without any noise, and make a very fast escape. Hermes also gave him a Harpe sword, so sharp that it could take off her head in one swing.

"The Hesperides gave him a *kibisis*—a special bag to put her head in."

Gabe raised a finger. "Who were the Hesperides?"

"They were 'the nymphs of the evening' or 'the sunset goddesses,' daughters of one of the Titans. They watched over a garden with golden apples in it—but those were probably really just oranges."

"Oh, probably *really.*" He gave a faux nod of understanding.

Nas went on, "And the last thing was a Helm of Darkness, of invisibility. He got that from Hades, the god of the underworld and the dead, because his name means, 'the unseen one.' Then, after he killed Medusa, Perseus went around the world and hid all of these things, and someone wrote down on this stele *where* he put them."

This is the stuff that really gets Booker's pulse going.

Gabe looked back and forth between the Aslanis. "So what about it?"

Nas looked at her father. "We're going to find these things."

"These...magical things? Around the world?" said Gabe.

She shrugged. "They might be magical, but they're not really around the world we know today. 'Around the world' in ancient Greek times meant around the Mediterranean and some of Africa and some of the Middle East."

"Are you saying you already know where they are?" asked Ridley. "Or are you guessing it's just around that area?"

"We translated it," said Jimmy. "We applied the old words to our modern geography. Athens. Egypt. Morocco. Spain, and Italy."

"You're trying to..." started Gabe, "*go* to all those places? Looking for magical items?"

"They might not be magical," repeated Nas in exasperation, "but yes. We're going."

He turned to look at Ridley. "Oh, is this why you're here?"

She raised a palm up. "I'm ready for magic."

Not really, Samaras, but sometimes you just end up with it.

His expression dripped with annoyance. "Look," he said to the Aslanis, "my job is to keep you safe. That's it. Not safe running around Africa and Europe—just safe—where you are now."

"I'm sorry, but we have to go," said Nas, shaking her head as if she pitied him.

"Come on, Gabe," said Ridley, happy to needle him. "Could you really resist finding out what this trail of breadcrumbs is all about?"

"I happen to find it completely resistible."

"I thought they picked you because you were the readiest officer for the job."

"I'm ready to do *my* job."

"So do it. Wherever that means."

They stared each other down in a moment that was becoming increasingly uncomfortable for Jimmy Aslani.

"We told the State Department that we had to go somewhere," said the older man. "They knew we had to travel."

"Traveling to Egypt is kind of different than a wine and pasta tour in the Italian countryside," said Gabe.

Ridley's eyes roved the dig site.

In the slanting golden light of late afternoon, the workers were starting to wrap up. She wondered how the Greek ones fared with the rigorous dig schedule, not able to take their traditional leisurely lunch or late nap. She hadn't even seen any coffee on site.

Monstrous.

"What about the dig?" asked Ridley. "Why leave now after such a huge discovery?"

Nas brushed a thick tress of hair out of her face. Her expression sobered.

"Because we don't have all the time in the world," she said. "This is the discovery that needs to be made now. If we don't go...someone else will, eventually."

Jimmy glanced away.

He has reservations.

"What's the point of all these things again?" said Gabe "You gonna shine 'em up—give 'em to a museum?"

"It would turn over everything we understand about history and mythology."

He arched a brow at her, but Nas had had it with his condescension. She leaned forward and delivered every word like a punch.

"Yes, we can actually change things in the world, Agent Tolkin, if we are not afraid. If *you* are afraid, then you can go back home or stay here and sit at the dig site. I don't care."

He sighed and looked off to the radiant cerulean waters.

"I'm gonna want souvenirs," he said, brushing something imaginary off his thigh.

A grin crawled across Nas' lips. "We will get you a *galabiya*."

Ridley chuckled.

"A what?" said Gabe.

Nas leaned forward and patted his arm. "Or a pharaoh's crown."

"Great, okay. And I'll get you 'not dead.'"

"This is going to be amazing," she said, wriggling upright in her chair. "The adventure of your *life*."

How many "adventures of my life" have I had already...

"Who's gonna run the dig?" asked Ridley. "They're not all stopping work on it, right?"

Jimmy glanced over at Yannis, still looking like a lion-tamer scouting his next job. "The Greek government steers the ship now."

"Now that we found something valuable," added Nas. "They take it over."

"And Nik will be in here," said Jimmy. "He's a very good archaeologist. A very good young man."

Gabe ran a hand over his hair, sweeping it back into place against the wind.

It was resolved. Ridley tried to conceal her satisfaction.

"So," she said, leaning forward in her chair to face Nas, "show me where we go first."

CHAPTER ELEVEN

ATHENS, GREECE

ATHENS WAS the oldest capital in Europe.

None of the four million people who were currently packed into the ancient city could really imagine life in 11,000 BC, but the pride of their history still thrummed in the streets.

Ridley and Gabe and the Aslanis landed back on the mainland late the next afternoon, getting off the ferry with their bags. Gabe wore an extra-heavy backpack.

They hailed a taxi and headed into the heart of the city, the smell of jasmine blossoms, grilled souvlaki, and diesel exhaust swirling hot through the open windows.

For such an old place, Ridley had always been surprised at how little there really was to see of historical sites. Within the city proper, it was basically only the famed Acropolis and the few stubborn columns that remained of the ancient Agora.

And everywhere—*everywhere*—there was graffiti.

The taxi dropped them off outside a cream-colored apartment building in the neighborhood of Makrygianni. Just above these lively and elegant streets, the Acropolis loomed in the background like a grand, faded emperor.

Clutching her bag, Ridley was heading for the main entrance when a voice called down from above.

"*Xadérfi!*"

She squinted upward to see a woman leaning over a third floor balcony, a cheeky smile framed by a cascade of mahogany hair.

"Cousin!" called Ridley, breaking into a grin. "You haven't looked *down* at me since I was thirteen!"

"*Karagiózis,*" laughed the woman, and vanished inside.

Clown.

"She's your big cousin?" said Nas.

Ridley nodded. "She used to dress me up like a Spartan princess when I was little."

"A Spartan princess?" said Gabe with a mock pensive face.

"It was a mashup look."

The door to the apartment building swung open. Tonia Georgiadis burst out into the sunshine and went straight for Ridley with open arms.

"*Theé mou,* you are a giant!"

They exchanged a kiss on both cheeks.

Tonia was several inches shorter than Ridley, though most women were. She had the same thick hair and dark carving brows, but it was her warm, majestic, lively voice that most resembled her cousin's. Other than the faint Greek accent, they could have easily passed for each other over the phone.

"Your friends want a tour?" said Tonia, glancing at the others.

"Just of the Acropolis."

"That's all anybody wants in Athens."

"Tonia, meet my friends. Nasrin, Jimmy, Gabe."

She reached to shake their hands as each of them said hello, but seemed to freeze when she looked at Nas.

"Wait, you're—you're Nasrin *Aslani*."

Nas smiled. "Yes, my whole life."

Tonia's mouth went slack. She looked back at her cousin, her expression a gigantic question. When Ridley cheerfully ignored her, Tonia clasped Nas' hand in both of hers.

"You're a hero. A hero for women, for freedom—"

"Women, life, freedom!" Nas exclaimed.

"Can I give you a hug?"

Laughing, Nas embraced her newest friend.

"Are you hungry?" asked Tonia. "What are you doing here together? What would you like to see? Come in, please, come inside."

She ushered Nas toward the door. Jimmy followed them with a proud chuckle.

Gabe muttered to Ridley, "Well, we're not quite undercover."

Any undercover identity would have shredded like tissue paper.

They followed the others inside.

Tonia could have leaned on the kitchen table for hours listening to Nas talk over coffee and baklava. She had followed the Iranian woman on social media for years, seen her interviewed on television and cheered her cause from afar.

She had heard about the archaeological discovery that Nas and her father had made right there in Greece, but could hardly believe that only days later, the renowned human rights advocate would be sitting in her apartment, regaling her with all the passion that had made Nasrin Aslani such a force to be reckoned with.

Ridley gave them a few minutes, but kept glancing at the

clock as she crunched her way through the honeyed baklava. Jimmy had indulged in the flaky pastry like a man eating his last meal, and Tonia took his enjoyment as the highest compliment. Persians and Greeks spoke the same language of food and hospitality.

Gabe had eaten half a piece and discreetly left the rest on his plate.

Who the hell is this guy?

"Okay, *korítsia*—ladies," said Ridley, "we have to go."

Tonia sat up and looked at her watch. "Oh! Yes, I'm sorry. We have to go meet my husband. His latest tour is ending in a few minutes, and his next tour is *you*. You're going to love the Parthenon! Let me get my things."

She excused herself from the room in a hurry. Jimmy leaned toward Ridley.

"You didn't tell her...?"

Ridley gave a quick shake of her head.

"Oh, no," he sighed, leaning back. "We're going to be arrested."

"We just have to lose Stavros," whispered Ridley. "Tonia's done worse."

Gabe shook his head like he was babysitting an unruly bunch of children, and muttered into his coffee, "This is so stupid."

"Come on," said Nas, nudging his arm. "Have a sense of adventure! You know what we're about to find?"

Forty minutes later, they were standing on the most magnificent plateau in the world.

The Acropolis was a crown jewel of the ancient world, a complex of temples and statues perched high above the city. As the sun began to set over the waters beyond, its slanting rays poured like molten gold over the giant marble columns. Though the crowds were beginning to thin at this hour, tourists were still swarming along the immense stairway.

Nas and Jimmy basked in awe. Ridley and Gabe—still wearing his backpack—were in work mode, their heads never still, eyes scanning, bodies shifting to keep the Aslanis within arm's length at all times.

Bodyguarding is terrible. Crowds are terrible. This is the worst assignment since the Navy's trash detail.

As they passed by the smaller temple of Athena Nike that loomed off to the right of the steps, Tonia slid in beside her cousin.

IN GREEK: *"What are you doing with them?"*

Ridley replied without meeting her eyes.

IN GREEK: *"They wanted to come to the Acropolis."*

IN GREEK: *"You work as a diplomatic translator,"* said Tonia, *"but you don't speak Farsi."*

IN GREEK: *"But I do speak Greek, and here we are!"*

Tonia gave her only an arched look of disbelief. "You are full of such bullshit, my cousin," she said in English.

Ridley finally met her eyes. "Okay. You know the regime in Iran is trying to have both of them killed. Gabe is her bodyguard. I'm along for the ride."

IN GREEK: *"Is he your lover? The man is—"* said Tonia.

IN GREEK: *"Not for a second, not for an inch."*

IN GREEK: *"Then what are you..."*

Tonia frowned, but then her face lit.

IN GREEK: *"You're a spy!"* she gasped.

Ridley snorted.

That was a really great game of twenty questions, Samaras. Well played.

IN GREEK: *"I've never spied for anyone."*

IN GREEK: *"But you're not a translator. Look at you. I should have known, you fucking badass. My God."*

In a sudden overflow of delight, Tonia grabbed the back of her head with an affectionate jostle.

"I'm so proud of you!"

Gabe, having missed the entire exchange in Greek and being well aware of the purposeful exclusion, glanced at the pair, trying to guess at what had prompted the declaration.

"Oh, there he is!" said Tonia.

Twenty feet ahead of them, at the top of the stairs, stood a man just under six feet, with dark hair that was gelled high into a pompadour. He wore hiking shoes, a linen button-up, and carried a satchel slung across his chest.

Stavros Georgiadis grinned when he saw them approaching.

"Welcome home, Ridley!"

Ridley greeted him with a huge hug and kisses on both cheeks. She'd always liked the man who married her cousin. He battled some demons within his own mind, and a sense of deep melancholy often shadowed his gaze, but Stavros loved Tonia as beautifully as any man she knew adored his wife.

Ridley made the introductions for the rest of her companions, and when Stavros was introduced to the Aslanis, he did a more subdued double take than Tonia's reaction. Of course he knew who they were. They'd made all the headlines in Greek cultural news. For a licensed tour guide, they were practically the rock stars of the moment.

"I'm honored to be your guide today," he said as they passed through the columns of the entrance. "If you see around us, we're passing right now through the Propylaea. It was the open-air building that looks like a temple, but really it's just a gateway for passing from the profane world outside into this sacred space."

As the path narrowed, Ridley grew tense. The proximity to the other tourists had tightened. Everyone who passed by the Aslanis felt like a suspect.

Then Stavros led them out into the vast sprawl of the Acropolis. Nas and Jimmy gazed about in wonder. Even Gabe looked impressed.

"You see here in the front," said Stavros, gesturing to the open plaza, "there stood originally a colossal statue of Athena Promachos, the goddess of wisdom and war. It was forty feet high and made of bronze in 456 BC. She stood with a spear and a shield and reflected the sun and looked out over the city that carried her name. And 'Promachos' means 'champion who fights on the front line.'"

And that warrior woman is what we're here for.

Ridley glanced at her tactix Delta watch. Only twenty minutes until the site closed.

"Stav, can we see the Temple of Athena Nike?" she said.

"You don't want to see the Parthenon first?" he asked, rather surprised. "If we only have a few minutes, I would recommend do that first. Or the Erechtheion."

Nas piped up. "I would love to see the Athena Nike."

Nike. *Victory.* Athena was always victorious, but they needed an extra temple just to celebrate that point.

There were statues of and temples for the goddess all over the Acropolis. She was the patron saint of the city who had beaten out Poseidon for the honors. His gift had been striking open a spring for the city to have water—only it was saltwater. Her gift had been an olive tree, which was said to be the same one standing beside the Erechtheion, one of the temples that housed yet another statue of Athena.

"Well, okay," said Stavros, puzzled and a bit deflated. "This way."

He trekked back toward the gate, but this time veered off to the edge. Gabe clutched at the straps of his heavy backpack. Sweat was dampening his shirt beneath. Ridley felt the sticky heat of her Glock pressing against the small of her back.

Tonia and Stav are going to hate you for this...

They reached the temple. It was a small, simple rectangle of marble, built on an even older stone bastion that jutted out at the front of the Acropolis.

The Aslanis immediately began canvassing, meticulously inspecting every foot of it. Nas placed a hand on one of the thick marble columns and gazed up.

"What's beneath the temple?" she asked.

"Beneath the Acropolis?" said Stavros.

"*Right* below this temple."

There are always things under other things in these old places.

"Old Mycenaean cave-like things. More like niches than tunnels. They were probably made for small shrines."

Tonia shot Ridley a look, as if she saw a balloon of secrets floating between her and Nas, about to burst.

"My young friend," said Jimmy. "We need to get into those."

"Oh, you can't," said Stavros. "They are completely blocked off."

Nas looked at him with those enormous dark eyes and gave a disarmingly warm smile.

"We did already know that, but we wanted to make sure, and to ask if you'll help us get into them."

He snorted. "I can't! I'm not going to break into those spaces. I would lose my tour guide license. We would all get arrested!"

IN GREEK: *"What the hell are you doing?"* Tonia hissed at Ridley.

Ridley spoke back in English. "It's part of their dig. You know what they just discovered on Serifos. You know they're onto something."

"I don't care! This is my husband's job! How can you ask this?"

Nas moved closer to their distressed Greek hosts.

"I'm sorry for what I'm asking, but I must. Greece has wonders beneath her, just waiting to be discovered."

"I know," snapped Tonia.

Gabe puffed out his cheeks and slid Ridley a side-eye.

She had set this all up. The violation was on her. She stepped up, hands raised, and spoke gently.

"I'm sorry for dragging you into this. We don't need you to set foot in those tunnels, Stav. We just need you to help us run interference."

The tour guide's eyes went wide. "You know the security here? They send guards through the whole place to make sure no one is hiding. They have CCTV. There is security on site all night. How can you do this?!"

Ridley put on a jovial grin.

"I've watched all the movies!"

CHAPTER TWELVE

ATHENS, GREECE

Dusk fell over Athens. Guards swept the Acropolis. The staff locked the gates. Overnight watchmen monitored the cameras from their hut.

As it turned out, it was a lot easier to watch Tom Cruise than it was to be Ethan Hunt.

But their team was the right one. Stavros knew the blind spots, and he knew the camera setup from a vandalism investigation he'd once been called into as a witness.

"There's one camera that's pointed at the front of the Athena Nike," he told them.

There would be no knocking out camera feeds. That would raise the alarms that something was wrong. It was far more effective to nudge a camera just slightly off track. In the monotony of watching dozens of screens every night, it was much less likely to be noticed by a bored security guard.

It was Tonia who found it, camouflaged in a nearby tree along the slope, its lens pointed straight at their temple.

It was Gabe who shucked his backpack and hauled himself up into the tree before Ridley could reach it.

The largest temples of the Acropolis were illuminated like beacons for the world to behold their greatness each night. The Parthenon was an epic sight to behold, the columns a blaze of yellow in the darkness. Spotlights shone up the cliffs all around the Acropolis, etching ragged shadows along its walls.

The six intruders gazed up at the only wall that mattered to them.

"You do whatever you need to from here," said Tonia, her arms folded across her chest. "We're not part of it."

Ridley knew she had stung her cousin, showing up after so many years only to use her and her husband.

Work can make you a real piece of shit to your own people, Samaras.

Ridley turned to her, and the shade of remorse in her voice was real. "Tonia, thank you. And I'm sorry. Stav—"

Stavros, looking more than a bit anxious, met her eyes. He was practically jittering to leave.

"—thank you. I know how much you just risked for us."

He nodded. Tonia shook Ridley's head and pulled her into a fierce hug.

IN GREEK: *"It must be important, you fool. I love you."*

Ridley squeezed her tightly. Tonia surely did love her, but she didn't know her well enough anymore to know which ear was the bad one. She'd spoken into Ridley's damaged right side. Her voice was little more than a muffle.

IN GREEK: *"You're my favorite cousin, you know,"* said Ridley as she pulled away.

IN GREEK: *"Of course I am. I crowned you first."*

Nas gave Tonia an especially gushing dose of gratitude, and

a moment later, the Georgiadis' went slinking quietly down the hill.

Gabe snatched up the heavy backpack again.

"Okay," said Jimmy with a deep breath of resolve. "Come on, children."

They hiked up the steep embankment to the base of the main entrance. Rising straight above them was the temple of Athena Nike.

"'Nike' means 'victory' in Greek," murmured Nas as she gazed up at the dilapidated stones.

Jimmy smiled at his daughter, "I think she knows that."

Ridley's eyes were fixed on the two doors cut into the marble rock at the base. "The mighty Greeks said: just do it. Just be victorious."

Gabe slid off his backpack. "So is this when you turn into Lara Croft?"

"I can feel it happening already. Boob job and a billion dollars."

From the bag, he pulled a short crowbar and offered it to her.

"I want the sledge," she said, refusing his offer.

"I carried this goddamn bag all day." He stood up gripping the handle of a sledgehammer. "It's mine."

He handed her the crowbar.

"*Malaka*," she muttered darkly, and took it.

They turned to the temple.

The two doorways were immaculately cut into the foundation structure, barely two feet separating them. They'd been bricked up with stones, walled off like the Cask of Amontillado.

Time to do away with that.

Gabe stepped up into the alcove, braced himself, and slugged at them. The sound of iron crushing against rock would have drawn out Pan himself from the caves. Jimmy winced at the volume. Ridley gave a quick scan of the slopes to see if anyone else had been alerted by the noise.

Just below them, the arches of the Herodeion glowed against the cityscape, the steps of its amphitheater unfurling downward. For a second, Ridley's mind flashed with a memory —*scampering onto the stage with Tonia and her friends, sweat trickling down their backs, hollering loud lines of Shakespeare that were surely butchered by their poor recollections.*

Gabe swung the sledge again and again, the giant mallet smashing until the rocks began to crumble. He pulled and pawed them away until there was an opening.

Darkness yawned.

He stepped down from the ledge.

"Probably no Iranian assassins hiding in there," he said. "All yours."

Ridley clipped a Nitecore flashlight onto her belt loop and climbed up into the doorway. She'd broken into more than a few tunnels in her lifetime that had been sealed for centuries, and she'd expected the draft of air that came out of this one to be musty and stale. It wasn't.

There must be a source of fresh air somewhere else.

"Okay," she said, hefting the crowbar in one hand. "Let's see if the gods come out to play."

Jimmy urged Nas to go on. Gabe offered her a hand as she climbed up into the doorway. As she crowded against the American's back, Ridley glanced over her shoulder.

"You know what we're lookin' for in here?"

Nas nodded. "I know."

Ridley climbed into the tunnel.

CHAPTER THIRTEEN

ATHENS, GREECE

THE SPACE WAS BIGGER than Ridley had expected.

The sides and ceiling were surprisingly smooth, giving it the appearance more of a palace passageway than a tunnel within a cliff.

Nas climbed in behind her. She pulled out a small flashlight and gazed about in wonder.

"Wow..." she breathed. "This makes it—it's all real!"

Irony. The archaeologist is amazed. The CIA operative is not.

"Tunnels?" said Ridley. "Real, and pretty common."

"I know this, but I know—" she said, pressing an impassioned fist against her chest. "We are in the right place."

"Shouldn't be hard to miss a big shiny shield, right?"

Ridley pulled the flashlight off her belt as she padded forward, sweeping the beam over walls and ceiling. A few yards ahead, the tunnel swerved.

"I don't think the shield is sitting in the middle of the

tunnel, out in the open," said Nas, following close behind, her own flashlight bobbing along.

"Would be refreshing, though."

Nas cocked a smile as she watched the back of the American's head.

"Do you do this a lot?" she asked.

"I've seen a few tunnels, yeah."

They rounded the bend and saw it stretch ahead for another fifteen yards before it curved again.

But there—on one of the walls—they caught sight of something small jutting out. Before Ridley even knew how to react, Nas had slid past her and gone straight for the odd object.

"They're leaves," she said.

Ridley got closer, peering closely with her light. They were indeed leaves, thin and silvery-green—and they were growing through a crevice in the wall.

"It's an olive tree," she said, frowning.

If you cut a Greek, they'd bleed olive oil. The trees were everywhere in Greece.

"Growing underground..." said Nas. "This is it. This is it!"

She tapped the wall.

These things never make sense.

Ridley re-clipped her flashlight to her belt, lifted the crowbar, and with all her strength, jammed it into the crevice. She wedged and wrenched at it until a sheen of sweat emerged across her brow—until a piece of the rock broke under the iron lever.

"Water from the leaves must have weakened it," she said.

She swung the claw end against the broken section until it crumbled away. Ridley brushed past the leaves and stepped over the pile of loose rock.

The beam of her flashlight landed in a small chamber. It

may have started as a natural cave, but it had been hewn and chiseled away until it resembled a small, circular temple.

In the very center sat a stone owl, perched on a dais. In the beam of light, its eyes glittered green.

Placing a hand on Ridley's shoulder, Nas stepped into the chamber. She gasped.

"Emeralds," she said.

"Oh, so is this a *treasure* treasure hunt?"

Both of them approached the statue. It was life sized, and to Ridley's eyes, the gems were genuine. And valuable.

Nas sighed. "Archaeologists can't dig to fill their own pockets."

"So it belongs in a museum?" said Ridley, her gaze roving over the rest of the space.

The olive tree had grown up along one of the walls and was almost melted into the stone. Its branches were reaching for the crevice like somehow it knew that fresh air lay beyond.

Impossible that it grew without sunlight.

"How old can this be?" said Nas, going over to run her fingers along the bark. "How could it grow down here?"

Something along the wall caught Ridley's eye. She lifted her flashlight and moved closer.

It was a spear carved out of the rock, nearly as tall as Ridley. The tip looked sharp enough to use in battle.

"In case we didn't know that this was Athena's temple," said Ridley.

"Look!" exclaimed Nas, crossing to another part of the wall.

There was a shield carved out of it, nearly the size of a manhole cover.

"Athena was the most fierce," she said in excitement. "Some say it was Ares, but he was so impulsive and bloodthirsty. She was strategic and thought ten steps ahead of everyone else, so when she committed to a fight, she *committed.*"

"Yeah," said Ridley, but her eyes had spotted the last symbol on the wall: the head of a gorgon.

It was hideous. Lips spread back from an oversized mouth... fangs that looked more like tusks...a wild tangle of snakes sprouting from her head...and a stare so lifelike that Ridley recoiled.

Nas looked from one carving to the next to the next...

"The spear and shield because she was the goddess of war. The olive tree for the peace and prosperity she gave to Athens—for a while—and the gorgon."

She stared at it for a moment, as though unsettled into silence.

"Perseus could never have defeated Medusa without Athena's help. You know after he used her head to turn King Polydectes into stone, he gave it to Athena. She put it on her shield, the most fearsome sight that anyone could see in battle."

"Mildly disgusting. What are we doing in here admiring this artwork?"

Nas pulled out a folded paper from her pocket, pulled it open and scanned.

"We have to use the owl," she said. "It's 'Athena's wisdom.'"

They turned to the jewel-eyed statue.

"To do what?"

"To..." said Nas, turning to look at each of the symbols on the wall, "direct her gaze to the right object, and the right object is...Well, I don't know if it's the shield or the gorgon, but I'm sure it's one of those two."

She glanced down at the copy of the stele etchings in her hand. Ridley swung the crowbar up to rest on her shoulder, propping her other hand on her hip.

Nas looked up, as if feeling her annoyance. "I couldn't figure it out before because I didn't know what symbols would be here. The stele says 'that repels.'"

Ridley looked at the gorgon head carved on the wall, this time determined not to look away.

Staredown with a rock. What a professional.

"I guess we can just try—" said Nas.

And before Ridley knew it, she'd stepped up to the statue of the owl and rotated its head to face the gorgon.

"Wait—"

Ridley lunged forward. She was too late to stop Nas, but just in time to avoid being crushed.

A chunk of stone the size of a suitcase dropped from the ceiling, smashing into the ground where she'd just been standing in front of the gorgon.

Nas' eyes ballooned. "Oh, my God. I'm sorry!"

"Tricks and traps," muttered Ridley, shaking it off. "I guess we can say...it's the shield?"

"Yeah, I guess *now.*"

This time, Ridley turned the owl's head, until the gleaming emerald of its gaze faced the symbol of the shield.

There was a cracking sound from within the wall. Nas took a step back, throwing her arm in front of Ridley as if shielding a baby in a carseat. Ridley slowly pushed it down.

The stone shield detached from the wall and fell to the ground.

Behind it, embedded in a small alcove, was a real brass shield. It shone so brightly that the flashlight beams coming back nearly blinded them. They had to point away from it.

Nas let out an exultant laugh of disbelief, covering her mouth with both hands.

"That's the shield of Perseus! I mean, Athena! *What?!*"

A little grin slipped across Ridley's face. This intrepid archaeologist had just made the discovery of her life a few weeks ago. Right in *this* moment, she'd made a discovery that dwarfed all her understanding of the world.

"Can we just...take it?" asked Nas, moving toward the wall.

"I hope so."

The surface of the shield was practically a mirror, it was so shiny. It was pressed deeply into a near-perfect indentation in the stone, so Ridley had to use the crowbar to pry it out. And it was heavy.

"Oh no, we have to carry this everywhere with us?" said Nas, feeling the weight of it.

"Well, the Greek gods were a little cruel," started Ridley, but then she spotted something on the back of the shield.

There was some device in the dead center of the circle, like a handle. She reached out to fiddle with it—and it turned.

The outer rim of the shield shifted, retracting until the entire thing had folded into itself like a circular fan. Within a moment, Ridley was holding a piece of brass that looked no bigger than a can of cranberry jelly.

This time, she laughed out loud. "Leave it to a goddess to go to war in practical fashion."

Nas gave her a funny look. "You don't actually believe that, though—about goddesses and gods."

She has no idea.

She couldn't tell Nas about what she'd seen in her work. She couldn't even articulate to herself what she understood of the world, but if this woman was dismissing even the possibility...

Much of Osprey's work was plowing into dark corners, working in deep shadows, and flying blind at breakneck pace.

Ridley had never been one to ruminate for long on the assignment at hand. Some of them had pushed her to the brink of her own sanity, had demanded she run her courage out onto the thinnest of ice, and had broken her body with cracks and cuts.

But once the mission was complete, she needed to go back to the world that made sense. Darts at the local bar, pickup basketball, taking Maddie on sniffy walks, laps in the pool, martial arts training, grilled cheese sandwich-making...if she couldn't shut away the gruesome and otherworldly horrors from replaying in her head all day, she would never be a fully functional person, or a useful operative.

And yet, none of it was ever really forgotten.

Ridley dodged her head and arched a brow.

"I don't rule things out," she said finally.

"You don't rule out *gods?*" said Nas, incredulous.

"What was it Howard Carter said when he saw inside King Tut's tomb?"

It was just the right reference to light up the eyes of an archaeologist.

Nas replied, "They'd just broken a small chunk out of the sealed door, enough so that Carter could lean through it with a candle. Lord Carnarvon was standing behind him and asked, *'Can you see anything?'* and he said, *'Wonderful things.'* It was the only pharaoh's tomb to ever be found intact, with all its treasure."

Ridley hefted the weight of the bronze block in her hand.

"I think you're going to see wonderful things," she said.

CHAPTER FOURTEEN

ATHENS, GREECE

When traveling on diplomatic papers, everything went through official channels. That meant that the Egyptian government knew they were coming.

Which meant they had to leave their guns at the embassy in Athens.

Laura Melden had been watching with one hand on her hip, the other clutching a coffee.

"We tried," she said. "They only allow it in 'extraordinary circumstances' and even then, they'd drag out the whole process going through nine fucking agencies over three weeks. Then they'd insist on escorting you around everywhere as *hosts* with their own armed brigade formerly known as 'spies.'"

She glanced in the direction of the lobby, where the Aslanis waited.

"They're not very happy about an Iranian dissident with

Nas' profile entering the country, either," she added. "So at least we got *that* concession."

Egypt was no friend of Iran, whom they saw as the most destabilizing force in the Middle East, funding terrorist proxy groups in every corner of the region. In recent years, though, the two nations had begun to thaw toward each other, with the Iranian Foreign Minister visiting Cairo in an attempt to reopen relations.

Iran could use Egypt's diplomatic clout. Egypt could benefit economically from trading with Iran. It wasn't out of the question that corrupt agents within the Egyptian government would tip off the Iranians to the presence of one of their most wanted former citizens.

And yet, no firearms allowed for them in Egypt.

"At least none of us will stand out," Ridley had grumbled, glancing at Gabe as they handed over their Glocks to an American officer.

"We blonde babes do have it hard," said Melden.

Gabe shot Ridley a sideways look. "Who gets further in the Middle East, a blond man or a brunette woman?"

"We'll lay a bet," said Ridley.

"Do you speak Arabic?"

"No."

Damnit. I need to learn.

"Then I'm in," he said, unclipping the holster from his belt.

CAIRO, EGYPT

They touched down on the hot runway that afternoon.

It had been some time since Ridley had been to this sprawling juggernaut of tradition and pollution that was Cairo.

They'd had to provide an itinerary to Egyptian authorities, but didn't want any diplomatic escorts from the host nation. The four of them passed through customs in an expedited line due to their diplomatic papers.

Ridley felt the suspicion lurking in every officer. She decided that she hated traveling on diplomatic passports. She'd rather sneak in and out of countries with fake IDs. The risk was worth it to fly under the radar, and cover stories were much more fun than feeling like customs was breathing down their necks.

Then there was the issue of traveling with a wanted woman. Nas' public profile was far greater than Jimmy's. Here in Cairo, the risk of being recognized was significantly higher. The Islamic Republic had maintained a network there for years, underground and deadly with ever-watchful eyes.

Thirty minutes after the plane had landed, they stepped out of the airport into the dry blast of sun.

As they walked toward the pickup line, Nas took out her mobile phone and waggled it in front of Gabe.

"Can I check the news quickly?" she asked.

"Quickly is thirty seconds," he said.

She turned it on and scrolled through a feed. Her brows knit as she looked at the screen.

Jimmy dropped back and spoke to her quietly in Farsi. Her response was sharp, grieved. They went back and forth with increasing frustration, until Nas shut the phone off and slid it back into her pocket.

Gabe, in his mirrored aviators, glanced back at them discreetly.

Beside him, Ridley muttered, "I don't like distress in a language that I don't understand."

"You think they're hiding something?"

She shrugged. “Some people call it privacy.”

But everyone is hiding something.

“Everything okay?” Ridley asked, turning around.

Nas shook her head, as if trying to restrain an emotion that couldn’t be tamed.

“The regime is about to execute a man in Iran. Mehrab Jalali. They accused him of *baghi*—rebellion against the government, but his trial was done in secret. He was tortured in prison, but he has not given up even while much of the world forgot about him. His mother, Pakhshan...she has sent me so many messages and is pleading with everyone who will listen to help her son. I’m doing everything I can—it’s not enough...”

The rest of the sentence strangled in her throat.

“You’re receiving messages?” said Gabe sharply.

“I didn’t answer her!”

Jimmy quietly took his daughter’s bag so she could wipe her eyes before the tears brimmed out.

Both the CIA and the State Department had Ridley and Gabe plugged into an alert system. Any chatter that emerged on the dark channels which referenced the Aslanis would be immediately alerted on their own phones.

A breeze riffled their clothes as they approached an SUV marked with diplomatic plates.

“You can message her back,” said Gabe finally, “but only this *one time*.”

Nas nodded. “I understand.”

But the look on her face was as though he had just announced the man’s death.

Their driver from the embassy, a middle-aged American named Tom, wound the SUV through the teeming mass of cars and mopeds and buses and tuk-tuks. Horns blared and the occasional stray dog scurried through the dusty streets. Ten million people lived in this clogged metropolis, and sometimes it felt like they were all in the same square block.

Tom gave them the most officious version of small chat that Ridley had ever heard, but he peppered it with enough tips on etiquette and suggestions for dining and shopping that she didn't mind.

They crossed over the Nile by bridge to Gezira Island, a small oasis wedged in the middle of the city. The scruffy streets around them melted into a leafy, quiet neighborhood. Bougainvillea and Arabian jasmine billowed over fences. Pedestrians strolled past stone villas, Asian bistros, and French bakeries.

"Well, *this* isn't Kansas," said Gabe, taking in the scenery.

The neighborhood of Zamalek was the land of old money and expats, and home to a handful of embassies. Ridley had been here before, though it always felt like stepping out of the Egypt of dreams and into a strange hybrid metropolis in the middle of a river.

Tom dropped them off on a street corner in front of a pair of arched double doors. Leaving their bags in the vehicle, they walked in.

The scene in the restaurant was almost a sensory overload. The walls were bold green, red, and yellow, with ornate tile flooring and chandeliers that looked like cascading lamps.

Ridley slid off her sunglasses. At a round table in the back, a young man jumped to his feet and started toward them.

"You're the friend of Fouad?" he said eagerly in a thick Egyptian accent.

She extended her hand and he shook it.

"I'm Tarek. Welcome to Egypt!"

Tarek Hanna was slender, in his late twenties, with dense brows, big lips, and jug-handle ears. His thick shock of dark hair stood almost straight up, and it seemed he was trying to grow a beard to make himself look more mature.

They settled down into the chairs, and within a moment, a cheerful server had brought over a massive platter of food. The smells of fresh bread, mint, and spiced meat made Ridley sit up straighter.

"Our friend is very sorry he cannot come to meet you," said Tarek. "He's not in the country now."

"He told me," said Ridley. "I didn't ask where."

She was sure it was Morocco, but she hadn't asked Fouad over the phone when she'd called him from Athens.

Fouad Elansary was the most reliable Egyptian she knew, for a mercenary. She had trusted him to run cover for her on deadly missions and all-out firefights. The last time she'd seen him, he had taken a bullet from the Order of Raphael in the salt flats outside of the Siwa Oasis. She and her partner Henri had rushed him to a hospital, and not a moment too soon.

They'd never discussed whether he held a grudge for it, but judging by his exuberant tone when he'd heard her voice, it was unlikely. Misfortunes like that were an occupational hazard of mercenary work, after all. Bullets sometimes included.

Fouad couldn't meet them this time, nor could his fierce little sister Aisha, so he'd referred them to a young associate of his who knew Cairo—and more importantly, the Giza Plateau.

"The man who can get anything you need. Anything," Fouad had told her over the phone. *"He has a magic rabbit hat."*

In person, Tarek seemed fidgety but excited. His eyes kept flitting to the Aslanis, but mostly to Nas. Gabe noticed it, too, as they tucked into the pita, kebabs, and baba ghanoush.

Egyptian boy has got a crush.

Or he recognizes her.

"Fouad told me it's tonight?"

"Two-thirty in the morning," said Ridley, dipping a crispy piece of *tarb* into the bowl of tahini.

Gabe glanced at the legs sticking out of the grilled quail. He winced almost imperceptibly, and reached past it for a veal kebab.

"We'll need some equipment," said Ridley, pulling a piece of paper from her pocket. "Can you get this for us by tonight?"

Tarek took the list and scanned it. He seemed dumbfounded for a moment. "You want...you want horses? And swimming goggles?"

He looked at Nas as if for help. She raised her hands without answer and took a bite of pita.

"Can you get it?" Ridley repeated.

"Yes. Of course. I'm your man. Are you looking for some treasure?" he asked.

It's not the kind of treasure you'd get a cut of.

Ridley smiled.

"Just a pair of sandals."

CHAPTER FIFTEEN

CAIRO, EGYPT

RIDLEY, Gabe, and the Aslanis had all afternoon to wait.

There was no way that Nas and Jimmy could be this close to some of the greatest antiquities in the world without seeing them up close. So the four of them ventured to the most splendid display in the city: the Grand Egyptian Museum.

It had been decades in the making, cost $1 billion, and sprawled over an area the size of ninety football fields.

With the soaring, angular ceilings, the museum looked like a modern temple worthy of the pharaohs.

As they wandered into the atrium, a stone statue of Rameses the Great towered nearly forty feet above them. Every visitor seemed drawn to it, their heads craned back. Unfortunately, that meant most of them didn't notice the shallow reflecting pool in which the enormous monument stood.

A middle-aged woman near them got too close, stumbled,

and fell into the water with a splash that echoed through through the vast lobby.

"It's a new kind of trap to protect great valuables," said Nas.

As the woman's companions helped her out through their own gales of laughter, Ridley spotted one of the museum workers a few yards away.

She was an Egyptian woman with a few strands of gray in her hair, leaning against the mop she was holding in a large bucket.

Not the first time this has happened.

Ridley caught her eyes and mugged a smile of clandestine amusement. The woman sighed and shook her head, then wheeled her bucket over to the new giant puddle on the floor.

Ridley, Gabe, and the Aslanis climbed a grand stone staircase, passing regal statues illuminated by accent lights.

As Nas and Jimmy drifted through the exhibit halls, exchanging the awestruck remarks of true archaeologists, Ridley and Gabe kept close by. Their eyes scanned the crowds milling about.

"Ever been sightseeing on a protective detail?" she asked Gabe under her breath.

He sighed, looking up at a gateway arch on display. "This is the craziest assignment I've ever had."

She slid around to his other side, so she could hear him clearly through her good ear. The looks they were attracting felt like they were becoming a problem.

With her unusual height and Amazon build, Ridley was used to some intrigued looks. But being out in public with this golden-headed, azure-eyed man felt like being perpetually on display.

Maybe that's his play. Distract them so they don't even notice whoever he's protecting.

"But my son loves hieroglyphics," said Gabe. "He would have loved this place."

Ridley didn't even try to hide her surprise. "You've got a son?"

"Yeah, he's nine. You know that's a thing that happens with grownups sometimes. When a man and a woman—"

"Oh no, my innocent ears, stop. But seriously, you just don't strike me as a dad."

There was a moment's silence.

Ah, shit. That was *mean, Samaras. You should have said that better.*

"I didn't strike me as a dad either, and then I just was one."

"Mother?"

"She resigned from my fan club a while back. It's aright. I'm pretty sure he likes me. That's what matters."

They followed the Aslanis into a huge hall where an ancient wooden barge seemed suspended mid-air. Oars bristled up its sides, forming a tent over the deck.

Nas looked back to be sure their protectors were taking it in with proper awe.

"This is the boat of Pharaoh Khufu!" she exclaimed. "Who built the Great Pyramid. It's the oldest intact ship in the world—almost five thousand years old—and it's such a masterpiece of wood that you could put it in the Nile today and row it downriver!"

"Pleasure cruising?" said Ridley.

Jimmy gazed over its steep prow. "Probably a funeral item. It was buried in a pit. They thought that ships would take them to the afterlife."

Of all the things in the world she'd seen that hadn't made sense—that had turned her upside down, that had been long hidden—there were still such vast mysteries standing right out in the open.

"This is all fascinating," said Ridley, "learning all about ancient Egypt while we're just being tourists, but why are we in this country at all? We're hunting the trail of ancient *Greek* myths."

"You know about the gods, right? The Greek gods? Growing up in Greece a little bit."

Gabe raised a hand as if in class. "Hi. Care to go back to square one for the class idiot?"

"Everybody knows about the Greek gods," said Nas, "but they were not the first beings in the mythology. At first, there was just Chaos, the Void. And from that—they say—came the primordial gods: Gaia who is the Earth, Tartarus who is like the Abyss, and then their children, like Uranus the Sky, and Nyx the Terror of Night, and Aether the Light.

"But then Gaia and one of her sons had twelve children together, and *those* were the Titans. I can't remember all their names...but then all of these Titans became the parents of the Greek gods that *we* know. It was Cronus the Titan who overthrew his father and had all these children with his own sister."

"He famously ate a bunch of them," added Ridley. "Thanks to Goya, it's the most famous thing about him."

"Oh, I've seen that painting," said Gabe. "Disgusting."

"Memorably."

"He *was* eating his kids," said Nas. "He was so paranoid that they would overthrow him like he overthrew *his* father, and take control of the whole cosmos."

Jimmy sighed and shook his head. "Not the way to do it."

"Not the way, baba," said Nas, giving him a playful finger wag. "But he had too many of them and couldn't keep up. *One* of those children was Zeus."

Gabe leaned against a nearby pillar, folding his hands in front of him like an attentive student.

"Well, just like the Titans, the gods didn't want to be ruled by *their* parents, either! So Zeus gathered his siblings and they went to war against the Titans. The twelve gods of Mount Olympus battled them for years, and *just* when it seemed like they had won—Zeus had taken the throne and given Hades the underworld and Poseidon the ocean—the primordial mother god of the Earth—Gaia—just could not stand watching her Titan children be defeated and imprisoned."

Jimmy pulled out a water bottle and offered it to Nas. She shook her head with a smile but was too swept up in the story to break for it.

"So she gave birth to another son, who was the most terrible thing that had ever been born into the universe. Typhon. He was a man and a beast, the biggest and strongest thing in all the earth, with a head that brushed the stars. He didn't have legs—just massive coils of vipers—and wings that could cover the sky."

Seen that sort before...

"His eyes were like lava," said Nas, "and a hundred dragon heads came from the ends of his fingers. And he also breathed fire."

Gabe gave a slow, indulgent nod. "Sounds like a Dungeons and Dragons big boss."

"He scared the hell out of the gods," said Nas, her eyes gleaming with excitement. "Typhon stormed Mount Olympus and everybody ran away except for Zeus and his daughter, Athena. The other gods fled to Egypt and disguised themselves as animals."

She leaned back, punctuating her story with a grin.

"So..." said Ridley, "the Egyptian gods were like the Greek gods?"

Jimmy spoke. "There are a lot of things in common with the gods of many ancient civilizations."

"So I've found."

"But all the gods had to go back to Olympus, right?" said Gabe.

"Yes. Hermes and Pan went back to help Zeus and Athena," said Nas, "and they finally overpowered Typhon together. Zeus threw him into the bottomless pit of Tartarus, the deepest region of the underworld, even below Hades. They said it was a pit so deep that if an anvil fell from earth, it would take nine days to hit Tartarus."

An elderly tourist couple stopped awkwardly close to Ridley to take a photo. She scooted aside. They remained oblivious.

Nas went on, "If that wasn't enough, Zeus also threw a mountain on top of him so that he could never escape. They say that was Mount Etna."

"Ah," said Ridley. "The ancient explanation for why it erupts so often?"

"Exactly! They thought Typhon was trying to escape."

"But back to why we're in Egypt..."

"Because Hermes was here, and Hermes was the god who gave his winged sandals to Perseus so he could escape quickly after beheading Medusa."

Gabe pressed two fingers to his forehead as though he'd just hit overload, and muttered, "Oh, my God."

"And we need those sandals," said Nas firmly.

Just then, a man came circling around one of the nearby columns. Middle Eastern, a scarf around his neck, athletic build. He glanced at Gabe, then at Jimmy and Nas.

Ridley and Gabe both moved in the same instant. As she stepped toward Jimmy and he stepped toward Nas, her hand flinched instinctively toward her waistband—

NO GUN.

Just then two kids came barreling around the column, knocking into the man. He caught one of them by the shirt and scolded her in Arabic. A woman emerged, calling to the boy and girl like a mother who was properly fed up.

Ridley's hand relaxed as the young parents moved on, attention now entirely on their children.

Nas turned to Gabe with a nervous smile, shaking off a surge of fear.

"Oh, you were ready!" she said, grasping his arm in relief.

Jimmy looked at Ridley. He was rattled by something else.

"I—I cannot have a woman die to save me," he said quietly.

"Okay," said Ridley—

—Iranian patriarchal—

"I'm not going to die," she said. "So we agree on that."

She smiled. He did not.

Gabe looked at Ridley, and she met his eyes.

"You don't protect your principal by dying," she said to him. "You protect them by making the other guy die."

"Sometimes," said Gabe.

She didn't like protection work, but nudging somewhere in the pit of her stomach was a feeling that she didn't like being *here* on this assignment. She'd been to Egypt several times before, but something here, now...

Whatever that feeling was, the mission did not change.

CHAPTER SIXTEEN

CAIRO, EGYPT

It was dusk when Tarek met them by the Giza Plateau. The last smudges of a peach-colored sunset were fading behind the pyramids.

Their embassy driver Tom had dropped them off by a small hotel at the edge of the sands. It wasn't their final destination, and Gabe had frowned off Ridley's push for secrecy.

"It's our own embassy," he'd said. "You know we're allowed to be here."

"In Cairo? Yeah. In the Giza Plateau? Sure. But you think they're gonna be okay with how we leave it?"

She gave him an obvious look and hoisted up her bag.

They didn't go into the hotel, though. Moments later, Tarek arrived in an old white Mercedes van. They climbed in and he drove them a few blocks to a horse stable.

"I haven't traveled in Egypt before," Jimmy said as they

stepped out into a yard that smelled of hay and manure, "but is it normal to ride horses out here to the plateau?"

Ridley had cocked her head. "It's...gonna make us harder to catch."

"Not when I fall off."

"Nas said you rode."

"Once. In Montana, when we went to a cowboy ranch."

"It'll be just like that," she said, giving him a clap on the shoulder and heading around the back of the van.

The older man stared miserably after her.

Tarek beckoned Ridley to show her what he'd gotten.

In two separate bags were pickaxes, chisels, small shovels, trowels, mallets, flashlights, and rope. It was common enough in her line of work to need such digging materials, but she was always aware that it was basically one tool short of a murder kit.

He had also packed in swim goggles, a snorkel, and an ultraviolet light wand.

"This is good," she said. "How 'bout the weapon?"

From his pocket, he pulled a small curved sheath.

"You can cut off a man's pieces," he said, handing it to her.

Ridley pulled out the knife. It was a curved blade and handle with a ring at the end of the hilt. A karambit for her. She'd had to leave behind the one that Melden had given her in Greece.

This one had a tie-dye rainbow pattern all across the steel.

"What is this, a video game knife?" she said with a frown, testing its sharpness.

Looks like a weapon out of some manga comic, but it would *be able to cut off a man's pieces.*

"You asked for something very strange. What could I do in a few hours? This is the best I have."

"Good, okay," she said, sliding the sheath onto the belt loop of her pants. "And the rest of it?"

Tarek knew discretion. He opened a smaller satchel for her to peer into. Inside lay two CZ 75 pistols and several boxes of 9mm ammunition.

She called over Gabe to show him the stash. When he saw the guns, he gave her a look of arch, irritated disappointment.

"You know what those will get us?" he said.

"Not dead?"

"Not employed. With a side of 'international incident.'"

"I don't wander around in the open under threat from assassins with a couple of helpless marks and *not* have access to equal power," she said, throwing both hands toward the satchel in a 'look at it' gesture. "Fire. *Power.*"

"Fired."

Tarek looked like he wanted to be anywhere other than in this argument.

"Do you want one or not?"

He actually sighed, looked away and shook his head. But he reached in for one of the CZ 75s, checked the chamber—empty—then grabbed a box of ammo.

Ridley rolled her eyes. She took the other. Tarek shrugged at her with a queasy smile.

It was one-thirty in the morning when the five of them mounted up on their high-stepping steeds. The owner of the stables watched them go off without an escort, tallying up the wad of dollars in his hand that was triple the regular fee.

As they rode out under the canopy of night, Ridley gazed up. The creak of the saddle, the dapple gray shoulders of the Arabian rippling beneath her, the rhythmic pulse of his steps...

she could almost hear her grandmother calling her back to the house.

Nas gave a nervous laugh. "I feel like Gertrude Bell, an explorer riding across the wild sand. You know Lawrence of Arabia is only more famous than her because he got a movie."

"Fell asleep during that one," said Ridley.

Gabe, looking deeply uncomfortable in the saddle, was struggling to rein in his jittery horse. The more he flailed, the more exasperated the horse became.

"Sit up straight," Ridley told him. "Don't pull on the reins."

He shot her a look and nearly snapped, "ATVs."

She gave him a scolding look for an idiot. "Loud and *also* require instruction."

But he took her advice—sat up straight and stopped pulling. His horse quieted, only champing at the bit to convey its lingering annoyance.

Ridley led the pack through the darkened streets and beyond—into the Giza Plateau. The clop of hooves became delicate thuds in the sand.

Ahead in the distance, the pyramids loomed, lit from below for all of Cairo to see. Even to Ridley, it felt surreal to be approaching them on the back of a horse like some warrior of the past. She could only imagine what they had looked like in ancient times—covered in smooth, gleaming white limestone, with a golden cap at the peak that would have burned like the sun.

"I cannot believe it," she heard Jimmy murmur beside her. "I gave up to believe that I would ever see this in person."

All it took was a supernatural quest.

They strode past the Great Sphinx, and even Tarek craned his head to gape at it. The mammoth paws seemed even bigger in person.

The riders passed small stone temples and funerary monuments half-buried in the sands. There were *mastabas* clustered around the Great Pyramid of Khufu, a cemetery for members of the royal family and noble officials. A few scruffy dogs loped about the plateau.

The entire place seemed like an epic graveyard of the most glamorous ancient history on earth.

But they were not headed for any of the monuments or tombs.

Instead, Tarek steered them toward a small shack where an open doorway glowed. As they approached, the silhouette of a man stepped out.

Tarek dismounted and greeted him in Arabic. The guard seemed to be expecting him, though he looked over the rest of the riders with a black-browed squint. The two Egyptians exchanged words, until finally Tarek pulled out a clump of dollars from his pocket and stripped off a few of the bills.

Dues paid. The guard waved them on.

Tarek returned.

"We have two-and-a-half hours," he said, clutching the reins as he stood by his horse's head.

"Before what?" said Gabe.

Tarek shrugged. "Before somebody from the government shows up for the tours. Very early morning, before the heat."

"Where is it?" asked Ridley.

Nas' gaze was fixed in the direction of the pyramids. "It's along the causeway, between the Sphinx and the pyramid of Khafre."

Ridley urged forward her gray Arabian. The others followed, until they reached a slab of bedrock that rose up like a small cliff before them.

There was a channel dug into the sand in front of it, ramping down to the base of the rock.

"This is it," said Nas, leaping down from her horse.

The others dismounted. Nas, Gabe, and Ridley all pulled out flashlights. In the shine of their beams, they saw an iron gate at the end of the channel.

Ridley grabbed the bag from the back of her saddle.

"Just watch the horses," she said to Tarek. "We'll be back before our time is up.

He looked agitated already, glancing around the plateau as if expecting trouble. But he nodded.

The grated door was locked, of course. This time it was Gabe's turn with the crowbar. He jammed and pried and strained, the muscles of his forearms taut as steel cords.

Finally the old metal cracked. He pushed the door open with a relieved exhale.

A smile broke over Nas. She touched Gabe's arm as she entered the tunnel.

"Welcome to the Tomb of Osiris."

CHAPTER SEVENTEEN

CAIRO, EGYPT

THEY SAW the top of a ladder only a yard past the entrance.

Nas was first to it, pointing her flashlight down into a shaft cut out of the limestone. It was wide and square, clearly manmade.

"That does not look safe," said Jimmy, peering at the rickety metal ladder built into the bedrock.

"Of course it's not safe, baba," said Nas, slinging her bag across her back.

He muttered something in Farsi that his daughter ignored. She lowered herself down the narrow rungs. A frustrated Jimmy followed her down, nervously clutching the iron rails.

Gabe gestured to Ridley with the crowbar. "After you."

"I'll take that offer," she said, and swung over the edge.

"There's so much trash down here!" called Nas.

Sure enough, when Ridley's feet touched down, they crunched onto an empty plastic bottle.

"Egypt and trash," she said, sweeping her flashlight about, "have an intimate relationship."

There was little more in this chamber than another set of metal rails and another hole in the ground.

Gabe dropped down into the chamber with a puff of dust as the rest of them peered into the hole.

The walls of this vertical shaft were cut perfectly straight and square. Two ladders led down side by side. It looked both narrower and longer than the first shaft.

"Okay," said Nas, steeling herself. "Lots of people have gone down there before. We're fine."

And she started down the next ladder, into the Tomb of Osiris.

A mysterious set of vertical shafts and descending chambers, they were likely built some four thousand years ago in "the Age of the Pyramids." It was all buried beneath the stone causeway which linked the Sphinx to Khafre's pyramid.

Though it had first been discovered by an Italian explorer in 1816, there was too much flooding in the chambers to even excavate it. It lay quietly for years and decades and centuries, only referenced in certain obscure maps and records.

That was until the most famous archaeologist of modern Egypt took on the project.

Zahi Hawass, backed by the Antiquities Department of the government, used all the technology that the 1990s could afford. His workers managed to pump and clear the shafts to the very lowest point of the structure, one hundred feet down.

And still, no one knew why it had been created.

The four of them climbed down the rungs with care. Thirty...forty...fifty feet...it wasn't until they'd descended a further sixty feet below the first level that their shoes hit stone.

They spun around, their flashlights sweeping.

This new level had six small chambers dug into the walls. Each was about six feet by six feet.

"Is this where they kept mummies?" asked Gabe, peering down at a pile of broken pottery shards and shattered bones.

"They were probably burial chambers," said Nas, "but nobody knows who. There aren't even any hieroglyphics or paintings down here."

A mouse skittered through the beam of Ridley's flashlight so suddenly that she nearly threw her knife at it.

What are you spooking at, Samaras?! Get a grip.

Jimmy and Nas stepped toward one of the chambers where an immense sarcophagus lay. There was no kingly ornateness to this one, though. It looked like nothing more than a stone burial box...though its top had been slid partially off.

"What the fuck is in that," said Gabe, his voice tight.

"Nothing," grinned Nas, sidling up to it and shining her light in. "Robbed long ago. All of this. There are almost no tombs intact in Egypt anymore."

"But here we are still trying to find things," said Jimmy, examining the top of it.

There was something black and oily coating the surface.

"Well what the fuck is *that*," said Gabe, now pointing to the strange substance. "I'm not here to cosplay *The Mummy*."

"The ancient Egyptians sometimes covered their coffins with black goo." said Nas. "Animal fat, plant oil, tree resin, and *crude oil*...It's so fascinating!" She looked at their very tense bodyguard. "But it won't get you."

He returned a sarcastic smile and turned away.

"Why did they do it?" asked Ridley.

"Maybe to honor Osiris, the god of the underworld. In most paintings, he was shown with black skin."

"Blackface for mummies. Fascinating. Okay, let's move on."

Ridley turned away, scoping the rest of the chamber with

her flashlight. Near the shaft they'd come down was another metal rail.

And another ladder.

Let's see what this underworld has got.

She clipped her flashlight to her belt and began the climb down.

This shaft was shorter than the last, though a dank stink was wafting up it. As Ridley lowered herself on the last few rungs, she saw the bottom that awaited her: a pool.

She stepped down into the gray-green water. It was shin-deep, with dark flecks floating across the surface. Broken beams of wood lay scattered off to her right. The entire chamber was flooded, leaving little head room.

"Pool day," she called back.

Nas splashed down behind her.

"Nasrin, leave the swimming for the others!" came Jimmy's voice down the shaft.

Nas gave Ridley an exasperated glance. "He thinks I can't swim because *he* can't swim. He's going to stay up there."

As Gabe stepped into the water, he grimaced but then gave a laugh. "Well, to hell with these shoes."

"Flooding in Egypt is...weird," said Ridley.

"We're a hundred feet below the earth," said Nas. "This is the water table. It's why they have never been able to really excavate it properly. They pump and pump but they can't get rid of the water."

"How deep is it?" asked Gabe.

Nas shrugged. "Depends on the day."

Ridley was scoping out the roughly cut chamber.

"How can there be anything in here that they haven't found yet?" she said. "Unless..."

At the far end was a crevice in the rock.

Nas followed her eyes. "That's the mystery shaft."

"They don't know where it goes?" said Ridley.

"No. It's too small for anyone to climb through. Archaeologists wonder if it's part of an underground tunnel system that links the Sphinx and the pyramids. People go *crazy* about ancient Egypt."

"Well I'm not fitting in there, if that's what this comes to."

"I left my dynamite at home," said Gabe.

They each tied their bags to a rung of the ladder to keep them dry. Nas pulled a notebook from hers, checking back to the inscriptions written on the stele. Ridley stripped off her linen button-up shirt to her tank top underneath. She pulled out the CZ 75 from her waistband and tucked it carefully into her backpack.

Then she pulled out the snorkel and snapped on the goggles.

"Because this water is *disgusting*," she said.

"You look like a bug," said Gabe.

"Wow, your pronunciation of 'Katie Ledecky' is so terrible."

He pulled out the ultraviolet light wand from his own bag and handed it to her. "Go raid the tomb."

She turned to face the chamber.

There was no record of a burial here, and yet there was a colossal sarcophagus in the center of the flooded chamber. For all of recorded history, it had been empty.

Ridley waded into the pool and was quickly chest-deep. She made her way to the center as the water rose to her neck.

"It should be on the top," Nas called to her.

"Yep."

She took a breath and ducked under the water.

Directly beneath Ridley was the ancient coffin. The top—a massive slab of granite—had been lifted up by modern excavators. It lay on two thick stone support beams suspended above the sunken trench, where the belly of the empty coffin still rested.

She flicked on the UV light and swam down. She had been told what she was looking for.

The gods eye writing...

She passed the wand slowly over the surface of the lid, peering close for any sign of a glow.

Nothing.

Counting on the lung capacity that had earned her the name "Aquaman" as a teenager, Ridley pulled herself across the entirety of it again.

Nothing. Damn this whole mummy underworld.

She surfaced, spouting water off her lips in frustration.

"No, there's nothing on the top."

"That's..." Nas trailed off, suddenly doubting. "That's not possible. This *is* the place. It's the only place—written so clearly on the stele! 'Written for the gods eye.'"

Gods eye...gods eye...

Ridley called, "Did they really think Osiris was buried in here?"

"*Something* must have been buried here. It's a sarcophagus. If you believe in the underworld—"

Gabe, hands propped on his hips, looked around. "This is probably it."

Ridley went on, her brain ticking. "And Osiris was a god."

"One of the most important ones," replied Nas.

"What did he see?"

She looked at Nas. Realization pricked them both at that moment.

"The inside," said Nas.

Ridley drew a breath and plunged below the surface again.

There was space between the top and the bottom of the

sarcophagus, below the stone support beams that separated them—but it wasn't much.

She swam down, slithered between the beams, and pulled herself under the massive granite slab. Facing up, she felt a twinge in her gut.

Literally lying in a coffin a hundred feet beneath the pyramids.

But then she held up the wand, and all of those thoughts dissolved.

Glowing in the ultraviolet light was a simple diagram. It took Ridley a moment to realize that it was the layout of the chamber they were in—the shaft leading down, the four sides, the rectangular sarcophagus in the middle, the four pillars around it that had crumbled over time.

And far from the center of the chamber's layout, in delicate brushstrokes—*were they brushstrokes?*—was a pair of Greek strap sandals. There were two faint lines leading to the sandals...

Ah, shit.

Ridley swept the wand again over the rest of the stone, but there was nothing else to be seen. She slid out from the sarcophagus and breached the surface.

"Are they here?" pressed Nas.

"Yeah," said Ridley. She pointed to the shaft at the far end. "There."

The archaeologist wilted.

Ridley pulled off her goggles. "And I'd fit through that like a rhino down a playground slide."

"I can do it. I'm the smallest here."

"No. If you get stuck in there, this'll be *your* tomb."

"We can't leave here without the sandals!"

"I'm thinking!"

Gabe was about to throw up his hands in exasperation, when a faint sound from behind made him turn.

The fabric of Ridley's backpack was quivering.

CHAPTER EIGHTEEN

CAIRO, EGYPT

As Ridley and Nas went back and forth, Gabe stepped away toward the ladder.

The faint sound was definitely coming from Ridley's backpack. He reached for it and slowly pulled the zipper back. He peered inside.

There was the collection of work material, digging tools, a bottle of water...it wasn't until he moved aside the extra scarf that he spotted it at the very bottom.

The bronze block—the shield of Athena that had collapsed into a small solid mass—was vibrating.

"Hey," he called to the others, trying to get their attention over the increasingly testy exchange. "Ridley!"

She turned to him and snapped, "Speaking!"

He pulled out the chunk of burnished metal and held it up. The vibrations were more intense than he'd thought, and made his forearm feel like jelly.

Nas gaped at it. Ridley cocked a brow and leaned away as if it might explode.

"This is your kind of strange, isn't it?" Gabe said to her.

"I never know my kind of strange until I'm looking at it."

"Look at it."

He offered it toward them both. Nas touched the top of the brass. The vibrations had intensified.

"Why?" breathed Nas, peering at it. "There's nothing inside. It was just a shield—we saw it collapse into this."

Jimmy's voice echoed down from the top of the shaft. "What's happening down there?"

Nas answered him excitedly in Farsi.

He called back. "Get it right. Then hurry."

Ridley reached to take the block from Gabe's hand. It began to shake. She felt like her hand was being spun through a dryer.

He looked to the back of the chamber, to the mouth of the tunnel, then back at the piece of bronze. Without a word, he slipped his gun out of his waistband and handed it to Ridley. Then he took the bronze piece back from her and stepped into the water.

The metal began to shake so violently that he had to grip it with both hands. The water reached his chest, a cool slip of weightless embrace.

Ridley tucked his CZ 75 into her own waistband as she watched.

Now he has ideas to contribute.

As Gabe waded deeper, Nas and Ridley beamed their flashlights in his direction. They could see the muscles in his back knot with tension beneath his wet clinging shirt.

He was five feet away from the tunnel entrance.

He felt like the vibrations were about to liquefy the bones in his hands.

He dragged his legs through the water, reached the opening of the shaft—

And the block in his hands burst open—blades of bronze fanning out and locking in place—to form the gleaming shield of Athena.

Gabe gave a bark of astonished laughter when he realized what he was holding.

Then something slammed the shield backward.

Whether the shield blasted *out* an otherworldly force, or it was hit with a sonic boom, Gabe was launched clear out of the water.

His head cracked against the stone ceiling before he hit the back wall. He crumpled into the shallows.

The force knocked Ridley back into Nas—and they both slammed into the ladder.

Ridley clutched at her charge who was gasping for air. "Are you okay? You okay?"

Nas nodded, woozy.

"Nasrin!" came her father's panicked yell from above.

"I'm okay, baba!"

Ridley dropped down to Gabe's side and hauled out his half-submerged head.

He spewed a mouthful of water into her face, then winced as he felt the top of his skull.

"That was an idea," said Ridley.

He patted the bronze shield that had landed next to him. "I thought it was good."

"Guys."

There was something about Nas' voice that stilled them both. They looked at her—then followed her eyes to the back of the chamber.

The wall of rock had split—the opening of the mystery shaft now double its original size.

There was a clanging on the ladder, and Jimmy stumbled down into the water.

"What happened, *dokhtar?*" He clutched at Nas, who turned to him with shining eyes.

"There are surely gods!" she breathed.

With that, she turned and splashed into the pool, her arms swinging as she launched herself across the chamber.

"Wait!" yelled Ridley, shooting to her feet.

"You're still too big!" Nas called back. "I'm going in."

The water was so deep that it lapped at her throat, slowing her down considerably. Ridley, still soaked through, went after her.

They reached the opening of the shaft at the same time.

"You see it, right?" said Nas, squeezing her waterlogged hair back behind her shoulder. "This is why it happened—to open it for us."

"Yeah," said Ridley, grasping the edge of the rock, "but you still need someone to pull you out if you get stuck."

"You can't go in there!" cried Jimmy. "It's not safe—the tunnel will collapse."

That is also...right.

"I'm going."

"Wait," said Ridley.

She sloshed back to the bags, grabbed a length of rope, and tied it around Nasrin's ankle.

"Okay. Green light," said Ridley.

Nas flashed a nervous grin and crawled into the shaft.

Her flashlight wobbled as she made her way on hands and knees, her soaked clothes turning to mud. She could see where the tunnel narrowed, but also where the split in the stone had widened it just enough for her to scrape through.

She glanced above at the deep cracks as she passed. Her father was right—the entire structure had just been violently compromised. A sprinkle of dust from the ceiling echoed that truth.

The shaft bent just slightly ahead as the walls tightened around Nas. She could feel the rock scraping at her shoulders as the beam of her flashlight wavered.

“Still okay?” Ridley’s voice called from behind her.

From an unnervingly long way behind her.

“Okay! I don’t see anything yet...”

How far could this go...? All the way to the pyramid?

Nas had never thought of herself as claustrophobic before, but the farther she went, feeling the rope slithering behind her, the more she felt like her stomach was beginning to boil.

Back at the entrance of the tunnel, Ridley watched the rope unspooling rapidly in her hands.

Why did you get such a short line? Why would you do that?!

She climbed up into the opening of the tunnel to get a few more feet, edging in as far as her five-foot-eleven frame would allow.

“The line is running out,” she called down the shaft.

Deep within it, Nas stopped. She closed her eyes and drew in a deep breath. Exhaled it slowly.

This was not the kind of archaeology she had ever envisioned. She wasn’t one of those kids who grew up idolizing Indiana Jones. She was just a passionate and nerdy girl from Tehran who wanted to discover the epics of history and the humanity of her ancestors. She was honest with herself that the idea of an ancient treasure hunt thrilled her like it would any archaeologist, but the reality of it...was unfurling risks right before her face that she had never really imagined.

Like dying in a tunnel a hundred feet underground, somewhere between the Great Sphinx and the Great Pyramids.

Without so much as a proper mummification.

But now it was time to move again.

She dragged herself forward on her forearms. Just as the tunnel bent again, she saw it also seemed to slope down.

Nas crawled closer...and noticed that a fresh chasm had opened in the floor. She inched forward.

The drop-off was nearly five feet, a ragged tear in the rock. And there, dangling off of a craggy outcropping, was a pair of sandals.

She scoffed in disbelief. Laughed—looking around as if there could be someone else to witness this surreal sight.

They were in shockingly good condition. Supernaturally good, she realized. They were fairly simple, with leather straps and a thin sole. She realized she was a little disappointed that they didn't have the wings on the ankles, as so many depictions of Hermes over the millennia had portrayed.

Nas scooted forward, stretching her arm out across the chasm. She knew she wouldn't have the raw upper body power to haul herself out if she fell here. She could almost reach it... almost...

A rumble overhead jerked her back.

The bedrock had surely been split. This tunnel *wasn't* safe.

She reached again, straining, her fingers aching toward the sandals—

Something cracked deep in the earth.

Nas threw herself forward, nearly pitching off the edge, but caught herself with one hand scraping to grab the wall.

And she had them—but there was no time to marvel at the godly apparel in her hands. Something rumbled faintly overhead.

Sandals clutched in one hand, Nas shimmied backward with all the speed she could muster. Wriggling around bends, her sides scraping along the walls, the rough rock bloodying her forearms—

Until she heard Ridley's voice like a beacon.

"You're almost out! Come on!"

She scrambled. The noises were growing ominously louder around her. Backing out now on all fours—

Until she toppled back, tumbling into Ridley who half-caught her in the water.

"I got them!" she exclaimed, gasping against the adrenaline and holding up the sandals.

"Come on!" called Jimmy from across the chamber. "It's *not safe!*"

The rumblings grew louder. They seemed to be coming from all around. The older man looked frantic.

Near him, Gabe was holding the shield, which had collapsed itself once again into an innocuous bronze block.

"Even more powerful than I look," he said, but he was glancing around at the chamber in concern.

Ridley and Nas ran-waded through the water, back to the entry shaft. Ridley took the sandals and the block and shoved them into her backpack.

"Go," said Gabe to Jimmy.

"No."

This man would never go before his daughter. He tugged and pushed at Nas to hurry up the ladder. Then he followed, trying to rush even as the arthritis in his thumbs twinged with pain.

Ridley went next, agonizing at the pace she was reduced to.

This is not hurrying—

She could feel Gabe on the rungs below her. Halfway up the shaft, they heard a crack, a muffled scraping, and a massive splash.

The iron ladder trembled.

"Expedite," said Gabe.

"Jimmy, I'm gonna need you to go faster," said Ridley, her voice taut with frustration.

Don't be an ass—he's trying.

Just as they reached the top of the shaft, something else crashed in the lower chamber. Nas was already on the next ladder—it was even longer.

They climbed for their lives. When they reached the second chamber, they dashed to the next shaft upward. The rumblings beneath them had not stopped. It sounded as if the entire tomb was collapsing.

Jimmy's breathing was ragged as they raced up the final ladder, tore down the tunnel, and finally burst out into the moonlit night of the Giza Plateau.

Nas rushed them away from the entrance.

"It's not sound," she said. "More of the area could collapse."

Ridley began prowling the sand to draw down her adrenaline. They were all still soaking wet, their pants sucked tight against their legs, their thin shirts clinging to their torsos in the dark.

"So," said Gabe, "*magical* sandals."

Nas gave him the first deadly look that Ridley had ever seen on her face.

"Can you believe there were sandals in there? And you found them by using a magical shield to explode a tunnel?" she shot back.

He made a face as if he'd stepped perilously close to a landmine, but stayed quiet.

Ridley gazed out across the plateau, looking for Tarek. The breeze felt cool against her damp clothing.

She saw the horses milling about and snorting softly a dozen yards away. The silhouette of the pyramid behind them seemed to blot out the sky with its own glory.

Where is that jittery Egyptian?

Then she saw movement by the guard shack on the other

side, three dozen yards away. In the half-light, she spotted Tarek, and then the guard...and then two other men.

She tensed.

"Gabe," she said, her voice low.

He followed her eyes to the shack. Immediately, he started toward Nas and Jimmy. The two archaeologists realized what they were looking at.

"Oh, my God," murmured Nas.

CHAPTER NINETEEN

CAIRO, EGYPT

Ridley had snatched the gun from her waistband before another thought even crossed her mind.

"They found us," said Nas in a strangled voice. "No!"

They were fully exposed out in the open.

Gabe had already lunged in front of Nas as Ridley called to him, "Gun is in my bag!"

The two other men rushed out of the guard shack, pulling up weapons that were bigger than their own CZ 75s.

"Horses!" yelled Gabe.

But he wasn't close enough to get to Ridley's backpack, and the Aslanis were priority. He shove-rushed them to the horses as Ridley took aim and fired.

Four shots—they seemed to explode the entire Giza Plateau.

Shouts echoed from the men, who ducked behind the shack again, then burst out with their own rifles bristling.

The horses startled as Gabe tried to launch Jimmy up into the saddle. Nas had mounted her own and was trying to keep control of the skittish Arabian, strafing and stomping with alarm.

The men fired into the open. Burst rounds, three at a time.

Ridley was moving, backpedaling, zig-zagging as she shot, forcing their attackers behind cover.

Gabe swung up onto his horse and grabbed the reins of the last one to hold for his partner.

"Go!" he yelled to Nas and Jimmy.

They squeezed on their mounts, who shot out from under them so fast that they nearly toppled off. The Arabians couldn't gallop away fast enough from the ear-cracking blasts.

Ridley fired again—

Only five rounds left—

"Come on, get on!" called Gabe.

She had to finally turn and grab onto the saddle. The horse skirted away from her just as she went to swing up.

"Shit!" she stumbled back.

A bullet grazed her calf with a strip of heat.

Ridley fired back with one hand—*three more bullets*—and launched herself up onto the saddle.

Gabe let go of her reins. He kicked his heels into his horse's flanks. It bolted so hard that he had to clutch onto its mane.

Ridley snatched up her reins, urged her horse into high gear, and shot off two more rounds as the Arabian launched after the others.

Nas and Jimmy were hurtling ahead in the darkness, their horses dipping and rising in the sand. Gabe was holding onto a bumpy gallop, but he slowed until Ridley caught up to him.

"Bag," he called to her, though she had already begun to shuck it.

He grabbed it, pulled out the other pistol, and handed her

an extra magazine. She reloaded and yanked the straps back onto her shoulders.

From behind them, the sound of an engine started.

They looked to see two ATVs roaring up on the plateau, headlights bouncing in the darkness.

Gabe shot at them.

"Go!" yelled Ridley, kicking her horse into a full gallop.

He followed. They flew across the plateau, toward the Aslanis.

Horses can't outrun ATVs. Agility is only slightly better.

The two men were gaining on them. Shooting.

The roar of thundering hooves and revving engines filled Ridley's ears, even the damaged one. Her mind was tearing through the options—

Split up. Reverse direction. Zig-zag.

—but then there was a break in the gunfire.

Reloading a rifle.

She moved so fast that it was almost inconceivable her brain had done the calculations. When Ridley sat back and hauled on the reins, her horse thrashed his head and skidded to a halt in the sand. She pivoted—his delicate hooves jamming the sand—and spurred him into a charge.

Straight into a gallop. Straight at the ATVs.

Timing is godly.

She raised her gun and fired.

Both sets of headlights swerved.

Pretty hard to reload a rifle while driving an ATV.

Gabe whipped his head back to see his partner tearing toward the enemy like the Charge of the Light Brigade. He realized the second ATV was peeling away, bearing down on Nas and Jimmy.

He leaned forward off the saddle and kicked his horse's flanks. The Arabian surged. Gabe was no longer racing to catch the Aslanis. He was cutting off the enemy's path to them.

Fighting for balance on his galloping mount, he raised his pistol and fired.

Behind him, Ridley's horse was sprinting full tilt at the other ATV. She could see nothing else but the shine of the headlights and the faint silhouette of the rider.

Twenty meters...

He couldn't reload fast enough. The shock of having a rider turn and charge straight at him must have earned her an extra few seconds as well.

She saw him drop the rifle and reach for something at his waist.

Ten meters...

He was drawing his sidearm—but Ridley beat him. She squeezed off five rapid shots.

The headlights wobbled.

She swerved her horse off at the last second to miss the vehicle. When she pulled up and turned back, the ATV was slowing.

The driver slid off the seat and crumpled to the sand.

Ridley lifted her eyes to the second attacker.

Gabe was hurtling into the pathway of the other ATV, racing to put himself between the Aslanis and their enemy.

He was shooting. The driver had pulled his own sidearm and fired back, but couldn't aim for anything as he tried to run a zig-zag.

Finally, the driver peeled away, speeding across the plateau as sand puffed in his wake.

Not today, you devils.

Ridley scanned about for any other threats. It was dark and quiet once more. She galloped to join the others.

She whooped and clapped her horse's neck as she rode up. "Agile little battle steeds!"

Nas and Jimmy had slowed and stopped with Gabe. All of them looked as if they'd just gotten off a Millennium Force rollercoaster. Their horses were stomping and dancing with adrenaline.

"You're okay?" Gabe asked father and daughter. "Check yourself. Sometimes adrenaline can mask pain at first."

Ridley could feel the blood dripping down her calf. Nothing urgent.

"Nasrin?" said Jimmy, his voice tight with worry.

"No, baba, I'm okay," she said, looking herself over.

"We have to leave," said Ridley. "All those gunshots will bring company. We'll go wide, around the other side of the Sphinx."

Gabe scanned the expanse, to the dense wall of Cairo in the distance, twinkling and rumbling even this late into the night.

"How..." he muttered to himself.

Ridley heard him, and her brows contorted into a scowl.

That rancid rat—

"Tarek."

CHAPTER TWENTY

CAIRO, EGYPT

THEY HAD to get out of Egypt.

The dead would-be assassin that lay on the Giza Plateau was most likely Iranian, but there was no way to find out by the time the sun rose on the pyramids. If he was Egyptian, and any one of the authorities found them out, it would be a diplomatic trainwreck involving at least three countries.

And so, despite the fury burning in Ridley, there would be no confronting Tarek.

Gabe had the embassy purchase airline tickets for them on the first flight to Morocco that morning. They dumped their disassembled weapons in the Nile, then arrived at Cairo International Airport at five in the morning to set up camp in the corner of their gate.

After their deluge of adrenaline out on the sands, Nas and Jimmy fell asleep nearly as soon as they hit the chairs. Gabe stayed on duty. Whenever he felt the tide of fatigue surging too close, he would paw at his face and stand up to shake out his limbs.

Ridley had some phone calls to make.

She went over to a deserted gate nearby, pacing as she punched out Fouad's number. It went straight to voicemail.

"*Habibi.* Your little friend thought he could cash in on a bounty last night, and almost got us killed," she nearly spat. "If I see him again, I will chop off every one of his fingers. And maybe a toe. *Deal with him.*"

The next person she dialed was Booker Douglas. He picked up on the second ring.

"Sir," she said, her voice tight.

"Oh, no," came the basso tone on the other end. "Tell me."

Under her breath, with eyes on passersby at all times, she relayed the night's events in cloaked terms. They had developed enough of a shorthand over the years that she could respond with mostly yes or no questions. At times, she could practically hear him draping a hand over his face in exasperation.

She skipped right over the destruction of the Tomb of Osiris. He did not love destruction of ancient monuments. It was really the dead assassin—and the surviving one—that were the problems here.

"What's your exposure?" he asked.

"As far as we know, none. The guard at the shack couldn't identify us in the dark. Only that treacherous assface who supplied us," growled Ridley, "and I'll bet he says nothing to any authority."

"Unless there's a reward."

Unless there's a reward.

"Where are you heading now?" asked Booker.

"Morocco."

"You got clearance for the Aslanis through State?"

"Gabe took care of all that. He can actually be helpful in some ways."

Unfair, Samaras. He was your wingman last night.

"I'm a bit surprised," said Booker. "They don't take kindly to Iran, either. If they think the Aslanis will bring trouble to their country...that's big trouble. Just stay low and quiet. Don't mess with their tourism prospects and you should be fine."

"I don't know how that last man standing could possibly track us," said Ridley.

"Well, the mission doesn't change. Two items down. You go get some sleep on that plane now."

"I've added that to the mission, sir."

An hour later, Ridley was sitting in an aisle seat with Jimmy beside her. Gabe and Nas were in the emergency exit a few rows ahead.

Both the CIA operative and the State Department agent had scanned every row of passengers for potential threats. The flight was full, with tourists in their linen travel shirts, white women with colorful local scarves draped around their necks, dark-skinned Egyptians yammering in Arabic, a few businessmen with their laptops out already, and some young kids who were having trouble staying still.

No alarms going off from this crowd.

She did wish that she'd gotten a look at the runaway assassin's face the night before.

That bounty went wide. There can be more hunters after them, anyhow.

Her head started to bob and drift even as she churned through her own personal situation report. Jimmy noticed.

"You can sleep," he told her.

"Sure, I know. Yeah."

"We're safe here, I think."

"Not a word I use very often."

He nodded solemnly. "I understand this."

Ridley straightened up, fighting her exhaustion. "Sometimes you're just lucky and your enemies have the aim of a stormtrooper."

He crinkled a brow. "What—oh, oh yes, Star Wars!" Then he laughed, "You're right."

"Could you watch Star Wars in Iran?"

Jimmy nodded. "It came to our theaters the year before the revolution. Then the Shah fell and the Ayatollah took his power, and the screens went black. I did not see another one until I came to America."

That was nearly twice her lifespan.

"Then I'm not spoiling it for you with any Darth Vader references, right?" she said with a tired grin.

"Oh, no, we Iranians all know Darth Vader very well. He sits at the head of the regime in our country. Same as the last Supreme Leader. But his stormtroopers don't miss nearly so much. The Basij—they're militia. They are *volunteers* who go into the streets and slaughter innocent people. They have killed tens of thousands. They don't miss very often."

Over the speakers, the flight attendant announced they were shutting the cabin doors and preparing for takeoff.

"How did you get out?" Ridley asked.

"Ah. That's a long story. But I wish...I wish I had done it...I wish many things did not happen the way they did happen."

She broke the lingering silence. "You followed Nas to America?"

"My daughter," he said, lifting a finger to stab the air, "is the bravest person I have ever known. She got it from her mother. I was not so brave. I—I got used to the way things were, after the revolution. I didn't fight it. But Nasrin...she had the blood of the

Persian lion in her. She protested. She spoke against the regime."

The plane lurched and shifted as they taxied out to the runway. Ridley was surprised he was speaking so personally, but the adrenaline of the night before and the lack of sleep had worn him thin. Now she feared he might stop speaking at any moment. It seemed as if the words were physically painful to him, yet he went on.

"I tried to stop her," said Jimmy, his voice strangling into quiet. "I knew they would come for her. Arrest her, beat her, maybe kill her. So I tried to make her quiet, but she would not live that way. Nasrin escaped the country in 2012. I saw it too late—what my beloved Iran had become. What the Islamic Republic had *done* to the country that I loved, that was *ours.*"

The plane began to build speed.

"But then you left," said Ridley.

"My wife was also a lioness, but we had three other children in Iran. Only one of our sons wanted to go, but then Shohreh got sick, with leukemia, and I stayed with her. And she died in her homeland."

He stared down at the seat pocket in front of him.

"And then I left."

The G-force pinned them back as the plane nosed upward.

Ridley knew, from reading their files, that the rest of Jimmy's children had remained in Iran. She also knew what had happened to them.

The regime had seen them as hostages—leverage to use in their attempts to silence Nasrin Aslani from afar.

Reza, her older brother, was a dentist in Tehran. He had been arrested shortly after Jimmy left, kept in Evin Prison, and tortured. His jailers took especially sadistic glee in drilling his teeth without anesthetics, and then yanking them out with bloody pliers.

When Reza was released a few months later, he was forced to record a video that was broadcast to the nation. In it, he disavowed his sister's and his father's treachery toward Iran. He had two small children. There was nothing else he could do.

Varisheh, Nas' younger sister, worked as a pastry chef. She had been followed and threatened by the regime's enforcers, but she had never caused trouble herself. When she got engaged to the son of a judge, the harassment melted away. She had learned how to keep her head down, how to stay on the right side of the powers that ruled.

Edris, the youngest son, had at first worshipped his older sister Nas. He wanted to do everything she did and go everywhere she went. When she escaped Iran, he was heartbroken, but even more awed by her. There went his hero.

That was until his father left to join her. Edris had been barely a teenager when he lost his beloved elder sister. He was just beginning to drive when his mother died. Though his father offered him a chance to escape to America—to be reunited with Nasrin—he was so drowning in his own rage and pain that he refused. He thought his father would stay with him to grieve, but Jimmy did not. Two days later, his father was gone.

Edris found a love for motocross and began competing. Substituting physical bravery for moral courage paid enough to make a decent living. So far, the regime had left him alone, yet there was never a moment of peace for his father and sister. As long as any family was still in the clutches of the Islamic Republic, no dissident could sleep soundly.

But Ridley would not ask Jimmy about any of this.

The plane began to level out. The roar of the engines became a steady background thrum.

"A father protects his children," said Jimmy, his voice small.

I didn't know that when I was a child.

Ridley set her head back against the chair. “You’re protecting your daughter.”

He smiled sadly. “*You* are.”

As sleep began to haul her under, she could see the waves of the Mediterranean sloshing at the edges of her mind.

Forewarning of how deep they would have to descend into its waters.

CHAPTER TWENTY-ONE

TANGIER, MOROCCO

THEIR PLANE LANDED in Tangier-Ibn Battouta Airport at midday. The four of them collected their carry-on bags, filed through the expedited customs line again, and met their embassy car outside.

Ridley had slept until the final hour of the flight, when she pulled up a map of Tangier's streets. It was her diligent practice to study the layout of any new city she found herself in. Yet with Tangier, a city stuffed with winding alleys, labyrinthine souks, and ancient quarters, it was only the main thoroughfares that she'd be able to memorize.

She wasn't the only one. The essential foundation of all protection work was done in advance. Gabe was also studying every city for its layout, traffic patterns, neighborhood behavior, secure hotels, restaurants that were off the beaten path, and any potential ambush points. He rapidly briefed himself on the political attitudes, current conflicts, ethnic tensions, and economic unrest. He would not land unprepared.

Their American chauffeur, Jordan "from Houston, and God's honest truth, the Cougars rule Texas," soared up the highway in a white SUV. He was rattling off his favorite places to eat as if he would make a commission. Nas tried the hardest to engage him with earnest listening, but even she couldn't keep it up.

"Jordan," said Gabe finally, leaning forward in his seat. "We'll go to the last place you mentioned."

Jordan brightened. "Yeah? Y'all hungry?"

"*Yes*," said Jimmy. "Please."

"That would be great," said Nas.

Jordan slapped the wheel. "Aright, then."

Ridley just propped her chin on her hand and took in the scenery.

She'd been through Tangier once, coming across the Strait of Gibraltar on a ferry from Spain. It was exotic, alluring, and brimming with a hundred different tales of conquering power.

Twelve thousand years ago, it had been Phoenician, then Carthaginian, then Roman and then won in battle by the Vandals. The Byzantines conquered it, and then it was taken over by the Arabs. It juggled through the Portuguese and the English, but then the French and Spanish fought over it, until finally it was declared an International Zone overseen by nine separate countries. The game of conquest snatch-and-grab was over.

Those were the glory days for artists, traders, writers, eccentric bohemians, and diplomats. Everyone from Ian Fleming and Patricia Highsmith to Yves Saint-Laurent and Truman Capote came to Tangier.

It was full of glamour, flavor—and espionage.

You missed the golden age for spies, Samaras.

Morocco had asserted its independence in the 1950s, and reverted to a monarchy. It was now flourishing.

For all of the culture and architecture around them, Jordan gabbed like he was heading to a tailgate party for a Big 12 football game. It was a long thirty minutes from the airport to the restaurant.

They left the SUV parked on a boulevard and headed into Petit Socco on foot.

The old medina was a labyrinth of sloping stone streets and whitewashed buildings with wrought iron railings. Jasmine and bougainvillea cascaded over walls and balconies. Merchants spilled into the alleys, their shops bursting with colorful rugs, knockoff designer bags, and soccer jerseys that fluttered in the breeze. Tourists milled through the streets and lounged at outdoor cafés.

It was all tranquil, just a scene of leisure under the hot azure sky.

But that was never really the case for bodyguards on a protective detail.

Since there had been no way to memorize anything about this place from a map, Ridley had to stick with visual markers and her sense of direction to track their path.

Jordan led them to the eastern side of the medina, to a small restaurant with high ceilings, rustic wood, and tile mosaics on the wall. Ridley and Gabe sat with their backs to the wall so they could see the door.

Weaponless.

Then again, everything in sight could be a weapon.

They were sipping mint tea when Ridley's phone buzzed—*Fouad.* She let it go to voicemail.

The table conversation was so heavily filtered due to the presence of their diplomatic escort that it almost felt like a relief.

Over chicken pastillas, Jimmy and Jordan argued over whether football or American football was a better sport. Ridley sat across from Nas, sipping Moroccan spiced coffee and digging into a fig and honey tagine like it was her last meal. She noticed the Iranian woman's eyes flitting to Gabe more than a couple times.

No. No, we are not reenacting The Bodyguard *in the middle of Morocco.*

It was obvious why anyone—woman or man, straight or gay—would need a few extra moments to take in that man's appearance. Even those few hours in the Egyptian sun had given his skin a tawny glow, which in turn made his blond hair look like spun gold and his eyes pop like chunks of azure.

Mr. Stand-Out-in-a-North-African-Crowd.

Thankfully, he was being a consummate professional. He didn't return the glances from Nas.

When she stood up from her chair, Ridley popped to her feet as well.

"I just need the restroom," said Nas.

"I know."

Nas rolled her eyes but suppressed a grin. She waved at Ridley to join her. "Let's go, girls!"

"It's a rallying cry," said Ridley as they walked first to the tiny hallway.

She kept her eyes on the entrance of the restaurant as Nas stepped into the bathroom. For a few moments, she just watched the diners, the servers, the tourists passing by.

Then Nas opened the door. She stepped out with her face angled away, but Ridley stopped her with a hand.

"What?" she said, her voice tight.

Nas looked up. Her eyes had welled with pain, and the expression on her face was stricken.

"My best friend from being girls together, Elnaz—she's

gone. They don't know where she is but her husband thinks she was taken—"

"Taken by the regime?" said Ridley.

"Yes, of *course!* It was just a few hours ago. This was because of me!" Nas cried. "Because I lived last night."

Ridley held onto both of her shoulders. "You were always gonna live through last night."

She worried that the woman may have an emotional meltdown right there, but suddenly an anger blazed in Nas' eyes.

"I *love* the people of my country. They believe in me. I would be betraying Elnaz and Merab Jalali and all of the women of Iran if I let them silence me."

A smile crawled across Ridley's lips.

She really is that fighter.

"Let me just—I forgot to wash my hands," said Nas.

She went back into the bathroom. Ridley turned away, moved to the end of the hallway, and glanced over to check their table. Jordan was relaying some amazing tale that apparently required both hands and arms.

Nas emerged again, newly composed. She brushed back her wavy mane and lifted her chin.

"Okay. We have to go find an ancient sword."

Ridley followed her to the table. They paid the bill and headed back through the bustling medina.

Jordan was just unlocking the SUV for them when Ridley and Gabe both felt a buzz in their pockets. She was quickly scanning the vicinity, but he immediately pulled his out to check.

Gabe looked up at Nas, his brows knitting together.

"What did you *do?!*"

CHAPTER TWENTY-TWO

TANGIER, MOROCCO

For a moment, Nas flushed like a scolded child, but then she raised her head.

"I had to show them that I'm not afraid."

Ridley pulled out her own phone to check. It was an alert from their tech, Ted, at the Osprey office. Nas had posted a video.

"You did this from the *bathroom?*" she exclaimed.

"Nasrin!" cried Jimmy, with the harsh edge of a disappointed father.

Gabe stepped closed to her, anger tightening his sculpted features. "Your phone isn't encrypted! We just escaped assassins—left them behind—and you broadcast your location?!"

"I didn't say where I was! Of course not! It was the inside of a room. They don't know any location."

"Yeah, there are ways," said Ridley, her own frustration flaring.

On your watch, Samaras. She slipped that one right by you.

"I told you not to post anything," said Gabe.

Jimmy unleashed a furious torrent of Farsi at his daughter. She snapped back at him, but rubbed a palm to her forehead as though trying to stave off regret.

"Give me your phone," said Gabe.

"No. What do you think I am, some child?"

"I'm here trying to protect your life and I can't trust you to not put mine in danger. Give it to me."

She glared at him. "I'm not doing that."

Gabe was about to launch another rebuke, but Ridley caught him. "Gabe. We need to just go. Enough."

Jordan slipped into the driver's seat as if he hadn't heard and didn't know anything.

"I don't care only about my own life," said Nas, her voice quiet.

Jimmy snapped at her. "*I* care about your own life! Do not do this to me, Nasrin!"

She shook her head and looked off down the street—before climbing into the car without another word.

Ridley got in behind her.

Two hours later, the four of them were walking down a marina on the glittering Mediterranean. A warm breeze swept through the bay. The clank of rigging and the slosh of waves against the hulls soothed Ridley's irritation.

She'd grown angrier at Nas over the course of the ride there.

Damn babysitting...except a kid screws up on purpose and risks everyone's life...the worst mission...

On the way, they had stopped off at a beach shop to buy swimsuits and wetsuits.

"The Harpe Sword," Nas had told her as they tried on their

picks in the dressing room. "The sharpest sword that any man could use. Hermes gave it to Perseus to cut off Medusa's head."

"It's harder than you'd think to cut off someone's head in one swing," muttered Ridley.

She'd seen it tried.

"I know," said Nas from the next stall over.

She's seen it, too.

"Hopefully we won't need to use it for that," said Ridley.

She almost instantly cringed at her own bad taste, and tugged the swimsuit straps up over her shoulders.

Nas ignored her crack. "It must be like, uh...some *attraction* between the items. The shield led us to the sandals. The sandals have to lead us to the sword."

"We're not finding this thing otherwise."

She heard Nas emerge from her stall. "Do you like yours? Let me see."

Ridley stepped out, adjusting the top of the turquoise Lycra suit. Nas, in a magenta two-piece, appraised her statuesque bodyguard.

"You look like you're ready for the Olympics!"

"I swim," offered Ridley.

"But you're not diving with us..."

She shook her head and flicked a finger at her temple. "Diving accident, back in Navy training. It burst underwater, I lost my bearing, I lost some hearing, and I washed out. First woman into BUD/S training, first woman to fail BUD/S training."

It was worse than that. You lost your goal. You lost your way. You lost your dream—traded it for a muffled right ear and a chip on your shoulder the size of a tractor.

Save the world as many times as you like. You'll never be satisfied.

"That's not failing, but I'm sorry," said Nas, the dark pools of her eyes fixed on Ridley—

—who hated sympathy.

"It's not all bad," said Ridley, turning back to her stall to tug her shorts on over the suit. "I'll be in the water with you. The hired man will do the deep stuff. Gabe can...doggy-paddle, or whatever he likes."

Nas laughed. "I don't think he's very excited about the water."

"Well, I don't think there will be any assassins swimming for red coral, even if you did signal to them where we are," said Ridley, unable to keep the bite out of her voice.

"I heard you! I know. You don't know what it's like...I know you're risking your life. But you're not the only one."

Touché.

An hour later, Jordan dropped them off at Port de Tanger Ville.

As they headed down the long dock, Ridley squinted out at the sea. "We're sure that GPS coordinates were not a thing in ancient, mythological Greece?"

"It's like looking for a needle in a mountain of haystacks," said Gabe, adjusting the straps on his backpack, which was growing heavier with each item they collected.

"Maybe I read the stele wrong," grinned Nas. "You're welcome to check my work."

They had gone over and debated the clue to the next item's location. *This* one felt like the impossible task, which only made Ridley hungrier to start.

Forty minutes after that, they were looking for a boat named *An-Najah.*

They spotted a thick-waisted man in a white polo shirt stepping off the back of a dive boat.

"You're Samaras?" he called.

"Yes," replied Ridley.

"I am Ayoub Chibi."

As they approached, he extended a hand—first to Jimmy, then to Gabe, then to Ridley and finally Nas.

And that's the kind of country we're in. Senior males, then younger males, and then *women.*

"You have our equipment?" she asked.

Ayoub gestured to the boat. He wasn't much older than forty, with dark hair that looked like steel wool, and skin that looked like it was too heavy for his face to bear.

"And your diver," he replied.

The four of them followed Ayoub onto the *An-Najah.* The dive boat was just over thirty feet, a weathered vessel but well cared for, with a small top deck. On the lower level, another man was laying out scuba gear.

Ayoub got his attention in Arabic. The man straightened up and turned to them.

He was in his twenties, big, with close-cropped hair and a scar through one black brow. His jaw and chin looked like those of a Disney hero, and he had the unmistakable broad shoulders of a swimmer.

"Munir," he said, extending a hand to Ridley, who was closest.

She shook it. "I'm Ridley. You're the diver?"

"Yes. You know how to swim?"

This pulled a grin from her. "Yes, and I'm getting in with you. But I can't go below ten feet right now. A problem with my ear."

This is going to be hard for you, Samaras...don't even get in...

"The rest of you? But *you* are not diving," he said to Jimmy.

"I won't get seasick!" declared Jimmy.

Nas jumped in. "Yes, I'm the one going down with you. I dived once in Hawaii. The manta rays were amazing."

"I got scuba certified a few years ago," said Gabe.

"Okay. Very nice. The captain knows where we go," said Munir, nodding to Ayoub.

Ayoub beckoned them to a gear bin where they could stash their belongings. "You're diving for something very specific?"

"We just want to find this red coral," said Nas.

"But we're not taking any," Gabe added quickly.

"I'm not for trouble," said Ayoub. "No red coral in my boat."

Red coral harvesting was heavily regulated. The "Mediterranean gold" was highly prized for its use in jewelry, but it grew so slowly that replenishments could barely keep up with the reaping. Most countries, including Morocco, now required a license to extract it from their waters.

But none of them were about to explain what they were actually after, especially after what had happened with Tarek on the Giza Plateau.

This location had been the most difficult to map. The stele had told them "Where blood spilled on Poseidon's flowers," but poetic lines were not enough to find a section of coral in the Mediterranean.

There were three *stades* provided in the ancient script, which did leave a huge margin for error in geolocating. The Greek *stade* was a unit of measurement between one hundred-fifty and two hundred-ten yards. Gabe and Nas had worked out the triangulation of the three directions during their flight from Egypt.

From the southernmost tip of Spain, from the tip of the Bay of Tangier at Malabata, to the northernmost Dalia Beach, they had circled an area for exploration.

What they had to count on, though, was something they couldn't explain and didn't understand.

Just as the shield had led them to the sandals, they could only hope, wish, and pray that the sandals would lead them to the sword.

Or we'll be swimming 'til we're shark bait.

Ayoub climbed up to the flybridge on the small top deck and started the engine. Munir cast off the mooring lines, and the *An-Najah* glided out toward the open water.

Gabe, in a pair of wraparound shades, held onto the railing as they started to surge across the waves. Ridley took a seat on the bench beside him, unfurling her arms along the siding like it was her throne.

"Doesn't it feel good to not have to keep scoping for threats?" she half-yelled over the roar of the engine. "Good to relax a bit."

"We sure about them?" Gabe nodded to Munir, who was cracking open a water bottle up by the bow. "Captain Chibi?"

"They don't know a thing," she said, her pride still stinging over Tarek's betrayal.

That was your fault, Samaras. Even if it was Fouad's fault, it was really yours.

She tried to shut down her yakking inner voice and take in the full glory of these glowing blue waters.

Back at the Osprey office, Ted had run thorough background checks on both of the Moroccan crewmen. Still, Ridley couldn't help but eye Munir again, and glance up at the flybridge where Ayoub had the wheel.

If it turned into close quarters combat on a small boat?

I'd turn them into shark bait.

CHAPTER TWENTY-THREE

TANGIER, MOROCCO

THE *AN-NAJAH* CRUISED into the Strait of Gibraltar.

There was little talking onboard, as the rumble of the engine was so loud. Ridley basked in the salty spray and the wind. She occasionally glanced over at Gabe, who was still white-knuckling the railing.

Nearly a mile offshore, Ayoub throttled the engine back. The boat drifted to a stop.

"These are your coordinates," he announced as he climbed down the ladder.

Nas was so nervous that she almost seemed like a kid. She looked to Ridley and Gabe.

"Okay," said Jimmy, standing up at her side. "Come on."

Ridley slapped Gabe's knee as she got to her feet. "Suiting up time!"

Munir stood in the middle of the deck, holding his own wetsuit.

"Okay, everybody," he said, "listen to me. Watch me—how I put this on."

He pulled off his tank top and stripped down to a pair of neoprene swim shorts. It made Jimmy squirm, but he couldn't well clamp a hand over his grown daughter's eyes at the moment.

Munir gave the full demonstration of pulling on a wetsuit. He got passing marks from Ridley, who had done this a hundred times if once, on a clock, in the dark, sleep-deprived, under the battering howls of her Navy instructors...

It was time to don the gear again.

Everyone except Jimmy stripped down to their swimwear. Gabe hardly looked like a real person with his shirt off.

She left him to Munir's supervision while she helped Nas into her suit. The Iranian woman's nerves had blended with her excitement, morphing into something like a giddy high.

Ridley rattled off her safety tips like bullet points. "...and never hold your breath. Breathe continuously."

"I know, I remember."

Ridley rolled her own suit up to her waist and went to check the tanks. Munir had already buckled on the Buoyancy Control Device vests, but she had to check everything for herself.

O-ring, valve, inflator hose check...

Nas strapped on her weight belt. Ridley arranged the hoses and the regulator onto the BCD vest, then lifted it and slipped it over the other woman's shoulders.

"Okay, mask and fins," said Ridley. "You'll have fun down there!"

When they had Nas and Gabe ready to go, Ridley and Munir suited up.

As Ridley took a few test puffs from the regulator, she felt a twinge of emotion, a wordless missing. This had been an essential part of the life she had wanted—of the profession she would have died for.

Once upon a time, she could have been the first female Navy SEAL.

Except you couldn't even make it to battle with any rogue terror elements. You got taken out by a rogue underwater wave.

Jimmy pulled one of their bags from a deck compartment. He took out the sandals of Hermes, which had been tied together with a short rope.

He held them out to Nas, but she said something in Farsi and nodded to Gabe. Jimmy raised a brow but handed them to their bodyguard instead. Gabe took them and tied them onto his chest strap.

"What are you doing?" said Munir, eyeing him suspiciously.

"Lucky sandals," replied Gabe.

Munir muttered something in Arabic as he pulled on his mask. They all moved to the dive platform at the end of the deck, and donned their flippers.

Ridley spotted the aluminum boat hook pole standing upright in its rack nearby. She grabbed it.

One by one, they stepped off the platform.

She was the last one in. The water felt amazing, like a warm dip into heaven. They spent a moment finding their buoyancy—so they neither sank nor rose to the surface, but simply floated.

Munir signaled when it was time to descend. They swam after him—

But Ridley had to stop short.

Only four meters down?!

She could feel the pressure already. The others cleared their ears of it, but she just shook her head at them. Her damaged eardrum simply couldn't take any more without intense pain, and even if she could withstand *that*, the risk of severe vertigo and further hearing loss was too great.

Not for a mythical sword, you idiot. STOP HERE.

Ridley waved them on. Nas seemed to hesitate, but finally gave the thumbs up and continued down after the others.

Visibility was about eighty feet, which allowed Ridley to follow their descent in the smooth blue. As she watched the sway of their flippers grow smaller, she felt the almost overwhelming pull to swim down after them.

You knew this would happen. Don't compromise the team by compromising yourself. Stay on your task.

She refocused—the weightless float...the steady Darth Vader sound of her regulator...the flashes of bright fish squiggling by...

Munir led Nas and Gabe downward. He stopped every few meters to remind them to pinch their nose and clear their ears of pressure.

As they swam closer, the smudges of color below sharpened. A coral reef sprawled across the seabed, hills and crags and caves and jagged edges. There were rope-like formations and giant fans—indigo, magenta, and orange. Schools of fish glided and darted about.

Nas drifted to an enormous blue clump that looked like a mass of bristles. She was only a little superstitious, but when she'd learned that these soft corals were called *gorgonia*, she was certain they would find what they were looking for here in the depths.

Gabe kept glancing down at the sandals floating in front of his chest. He didn't know what exactly he was expecting them to do, but as of now they were inert. Useless.

They swam lower, and spotted it.

There was the famed red coral they were searching for.

Nas and Jimmy had been sure that it was "drops of the

monster's blood" that had fallen into the sea after Perseus cut off Medusa's head. The dripping blood had stained the ocean floor where the sword fell, so the coral that grew there would forever mark his great and deadly deeds.

Munir signaled that he was going under the overpass of coral. Nas and Gabe swam after him.

Far above, Ridley watched as the faint dark blobs of all three divers disappeared into the reef. With the long boat hook in hand, she rotated herself slowly in the water, surveying the blue expanse.

The shadow of the boat bobbed a few meters away. She watched a silver school of fish circling up from the reef.

Then she spotted a silhouette—

It was thirty or forty feet away, hard to tell the size.

But it was big. With a dorsal. A sharp nose. And oar-shaped fins.

Munir glided below the huge arch of the reef. Nas followed at his side. Gabe brought up the rear.

There was the coral.

It fanned out, a web of scarlet fractals. There was a thin layer of white covering it, like dandelion pappus that had been scattered across the sea floor. The blood-red polyps were everywhere on the underside of the arch.

Gabe felt a strange sensation against his chest. He glanced down.

The sandals, which had been floating along in front of him, were suddenly extended. He signaled to Nas, who saw the taut rope. She got so excited that she gurgled something through her regulator.

He swam forward, following the tug of the sandals. The tug became a pull. Munir looked at him in bewilderment.

Gabe tried to steer himself with his flippers, but the sandals were pulling harder. He felt the pressure of the water on his mask as he sped forward.

Nas and Munir went after him.

He veered out from the overpass, then up around the arch. Another cluster of red coral appeared.

Gabe was yanked toward it, but then the rope on the sandals went slack. The pulling stopped, and he was staring at something wedged into the reef.

An electric surge coursed through Ridley as she stared at the creature in the blue.

Oceanic whitetip.

The "shipwreck sharks." They were the killers behind the most infamous shark attack in history.

When the USS Indianapolis was struck by a Japanese submarine in WWII, the Navy cruiser sank into the Philippine Sea. Over a thousand men went into the water that night, stranded, floating on their life jackets or treading water for their lives.

And then, the sharks came.

So began the massacre from below.

For two days, the sailors watched their mates be yanked under the water, only to see disemboweled corpses pop back to the surface with life jackets still on. Dorsal fins cruised around them.

When those disappeared from the surface, all they had to do was look down to see the hunters circling in the water beneath them.

The blood from the attacks only drew more sharks. Screams, hallucinations, men disappearing from the surface.

On the fourth day, a patrol plane spotted the survivors.

Nearly nine hundred men had gone into the water when the USS Indianapolis went down. Only three hundred came out.

They're not afraid of humans.

This shark was gliding closer. Ridley extended the boat hook to make herself appear bigger.

Eight feet? Ten feet? Altogether too big...?

And then she saw a second shark emerge in the blue.

CHAPTER TWENTY-FOUR

TANGIER, MOROCCO

Gabe floated closer to the reef as Nas swam up beside him. They both peered into the cluster of red coral.

Deep within the web of blood-colored spires was a bright glint, a knob of some sort.

He reached in carefully, grasped the end of it, and tugged.

It didn't budge.

He braced his other hand against the reef and pulled, straining—until it gave a bit—and then a bit more...and finally drew it free.

Gabe floated in the weightless blue, holding a curved sword like he was King Arthur himself.

Nas almost sputtered her regulator out of her mouth. She reached for the sword, brushing her fingertips along the dark blade.

He offered it to her. She gripped the golden handle and swiveled it about, taking in the sparkling metal.

From a yard away, Munir stared at them. He signaled a question: *Up?*

Gabe nodded and confirmed: *Up*

Ridley's breathing was calm. A steady stream of bubbles rose up from the exhaust valve of her regulator.

Making sure to stay upright, she watched as the sharks circled closer.

I'd rather be facing a single great white than multiples of these bastards.

The second was still farther off, dipping a few meters beneath her. She could not afford to lose sight of either of them.

Are there more down there?

She glanced below but couldn't make out her companions. There was no way to signal to them what they were about to swim up into.

The first shark glided toward her at an angle. She could see now the white on its belly and its fins. It looked ten feet long.

There was a thin line with some sharks between curiosity and deadly aggression. Oceanic whitetips were known to bite divers even when there were several people in a group. Worse still, they were known for their persistence. If one of these went for even a "test bite," it would spill blood in the water.

A beacon for every other shark in the area.

Ridley clutched the boat hook.

I'm not your prey. I'm another predator.

Nas slid the sword into her weight belt as a makeshift scabbard. She began the swim upward with the others.

Munir, who was checking the rate of ascent on his Peregrine

watch, kept their pace slow—no more than nine meters a minute.

Once more, the sandals floated in front of Gabe's chest, inert.

Nas could feel the long blade against her leg each time she kicked.

The first shark turned to Ridley—and swam straight toward her—

She jabbed at its snout with the long end of the boat hook—

But missed as it veered off at the last second.

Where's the other one?!

Focusing too much on one could spell disaster. She spun around.

The other was coming up from a meter below her, circling closer. Its light gray beady eyes flashed in a ray of light from above.

She angled herself in the water so she could keep both in her line of sight.

She glanced down...she could see Nas and Gabe and Munir now.

They're gonna be so damn slow. Can't rush the pressure.

Have the sharks seen them?

The second whitetip got within a meter of Ridley—then turned and sped off. It left, swimming thirty...forty meters into the blue until it had vanished from sight.

The first one was loitering at a distance.

She gave a quick look down again. The other divers were almost halfway to her.

As she looked back up, the first shark was coming in—speeding up—

She tried to swing the boat hook around but the water drag

slowed it—she barely got the broad side of the pole up to deflect its nose—the shark butted past.

Testing attack speed.

Very bad.

She swiveled around, looking for other sharks. There were none in sight.

Her three companions finally reached her. They had to stop for a few minutes at the five meter depth to safely decompress.

But they had clearly seen the shark by now, lurking quietly only a short ways off. Munir pointed to each of the divers, then motioned for them to cluster together as a group.

A burst of muffled sound escaped from Gabe—pointing behind Ridley—she turned her head.

The second whitetip was speeding straight at them, a gray missile exploding out of the blue.

She had only enough time to stab the boat hook out from under her arm.

It snapped against the creature's snout, just inches away from her—

Stung, the shark jetted off.

It had consumed all of their attention...taking it away from the bigger of the two predators for only *seconds.*

And the huge predator seized its moment.

A gurgling cry broke through the water—

Coming up behind them, the first oceanic whitetip had bitten down.

Its shovel-sized jaws clamped around Gabe's back. It began to thrash. A cloud of bubbles exploded from his mouthpiece as he tried to free himself.

Munir tried to round the shark and beat it away. Ridley struggled to get an angle—to stab at it with the boat hook. Nas pulled the Harpe sword from her belt, but it was too unwieldy underwater.

Small clouds of blood plumed from Gabe's torso. His howls were muffled gurgles.

Finally, the assault from the rest of the divers became too much for the shark. This wouldn't be his meal today.

The creature released Gabe and darted off into deeper waters.

No more time for decompression.

Munir grabbed Gabe's vest and hit the button for the power inflator. The vest filled with air and pulled Gabe to the surface. Munir swam after him. Ridley pushed Nas ahead of her.

They broke the surface only a meter from the boat. Munir called urgently for Ayoub, who rushed to help Gabe up onto the diving platform.

As Nas went next, Ridley sank below the surface again, scanning the blue abyss for any sign of their attackers. There was nothing in sight but the shifting beams of sunlight slanting downward.

She resurfaced.

They stripped their gear in a rush of adrenaline and worry. Ayoub pulled off Gabe's tank and BCD and grabbed the medical kit.

Jimmy helped him pull off the perforated wetsuit.

Watery blood streamed down the right side of Gabe's torso. He winced as Ayoub made him lie flat on the bench and began to wipe away the fluid.

There were multiple lacerations, jagged as sharks' teeth, but they weren't as deep as expected. The captain rinsed everything with fresh water and hydrogen peroxide. As he bandaged the wounds, Munir inspected the scuba tank.

"Lucky," he said, tracing over a series of dents and scratches on the aluminum. "Sharks don't like metal."

Gabe sat upright so that Ayoub could finish wrapping the bandages.

"But we got it," he said, grimacing.

"You got it!" said Ridley.

"Yeah," said Nas, as though remembering through the dreamy grin of her adrenaline dump. "We got it."

Brushing locks of wet hair back from her face, she bent and picked up the item that she'd dropped on the deck. Ridley and Jimmy drew closer in.

The Harpe sword.

A gilt pommel gleamed as if new. The hilt looked like it was wrapped with black leather, yet somehow it was undamaged from millennia in saltwater.

The blade, though...it was a dark gray that glittered in the sunlight. The top half of it swooped and curved almost like a sickle.

Jimmy reached for the hypnotizing metal. "Adamantium?"

"Maybe it is real," said Nas.

"The skeleton they put into Wolverine, adamantium?" said Gabe.

"The comic book writers got it from Greek myths," she told him. "It's where the English word 'adamant' comes from. You can't beat it. They say it was used by the gods to make weapons and forge chains."

Ridley cast an eye to Munir and Ayoub, who seemed to be sizing up the sword for potential value.

"Did you feel like King Arthur down there?" Nas grinned at Gabe. "Pulling the sword from the stone?"

"Kinda." Gabe sucked in a pained breath. "Give me a crown with my stitches."

That thing had better collapse like the shield.

"Okay," said Jimmy, turning to Ayoub. "Captain Chibi, we can go back to shore, please."

The Moroccan nodded, turning slowly back to the flybridge.

Ridley pulled out her bag from the deck compartment and grabbed her phone.

"First time getting bitten by a shark?" she asked Gabe, sitting next to him on the bench.

"First time watching your partner get bitten by a shark?"

His words felt like a punch to Ridley. The boat motor gunned to life.

You failed your teammate. You were the only one with a defensive weapon and you didn't have his six.

But she was angry at him for pointing it out. "Well, I won't let you die."

He frowned. "I'm not even close to dying."

"Exactly. You're welcome."

She unlocked her phone to summon Jordan with the car, but saw she had an encrypted message. She opened it.

Meet me - Aunt Bea

CHAPTER TWENTY-FIVE

TANGIER, MOROCCO

Aunt Bea was not Ridley's aunt.

She was a CIA legend. Or a myth, depending on who you asked.

Ridley had only met her once in person, at a high-level meeting involving Booker, the Deputy Director of the Directorate of Operations Ben Conway, and a few other administrators within the DO—formerly the National Clandestine Service. Aunt Bea had been formally introduced by her title as they opened the proceedings. Technically, she was the Chief of the Liaison Division, but throughout the meeting she was referred to by everyone as "Aunt Bea."

That was the only interaction Ridley had ever had with her. Now she was sending a summons by private message.

She couldn't figure out how she felt about it. The fact that Aunt Bea even *knew* about Osprey and its work was a sign of the woman's significance.

So Ridley answered her message as the boat sped back to shore, as Gabe lay grimacing on the bench, as Nas and Jimmy bent over the sword, examining it with awe.

Abroad. Can we meet in Spain?

Seconds after she sent it, Ridley shook her head in frustration.

Of course she knows you're abroad, you idiot. She's—

"That!" exclaimed Nas.

The sword in her hand was simply not there anymore. She held the grip, but there was no longer any blade. She hoisted it aloft and waggled the hilt.

"It did collapse. You press the end of the handle—the pommel?"

Ridley gave a short fist pump. "Who knew the Greek gods were into travel size?"

She clutched the phone for the rest of the ride, waiting to hear back from Aunt Bea.

The reply didn't come until four hours later, when Ridley was sitting in a hospital waiting room in Tangier.

Can you be in Sevilla tomorrow?

She set her water bottle down between her feet and typed back:

Yes, tomorrow afternoon.

Aunt Bea's next message came through instantly.

Good. I'll send you time and place.

Ridley shut down the phone and slid it back into her pocket.

Nas was curled up in the chair beside her. The surge of adrenaline from their dive and the close escape that afternoon had left her exhausted. She'd been dozing for the last half hour, the bag of treasures nestled between her and Ridley.

Jimmy sat cross-legged beside his daughter with an issue of

National Geographic on his lap. He was not exactly absorbed in it, though. Ridley noticed him glancing up often, giving a quick scan of the strangers moving around them.

A television on the wall across from them was broadcasting scenes from some catastrophic flood in northern India.

The thoughts that churned through Ridley's mind were putting her on edge. She wanted to go for a run, but there she was—stuck—playing babysitter every minute of the day.

She couldn't dive with the team.

She'd let her partner suffer an attack underwater.

She'd let their protectee send up a digital flare that would surely sic assassins on their trail again.

And now Aunt Bea had summoned her to meet in person.

"Ms. Ridley?"

A thick Moroccan accent cut through her brooding. She shot to her feet to face the doctor, a slight man in scrubs with a clipped manner.

"Yes," she said.

"Mr. Tolkin is okay. There were a lot of bites but they were shallow. It looked worse than it is. The tank on his back definitely saved him from a lot worse. We gave him stitches and they're bandaging him now. You will need to help him change the bandages one time per day for two days. The stitches cannot get wet. We'll write down all of this for you in the paperwork. Okay?"

She nodded. "Okay, yeah. Thanks."

"Okay," said the doctor. "Maybe an hour. Please wait."

He strode off to his next appointment.

Behind her, Nas mumbled, "He's okay?"

"He's okay," said Ridley. "Stitches and bandages."

Jimmy glanced up at the television. The screen was now playing footage of the Iranian Foreign Minister greeting an American envoy in Oman.

His face darkened. "They're doing it again," he muttered.

"Doing what?" asked Ridley.

"Every president of the United States thinks that they can buy good behavior from the Islamic Republic. There is no such thing as *good* from this regime. There are only the fools from the West. We don't want America to save the people of Iran. We want them to stop helping the regime."

He spoke with such venom that it took Ridley aback.

He's not so *unlike his firebrand daughter.*

Jordan drove them to a hotel that evening that looked out over the Bay of Tangier.

As the four of them checked into two adjoining rooms, the enthusiastic Texan went out to get them food. Gabe didn't want any hotel staff knocking on their doors with room service.

He couldn't get his new stitches wet, but the others showered and cleaned up.

Ridley had to work to scrub the salt out of her hair under the thin drizzle of the shower head. The bullet slice on her calf still stung, though it already felt like the firefight on the Giza Plateau had been months ago.

She replayed the day in her head...the muffled sound of the regulator in her bad ear...the shark appearing out of the blue gloom...Gabe's gurgled cry as its jaws clamped around his torso...Aunt Bea's message...

What does she want?

By the time Ridley toweled dry and pulled on a T-shirt and shorts, she'd stormed out of the looping relays in her head. It was time to get back to work.

No sooner had Nas stepped into the bathroom than Jordan returned with two paper bags in hand.

"Enough for everybody who might be extra hungry, and six water bottles," he said, handing them to Ridley.

She peered inside. "You got—burgers?"

"People love burgers everywhere! It's a beautiful piece of cultural appropriation that they got *Texas barbecue burgers* in Morocco. You're already welcome for how much you're gonna love those."

"Thanks, cowboy."

He left for the night, promising he'd be back in time to chauffeur them to the airport.

After Nas showered and dressed, she and Ridley took the food and the backpack and went next door. Gabe answered their knock, moving gingerly.

When Nas saw his damp golden hair, she exclaimed something to her father in Farsi. Jimmy was sitting on the edge of his bed, and snapped back in a scolding tone.

"What?" said Gabe, looking between the two.

Nas shook her head as though embarrassed. "I thought you took a shower, I'm sorry. The doctor said you can't for at least a day."

"Yeah, I was there. Good thing the sink is big enough for my head. Thanks, though."

He gave a little smile and moved aside to let them in.

The men's room was small but impeccably decorated. The floors were made of polished wood, and Arabian arches loomed on the headboards of each bed. Their balcony doors were open and a warm sea breeze billowed the gauzy drapes.

They unpacked the food on a table, where Gabe and Jimmy were equally surprised by the choice of cuisine.

As they tucked into the messy brisket burgers, Ridley was struck in a moment by how these meals with the Aslanis felt like...being in someone's home. Despite the physical demands, she normally had little of her regular appetite when on a mission. Yet for these Persians, food was social. It was hospitality. It was bonding. Jamshid and Nasrin were warm and genial and full of laughter when they shared a meal. It was becoming infectious, even for the laconic, cynical Gabe.

And Jordan had not been wrong. The burgers were damn good.

After they'd washed the mess of barbecue sauce off their hands, Jimmy took the backpack and began emptying it. On his bed cover, he laid out each of the items they'd collected.

The bronze brick that was the shield of Athena.

The strapped sandals that belonged to Hermes.

The hilt of the sword of Hermes.

Ridley took a swig of water and looked down at them. "One bag and a hat still to go."

"Yes," said Jimmy.

Nas gazed over the items. "I cannot believe...are we really looking at these things from Greek *mythology?* That came from gods who don't exist? I *cannot* even understand..."

First timer at the weird rodeo.

"I told you you'd see wonderful things," said Ridley.

She'd seen her share of things that couldn't be real, that came from beings that *couldn't* exist.

"Riddle me this," said Gabe, wincing as he lowered himself into an armchair. "What the hell do these things do *now?* We're not slaying monsters anymore."

Something sparked in Nas' eye.

"You think Medusa was a *monster?*"

He blinked. "We are talking about the snake-headed woman who turned any man who looked at her to stone? Yeah, I know about gorgons. I'd call that a monster."

Nas grabbed a water bottle and took a sip.

"Oh no," she said. "You might know gorgons from a video game or a movie, but Medusa was not born with snakes for hair, or claws, or wings, or a gaze that turned men to stone. She was made *into* that."

This rings a bell...though Yaya would be ashamed of how faint...

Gabe swept a hand across the room. "Tell me a story."

Nas gave him a sly look.

"The villain of this story is not who you think."

CHAPTER TWENTY-SIX

TANGIER, MOROCCO

NAS SAT on the edge of the bed, clutching her water bottle.

"There were three gorgon sisters born to deities of the sea—before there were even 'gods.' Two of those sisters were immortal: Stheno and Euryale. The third was mortal: Medusa. I don't know why. No one explains.

"*Medusa* was famous for her beauty. She was the most charming and the most confident of the sisters, and had men everywhere lining up for her. One of the *men*, though, was Poseidon, the god of the ocean."

Her eyes were shining as she spun the tale.

"But Medusa would not have him. That really offended his ego, so one day he captured her in the temple of the goddess Athena and raped her. Athena caught him. The stories don't say if she thought it was mutual, or if she knew Poseidon was violating her, but she was so angry about the desecration of her temple that she lashed out.

"She couldn't take out her anger on Poseidon, though, because he was her uncle and another god. So she poured *all* of her punishment on his victim. She turned Medusa into a monster. Even her appearance to others became a curse—anyone who looked at her would instantly turn to stone."

It was not the same story as Ridley remembered. "What about her sisters? Because doesn't 'gorgon' mean they were all snake-haired?"

"Well, Stheno and Euryale tried to intervene, to defend their sister. Stheno especially—the oldest—was ferocious. But Athena turned both of them into monsters, too."

"So Athena's the asshole," said Gabe.

Nas looked at him. "And Poseidon, don't you think?"

"Yeah, of course him, too."

She gave Gabe a side-eye, but went on. "Medusa and her sisters were *devastated*. They fleed—fled?—to a distant cave so they wouldn't be a threat to anyone. If no one could see them, no one would die by turning to stone.

"But of course, when the men of Greece found out, they had to go try to find her. Once they chased her beauty to sleep with her, and then they chased her ugliness to kill her. What a prize, then, to *slay a monster like that!*"

Jimmy was listening gravely to his daughter. He gave no indication of what he thought about these stories.

"But all of these men failed," said Nas. "They obviously had to look at her to try to kill her, so they all turned to stone. She killed *them*, but not on purpose."

Ridley spoke up. "But it was Athena who helped Perseus kill her. She gave him the shield...after turning Medusa into a monster in the first place. What the fuck, Athena."

"*You* know," said Nas, "the Greek gods were cruel and full of vengeance. They could be good, but...they could be very, very bad. Athena gave her shield to use Medusa's reflection instead of having to look at her directly. Hermes gave flying sandals and the sharpest sword in the world. The Hesperides gave a special bag to keep her head in. Hades gave a helmet of invisibility."

"What happened to the sisters?" asked Ridley.

"Stheno and Euryale were there in the cave when Perseus found them all sleeping. He used the shield to spot Medusa, chopped off her head with the sword, but accidentally woke up the sisters. He had to use the helmet to make himself invisible while he escaped with the fastest flying sandals ever made. Then he took the head to King Polydectes in the special bag, used it to turn *him* to stone...and then gave the head of Medusa *to* Athena."

Gabe leaned forward, exclaiming, "She got Medusa's *head?*"

He winced hard, having momentarily forgotten about his stitches.

Nas leaned in as if she couldn't believe it either. "She put it on her shield to carry into battle, to turn her enemies to stone."

Ridley offered up a hand. "That was actually a really smart thing to do. Goddess of wisdom and war. And a bitch. A smart warbitch."

"I thought Ares was the god of war," said Gabe.

"He was the wrecking ball," Nas told him. "All fiery, passionate, impulsive violence. He was more like the god of *combat.* War is courage and skill and strategy."

Jimmy spoke for the first time, his brows knit tightly in thought. "What happened to the two immortal sisters? Did they not try to take revenge against Athena?"

Nas took a sip from her bottle and puffed out her cheeks before answering. "There's nothing written anywhere about them ever again. But they weren't the only survivors. When Perseus cut off Medusa's head, a son leaped out of her neck—a man with a golden sword. I think his name was Chrysaor...but with him was a much more famous creature: Pegasus, the winged horse. Born out of a neck."

"Let me guess," said Ridley. "Their father was Poseidon."

"Your guesses don't count," said Gabe. "You're Greek."

"Half. So, half the answers. You give the other half your best try."

He rolled his eyes.

Grouchy prick.

Gabe looked back at Nas. "And now you think...as an archaeologist, that all of those insane stories are true."

Before she could answer, Jimmy said, "You tell me. Tell us what happened in the Tomb of Osiris. Tell *us* what happened at the bottom of the sea."

Gabe said nothing, but his bright eyes were rippling with doubts.

"*As* an archaeologist," said Nas, more gently, "I am only following the trail left by history. *Somebody* put these items in very specific places. They are the items of the story. They are in the places that the ancient stele says. They speak to each other and I—I can't understand that. Can you?"

Gabe glanced at Ridley, as if aware in that moment that she knew more of this world than he did.

She raised a dark, arching brow at him.

A whole new world...

"Yeah," he muttered, pushing himself slowly up out of the chair. "This is all your stuff. I'm just here to keep you among the living."

That was curtains on the group conversation. The two women collected the items and headed back to their own room.

When Nas wanted to step out onto their small tile balcony, Ridley insisted on going out first. They were on the fifth floor, so there was little to see below the canopy of thick rustling palms.

Only one older couple was out on their balcony, three doors down. A thick vine of Arabian jasmine wound up the railing.

"Okay," she told Nas behind her. "You can come out."

The Iranian woman smiled with a touch of bemusement and nerves.

"Strange times," she said, "that I can't walk out to see the ocean without wondering if I will die doing it."

"I can't vouch for the construction here," said Ridley, gripping the wrought-iron railing.

Nas leaned over and plucked one of the white jasmine blossoms. The scent was unmistakable—rich, silky, honeyed sweet. She tucked it into her thick hair, just behind her ear, and gazed out at the glint of sea in the distance.

"Don't tell Agent Tolkin, but this was a *great* day."

She smiled.

Before Ridley could respond, her phone buzzed in her pocket.

Aunt Bea.

Ridley had her meeting.

CHAPTER TWENTY-SEVEN

SEVILLA, SPAIN

The four of them took a ferry the next morning across the Strait of Gibraltar. They arrived in Tarifa an hour later, where green hills rolled up from the bay. The wind whipped at their clothes as they disembarked. In the distance, flocks of brightly colored kitesurfing sails soared and banked over the bright blue waters.

They passed through their expedited customs check and found their official driver waiting by a silver Mercedes-Benz GLS. She was a thick-waisted, cherub-faced woman with light brown hair tied back in a messy bun. She greeted them brightly and introduced herself as Sadie.

"Pleasure to meet you all," she said, shaking hands, but slowed deliberately as she looked each of the Aslanis in the eye, "but a special privilege to meet both of you."

Jimmy seemed taken aback. Nas smiled in thanks.

Sadie helped them load their bags into the back. Gabe was moving stiffly, his jaw clenched in pain as he climbed in with the others. Ridley had offered the front seat, but he'd given a terse shake of his head.

"You must already know," Sadie told them as she slid in behind the wheel, "I'm not with State. I'm from the agency."

Gabe glanced sharply up at her in the rearview mirror.

Ridley buckled her seatbelt. "Did she send you directly?"

"Yep, she did, and don't worry. Your boss knows about the meeting."

Ridley felt a pang of guilt, as though she'd been caught out. She *hadn't* told Booker about this meeting yet.

Sadie gave her a smile and dodged her eyebrows upward. "To the matriarch."

She started the car, and Taylor Swift exploded through the speakers mid-ballad. Sadie turned it down with a grin.

"You didn't happen to see any terrorists on the ferry, huh?" she said as they pulled out of the lot. "Things are getting a little hot on our channels right now."

"No one put up their hand when we did a roll call," said Ridley.

"Probably hadn't had their coffee yet," said Gabe.

Spain was separated from Morocco by only eight nautical miles. For Spanish authorities, it was a tense and dangerous distance.

Islamic terrorism had long simmered and festered within the kingdom of Morocco.

In 2003, twelve suicide bombers dispersed through the city of Casablanca on a warm evening. Their targets: a luxury hotel popular with tourists, a Spanish restaurant, a Jewish restaurant, a Jewish community center, and a Jewish school.

They slaughtered thirty-three people that night and injured a hundred more. It rocked the nation's sense of itself and sparked an overhaul of the country's approach to radical Islam. Morocco massively expanded the capabilities and intelligence-sharing of their law enforcement agencies, passed much stricter legislation that widened the definition of "terror," cracked down on radicalized neighborhoods, kept prisoners for indefinite detentions, and brought mosques under state control to prevent them from fomenting jihadism.

Even as they began to coordinate their counter-terrorism efforts with France and Spain, they were too late to stop one cell that had already taken root in the Spanish homeland.

On March 11, 2004, during the morning rush hour in Madrid, Islamic terrorists blew up four commuter trains. They killed one hundred and ninety-one people and injured nearly two thousand.

The city was shattered. All of Europe was rocked. The terrorists had been members of the Moroccan Islamic Combat Group, who had been living in Spain at the time.

It was only the beginning for Europe.

In Barcelona, jihadis used a ramming van to murder over a dozen people.

In Brussels, terrorists blew themselves up at the airport, injuring hundreds.

In Paris, another terrorist cell tried to suicide bomb an entire stadium of football fans. They *only* managed to massacre one hundred and thirty-seven people, on sidewalks, at restaurants, and in a concert hall packed with people.

In France, terrorists killed seventeen people at a newspaper office and a Jewish supermarket...after a terrorist rammed a truck down a promenade in Nice on Bastille Day, murdering eighty-six people.

Far too many of these terrorists had come through Morocco. As the primary and simplest route into the European continent, the Spanish authorities knew that the danger was always at their threshold, like a lion crouching at the door.

Now, we have to be on alert for Iranians, too.

Sadie drove the four of them up to Sevilla. It took two hours, though her easy laugh and casual chatting helped lift their moods. Even Gabe relaxed, though any jolts on the road would still make him wince.

"In my humble, well-traveled opinion," said Sadie, "Andalusia is the most beautiful part of Spain. I don't know what your work here entails, but I hope you get to see some flamenco. And the horses are spectacular, but the bull-fighting —" she shuddered. "Been here four years and I still can't accept that. Horrible stuff."

"Do they still actually *kill* the bulls?" asked Nas.

"Right there in the ring. Like barbarians—trapping an animal and torturing it before stabbing it to death."

Ridley had been once as a young teenager. Her father, Nikos, had taken her and her brother on a rare family outing, but the ending was grisly. She'd been ready to climb over the rail, dash across the ring, and fight on behalf of the bull. If only she'd had some gladiator weapons.

Their father, realizing how dreadful it had all been for his children, took them for churros afterward. No one ate them.

In the backseat, Jimmy murmured something to Nas in Farsi. A smile broke over her face as she looked at him, as though surprised with delight. She replied, and made her father laugh.

Ridley couldn't remember the last time her father had laughed with her. Jimmy's easy warmth with his daughter was unusual.

No—rare.

They weren't just coworkers, but friends. That was the richest addition to a family bond that she could imagine.

But *only* imagine. That just wasn't part of Ridley's story. Her father had provided for the material needs of his children all his life, and that was it. It had been enough for her in the moment.

She and Alexios had been their own family, like two Artful Dodgers scampering about and getting into scrapes in a dozen different countries.

She missed her brother, who had gone back to live an ordinary suburban life in Chicago.

She didn't know how to miss her father.

She knew that he loved The Beach Boys and cigars and the movie *Alien.* He sometimes played soccer with her and Alexios, teaching them to be strong when he body-checked them off the ball. He hated laziness and thought that gullibility was a character defect. He liked cats, though they never owned one. He rarely shared memories with his kids of their mother. He rarely spoke of her at all, but Ridley and Alexios knew that he kept photos of her in his room. Every time they moved, those pictures were the most safely packed of all his possessions.

Ridley shook out of her thoughts when Sadie pulled over the SUV by a leafy, shaded avenue.

"Okay, we're here—Plaza de España." She turned to Ridley. "I'm relieving you. Go see the queen bee. We'll all get lunch or something. You want anything?"

"Uh...*montadito de pringá,*" said Ridley, reaching for the door handle, absent-mindedly listing the only sandwich in Sevilla she could remember.

She had hesitated on whether to take the backpack...the Perseus collection of magical items. Aunt Bea was CIA, but had nothing to do with Osprey. If Booker had wanted to read her in to the mission, he would have told Ridley directly.

Unless something happened to him?!

She swallowed back the notion and got out of the car—without the backpack. Sadie pulled away into traffic.

Ridley walked to the the Plaza de España.

The courtyard that opened up across from the leafy park was a sprawling, palatial vision. Ornate, painted lampposts rose high above the stone railings that lined a moat. The manmade river encircled the plaza, making it look like something out of Venice. A handful of small rowboats even floated around it, under the stone arch bridges and around the thick magenta blossoms of the Judas trees.

Ridley crossed the expanse of tiled mosaics underfoot. Tourists wandered about, taking in the sprawling complex. The building itself was a massive half-circle. A series of alcoves and towers displayed a spectacle of Baroque and Moorish and Art Deco styles. It was one of the great wonders of Spanish architecture and the most photographed location in Sevilla.

And one of the most conspicuous possible places to meet outdoors.

She took up her place at the enormous fountain in the center of the plaza, leaning against the thick stone edge.

The scent of orange blossoms wafted by. Ridley felt the cool spray from the plumes of water behind her. The distant twang of a Spanish guitar echoed from one of the pavilions. A couple passed by pushing a baby carriage, speaking some Eastern European language.

Ridley squinted about in the high sun.

Then she heard a loud wet plop behind her, and she turned.

CHAPTER TWENTY-EIGHT

SEVILLA, SPAIN

A MAN in his forties was leaning on the fountain a few yards away from Ridley. He had a shock of black hair and a dense, trimmed beard.

"You know what's amazing?" he said in a faint New York accent.

"Grace?"

"Silver dollars." He nodded to the shiny disc that glinted beneath the water.

"Only the originals," said Ridley. "Lady Liberty reigns."

He pushed himself off the stone edge and gave a dark chuckle, "*That* remains to be seen. You ready?"

"Lead the way, Luigi!"

Whatever-his-name-was led Ridley across the plaza, over one of the stone bridges, and up the steps of the south wing. They walked the colonnade almost to the end, where not-really-Luigi walked her to a set of grand, carved wooden doors. There he paused and looked back at Ridley.

"You met her before?"

"Sort of. She's the queen bee?"

He shook his head at her pun, then grasped the handles and pushed open the doors.

They stepped into a high-ceilinged lobby, full of ferns and Oriental carpets and brightly colored tiles. A taller, younger man stood at the far end. He nodded to them as they entered.

"Great success!" said not-Luigi in his best Borat accent, lifting his fists in mock triumph.

The taller man didn't even crack a smile. "You can go in."

Ridley went to the closed door beside him and knocked.

"You can come in," came a woman's muffled voice from behind it.

Ridley entered.

Sitting at a tidy mahogany desk in a wood-paneled ministerial office was a woman in her fifties. She was leaning back in the chair, scrolling through a tablet.

Aunt Bea's thick auburn hair was pinned back in a messy-but-still-fashionable bun. She wore tortoiseshell glasses over a heart-shaped face, a loose navy blouse, and boat shoes.

She looked up and gave a high-wattage smile.

"Hi, Ridley Samaras. Take a seat." Her tone was slightly nasal but calm and articulate.

Ridley didn't often get nervous around high-ranking agency heads, or heads of state, or royalty, or fiery demons, but Aunt Bea made her feel like a kid in front of the coolest teacher at school.

"Hi," she replied, lowering herself into the cushioned chair.

"Most people never see their own files," said Aunt Bea, going back to scrolling. "You wanna see yours? Performance evals are kept separate."

She smiled again and held up the tablet.

"No, no, thanks. I was there. I know if I failed or succeeded in my missions."

Goddamn, lady, who says yes to that question?

"Eh, thought I'd ask," said Aunt Bea, setting it facedown in front of her. "Always interesting to see who says 'yes.' That's your water, by the way."

She pointed to a bottle on the edge of the desk.

"No, thanks," said Ridley. "Just thirsty to know why I'm here in front of you...ma'am."

That was awkward. Don't do that again.

"I'm read in on what happened in Egypt. Obviously." She waved a hand. "Whatever you're *there* for, I don't think I really care. Osprey does its own thing and I don't understand it and I only cross Director Douglas when I have to. He's good at his job, and it seems like you're good at yours."

Ridley didn't know what to say.

Her superior went on. "I'm here because of who you killed in Egypt. And who's coming after you next."

"Let me guess. Iranians."

"There she is," said Aunt Bea with a real smile. "Smartass. Those Iranians you shot were flunkies. The infantry. First on the line, with the least planning, the least precision, the most dumbassery. Don't expect it to be that easy ever again. There are others coming."

She pulled up something else on the tablet and handed it to Ridley.

"We're monitoring some channels. Don't tell anybody."

On the screen were two photos. The men in both were black-haired and olive-skinned, in their thirties or forties.

"Meet the Bash Brothers," said Aunt Bea. "The one with the shaggy hair and Eugene Levy eyebrows is Esmail Fadavi. He used to work in Evin Prison before becoming an entrepreneur in the mercenary space."

Evin Prison. The worst place in Iran.

"And the second one with the glasses is Qassem Hedaji. He's the son of one of the Ayatollah's bodyguards. He has a knack for assassinations."

Ridley studied their headshots. "How recent are these?"

"Fadavi—two years old. Qassem—that was just a few months ago." She leaned forward onto the desk. "They're good at what they do. Not better than you, but they're clever. And patient. And savage. Fadavi's favorite method of torture is acid. In the face."

Ridley had seen photos...women who were punished for their "immodesty" by having their faces disfigured.

"You're monitoring their communications though?" she asked.

Aunt Bea cocked her head. "Not anymore. Once they took the bounty, they became ghosts. We have INTERPOL alerts out across the Middle East and Europe. Facial ID is advancing our surveillance, but any idiot with cash can get prosthetics and a wig. Swipe left for some of their glamour shots."

Ridley swiped, and saw an array of dramatically different looks. Bleached blond. Buzzcut with fake neck tats. Combed and gelled hair with professorial glasses. Even the shape of the eyebrows, cheeks, noses, and chins varied.

Prosthetics beat facial structure identification.

"Qassem is better with disguises. That murder-boy is *deep* in his closet, but everyone has different ways of coping with being born into an oppressive fundamentalist Islamic theocracy."

"So many gay powers he could have used for good..." said Ridley.

"Okay, enough *Queer Eye*. If it was up to me, I'd pull you all from the field."

Ridley looked up to meet her eyes. Aunt Bea's authority had its own field of gravity.

"I'd bring the Aslanis home, lure Qassem and Fadavi to the States, and take care of them there. It's my recommendation that you all report to the embassy in Madrid immediately and wait for transport home."

Ridley straightened up to protest. "They won't leave—"

"But your director does his own very *special* thing, and he runs a *specialized* division, as I understand. So at this time, I'm not going to interfere with his instructions to his operatives. There's still a problem, though."

Aunt Bea brushed back a stray lock of hair.

"The State Department. This fun little dual operation is gonna crack if something happens to either Nasrin or Jamshid. I spoke with Secretary Rhodes yesterday. He's in the UAE trying to clean up some absolute shit that our president vomited up, but he's giving his own adjusted parameters. Agent Tolkin will be informed directly that he has five days. After that, they'll send their own plane and bring home the most famous dissidents in the world."

Ridley's head was racing.

They already had three of the items that the father and daughter archaeologists were after. There were only two more out there.

And then what...?

It was a scraping small voice at the back of her mind, but there was no answer. No point in dwelling on it.

"Maybe five days for him, but the CIA doesn't have to follow a State Department directive." said Ridley.

Aunt Bea snorted a laugh. "Welcome to the bureaucracy, Ridley Samaras. You think CIA Director Jude Fraser is closer to the president than Neal Rhodes? State takes this one, sweetie, 'specially because those at risk are naturalized citizens."

Shitsacks.

"Why didn't Booker tell me all this?" she said, her frustration starting to make her feel trapped.

Aunt Bea's look could have tipped over a building.

"Osprey runs its own missions. I run the people who run the missions."

"So you're gonna tell him?"

"He'll be notified. I'll speak to him. I like Booker Douglas. He's just running against a bigger, faster horse in this race."

He's gonna hate this. You *already hate this.*

Is this what Aunt Bea really does? That's actually...sort of a lot of power.

"Get your shit together, Samaras. We cleaned up your mess in Cairo, and your partner was bitten by a shark yesterday."

How did she know that?!

"And now you're being hunted by a very deadly, very capable duo. There are no more margins in which to fuck up."

A deep burn twisted in Ridley's stomach. "I understand, ma'am."

"I've sent the dossiers on Fadavi and Qassem to your device. You all study those faces until you can draw them from memory. What else do you need?"

"Weapons."

Aunt Bea smiled at her.

"My kinda gal."

CHAPTER TWENTY-NINE

ANTEQUERA, SPAIN

Gabe got a phone call that afternoon from his boss at the State Department.

Ridley got a message from Booker.

B called it. Rhodes isn't budging. You have five days. Status?

She rubbed the back of her neck as she stared at the phone. They were stopped on a hilltop overlooking the small town of Antequera.

Nas and Jimmy were wandering around nearby, gaping at the entrance of a tomb constructed of massive stones. Gabe stood guard, feeling far more confident in his professional capabilities now that he had a Glock tucked under his shirt.

Ridley had picked up their new arsenal from Aunt Bea that afternoon. Two Glock 19s, an FN SCAR 15P with a suppressor on the barrel, a Trijicon red dot sight and a sling to carry, two black steel Benchmade daggers, and a handful of tiny tracker devices.

They tagged both of the Aslanis, pinning the tracking buds

discreetly into their clothing. Ridley and Gabe holstered the Glocks inside their waistbands, slid the SCAR into the spare backpack, and took over the SUV from Sadie.

The drive from Sevilla to Granada was two-and-a-half hours, but Jimmy had lobbied for a stop along the way. In all the months she'd spent in Spain as a teenager, Ridley had never heard of Antequera. Yet when they arrived, she realized why archaeologists even knew the name.

Just beyond the town limits was a series of hills—burial mounds. Embedded into them were *dolmens*, megalithic cave tombs. Nas and Jimmy had found their nirvana. Thankfully, there wasn't a single other tourist or visitor in sight.

Ridley watched them enter one of the immense tombs with Gabe, then squinted back at her phone.

3 out of 5. Almost in position for the 4th.

She slid the phone back into her pocket and went to the cave's entrance. The overhang was a mammoth slab of stone, a ceiling that was chiseled flat and propped upright by rock pillars throughout.

"This place is maybe six thousand years old," said Jimmy. "And the ceiling here—one big stone—one hundred and eighty tons. How did they do that?"

"They found a hundred bodies in here!" exclaimed Nas.

Ridley glanced around. Despite her focus being elsewhere, she had to admit it was bafflingly impressive.

"I guess that's exciting for some lines of work," she said.

Booker would love this place.

As the Aslanis wandered deeper into the cavern, Ridley went over to Gabe.

"What did you get from *your* boss?" she asked, keeping her voice low.

"A lot of shit for getting into a fight with a Great White."

"It was an oceanic whitetip."

"Oh, I should have clarified for him. Maybe he would have given me a little shit instead."

"Wasn't even ten feet long."

A wry smile crept over his face. "Coolest thing that ever happened to me on the job."

"You've been a pretty cranky bitch about it, though," said Ridley, but grinned back.

"Maybe I got a little shark in me."

Memory struck Ridley like a hurricane gust.

Dark wavy hair...deep-set blue eyes..."He's got some shark in his soul..." in that burr-ish Glasgow accent...

Then that dark wavy hair soaked in blood, spilling against the snow—

Iain.

She had to blast the memories back.

You're on a new mission. This is all you have right now. All you're doing.

"My boss said, 'keep up the great work,'" said Gabe, glancing at the entrance as a couple passed by outside. "For five more days. Then bring 'em home. The risk factor just blew up."

She'd given him the full file on Esmail Fadavi and Qassem Hedaji. He'd studied it as intently as she had, putting to memory the eyes of both Iranian men. Whatever costumes one could don, it was eyes that were the most distinct, the most difficult to disguise.

They'd also passed the photos to Nas and Jimmy to memorize. Ridley had kept the rest of the file from them. No doubt they knew more about the horrors of the regime's torture than Ridley or Gabe ever would, but there was no need for specifics on the men hunting *them*.

Ridley glanced at the father and daughter, wholly absorbed in the wonder of engineering around them. "If we don't get what we need in five days—"

"If *you* don't get what you need in five days," said Gabe.

"Yeah, we're on different missions, but what are you gonna do? You think they're going to give up the biggest discovery of their life? Especially when they're so close to getting all the pieces?"

He shook his head in aggravation. "It's just stuff."

Operatives in Osprey did not usually have to play nice with other American agencies. It was such an independent and clandestine division that bureaucratic power struggles were rare.

"You have no idea how much 'just stuff' has done in this world," muttered Ridley, walking away to collect the Aslanis.

BARCELONA, SPAIN

They arrived in Barcelona that afternoon.

The jewel of Catalunya, the city basked in a warm summer breeze. The waters sparkled and the beaches buzzed with tourists.

"Here's a city I've actually been to," said Gabe as they drove north along the shoreline.

"No kiddin', Agent Tolkin," said Ridley from behind the wheel. "Is this where you learned all that Spanish to pick up chicks?"

Though she couldn't imagine he needed to do much more to impress most women than just walk into a room.

"I tried learning Catalan to really impress," he said. "That one's pretty useless."

Ridley knew a few words of the native language, one that had been proudly preserved for hundreds of years. Even under the oppression of the dictator Francisco Franco, who had outlawed its use for decades, the pride of a people survived. It *was* useless outside the region, though, and everyone within Barcelona spoke Spanish anyhow.

But it does *impress the local girls—and the guys.*

They drove to their waterfront hotel, a posh, upscale place that towered and glinted in the ever-present sun. Being one of the most secure accommodations in the city, it was the first recommendation of the State Department.

This time they'd gone high, with a suite on the seventeenth floor. For a few minutes, they relaxed into the bright, plush rooms, admiring the stately granite in their bathrooms, the modern art hung on the walls, and the spectacular view. Blue as far as one could see.

Still, it didn't take long for Nas to pull out the copy of the stele's inscriptions and settle in front of the coffee table. Jimmy spread out the map of Barcelona that he'd picked up at the front desk.

Ridley picked up a banana from the fruit basket and sat across from them, unpeeling it. Gabe sank into the armchair and propped one hand under his chin.

"Well, I think this one will be much harder," announced Nas.

Ridley chuckled. "You must work for the government to start a briefing with that. If this is harder than finding a sword at the bottom of the ocean, I think we might need to call on at least one of these ancient gods."

Gabe raised his hand. "I missed this in history. Why are we in an old *Spanish* city?"

"Mythology has a lot of stories," said Jimmy. "One of them is that Hercules founded this city."

Through a mouthful of banana, Ridley corrected him. "Heracles. Let's keep it Greek, please."

"Yes, the Roman name won in history," he said.

Nas interrupted excitedly. "The myth that says Heracles-Hercules founded this city...For a long time, people thought it was made up by a priest hundreds of year ago, but it *feels—now*—like maybe it was true. I've learned a lot of strange things recently..."

She waved a hand over the table.

"Okay, I don't remember this part of the mythology," said Ridley.

"I've just learned about it," said Nas with a reassuring smile, "but Hercules was with his brother Hermes and they were traveling with Jason and the Argonauts. They were in a fleet of ships, but when they got caught in a terrible storm off the coast of Catalunya, one of the ships wrecked.

"When the storm passed, they found it, destroyed against the shore at the foot of a hill—"

"Montjuïc?" said Ridley.

It meant "Jewish Mountain" in Latin and Catalan, a broad hill that housed an old fortress overlooking both the city and the sea. It had also been mined for stone by the Romans, leaving massive quarries behind, and in the modern era, had become a tourist favorite by cable car.

"I believe that was it," said Nas. "Hercules thought it was an amazing place and I can see why. So he named it '*Barca Nona*' which means 'ninth ship,' for the one that wrecked."

Gabe piped up. "That's why there's a Hercules statue in Barcelona then."

Ridley gestured to him. "Watson speaks!"

He yawned, unfurling a middle finger toward her.

"We are just looking for a bag," said Jimmy. "It's one of the reasons this may be more difficult."

"Where is it supposed to be?" asked Ridley.

"Under the city, of course," said Nas. "The old ruins. There are all of these old quarries on Montjuïc, and they have dug out the Roman sewers beneath the Gothic Quarter. The stele says—"

She leaned forward over the papers in front of her.

"The oars of the nine lie with the shadow of the gorgon—under the mount of Zeus—from the face of the south, from the bottom of the land."

As she finished, she cradled her head in her hands and groaned. "Oh, my God, it's so vague and also so complicated."

Gabe sucked air in through his teeth. Ridley took the last bite of her banana.

Jimmy pulled the map of the city closer to himself.

"We know the mount of Zeus," he said. "It is Montjuïc, because some people thought the name came from *Mons Jovicus*, that is 'mount of Jove,' and Jove is Jupiter—"

Ridley finished his sentence, "And Jupiter is Zeus."

"On the south side, the lowest part. Nasrin, we have already the parts to find it. And we have the sword. That will guide us."

She gave a tired glance up at her father.

"Baba, you're a wise man."

"The idea—that you can still listen to your father."

Ridley's eyes swept over the stele...over the map...recalling the placements of each of the items they'd found...

Her voice came out low and slow. "Who did all of this? Buried the items, wrote the stele...who wanted someone to find it? *Why?*"

Nobody spoke for a moment.

Then Nas said, "The stele doesn't tell us. But it was found on the island where Perseus went with Medusa's head, so I thought that it was Perseus himself who hid all of them."

"But why," murmured Jimmy, now caught in the wondering himself. "Why would he go around the world again to bury the things that the gods gave him?"

"Who else could it be?" said Nas.

And yet, assumptions can kill.

"I'd like to know," said Ridley, looking at each of them. "We're playing a game here, following a trail to God-only-knows-what. I'd like to know whose game—whose trail we're following."

It may matter a whole lot in the end.

Gabe felt his phone buzz, and pulled it from his pocket to check.

"No going yet," he said. "Everyone stay in this room. I've got an appointment."

"Right now?" said Ridley in surprise.

He got to his feet. "Yeah. The RSO from Madrid is downstairs. He wants to meet."

From Madrid. All the way from the embassy?

Gabe gave her a knowing look of dread.

She could understand this one. The bosses never showed up in person to deliver good news.

Something had changed, and not for the better.

CHAPTER THIRTY

BARCELONA, SPAIN

GABE DIDN'T RETURN for an hour.

He knocked the entry signal at the door before letting himself back into the suite. Another man stepped in with him.

Ridley tensed, her hand flickering immediately to her waistband.

"Everyone," said Gabe, "this is Jeremy Kerik, DSS agent. The State Department wanted him to be our new guard dog."

Kerik shot Gabe a look of "really?"

The new agent was in his mid-thirties, barely five-foot-ten with dark, scruffy hair. He had a short face with a square jaw, sly eyes, and a wide grin. He stood with his hands propped on his hips, surveying his new detail.

"Pleasure to meet you all," he said.

From the kitchen, Nas said hello. Jimmy stiffened a bit in his armchair seat, but nodded a greeting.

"Kerik," said Gabe, "meet Ridley. CIA."

The new guy gave a small wave. She gave an even smaller one in return.

"Make yourself at home," Gabe told him. "We're just gonna be talkin' about you like you're not here."

"Oh, okay. Great," said Kerik.

Ridley got to her feet. "You carrying?"

"Of course," he said, patting the small of his back.

"Useful. Agent Tolkin?" she said, pointing to the balcony.

Gabe followed her out into the bright windy afternoon. He slid the door shut behind them.

"What the fuck," she said.

"Pretty much."

"Why?"

"They think Fadavi passed through France last night. Almost sure Qassem did, too, so the threat just hit a new level. Now at least our detail outnumbers the protectees."

It had been bad enough being assigned to a partner outside of her division—outside of her *agency*—but at least the operational need-to-know included only one other person. Ridley bristled at the idea of another State Department body meddling in a highly classified CIA mission. What Osprey did was not for outside eyes.

At least, not if everything went well.

"He's not getting read in," she hissed.

Gabe shook his head in agreement.

"Does he even speak Spanish?"

"His mom's from the Basque, so, yeah."

"A trained driver?"

"Not his specialty but I asked that. Got high marks from the RSO."

"Great. He can stay in the car."

Gabe cocked his head. "You remember the *primary* objective here, right? Keeping our assignments alive and in our custody?

The point isn't to live on the edge for your sense of adventure. We're not taking risks we don't have to."

"Fine, he can come eat with us."

"Fuckin' Martha Stewart hospitality."

She scowled. "He's not getting into relic hunting with us. You find him something else to do to be useful and protective."

"No room at the mystic party, huh?" he smirked.

"Fuckin' *none*."

To be fair, Kerik was as easygoing as Ridley could have asked for. He had a cowboy vibe, perfectly content to keep to himself, asking almost no questions outside the structure of the detail and their travel plans.

Nas and Jimmy adjusted as easily as they had to Ridley and Gabe, though they kept quiet about anything related to magical items or mythology.

They had together determined it would be better to go exploring at Montjuïc in the early hours of the next day.

That left the Aslanis itching for a taste of the legendary city tonight.

In their shared bedroom, Nas pleaded her case to Ridley.

"I don't want to die," she said as she sat on the edge of the bed, tying her shoes. "I am afraid, but I won't hide from the world. I want to see the world."

Ridley leaned against the wall and crossed one ankle over the other.

"How does your dad feel about that?"

For a few seconds, she didn't answer.

"Of course he wants me to not die, but also to live. And he tries...he was a proud man. Once he didn't like having a daughter like me. He was ashamed in our community because he couldn't keep me in line. Then he was ashamed because he couldn't protect me. I think he's ashamed now because he didn't speak out and fight for freedom before. I love him, but—we've had to love over a lot of hurts."

She looked up at Ridley. Her dark eyes held another world of suffering.

"I want us to do something great together," she said. "I want him to be proud again."

Ridley didn't know what to say about such fathers and daughters. She straightened up.

"Well, let's see what he wants to do," she said, "or whatever these guardians of the State Department will *let* you do."

She looked up with a flash of defiance. "We're not prisoners!"

"No, of course—just—I didn't mean that." Ridley flushed. "It's an amazing city. We'll do what we can."

What Jimmy wanted to do more than anything else in Barcelona was to see La Sagrada Familia in person.

"No," said Gabe. "Protection detail nightmare. Textbook 'no go' location."

"We have extra protection now," Nas exclaimed. "We're *even safer*. Isn't that what you do, anyway? You don't just sit in hotel rooms with people, right? You guard them when they go outside."

Gabe leveled her with a glacial blue gaze.

"No. The compromise is goin' out for dinner. I think you should take it."

Thirty minutes later, the five of them crowded around a table in a small tapas café near the water. A pitcher of red sangria glistened on the table. Plates of *jamón*, *patatas bravas*, stuffed peppers, calamari, and croquettes paraded to them.

For as much as their risk factor had risen, Nas and Jimmy

seemed even more jovial, determined to enjoy themselves. Ridley, Gabe, and Kerik tried to keep up, but their attentions were elsewhere. Their heads whipped up at any sudden movement, and every person that entered the café got a full visual scan.

Ridley was surprised by how she'd adopted their mindset. Every former military or active intelligence operative worth half the price of their training was situationally aware at all times, but this had begun to feel different.

Listening to Jimmy try to convince his daughter that he had once given her anchovies as a kid and she'd loved them—

Watching Nas slide down in her chair, laughing as she hid behind her glass of sangria to avoid even looking at the anchovies—

They're not 'the mission.'

They're a father and daughter.

They're ours to protect.

Reaching for a *pan con tomate*, she felt the dislodging of something inside her. If it would make her better or worse at this, she couldn't possibly know.

After they'd finished their dinner, the party of five ventured out into the darkening streets of the Gothic Quarter.

They ran a Surveillance Detection Route as they left the restaurant. They would double back to make a turn, to throw off any potential tails. Once they stopped at a shopfront where Ridley pulled out her phone to take a selfie with Jimmy, posing like her "father." As she set up the shot, she scanned the screen for pedestrians behind her.

Kerik was not very skilled at blending in or looking casual in a European city, but nothing escaped his scrutiny. He walked just slightly behind them, and Ridley had to engage him in occasional conversation so he didn't look so obviously like a bodyguard, or a stalker.

Pedestrians wound through the narrow streets. Most of them looked like tourists, pointing and taking photos as they ambled across the flat stones. More than a handful wore the blue and garnet stripes of the Barcelona football team, with "MESSI" or "LAMINE YAMAL" emblazoned on the backs of their shirts.

They passed under wrought-iron lanterns, thick green vines spilling over balcony rails, and the red-and-yellow flags of Catalunya fluttering against chipped walls.

Over the murmur of nightlife, a clacking sound echoed.

Ridley, Gabe, and Kerik flinched, their eyes darting, closing ranks around the Aslanis—but then they heard the strains of guitar music drifting through the alleys.

"Is that..." said Jimmy, whose eyes were beginning to light. "We need to go see!"

Gabe put his arm out discreetly to prevent the older man from passing him, but led the way toward the sound.

When they finally emerged into a cobblestone square, they stopped.

In a pool of lamplight, a flamenco troupe had burst into life. The musicians sat in a semi-circle, thudding on a wooden box drum, fast-plucking the strings of a guitar, while the rest of the troupe clapped out a rapid rhythm for the dancer.

She was poised on a wooden platform, her hair pulled back tight with a blood-red carnation tucked into it. The woman stomped—and then became a dizzying sight of clacking shoes and swirling hands, her arms flying in arcs while the ruffled black dress swept around her.

Jimmy was drawn forward as if magnetized.

A small crowd had gathered around the makeshift stage. Ridley, Gabe, and Kerik scanned the square.

Eight entry-exit points, by car, bike, or foot.

No visible threats. No suspicious persons.

As they approached the performers, they could feel the sheer passion that radiated from the dancer. Jimmy watched it unfold.

Nas glanced at her father and smiled. Women were forbidden to dance in public in Iran. They were arrested and executed for it. Once he would have frowned upon this, the impropriety of it all.

Now...

The rapid clapping and stomping and twanging of the guitar...the red tassels of her shawl swirling as her heels rattled on the wooden boards...

Ridley had to drag her eyes away to scan the perimeter again. Kerik was slowly swiveling his head. Gabe was watching the small audience that had gathered around.

She and Kerik saw it in the same moment.

Forty feet away, leaning against the wall of one of the side streets, was a man of average height. He was dark-skinned—*or maybe that's just the shadows*—wore glasses and a gray T-shirt, and sported a close-cropped mustache. He held a backpack slung over one shoulder, and seemed satisfied to take in the flamenco show from a distance.

Ridley tightened. Her hand slid toward her waist, ready to snatch up the hem of her shirt to reach for the Glock. She could tell Kerik had sighted the man, too.

"Gabe," she said, just barely loud enough over the strumming and clacking. "Your five o'clock."

Without even looking, he repositioned himself between the Aslanis and the corner, where their person of interest was loitering.

Ridley raked her gaze over the rest of the square, turning every way.

Where's the second man?

CHAPTER THIRTY-ONE

BARCELONA, SPAIN

THE TAP and clack and strums and claps suddenly felt like Ridley's pulse.

Don't engage. Extract.

"We're moving," said Gabe.

Nas turned. "What?"

"What's wrong?" asked Jimmy.

"Potential threat on the other side of the square," said Gabe. "We're going to exit the way we came in. Follow me—right now."

He led the way. Ridley flanked the Aslanis, who were glancing about in alarm. Kerik brought up the rear, his eyes never leaving the man with the backpack.

They rushed down the narrow, dimly lit street, drawing a few odd looks as they barreled past other pedestrians. Running would draw too much attention, but speed was vital.

Every shop door and alley offshoot was a potential ambush,

but Gabe knew the way. He had marked it all mentally as they'd wandered through the labyrinth of the Gothic Quarter, in case they needed such an extraction.

"Going left!" he called, just before veering down a side street.

Jimmy kept a hand on Nas' back, adamantly keeping her within reach.

"Clear in the back," said Kerik.

Then Ridley heard something—a faint buzzing.

She whipped around. It grew louder.

She looked up.

Overhead, a small spider-like silhouette hovered.

"Drone!" she called.

The others looked up. The thing was several stories above, flying just over the buildings.

Kerik stared at it. "Not weaponized or it would be closer!"

But there's no way to outrun a drone.

"Take the right," said Gabe.

He grabbed Nas' arm and hauled her around a sharp turn, into a narrower street. Ridley shuttled Jimmy into it.

She wanted to reach for her gun, to shoot that giant motorized bug out of the sky.

And bring the entire Barcelona police force down on our location. It's not that kind of mission, Samaras.

They were half-running now, and quickly emerged into a small plaza. A cathedral rose up at one end of it. The heavy wooden doors were propped open, welcoming worshippers.

"Into the church," called Gabe.

They burst through the darkened doorway, coming to a halt in the narthex.

In the cavernous gloom of the sanctuary, candles flickered and glowed. A dozen of the devout were scattered amidst the pews, heads bowed.

"There's another way out of here," said Ridley, realizing which church they were in. She had also done her homework.

As they hurried down a side aisle, she locked eyes with Nas, whose face had flooded with fear.

"We're okay," said Ridley. "They can't see us."

They drew glances from the parishioners as they rushed toward the transept at the front.

"There," said Gabe, pointing to the south end, to a door in the shadows.

They bolted for it. Gabe threw it open first, eyeing the street in both directions—then overhead.

"Clear," he called back.

They made a break into the open.

No sight of the drone.

No sound of the drone.

They made their way down the next few blocks on high alert, but there were no more signs of danger. No man with a backpack. No overhead surveillance.

No Qassem. No Fadavi.

When the five of them finally reached the safety of their hotel suite, Jimmy's polo shirt was damp with sweat. A light sheen had appeared on Nas' forehead. Kerik's breathing was labored.

He and Gabe pulled their weapons and did a sweep of each of the rooms.

Jimmy looked rattled. He kept checking in on his daughter. Nas said little, but went to the sink and chugged an entire glass of water.

She leaned her hands on the edge of the counter.

Gabe emerged from one of the rooms, holstering his Glock. "Clear."

Nas burst into a strange, strangled laugh, and turned around to face them.

"Now we're really on a treasure hunt."

That night, Kerik stayed in the suite while Ridley sat out on the balcony with Gabe, debriefing.

She had been surprised by how smoothly they'd worked together to extract the Aslanis.

"You were like a real member of a detail," said Gabe with an approving nod. "You've got range."

Range to improve...

She pushed aside the one voice that never stopped.

"Speaking of range," he said, "that drone was just doing recon. Getting a look at us and how we operate."

She frowned. "Why would they tip their hand? They just escalated the threat perception without executing."

He tapped his fingers along the arm of the chair. "It's sloppy, or an ambush. The drone took up all our focus."

Shit. He's right. We let them control our attention.

"I want an extra security escort tomorrow," he said. "We have to alert the Guardia Civil about Qassem and Fadavi anyway. Get out a citywide alert."

She held back a grimace.

Inviting local authorities to any part of an Osprey mission was typically anathema to their ends. It was only to be done in the most extreme and essential of situations. Too much of their work seemed to inadvertently involve desecrating national landmarks and historical sites. Best not to invite the cops along as witnesses.

"You give 'em the State Department alert on the team of assassins," she said. "*Do not* tell them where we're going tomorrow."

"Ridley—"

"You tell them? It's over. And I can't have that. This is a CIA mission, too. You know that. Really, that's why you're here at all."

"You're a real goddamn hardass. You know *that.*"

"Yeah. I guess that's why I'm here at all."

They stared each other down.

"Okay," said Gabe finally. "But Kerik is comin' with us."

He stood up.

"Okay," said Ridley.

He went inside and slid the door shut behind him. Ridley leaned back in her chair, taking in the view.

Dark waves frothed up along the beach. This city sparkled and buzzed late into the night. Up here she felt isolated—caged.

In a luxury hotel.

She pulled out her phone and dialed Booker. It was time he knew.

The threat level was now red.

CHAPTER THIRTY-TWO

BARCELONA, SPAIN

THEY WOKE before dawn the next day.

"Don't you waste a minute," Booker had told Ridley the night before. "I'll have a bag dropped at your hotel overnight. What do you need?"

That was always a question—how to pack when you didn't even know what you were about to find or face. For an ancient rock quarry, it came down to the basics.

So the next morning, she picked up a heavy black duffel bag at the concierge desk. The essentials: flashlights, headlamps, two pickaxes, a sledgehammer, a hammer, and two crowbars. Each of the tools was wrapped in cloth to muffle any clanking. Ridley had also added a length of rope and five pairs of utility gloves to the mix.

She didn't want any hotel valet in the car, so she walked to the garage. There was no one else getting such an early start with their vehicles. The only sound was the faint echo of her footsteps in the dank space.

Gabe and Kerik were waiting in the lobby with the Aslanis. They all slid into the car, still fuzzy for lack of sleep. Gabe handed Ridley a coffee.

"Flat white?" she checked.

"Yeah, your Majesty."

They drove in loops to throw off any tails. There were so few vehicles out at that hour that it was clear they weren't being followed by car. Gabe kept glancing up at the skies for any sign of a drone, but it was clear.

Ridley turned them along the coastline. A lilac smudge appeared on the gray ocean horizon. She steered inland and drove up a quiet, wooded road. Up and up, until they could see the city stretch below them.

They passed the stadium that had once been host to the Olympic games, and then the old stone fortress that overlooked the sea. Finally, they turned back down to the base of the hill.

As they made their way onto a broad sloping street, Ridley spotted a car parked alongside the curb ahead of them.

White body. Green doors. A short rack across the top—

She whipped on Gabe. "You son of a bitch. You called the cops?!"

"Calm down. They're just here for street surveillance. They're not coming in the cemetery with us."

Ridley didn't want to upset the Aslanis, but muttered under her breath, "You suck-rotten liar...what an asshole."

"Why is this bad?" asked Jimmy from the back seat.

"Just pull up behind him," said Gabe, gesturing to the Guardia Civil vehicle.

She did, then smashed the brakes to jerk the car to a halt.

Gabe got out—looking each way—and approached the cop. He was a tall man with a blank expression on his young face.

"Let's go," said Ridley.

She shut off the engine and climbed out. Kerik and the Aslanis followed suit. Jimmy grabbed the backpack with the ancient items.

Ridley was wearing trim gray pants—stretchy enough to crouch in, tough enough to crawl in—and a cropped cargo jacket over a navy T-shirt. For efficiency, she had braided her dark hair back into a thick lock. A pair of Salomons completed her "we're-going-discreetly-tactical" look, but an average cop wouldn't take any note.

Kerik walked a small circle around their Mercedes, scanning for threats. There was no one else in sight.

Gabe thanked the cop and walked back to join them. "He's drone-aware. Good to go."

Ridley pulled out the duffel and heaved it over her shoulder. She gave a curt nod and brushed past Gabe.

A grand, decrepit stone wall lined the sidewalk. The engraved faces of niche tombs lined it.

"Geez, did they run out of room?" said Jimmy.

Though Ridley had done her best with the maps, the cemetery itself was a huge, snaking labyrinth with no street signs.

And we have no idea where the hell we're going anyway.

They went up the broad stone steps, past the rows of cypress trees, past the mausoleums so grand and ornate that they looked like mini cathedrals.

"This is like a palace graveyard," said Nas.

There were monuments and chapels, statues and slab tombs and giant stone crosses. Bouquets of flowers were scattered about the rows.

Kerik looked around with apprehension. "Y'all are grave-robbing, are you?"

Ridley shook her head. "No, no, this isn't *The Mummy.*"

Nas scoffed at the idea, then darted a nervous glance at Ridley.

"We're looking for something much older," said Jimmy. "Much older than these graves. This has only been here since the 1800s."

"So what are you doin' here?" asked Kerik.

Gabe came up and clapped him on the shoulder. "Great questions, great questions—but you just slid up into the wrong pit box. Find your lane, agent."

He gave Kerik a hearty pat on the back, then strode ahead.

Ridley watched Gabe, surprised that he would intervene to protect her mission secrecy.

Doesn't make up for him calling the cops behind my back.

Once they were out of sight of the entrance, Nas pulled Jimmy to a stop.

"Okay, wait, everybody," she said. "I think we need the Harpe sword. I have no idea where we're going."

Jimmy pulled off his backpack, rooted around in it, and pulled out the sword. It was currently nothing more than a handle, the blade having so oddly collapsed into the hilt.

Nas raised it up, gripping it tightly.

"We have to trust it'll take us to the right place," she declared.

They all stared at the handle as she held it aloft. Kerik looked bewildered.

Nothing happened.

"Maybe we should walk around a little," said Ridley. "Give the dog some scent to work with."

"Yeah," said Nas, frowning at the hilt. "I guess so."

They began to roam the avenues of the dead, watching the gold pommel in her hands for any sign of agitation. Kerik followed behind, watching them all like they were slightly mad.

The group wandered down the dusty avenue, past mausoleums with lavishly wrought iron gates, past a giant stone pyramid tomb and even one crafted to look like the Parthenon.

Ridley, Gabe, and Kerik kept glancing around. There was still no one else here in the dawn light.

They had just passed by an enormous winged angel standing guard over a sarcophagus when Nas cried out—

"Hey! Oh! It's here!"

The pommel was vibrating just slightly.

"You can hold it?" asked Jimmy.

"Yes! Here..."

She wandered forward, holding out the hilt like a drug-sniffing K9 on a leash. The rest of them went after her.

She rounded a sharp bend to another road leading upward, where Nas stopped short. Her hands were almost blurry now, the grip was shaking so fast. She took a step forward, her face screwed up with the physical strain of holding it.

Ridley reached out.

"I got it. Let me," she said gently, but Nas gritted her teeth and shook her head.

The power of the pull was immense. The only thing to do was follow it.

Some unseen force tugged the hilt forward. Nas lurched after it—straight toward the curve of the rock wall—

—until she was skidding to slow herself down—

Unsuccessfully.

She slid into the stone hands first, the hilt clanking against it.

"What the fuck?" blurted Kerik.

Nas used one hand to push off the wall. In her other, the sword grip was vibrating with almost unbearable force.

Then she spotted it.

In the rock, about chest height, was a narrow slit, nearly the size of a sword.

She dragged up the hilt and pressed it against the slot. The blade shot out, straight into the rock—

—and the rock split.

CHAPTER THIRTY-THREE

BARCELONA, SPAIN

The crack of stone echoed through the cemetery. A deep crevice appeared in the wall where the sword had cleaved it open.

Nas stepped back, drawing out the sword. It dangled from her hand, dark and glittering and sharp.

They all stared in shock at the destruction. It was an opening that had rent the rock from top to bottom, but was only a foot wide.

"Oh, my God," she murmured.

"Pardon me?" said Kerik. "But what the actual for real fuck."

"So this part?" Ridley said to him. "This part is *my* mission." She pulled the duffel off her shoulder so she could slip through the rock.

Gabe looked at his fellow agent. "Hold position here."

"Yeah," said Kerik. "No problem. At all."

Jimmy was looking at the rock with wide eyes and a clenched jaw.

“Baba,” said Nas gently, “you don’t have to go in. The space could be very narrow.”

He replied with something sharp in Farsi, and his daughter backed off.

“It’s claustrophobia,” Nas whispered to Ridley as she drew up to her side.

What’s not to look forward to?

Nas held up the sword like it was a defensive option. “You think this will—”

—and the blade collapsed as if it had been sucked back into the hilt.

“An ancient lightsaber,” laughed Nas, and started for the crevice.

Ridley grabbed her arm. “Nas, you’re brave as hell, but you’re not going first.”

She held up the sword hilt as an option.

Ridley chuckled and shook her head.

She took the headlamps from the duffel and handed them out. She grabbed an extra handheld flashlight to clip onto her pocket. Then she picked up the bag, turned sideways, and slipped through the crack in the rock.

The passageway had clearly been dug out. It was bigger than the opening—just high enough for her to stand upright and just wide enough for her broad shoulders.

Ridley stepped forward as the others edged in behind her. She peered at the walls.

There were very faint carvings on them...

All of them were snakes.

And all of them were facing down the tunnel, as if slithering in the same direction.

This feels bad.

“It’s not so bad,” Nas said to Jimmy. “Bigger than I thought.”

Ridley's headlamp beamed through the blackness. A dozen yards ahead, it curved out of sight.

Jimmy looked indeed relieved. "I'm—uh...closet—"

"Claustrophobic," said Nas.

"Turn back whenever you want," said Ridley.

She started down the tunnel, the others following.

From the back, Gabe asked, "You gettin' anything from the sword?"

"No," said Nas. "Like it died."

They reached the turn and saw that there was another one ahead, veering the opposite direction. Ridley led them on.

Gabe finally realized what was on the walls they were passing by.

"Are those fuckin' snakes?"

"You don't like snakes?" said Jimmy. "We have so many snakes back in Iran."

"No, I don't like snakes. I don't like sharks, either. I'm kinda having a bad run on this detail."

Jimmy went on like he hadn't heard. "*So* many snakes. Vipers—even one that can climb trees—and the Caspian cobra—"

"Baba!" Nas cut in. "Don't drive him off!"

"These aren't real snakes!"

"Look, he's scared of snakes—"

"I'm not scared of snakes," Gabe bristled. "I said I don't *like* them."

"Because they can kill you, right?" said Nas. "It's okay to be scared of things that can kill you."

"I'm not—"

"But you have a gun," said Jimmy.

Ridley rolled her eyes. "No shooting in a tunnel! I don't care what kind of snake you see. We're not doing bullet pinball underground."

She could hear Gabe muttering something in the back.

She rounded the next bend.

Ahead, in the light of her headlamp, the tunnel opened up.

"Hey," she called. "I think this is something."

Ridley stepped down into a cavern and gazed around. The others spilled in behind her.

"How *old* is this?" exclaimed Nas.

It was a ragged circular space, perhaps fifteen feet in diameter and ten feet high. In the center was a square-cut altar made of stone.

Nas crouched down in front of it. "Cows."

On each side of the altar, there were relief sculptures carved out of the rock—cows' heads—connected to each other by chains of laurel leaves. Atop the altar, there were a dozen square slots cut into the surface.

"I have never seen this before..." said Jimmy, frowning at them.

Ridley and Gabe had stepped closer to the walls, which weren't flat. They were cut into horizontal sections, each of which bulged outward. There was a faint hex pattern across the layers.

"Guys..." said Ridley, touching the stone. "We're inside of a giant snake."

"What?!" said Nas.

They all began to look around...to realize that they were in the middle of a massive python coil.

Gabe propped his hands on his hips, fighting to keep down his rising anxiety. "Shit."

"It's only rock," Jimmy assured him.

"A little unwelcoming," mused Ridley, setting the bag on the ground by the altar.

Spaced out along the floor were small stone boxes. On

them, words were carved in an alphabet that Ridley didn't recognize.

"Hey, experts. Is this the same language as the one on the stele?"

Jimmy came over to look. He bent down.

"Linear B. Yes, the script of the Mycenaeans," he said. "This one...says 'hydra.'"

Gabe scoffed. "Monster caves." He looked at Ridley. "Is this really the kinda work you do?"

A sly grin tugged at her lips. "Sometimes. How you doin', Agent Tolkin? I thought you played Dungeons and Dragons? Isn't this kind of exciting for you?"

"I don't—like—snakes." He threw out an exclamatory hand toward the wall, then toward the box. "And *that* has a lot of goddamn snake heads."

She chuckled and looked back to the altar, where Nas stood puzzling over it.

"The cow is Hera, right?" said Ridley.

"Right. She was the one who gave Perseus the *kibisis*, which is what we're here for. Vengeful woman."

"Zeus should have been more faithful to his wife."

"That's usually the case." Nas touched the slots on top. "What goes here?"

From across the room, Jimmy said, "These."

CHAPTER THIRTY-FOUR

BARCELONA, SPAIN

JIMMY WAS bent over one of the dozens of small stone boxes. He had opened it, and was holding up a carved figurine.

"It looks like a bull," he said.

He turned it over in his hands. The base of it was shaped like a tall rectangle. Jimmy carried it over to the altar and inserted it into one of the slots.

It fit perfectly.

"Baba!" Nas exclaimed in delight. "You got it!"

Ridley looked around. There were dozens of boxes on the floor...

"Why a bull?" wondered Jimmy. "Hera was for the cow, not the bull."

"Well, what else is in these?" said Nas.

She opened the box in front of her.

And a loud scraping sound rumbled through the cave—as the coils of the wall *tightened.*

They began to slide over the opening of the tunnel—rasping across the floor toward the four of them—

"What the fuck?!" shouted Gabe, losing his cool for the first time.

The walls stopped suddenly, having shrunk the diameter of the room by a foot.

"Okay, well that wasn't the right box then," said Ridley.

"We're gonna get trapped!" exclaimed Gabe.

"Yeah, but I promise you it's just until we figure this out. Look—" she said, "there are only twelve slots on the altar. There are more than twice that many boxes. Figurines, whatever."

Jimmy stared about in grim realization. "The bull was lucky, but we need to read them."

"So we don't get crushed inside of a stone snake?" said Gabe.

"Neither of us are very good at reading this script," said Nas.

Jimmy's voice was calming. "We have to read them."

"You're hardly better than I am at Linear B!"

"Nasrin. Together. We *can* do that."

She stood up and met his gaze. Her father seemed to emanate a new confidence. It calmed her.

She took a deep breath.

"We have to know what we're looking for," she said. "What are the other elev—"

"Hercules!" said Ridley. *Damn.* "Heracles. This was his city. The twelve labors. Hera sent them to try to destroy him."

She looked between the Aslanis.

"It makes sense," said Nas. "And the bull—it's the Cretan Bull that was the father of the Minotaur."

"Do you know the rest of them?" asked Ridley.

"Maybe..."

"But you're not sure if you can read them," said Gabe, "and

if you open the wrong box, the snake room squeezes us to death."

"Yeah!" said Ridley with spiteful cheer. "Thanks, teach."

He scowled back at her.

"Okay, what were they?" said Nas, pulling up a note on her phone. "We need to write them down."

"The Bull," said Jimmy.

"Thanks, Dad."

"The hydra," said Ridley, "The Nemean lion. A boar. Cerberus! The filthy stables."

Thank you, Yaya, for all your pride in the Greek stories.

"There were horses who killed," added Jimmy. "Mares?"

Nas checked her phone with a sound of frustration. "Of course, I don't have any internet service underground."

Ridley chuckled, "Yeah, classic problem. It would always be easier to look 'em up."

Nas started typing up a note on her phone.

"We have seven," she said. "There was a deer, too!"

"They called it a hind," said Ridley. "Just—in case that helps with your translations."

For the next two minutes, they argued and sweated it out. Jimmy wanted to collect all of the words first, to be orderly about it. Ridley wanted them to start translating the Linear B script on the boxes. She would scour her brain for the remaining labors.

Half the translations would be a useless waste of time, as half of the boxes were red herring traps.

Nas and Jimmy worked through the words.

What are the rest, Samaras?! Why didn't you pay more attention?

"Birds!" she called out. "He had to kill these man-eating birds."

The Aslanis had gotten two more correct—the lion and the stables—and set the figurines into the altar.

Then they got another one wrong. Too late did they realize that they'd mistaken the basilisk for the hydra.

The walls scraped closer, sealing the tunnel shut behind them. A glisten of sweat appeared on Gabe's forehead.

Ridley tried to reassure him. "At least it isn't an Indiana Jones snake pit."

He rolled his eyes into a glare at her, but then his head shot up.

"Hercules took the belt of the Amazons," he said. "The Amazon queen, Hippolyta."

She stared at him.

"Our Dungeonmaster ran a campaign once and threw in some Greek mythology," he said almost sheepishly.

"You haven't mentioned any of this?!"

"I don't remember much of it!" he snapped. "Look, I helped, anyway."

Nas opened another box, grimacing with trepidation...the walls did not move. She blew out a sigh of relief and placed the figurine of a boat into the altar.

Then another...and another, until they had completed ten.

"You are getting it," Jimmy said to his daughter, almost laughing in relief.

They went back to the boxes—*no to the griffin, and the manticore, and Scylla...*

"Baba," said Nas, "look at this one. I'm not sure...it could be the horses."

Jimmy frowned. He bent over it for seconds, which began to feel like minutes.

"I think it is horses."

Ridley glanced around her, trying to gauge how much closer the walls had gotten with only two boxes wrong.

How many more can we take...

Jimmy knelt and opened the box.

The sound of scraping reverberated in the cavern. The walls ground closer, and it felt like the air had been snatched from their lungs.

Do. Not. Panic.

The cavern was now no more than a dozen feet in diameter.

Jimmy unleashed a furious curse in Farsi. He looked up at his daughter.

"Now we have eliminated one more!" she said, bracing herself with positivity.

The walls were crowding the boxes now. Any more movement inward and some of them might be crushed by the rock. But they couldn't take the risk of moving any of them now.

Ridley's voice was calmer than she felt by about twenty thousand leagues. "Two more. What's left? The mares and the belt?"

"Yes," said Jimmy in a hoarse voice, climbing to his feet.

The four of them looked at the boxes left.

Hera was more vindictive than Hades.

Nas raised her head and shook out her thick mane of hair. "I have done harder things than this."

She crouched, studying each box. Ridley could see the struggle on her face.

Finally, she reached for one of them. Lifted up the top. She pulled out a stone-carved horse.

The walls didn't move.

Jimmy took it from her without a word and placed it in one of the two remaining slots on the altar.

"And then the belt," he said.

Nas knelt, looking between two of the boxes. Ridley heard her murmur something under her breath as she reached for one.

She lifted the top.

The grinding of the stone was nearly deafening. The walls crunched toward them.

"Shit!" yelled Gabe.

One of the last boxes was too close to a wall—

Ridley snatched it up, reeling backward.

The coils slid closer, crushing more boxes along the edge. They were closing in—pushing the team toward the altar—

Ten foot diameter...eight...seven...

"Baba!" called Nas over the grinding noise. "It's that one!"

She couldn't reach it—the walls were too close. She pointed at her father's feet.

Jimmy pulled open the box beneath him, grabbed the piece of carved rock inside, and jammed it into the last slot on the altar.

The noise stopped.

The walls halted.

For a moment it felt like there was no air in the chamber.

There's no way out. But there has *to be a way out!*

Nas was leaning back against the altar. Gabe was practically standing on top of it.

"Where is it?" she said. "Where is the *kibisis*?!"

Ridley glared at the walls. "Hera was a *bitch*."

There was no *kibisis*. And no way out.

She looked down at the altar. One of the pieces was askew, only half cocked in the slot. Ridley reached out and adjusted it.

The sound of a heavy rock sliding across rock echoed through the small space. They glanced about in dread...

Until the walls began to move *back*.

Nas choked on a laugh. Jimmy muttered something prayerful in Farsi. Gabe looked like he was about to melt.

"Where is the damn bag?" said Ridley, looking all around.

The entrance to the tunnel reappeared as the coils of the

wall shifted back into place. As they did, the entire altar shifted backward.

There was a small compartment cut into the floor below.

At the bottom of it lay a small pouch. It was a dark shimmering gray.

Nas reached for it slowly, and raised it up. "I thought gorgons were bigger."

Jimmy frowned. "That's not big enough to hold a head."

Ridley cocked her head. "You think it's like a Mary Poppins bag?"

Gabe was already moving toward the tunnel exit. "It's the only bag in here, so clearly—you've got it. Let's go."

Jimmy pulled off his backpack. Nas tucked the *kibisis* inside. She zipped it back up and looked at her father with shining eyes.

"There's only one more," she said. "We have the most *amazing* set of treasures in all of Greek archaeology!"

He chuckled. "And you were *already* famous."

"Come on!" yelled Gabe from the tunnel.

The Aslanis headed toward him. Ridley gave one last glance around the coiled cavern with its crushed stone boxes and shifted altar.

What happens when you get the last one...?

Whatever it would summon when the set was complete, she knew they would not be ready.

You never are.

She grabbed the duffel bag and followed them into the tunnel. They hiked up through the passageway, past the carved snakes on the walls.

Finally, the break of daylight beckoned them to the exit crevice. Gabe slid through first, then Nas, then Jimmy, then Ridley bringing up the rear.

Kerik was only six feet away from the entrance, looking relieved but once again bewildered.

"You good?" asked Gabe.

"Good," said Kerik, noting the thin layer of sweat on the forehead of his fellow agent. "You guys...?"

They could hear the distant droning of cars on the motorway.

"Yeah, good. Nothin' down there but a stupid snake cave."

"Snakes?" Kerik's eyes went wide.

"Not real snakes," said Jimmy, like an exasperated uncle.

"Almost killed us, didn't it?" shot Gabe.

Ridley rolled her eyes. "We're done he—"

But she never finished her sentence.

Because something dark dropped from the sky and Kerik's face exploded.

CHAPTER THIRTY-FIVE

BARCELONA, SPAIN

The flash of heat was blinding.

Ridley reeled, stumbling back, hauling Nas with her.

Gabe tackled Jimmy behind the edge of the stone outcropping.

Their heads spun—trying to figure out where the strike had come from. Ridley covered a gasping, shaking Nas as the realization hit—

She looked up.

"Drone!" she yelled at Gabe.

The hovering assassin was plummeting toward them.

Both drew their guns and shot upward. It might be like trying to shoot the moon, but at least they had the bullets.

What it just did to Kerik—

The drone began to flit and zig-zag as it descended—

Ridley had to yank out another magazine to reload—

It was descending on them, this terrifying motorized killer... *forty feet...thirty...*

The blasts of gunfire were a cacophony.

Until finally there was a *clink*—one of the bullets had hit.

The drone wobbled...then veered off, disappearing over the next row of mausoleums.

"Oh, my God," came Nas' wavering voice from beneath Ridley.

"Move!" called Gabe.

His head spinning, he hauled Jimmy to his feet. The older man was stunned. He looked down at the gruesome heap of Kerik's body.

The former agent's head was a mess of blood and brains and shards of bone. Smoke was curling up from the grisly mess.

Ridley scanned.

That can't be the only threat—

Gabe was already moving with Jimmy.

"Where?!" she yelled to him.

"I don't know—"

She finished his sentence, "But get off the X."

The X: the site of the attack, the location of the ambush. The place you cannot stay.

Gabe took the lead, sweeping everything ahead of them with his Glock raised. He kept Jimmy behind him as he rushed down a long ramping walkway.

Ridley yanked open the duffel bag and grabbed the FN SCAR 15P rifle. She slung it over her shoulder, holstered the Glock, then pulled Nas up to her feet.

"Stay close to me! Okay?"

Nas nodded quickly and they followed after Gabe and her father.

At the back, Ridley covered everything in sight. She gripped the small rifle, backpedaling as her eyes swept the statues, the graves, the columns and trees. It was like moving through a city of the dead.

They missed their targets—the assassins must be here in person—

"Shooter, two o'clock!" yelled Gabe.

He shoved Jimmy behind the nearest raised tomb. The older man hit the dirt with a stifled cry as Gabe dropped down beside him and opened fire over his head.

Ridley spun around and yanked Nas behind a stone altar. She couldn't see anyone—

Gabe realized that no one was answering his shots. He peered out again...and this time saw no one.

"Shit. False alarm?" he called back to Ridley.

"A trap?"

"Let's move!"

They dashed to the nearest mausoleum, taking cover behind the wall. Gabe and Ridley did a quick scan around each corner.

Where the fuck are they?!

"Clear," said Ridley.

"Clear," said Gabe. "Let's move."

He kept Jimmy low behind him and scurried out to the next mausoleum. Ridley pulled Nas behind her as they bolted out to the other side.

A crack split the quiet morning air.

A piece of stone splintered off the column beside Gabe's head.

"Sniper?!" yelled Ridley.

She had never been the best with sniping, but the *snap—boom—echo* of a distance shot from a high-powered rifle was distinct.

Gabe was on the street-facing side of the stone structure, and the bullet had hit the front.

“He’s ahead of you,” said Ridley.

“I know!”

She looked up the slopes behind them, scattered with graves.

The cemetery layout had been a maze to her eyes the night before, but she knew there was another access road at the top of the hill.

“We’ve gotta go up,” she said to Gabe.

“Do you think it’s a trap, though?” said Nas, clutching Ridley’s back.

It’s finding out time—

“We just have to move. We can’t stay in *this* trap.”

“Okay,” said Gabe. “You take lead.”

Ridley broke out from cover, leading the pack. Gun raised, head swiveling. It was a nightmare location for ambushes.

She rushed them toward the first steps in sight. Up.

Next level cleared.

Next set of steps.

Ridley reached the top, gliding through the tombs. She led them toward the next stairway—

Then glimpsed a flash of movement off to her right.

“Down!”

In that second, she slid in front of Nas and swung around—

Man pointing a gun—

She shot—he shot.

He was four yards away.

The bullets from his compact rifle sniffed her hair—

Hers exploded his chest with blood.

He collapsed to the ground.

*Black hair, dark skin...*but she couldn’t tell whether it was either of Qassem or Fadavi.

“Target down!” she called.

Gabe was trying to cover Jimmy, but had no idea the direction of the threat.

"Keep moving!" he said.

She scanned furiously for any sign of another threat—nothing.

By now she didn't need to pull or push Nas anywhere. Both the Aslanis were in stunned-action-mode, staying as close as they could to their protectors.

They stumbled up the next set of stairs behind Ridley.

As they reached the top, the sound of faint buzzing could be heard. It grew louder, and they realized it was coming from the sky.

"Shiiiiiit..." said Ridley, peering upward.

This level of the slopes was loaded with cypress and olive trees, so thick that it was hard to see much of the sky above.

But the sound was unmistakable now.

"Another drone?!" cried Nas.

The dark shape flitted overhead.

"Stay under cover," said Gabe.

"It's gonna come down," said Ridley. "We have to break after it passes."

The next set of stairs was out in the open. The road was at the top.

Under his breath, Jimmy muttered something in Farsi. Ridley could make out the only word he said in English, "evil."

Support assassin drones.

She wasn't prepared for this. She'd never been on the front lines of a war, never been anywhere near a weaponized motorized flying mega-bug.

She wanted a bazooka.

"Jimmy," said Gabe, "give me the bag."

The older man shucked it off and handed it to him.

There was a shout from somewhere down the slope, calling in Spanish, "Policia!"

Ridley yelled—

IN SPANISH: *"Watch out! Multiple shooters, and they have an armed drone!"*

The cop shouted something back but she couldn't make it out.

IN SPANISH: *"Call for backup!"* she hollered.

Gabe had been keeping his eyes on the sky.

"Ridley, can you hit it with the SCAR?" he asked. "It's going slow, stalling for surveillance."

"Yes," she said, clenching her teeth tight.

Even if I can't—I will.

"Okay, get ready," he said, staring upward. "We have to break for the street."

There was another shout from the policeman in the distance, and then a burst of gunfire.

"Oh, no," murmured Nas.

Suddenly, the drone veered off toward the sound of the firefight.

"Go now!" said Gabe.

They burst out from the trees, running for the steps. The broad stone staircase came up from both sides, met on a platform, then split again, going up each side.

Gabe ran to the right with Jimmy. Ridley went left with Nas, the FN SCAR braced tightly in her grip.

She heard Gabe yell, "Down! Shooter nine o'clock!"

He fired down into the cemetery.

Nas flattened herself on the steps. Ridley dropped into a crouch. She peered over the stone banister—

Saw a man emerging from behind a tomb, gun raised—

She fired off a volley.

No hit.

The man ducked behind the stone.

We have the high ground now. As long as the drone doesn't come back.

As if summoned, she heard the distant buzz of the flying demon.

"Drone!" she called to Gabe.

"Fuck!" he yelled back.

Ridley lifted the rifle as the drone came swooping over the trees. She fired again and again—

If I don't take it out, we're done.

The drone lifted and veered to avoid the bullets—

Another volley of shots came from below—

She didn't see it at first. She heard it.

A cry, then a series of rapid thuds.

Ridley and Nas looked across the long stairs—

To see Jimmy tumbling down them in a trail of blood.

CHAPTER THIRTY-SIX

BARCELONA, SPAIN

THE OLDER MAN hit the stone landing with a crack and a muffled yelp.

His arm bent the wrong way. Blood spooled from his stomach into the dust.

The cry that came from Nas seemed ripped from her gut. She started to rise up, to race to him, but Ridley shoved her back.

He was lying out in the open. Unmoving.

The buzz of the drone grew louder.

For a moment, Ridley was paralyzed.

You can't get him. You can't leave him behind. You have to protect Nas.

Across the stairs, Gabe was agonizing over the same, trying to fight his way through the dilemma. He reloaded his Glock and squeezed off more shots at the assassin below—who had a rifle with a very big magazine.

"I have to take her up!" yelled Ridley.

"Go!" shouted Gabe.

Nas screamed. "No!"

She tried to claw Ridley's arm away, but couldn't. Her protector was resolute, and stronger.

"You can't drag him up these stairs," Ridley said to Gabe. "They'll kill both of you."

Nas choked back a sob as she saw Gabe descending, trying to reach Jimmy.

The drone appeared above the trees. Ridley fired a volley at it.

Staying low, she grabbed Nas and half-dragged, half-pushed her up the steps.

She couldn't tell Gabe what to do, but a rescue attempt would be suicide.

Do your own job, Samaras!

She reached the street with Nas. It was deserted.

The drone hovered over the stairs, seemingly occupied with Gabe. Ridley kept the FN SCAR braced and ready, aimed at the top of the staircase...

"We need a car," she called to Nas.

Sloppy. Careless. Stupid. No backup exit plan.

The shots from the cemetery split the air in sporadic bursts. She slowed her breathing.

They heard the faint sound of a car coming.

"Here!" said Nas.

She rushed out into the road, waving down the oncoming van.

Ridley knew the sight of a rifle on a hitchhiker's shoulder was not a good start, but there was no way she was about to lower her sights.

Here goes—

So she swung it around, keeping the barrel pointed just below the hood of the van for maximum effect.

The vehicle skidded to a stop. She could see the driver's terrified expression behind the windshield.

She shouted at him.

IN SPANISH: *"We need a ride, please!"*

The man hesitated, then climbed out of the vehicle with his hands up. The blasts of gunfire below were frightening enough.

"I'm sorry," said Nas, "but we need your van."

The man stumbled over his words, protesting that he didn't speak English.

IN SPANISH: *"Go,"* said Ridley. *"Run up the street."*

He shook his head but took off at a clumsy jog, back the way he had come.

Nas looked at Ridley, and her face was a mess of desperation. "We can't leave *baba!*"

Ridley turned her sights back to the top of the stairs—and couldn't answer. Then they heard a shout from below—

"It's me! Don't shoot!"

Gabe came stumbling up the top steps, the bag with the items in it jostling against his back.

Alone.

"I'm out!" he said, waving his empty Glock.

The drone came soaring up from the cemetery.

Ridley snapped up the rifle barrel and loosed a hail of bullets at it. It zoomed higher.

If we stay, she dies, too.

Ridley locked eyes with Gabe—then glanced toward Nas—then back at him.

While she kept the rifle trained to the sky, Gabe barreled toward their only remaining charge. He half pushed, half hauled her into the van.

She howled. Her cries were the kind of terrible sound that Ridley knew she would never forget.

Gabe bodied her into the vehicle and climbed in after her. Ridley backed up toward the driver's side, trying to eye the top of the stairs without letting the hovering drone out of sight.

She had just slid behind the hood of the vehicle when something dropped from the sky.

She glimpsed the flash, the trajectory—and leapt backward.

It exploded with a deafening blast only a few yards in front of the van's passenger side.

Ridley's ears were ringing...her right one muffled.

A man appeared at the top of the steps—

GUN.

He sprayed the passenger side door with bullets.

She lurched forward and fired over the hood of the van—

He jerked and stumbled back—but there was no blood.

Bulletproof vest.

GET OUT OF HERE.

She jumped into the driver's seat and handed the rifle to Gabe behind her. Throwing the van into gear, she stomped on the gas.

They jerked forward and tore down the street. The sound of gunfire grew distant behind them.

Nasrin Aslani sobbed.

CHAPTER THIRTY-SEVEN

BARCELONA, SPAIN

A FULL SECURITY team reached the hotel within hours.

The American embassy in Madrid had received the directive that morning.

Dispatch—urgent priority.

Three men and one woman arrived at the door of the suite, their guns concealed under casual clothing.

Gabe answered the door. His golden-tan face now looked ashen. Stains of blood had seeped through his shirt when his stitches had ripped.

The agents entered a room so somber it felt like a wake. The curtains to the balcony were drawn.

"They have weaponized drones," Gabe explained.

Nas had wanted only to sit out on the balcony and gaze at the sea, but they could not let her.

They found her instead sitting cross-legged on the floor,

leaning back against one of the armchairs. Her head was bowed, her eyes closed. She did not speak. She did not cry.

The agents looked to the kitchen.

There stood an Amazon of a woman, her dark hair braided back, dust powdered across her navy shirt. She was gripping the counter, staring down at the FN SCAR rifle lying in front of her.

"Agent Samaras?" said the lead, a gray-haired man in a polo.

She looked up.

"I'm not an agent," she said, her voice barely containing the force of her emotions.

The new guy didn't know what to say, so he gave a nod and looked back at Gabe.

"Agent Tolkin. We're not here for debriefing, as you know. We'll be providing extra security until the suits arrive. All operational decisions will be suspended until then."

"Yeah, I got the message," he said, his voice hollow.

Another one of the agents, a baby-faced young man, spoke. "Do any of you need medical attention? Agent Tolkin, you look like you've got something there..."

He pointed to the blood along Gabe's ribs.

"Stitches. Yeah."

"I'll take care of that for you," said the agent, slipping a pack off his shoulders. "And Ms. Aslani...?"

"Leave her alone," said Ridley. "Of course we evaluated her. She has no physical injuries."

"Okay. And you, ma'am?"

"I'm fine."

The hours that followed felt like a dead swamp.

One agent was always positioned by the door. The others

tried to be as unobtrusive as possible. They were good at it, used to it.

It still felt like suffocation to Ridley.

After Gabe had gotten his stitches re-done, he returned to the living room. His eyes kept slipping to Nas where she sat on the floor, but he couldn't bring himself to say anything at all. Eventually, he went and sat at the dining table to watch two of the agents quietly playing cards. He declined their invitation to join the game.

Nas didn't move.

When two of the agents brought food back to the hotel for dinner, Ridley made up a plate of tacos for her. Gabe handed Ridley a stack of napkins for her.

She went and crouched by the armchair. As she set the plate on the carpet with a glass of water, Nas lifted her face for the first time.

Ridley thought that all the grief she'd ever felt in her life couldn't have amounted to the look in this woman's eyes.

"If you can," croaked Ridley.

She stood up and left the food to Nas.

Nas never touched it.

Eventually she got up and went into her room. She shut the door behind her for the night.

Occasionally Gabe would go put his ear to the door, listening for signs of life. He heard enough to know she was alive. They left her alone.

Ridley hardly slept.

Every swoop of the drone, every staircase, every step and stop in the labyrinth of tombs, the flight path of the drone, every shot she took—and the ones she didn't—played in her mind like game tape.

She was endlessly breaking it down, lashing at herself for every foolish thing, every miss, every half-thought-out move.

The game that ended in disaster. A man's life. Jimmy's life.

You didn't do enough. You could have done more.

She knew this whirlpool. It was always below her, always swirling, always waiting.

The smell of coffee woke Ridley.

Two of the embassy agents had gone out early to get coffee and breakfast for the group.

Ridley poured milk into her steaming cup but left the pastries alone. The only thing she could brace her stomach for that morning was the dressing-down she was about to get.

Nas emerged from her room freshly showered. The entire suite went quiet when they saw her, but she was composed. Her face was still, her big eyes sedate.

As she walked into the kitchen, an abashed Gabe nudged the box of pastries toward her. She took one.

Ridley's phone buzzed. It was Booker.

On our way up

She bit the rim of her paper cup, then went to sit on the edge of the coffee table.

Gabe eyed her apprehension. He had just taken his last bite of a ham and cheese sandwich when there was a distinct pattern of knocks at the door.

The nearest agent verified their password before he opened it.

Booker Douglas entered the suite like a draft horse. Behind his broad frame, Joe Lasch—the State Department's Division Chief of Overseas Operations—walked in.

Ridley felt a wash of relief to see her boss in the midst of so many Staters...then realized that this tide was also filled with sea urchins which raked and felt equally as terrible.

Booker greeted her with professional seriousness.

Then he went to Nas and offered her a gentle hand. He murmured his condolences quietly. She took his words with a grateful nod.

"Dr. Aslani," said Joe Lasch when Booker stepped away. "I'd like to invite you to join us for this discussion. You don't have to, but if you'd like to..."

He gestured to the sitting area.

"Thank you," she said.

Nas took a seat in one of the chairs. Lasch took the other, which evidently annoyed Booker, whose frame was not built for sharing the couch. He pulled over a chair from the dining table instead.

Ridley and Gabe took up either end of the couch. And so the debriefing began.

Gabe took the lead.

It was the protection part that had failed—his mandate, his job. So he recounted the totality, everything from the Iranian bounty, to the showdown in Cairo, to the CIA's alert about the pair of assassins on their trail, to the previous forty-eight hours in Barcelona.

Nas listened without reaction until the last part. Until her father fell. She couldn't lift her eyes as Gabe told them how he'd had to choose between saving her or staying on a suicide mission to save her father.

"Was he alive when you last saw him?" asked Lasch.

"I couldn't say, sir."

He couldn't bear to look at Nas.

"Agent Kerik's body is being flown home today," said Lasch.

The mess of bloody flesh that was his face—smoke curling up from it—

"The Department is monitoring all official and non-official Iranian channels," he went on. "We expect they'll announce something today. They wouldn't stay quiet about getting Jamshid Aslani."

Nas was trying to swallow back her grief.

"Since only half the bounty has been fulfilled," he said, "we believe you're still under the same level of threat from the same individuals. They would have handed off your father to some accomplices, or official state actors. The tracking pieces you wore were destroyed shortly after you were separated."

After we left him.

Nas nodded.

"Dr. Aslani," said Lasch. "Is there anything you'd like to add, or say?"

She shook her head. "Agent Tolkin told it correctly."

Ridley could sense Gabe burning to look at Nas, but he couldn't bring himself to do it.

"Director Booker," said Lasch, "Secretary Rhodes himself sanctioned this joint operation, but with an escalation like this, we're not seeing our interests as being on equal footing."

Booker gave a grave nod, as he was giving Lasch the respect of at least considering it.

He can't be...

"What happened..." Booker started, "is a 'worst case' scenario. Nasrin, the American government is deeply sorry for what happened to your dad, and to you. We offered you protection abroad and it failed."

Ridley felt a hot flush of shame.

"But abandoning you now would be the ultimate insult. It's up to you to go back to the States—or finish your objective."

Lasch tightened at the suggestion. They were not on the same page.

"Dr. Aslani," said Lasch, "your protection is *my* highest concern. The best way to keep you safe is to get you back to your adopted home country. These particular mercenaries have proven that. They try to come onto American soil? We'll catch these sons of bitches. Then maybe when things have cooled down a bit, you can resume your search for...your archaeology project."

Nas looked at him, almost vacant.

Lasch nodded assuredly. "We'll get the sons of bitches."

"You try to say something bad about a man by insulting the women who gave birth to him?"

Lasch had too much pride to wince, but embarrassment rippled across his face.

"I didn't mean that."

"Sometimes it's 'bastards,'" said Nas. "But no difference. It's the mother you insult."

His cheeks tinted pink. "Look, I apologize for using some English colloquialisms, but my point stands, Dr. Aslani. It's my request that you return to the States with us today."

She looked at him for a moment.

"I have only one more place I need to go first. If I give up now..." Nas raised her hands. "My father accomplished nothing. I accomplished nothing."

Lasch glanced down, setting his jaw in frustration as though dealing with a defiant child.

"I advise *against it*," he said.

"I know. And I know that you can't *make* me go home. And you won't cancel my protection detail."

There she is. Proud Nas who made a whole country of men fearful of her.

Lasch stared at her, as though he could intimidate her with severity.

He knows nothing.

Booker intervened. "Your decision is to resume your search, then."

"Yes, Mr. Booker," said Nas.

"Then Ridley will stay on your protection assignment."

Gabe spoke up. "Sir, please let me stay on. I owe Dr. Aslani this. I owe her father."

Lasch gave him a puzzled look. "Didn't you get bitten by a shark?"

"Yes—but that has nothing to do with this."

Booker dropped his head to chuckle.

"I would question your fitness, Agent Tolkin," said Lasch.

Nas piped up. "I would like Gabe to stay. Please."

His blue eyes shot to her in surprise.

She kept hers on Lasch.

"Agent Tolkin can stay on," he said, "but one agent is not sufficient. You're dealing with goddamn drones now!"

Ridley bristled. This wasn't her boss, and she felt no hesitation in telling off State. "Of course one agent isn't sufficient, *says the second member of the protective detail.*"

Lasch gave her a dark look.

She would never have made it through their political, bureaucratic pipelines.

"Are you trained in executive security, officer?" he said.

"I'm very well trained in killing the enemy, which is what got us out of Cairo alive, and what got us out of that cemetery alive."

"Got *you* out alive."

Like a poisoned barb to her chest.

"Chief Lasch," said Booker, his voice steeling. "Make your own decisions about your own personnel. My officer is more than sufficient for her assignment."

The tension in the room was stretching...

"Everything else will be on me," said Nas. "This is my decision, my life."

"It's not just you, Doctor," said Lasch. "Your wellbeing is very important, but the State Department also has to account for international relations. If Iran was to get ahold of you—it would be a diplomatic nightmare. I hope you understand how important you are to us."

She gave an enigmatic smile.

Ridley was sure there was some mockery behind it.

"I'm a symbol," said Nas.

"You know you are," Lasch replied.

One of the agents from the embassy team interrupted them—

"Sir? We got a hit on an Iranian state channel."

Nas shot straight up in her seat.

"Do you want to see it now...?" asked the agent, eyeing her with apprehension.

"Dr. Aslani?" said Lasch. "Do you want to see?"

She lifted her chin. "Whatever it is."

Lasch beckoned for the agent, who brought over his computer tablet and set it on the coffee table.

There on the screen was Jimmy Aslani.

CHAPTER THIRTY-EIGHT

BARCELONA, SPAIN

THE AGENT PRESSED PLAY.

Nas choked back a cry.

Jimmy was sitting at a table, nothing behind him but a white wall. His face was a mash of bruises and cuts. He wore no handcuffs, but he did wear the unmistakable expression of a hostage.

He began to speak, and it was immediately obvious that it had been rehearsed. The auto-subtitles flickered across the bottom of the screen.

IN FARSI: *"Praise be to God. Long live the Leader and peace be upon him. My name is Jamshid Aslani, and I have returned to Iran to confess my crimes."*

Nas leaned forward in her seat, her hands pressed to her mouth.

IN FARSI: *"I beg the Supreme Leader for forgiveness, as I was led astray, under the influence and insanity of my daughter."*

Ridley looked at Nas. She was frozen.

IN FARSI: *"Nasrin Aslani is an enemy of Our Sacred Land. She blasphemes Allah and the Prophet, and she has been working as an agent of the Great Satan to spread lies and propaganda. She promotes immorality and has corrupted hearts, to wage war against Allah."*

Everyone watching felt their chests tighten at once.

IN FARSI: *"I am now reunited with my true and faithful children. I condemn Nasrin for all that she has done in her wicked rebellion. I renounce her as my daughter. Long live the Supreme Leader."*

There was a second's pause, and then the corner of his swollen lip rose in a faint smile.

IN FARSI: *"Mongoose."*

The video went black.

They all sat in silence for a moment. Their eyes drifted to Nas. Her hands were still cupped over her face, her eyes stricken.

The agent who'd brought them the tablet spoke quietly. "This was published sixteen minutes ago...broadcast all over Iran."

Ridley didn't know what to say to Nas. She didn't know what to do.

It would have been better if he'd died on those stairs.

Iran wouldn't have a prize to flaunt.

Her own father wouldn't have just sliced open her heart.

Booker cleared his throat. "Of course, we'll have the video analyzed—"

Nas burst out, "He's not a coward. He's *not* a traitor."

"Nobody would—"

"They have my brothers and sisters. They would torture his own children in front of him if he didn't say those things."

"It's typical behavior of the IRGC," said Lasch. "No one blames him."

"What did that last word mean?" asked Booker. "That he said at the end, 'mongoose.'"

Nas laughed, and it was a broken sound.

"Baba called me mongoose when I was a little girl. I tried to fight a snake one time. So he thought I wasn't afraid of anything...that I would fight anything. Like a mongoose."

You would, wouldn't you?

She sat up straight, pressing her palms down on the tops of her thighs.

"They will torture him," she said calmly, "but they won't kill him. They want to use him as bait."

"They want you back," said Lasch.

Nas nodded at him. "They would rather take me alive, to make me an example. They would hang me from a crane in front of thousands of people and put the pictures on every television and newspaper in the country."

Ridley and Gabe met each other's eyes, and something flashed between them. An iron determination.

That will never happen.

"Dr. Aslani," said Lasch, his tone having softened, "I can only recommend our best option to keep you safe from that, but if you refuse it, then...godspeed."

Nas lifted her head.

"I'm going to finish this."

Booker took Ridley out for a walk.

Lasch wanted one of the State Department agents to go with them, but the CIA director rejected the extra protection. This was his time with his operative.

The morning was already warm, the kind of temperature that's a harbinger of afternoon sweat. The two of them walked through the line of trees along the seaside promenade. Joggers slid past them, dogs trotted by with their owners, and the occasional tourist stopped for photos of the waterfront.

Booker first checked in with Ridley, a cursory set of questions that were less about hearing her answers and more about watching her reactions.

She was skilled at presenting both exactly how she wanted.

"I'm not too fu—messed up to continue, sir," she said.

The boss didn't like swearing, which sometimes made it hard for her to think.

He nodded. "I wouldn't imagine so. You've been through worse and I've seen it. Where are you taking her now?"

"Italy. After that, I don't know. If we're done—back to the States, obviously."

"Not back to her dig on Serifos?"

Ridley gave him a look that left no space for dissent. "I'll lean hard on that one."

"She's a hell of a woman, huh?" said Booker, shaking his head in wonder.

"She's a hell of a woman. She was really shattered yesterday, but...she just showed back up today on her own mission. Some resolve."

"You really think you don't need reinforcements," said Booker. "There are two Ospreys I could assign right now to meet you in Italy."

Ridley watched a slick-skinned woman run past, whose sports bra was struggling to contain her.

"I'm new to the protective detail thing," she said, returning her attention to her boss, "but it's *not* actually easier to move around in a big group without drawing attention."

"I don't think attention is what you're really workin' against right now. You have their attention. It's their aim you gotta worry about."

"And their damn drones."

There was a moment's quiet, and Ridley felt something brewing in him.

"If you want to claim the rest of this mission on your own," he said, "you're gonna own the results. I know this hybrid protection thing can't fall on you completely. I know Agent Tolkin and Agent Kerik were on Jamshid's protection when this happened. State Department owns their own failure, *but*...like him or not, Tolkin's your partner and this is *your* team. You stand together—this lands at your feet, too."

The failure curdled in her gut.

"You have a tough record, Rid," he said. "You always accomplish the objective, which is why you get these assignments, but you don't make it easy—on you or anyone around you."

"I win my games," she said with some heat. "I put up the points that matter."

"Don't give me that crap," he rumbled. "This isn't a game. Jamshid Aslani is sitting in an Iranian prison being tortured right now. How many points is *that?*"

A hot blade of shame slid through her.

What the fuck is wrong with you, Samaras?

"Your arrogance and emotional immaturity aside," he said, "I know you're good at this. *I've* seen it...I'll let you go on here."

He had been out in the field with her before, partners on a dark chase through the snowy cities of Europe. He'd covered for her when she left a royal residence in a bloodbath. He had even helped with the most courageous act of them all—exposing elite figures in society for having engaged in child abuse, facilitated by the most notorious trafficker and blackmailer in the world.

Ridley had stolen the evidence of it, and though he'd had to do it incognito, Booker refused to do his "duty" and bury that evidence. He quietly made sure it went to the places where it would be properly dealt with, never to be swept under the rug again.

Men's lives were exploded around the world.

Though not enough of them.

But she had seen enough to trust him, and he trusted her.

"You haven't heard anything about the Order of Raphael trying to get in on this treasure hunt?" she asked.

"I don't *hear* anything about the Order," said Booker. "They don't put out soundwaves."

With all the threats of the Islamic Republic and their assassins, with sharks and ballistic drones and treacherous Egyptian guides, this thought had still been drifting in and out of her mind.

"This is what they do, though," said Ridley. "Like anything we want to get a hold of, they'd want, too, and this one was *public.* International news level public. So where the hell are they?"

Booker frowned. "I get the question, but I've got no intel. They're better than the CIA at keepin' their secrets."

She didn't want another Tiago Inacio taking her by surprise. There was enough to deal with on this mission already.

Shelve it.

"Did Aunt Bea turn down this powwow?" Ridley asked, shaking herself out of her spiraling paranoia.

"You wouldn't have wanted her here."

"Book, I met that woman for fifteen minutes and I can't understand how she doesn't actually run the entire agency."

Booker laughed, a rich booming sound from deep in his chest. "She doesn't see it either. What else do you need?"

She squinted out at the water and replied, "A blind eye."

"Wait a second...*where* in Italy are you going?"

Ridley wobbled her head from side to side—

"You're askin' for *both* eyes to go blind!" he said.

"If the Simon sisters find out I'm there, you know they're gonna make this mission hell. I have to tell them before."

Booker shook his head. "You have left your mark on this world, Ridley Samaras, and the world doesn't even know the half of it."

"I should tell the Simons that part."

"Mm, yeah, go tell 'em. Run up your flag with the cleverest criminals in Europe. *What* did you really do to piss them off, anyhow?"

Ridley gave an exaggerated scoff of offense. "Me?" But then she grinned, "I made them look *un-clever.*"

Booker smiled. "Would be a real shame for you to survive all the crazy things you have, only to get done in by a pair of rich English women living on Capri."

"I've got this, I've got this."

Yet she had no idea the kind of reception she would get...for the Simon sisters never forgot.

CHAPTER THIRTY-NINE

CAPRI, ITALY

The island was really as dazzling as its reputation suggested.

In the splendid mosaic of color that was the Amalfi Coast, Capri was the jewel of tourists, artists, and royalty.

Ridley, Gabe, and Nas had left Barcelona that afternoon. Lasch booked them first class tickets to Sorrento, where they picked up a private boat out to the island.

Tribute had to be paid before they set foot in Napoli.

Nas was quiet for most of the trip, though when she did speak, her voice was sure and strong. There was no wilt in her. There was no tell that she had just suffered one of the most agonizing events of her life.

As she had packed up her things that morning in their Barcelona hotel rooms, Ridley went to the door to check on her. She'd found Nas standing over the bed, looking down at the array of things they'd collected on this treasure hunt.

The bronze block of the collapsed shield.

The plain strapped sandals.

The hilt of the sword.

And now the gray shimmering bag.

Is it worth this?

The thought clanged in Ridley's mind as a sudden surge of emotion stung her eyes.

"We leave in ten," she said gently.

Nas nodded, not taking her eyes off the items.

"Did Agent Kerik have kids?" she asked.

Ridley had been so caught up in Jimmy's capture, his torture, his daughter's grief...she hadn't thought of the man who died trying to protect him from it. Somehow it was the one who was suffering the most here who even thought of the pain of others.

Ridley shook her head. "I don't know. I didn't know anything about him. I can—we can find out for you."

Send them flowers. Send them a toy. Send them...a futile and desperate attempt at consolation.

Nas spoke again. "You fought for each one of these, for us. I know what Gabe's mission is here—what Agent Kerik's mission was—to protect us from the regime, but I don't know why you risk your life here."

She finally looked up at Ridley.

"What does Mr. Douglas want? What's your final goal? What happens when we get the last piece, the helmet of Hades?"

It took her this long to ask.

"I don't know what happens when we get the helmet," said Ridley. "It's obvious these things have some kind of power, and that power compels them to reunite with the others. Strongly. Pretty strongly."

She leaned against the doorframe.

"I'm here to make sure nothing really terrible happens when the entire set comes together."

Nas looked at her with bemusement. "Like in Jerusalem?"

How the hell—

"So, you're clever," said Ridley.

"It was a guess, until now."

It seemed like the whole world had seen what happened that day. For those who could make out the tall brunette in the blurred footage of chaos...she might be famous.

Ridley blew out an exasperated breath. "You have no idea how much worse it could—*would* have been."

"And you think something like that might happen if we get a bunch of armor and weapons back together?"

A pause.

"We're always open to worst case scenarios."

Nas arched a brow and went back to packing.

Hours later, as their boat approached Capri, she sat with Ridley and Gabe, taking in the sight.

Craggy limestone cliffs rose high from turquoise waters. Gleaming yachts floated and speedboats flew across the sparkling surface. Houses were scattered along the coastline in bright colorful rows.

"*La dolce vita,*" murmured Ridley.

The warm Mediterranean wind billowed their clothes.

"It was originally settled by Greeks," said Nas. "Until the Roman emperor Augustus and then Tiberius moved here to live."

"*Romans.* Always drafting off the Greeks. Gods, islands, architecture, bastardized democracy," said Ridley.

Gabe was gripping the siderail, his golden hair whipping in the wind, his eyes as blue as the water. His expression was somber.

Ridley had been surprised that State was allowing him to stay on the detail without any more reinforcements. She didn't understand the workings of that department, but it felt...permissive.

Maybe he can atone.

"My father would love to see this." Nas smiled and leaned forward on the rail. "One day, I'll bring him here."

Ridley could say nothing, but reached out and squeezed her forearm. Gabe tried to smile but it quickly melted off.

They reached the docks and disembarked in a swarm of tourists fresh off the ferry. Ridley pulled on the backpack with their items in it. Gabe was carrying the weapons. Nas had her own overnight bag.

Their eyes scanned the crowds for Qassem and Fadavi. However unlikely, they couldn't help but search.

In fact, there were two men who were watching for them, but they weren't Iranian. A pair of Italians were standing by the first kiosk at the docks.

Ridley noticed them first, only twenty feet away.

"Our charioteers," she muttered to Gabe. "They're okay. Stay cool, man of the Shire."

As they approached, the taller of the two men stepped up. He was broad-shouldered and slightly balding, with a scruffy face, square jaw, and a Roman nose that made him look like a centurion out of Nero's guard.

"*Ciao,*" he said, his gaze sliding up and down Ridley's figure. "Are you Athena come to life?"

His accent was pasty thick.

"How did you know?" she replied, grinning back at him. "Your mother's been waiting for me."

He bellowed a laugh, glanced back at his companion and said something in near-Italian.

Ridley had forgotten. Though she could speak Italian with

ease, the Napoli contingent here spoke their own dialect: Neapolitan. And it was not in her arsenal.

He would still understand her, so she asked.

IN ITALIAN: *"Are you the new top boy?"*

The centurion-looking one actually recoiled in offense. It was so easy to prick an Italian man's pride.

"I'm the 'right hand man,'" he nearly spat. "You call me Cesare. You call him Gianluca."

He gestured back at the other man. Gianluca was younger, with high arched brows, thin lips, and a pair of dark eyes that stared unnervingly.

He's either trying to bore through everything with some super vision or he's working out how to murder everyone he looks at.

"Well, you already know who I am," said Ridley.

"Who are your friends?"

Cesare looked at Nas and Gabe behind her. Ridley did not want to disclose Nas' identity before she had to. That Iranian bounty was high. It might prove too appealing to the worst criminal henchmen in the country.

"You can just call them my friends for now," she said.

Cesare muttered something obscene but beckoned them to follow. He led the way out of the marina as Gianluca circled behind them to bring up the rear.

Ridley knew the encirclement was coming and it still unsettled her. Gabe hated it so much that he kept wanting to drop back into step beside the Italian, but couldn't separate that far from Nas.

Cesare went over to a blue Mercedes-Benz S-Class and opened the back door for them.

Cars were almost entirely forbidden on the island, especially during the summer. There were always service vehicles, a few small taxis, mini buses, and electric carts to transport heavier items, but even scooters were heavily restricted in the high tourism season. Only residents could get permits for exceptions, and only for small vehicles.

The Simon sisters were excepted from the exceptions.

As the trio piled into the back of the large sedan, Ridley kept the bag with the artifacts in it on her lap.

They wound up through the narrow streets, passing by the funicolare that glided down the steep hills, its cars packed with sightseers. They could see the yachts anchored offshore, so many that it looked like a gleaming white hive of luxury.

Cesare drove them past the town of Capri, bustling with visitors, shoppers, and travel vloggers wandering about as they filmed it all. The Mercedes took them higher, to the west side of the island.

Anacapri.

Most of the scant thirteen thousand residents lived here. There lay the wealth, the peace, and the views.

Their hosts had come for all of it.

The two Italians pulled up to a villa and the gate swung open.

"Wow," murmured Nas as the car rolled up to the front.

A long marble stairway led up to grand arched doors. A pair of stone lions were frozen mid-roar, perched on either side of the bottom step. Bougainvillea billowed off the long trellis overhead.

Ridley, Gabe, and Nas climbed out. Cesare led the way up the broad steps, with Gianluca again lurking behind. Instead of going inside, Cesare turned off to the right. He brought them around the back of the villa.

There, they emerged onto a veranda. Stone steps descended to a turquoise pool. Elegant lawn chairs lay out along the deck. Vines and flowers blossomed everywhere.

And there, taking cocktails off the bar cart, was the most unlikely pair of criminals in all of Italy.

CHAPTER FORTY

CAPRI, ITALY

As far as anyone knew, the sisters didn't have a drop of Italian blood in them. The Simons were blonde, blue-eyed Englishwomen with London accents and an impeccable sense of savagery.

The older one, Phoebe, had arrived in Milan as a nineteen-year-old hungry for a modeling contract. She got one from one of the most successful men in the fashion industry: Carlo Geloso.

But running a worldwide modeling agency was not his only business. The dapper man who never appeared in public with even one silver hair out of place was the heir to one of the most fearsome bosses in the Camorra.

This was the Neapolitan mafia, a criminal organization forged in the grimy gambling dens and brothels of 18th century Napoli. They grew and grew until they became power brokers in society. The "low Camorra" still dealt in crime within poor areas, but the "high Camorra"—the most ambitious and cunning members—began to deal in the bureaucracy of the state. They took up public contracts, flexed their influence in politics, and offered *quid pro quo* arrangements that turned many an official's head.

Though dozens of its members were prosecuted and even executed in the following century, the Camorra held. It was a hydra. Unlike the Cosa Nostra of Sicily, there was no head of *the* snake, but only more and more snakes. Territorial families became their own centers of control, but worked together to maximize their powers.

Yet, the decentralization also led to near perpetual feuding. Attempts to unify in the 1980s fell flat. The clans multiplied, finally eclipsing the great Cosa Nostra itself.

It was into one of these families that a young Englishwoman had been introduced. Her looks got her the catwalks and the photo shoots, but it quickly became evident to Carlo Geloso that he had a girl of unusual talents on his hands.

Phoebe was always watching. She was shrewd, audacious, and best of all, ruthless.

Carlo was bemused at first by her interest in his business affairs. He challenged her with small riddles and logistical complexities. She passed every test of his with aplomb.

By the time she was twenty-four, she was already halfway out of the modeling world. She had mastered Italian and Neapolitan. Her encyclopedic knowledge of Carlo's enterprises was unsurpassed. He had come to rely on her, and she repaid him in abundance.

Yet earning the respect of the rest of his organization had been hard-won. They scoffed at her, laughed at her, insulted her behind her back.

And then one night, she'd come back from meeting a traitorous drug dealer. She had been dispatched by Carlo himself to confront the rat in their organization. It was a test. So she took along two goons—and came back with the severed thumbs of every single one of the drug dealer's entourage.

And the head dealer's tongue.

She had dumped out the bloody bag in front of Carlo and his associates while they were all sitting around a table for a conference.

Carlo had smiled faintly and murmured, "*A sangue freddo.*"

There were no more sneers. Every man looked her in the eye. They listened when she spoke to them.

And if Phoebe Simon was brutal, her younger sister was barbaric.

When she was newly graduated from the London School of Economics, Ivy Simon had been looking for something that could satisfy both her crocodile instincts and her business savvy. So her sister had invited her out to Napoli, and she found her happy place.

It became a family business.

Over the next two decades, both women established their own fearsome reputations. They had to be harder, cleverer, and more vicious than the rest. And that they were.

Yet out here by the pool under a glorious summer sky, no one could have guessed the amount of blood on the hands of these blonde Englishwomen.

Ivy turned to see Ridley, an Aperol spritz in her hand.

"Ridley Samaras. I always knew someday you'd come walking back through my door."

Ridley pulled off a modest, crooked smile. "Hello, Ivy. Phoebe."

Both of them wore their hair tied loosely back. They had the same sly eyes. Though Ivy always looked like she was up to some mischief, Phoebe seemed like she was always analyzing, always reading.

The elder sister dismissed Cesare with a wave, then addressed Ridley.

IN ITALIAN: *"You left Amsterdam without saying goodbye* or *apologizing,"* said Ivy. *"You're lucky I liked you so much or I would have cut out your eyes."*

In case she had forgotten who she was dealing with, here was Ridley's refresher on the Simons.

Very few people actually come right out and say that to a CIA operative.

"I would have apologized in person but I was concerned you might cut my head off," she replied.

Phoebe's gaze drenched across Gabe, as if her own personal Greek god had just been delivered to her. Ridley knew she was married to some English broker, but they had an arrangement. He lived in London most of the year while she lived in the sun-soaked Mediterranean.

"Your friends?" said Phoebe.

Ridley gestured. "This is Gabe. This is Nas."

But now Phoebe stared at Nas. "Are you safe here?"

It felt like a steam valve had burst inside of Ridley's chest.

Of course she knows.

Nas swallowed back her own wave of fear. "I believe so. Nobody would dare touch me when I'm your guest, right?"

That got a smile from Phoebe. She could always appreciate clever plays.

"You're very right," she said, sweeping off the lounge chair to her feet. "While you're our guest, you *are* safe. Shame about your father."

The Simons paid attention. Their livelihoods depended on the power struggles and political shifts happening around the world.

They imported cocaine from Peru by way of the Netherlands, trafficked drugs into Spain, ran arms shipments through

Switzerland, and laundered money through their casinos on the French Riviera. In Napoli, they owned construction companies and restaurants, bakeries and music venues.

Ivy handed an Aperol spritz to Nas, who took it without any intention of drinking it.

"What are you doing here?" Phoebe said to Ridley. "Aside from begging forgiveness of my sister—not known as 'Ivy the Merciful.'"

Gabe was eyeing them with growing unease.

"You know Nas is an archaeologist?" said Ridley, her tone bright. "We're looking for something pretty old, and we think it's in Napoli."

Both sisters looked at her for a moment, then exchanged a glance.

"You're here to ask for something?" said Ivy.

Ridley raised up her hands in a peace offering. "I didn't want to sneak around in your backyard without you knowing I was here."

"What is this thing you're looking for, and where is it?" asked Phoebe, her tone becoming scalpel-sharp.

This wasn't curiosity. It was interrogation. Ivy began to make up another drink.

Nas spoke. "It's an old Greek helmet. I believe it's in the caves beneath the Temple of Apollo, by Lake Avernus. I'm sure."

"*Lago d'Averno*," said Phoebe. "You have a team with you, then?"

Nas glanced at Ridley. "No...it's not a dig, really."

Ivy handed the next Aperol spritz to Gabe, who cocked an eyebrow at it. Then she pointed at Ridley as though trying to remember something.

"Gin, wasn't it? Psychopathia Sexualis? Some sherry and vermouth in there...?"

"That's me," said Ridley.

Ivy grinned back at her before turning to mix it.

"Given the state of things," said Phoebe, "surely you'll need an escort. We can't have any unauthorized kidnappings on our territory. And certainly not by foreigners."

You're foreign.

"We'll be fine," said Gabe. "Thanks anyhow."

Phoebe completely ignored him. There would be no turning this one down. They would not be allowed to leave for Napoli without some of the Simon goons coming along for the trip.

"We'll have some of our lads take you by boat tomorrow morning. You'll spend the evening with us, then."

Ivy handed Ridley her cocktail.

"Are you going to destroy the world this time?"

CHAPTER FORTY-ONE

CAPRI, ITALY

THE WAIT WAS AGONIZING.

The food was not.

Ridley was reminded that despite all their villainy, the Simon sisters were charming and amusing company.

Sociopaths could be delightful in their element.

A couple of servers brought them dinner out on the patio that evening, and it was the best meal she'd had since being on Paros. Caprese salad, pasta, and grilled seabream paired with a local white wine.

Nas was quieter than usual, but smiled warmly at the bursts of laughter in conversation. Gabe was doing his mildly antagonistic, mildly dickish banter that she'd first encountered in the airport back in D.C. The Simons found it fantastically engaging.

Ridley had more glasses of wine than she usually would on the job.

We're already in the lion's den. No need to worry about falling into it.

The warm bloom in her chest was a welcome relaxation. She tried to not imagine Jimmy sitting at the table with them, chuckling and watching over the conversation like an elder lion.

She tried to not imagine him slumped in a cell, bleeding and broken.

The Simons hadn't wanted to spoil their own dinners with work talk.

As soon as the limoncello hit the table, though, they were back to business.

"You're CIA," said Ivy, pointing at Ridley with her glass, then to Nas. "You're an Iranian archaeologist that your own country wants to kill, and you must be..." she said, settling on Gabe, "from the American State Department."

He gave his most attractive smirk. "We take care of our naturalized citizens, too."

"They're giving her protection to run around the world on an archeology study?" said Phoebe.

Ridley could feel Ivy's sharp gaze on her.

"There's something special about this study," said the younger Simon. "That's why *she's* here. Ridley Samaras doesn't just—do protection work. Am I right?"

Ridley didn't answer. She sipped her limoncello.

"She's here for something else. Much more important." Ivy turned her attention to Nas. "What did you say that helmet thing was about?"

Nas shuffled in her chair.

"It's the final artifact in a series I've been collecting," she said. "Allegedly, the items that Perseus used to kill Medusa."

Why did you say that?!

The sisters exchanged a look. Phoebe grinned.

"You're a mythological archaeologist? That sounds fun."

"We've found everything else in the series," Nas retorted.

Shut the fuck up, Nasrin!

Ridley saw the Simons' eyes start to kindle and knew she had to jump in.

"Important for posterity," she said. "Worthless materially. A pair of old leather sandals? Interesting to poor nerds in university departments."

"Which is why the CIA got involved, I'm sure," said Phoebe —and her voice was frosted.

Goddamnit, Nas.

"You know me!" said Ridley. "I'm into the weird stuff."

Ivy smirked and murmured something into her glass.

"You have some nerve," Phoebe went on, her eyes piercing right through Ridley. "You're here to ask for our blessing to work in Napoli, but you've offered us nothing."

Ridley spread her arms and looked around.

"What could I possibly have to offer *you?*"

"You'll give this helmet to a museum?"

"Yes," she lied.

"I think we'll *sell* it to a museum. The whole lot of it," said Phoebe

There was a loaded pause. Nas looked at Ridley in near panic.

The devil wants his due, Samaras. Great job laying it at their doorstep.

"You can sell the helmet. The rest is not for sale."

Ivy leaned forward. "We'll see what the helmet is worth. Then we'll take our pick of the rest."

Gabe spoke up, stretching back in his chair. "Look, I'm bored. The sooner we can find this old iron hat, the better. Wrap up my job here."

"I'm sure Nas is flattered to hear you say that," said Ivy.

He shrugged and held up his hands.

"To your success tomorrow," said Phoebe, lifting her glass in a mock toast.

Ridley lifted her own glass with a flashing smile. "Great success."

Phoebe had invited Gabe to her parlor to offer him a cigar before she had to take an important call. It was highly unusual for her to share such a luxury with anyone other than an A-lister or a fellow don, but then again, he looked like a celebrity.

Beauty was the great seducer of men...but women fell for it, too.

He reemerged outside holding a cigar worth as much as a new mid-size car.

Ridley stayed out on the patio with Nas and Ivy, watching the twilight fade into a shroud of dark blue. Ivy made another round of drinks for them, but no one else seemed interested.

Nas eventually announced she was going to bed, and trudged up the steps.

She stopped, though, by a blooming bush, and bent over to pluck a yellow and pink flower. She tucked it behind her ear, drew herself up straight, and disappeared into the house.

"She's quite a dame," said Ivy, handing Ridley a vodka martini.

"She's quite a dame."

Ivy heard Phoebe calling her name from the house. She sighed and excused herself.

Ridley emptied her glass into the bushes nearby and went over to Gabe. He was sitting on the edge of one of the pool chairs, bunched and tense, holding a smoldering cigar.

"State Department agent meets the mafia," said Ridley.

"I've met worse *in* the State Department."

"Be tight-lipped tomorrow, okay? They catch a whiff of its value and they'll snatch that damned helmet right from us."

He sucked in a mouthful of smoke. "Damned is right."

She shrugged.

Everything Osprey gets into is damned.

"Why do you do this?" he asked. "Whatever it is...you do."

"Because a wave came along and wrecked my dream? I wasn't made for the little shit. All hail the ones who keep the aircraft carriers running, but finishing out my Navy service on one of those felt like a worse drowning than my accident."

Like my mother's drowning—

"Booker found me, had a wild job offer, and I found something I'm really good at it."

Except when you fail and get people killed or kidnapped. Never forget those parts.

She grinned past the dark voice inside of her. "I really took to it—saving the world."

He snorted. "You're a little warm on the drinks."

"And you on the smoke? Why are you a DSS agent?"

"Samurais went out of style."

"Knights, too."

He puffed out a ring of pungent smoke. "My son wants my sword collection when I die."

"That kind of noble violence just doesn't pay much these days."

He looked at her for a moment. "What's behind all this? Why are all these pieces trying to reunite using some...supernatural shit?"

She shrugged again. "Tends to be bad. I thought the Order of Raphael would be all over this, but I've only seen the murderous republic of Iran on our tails."

"An order, like some Dan Brown movie?"

"They're...some fanatics that broke off from the Templars

like eight hundred years ago. They have a surprising number of people in high positions around the world, and they like to collect the things that will give them *supernatural* powers."

"Like in Jerusalem."

"Right. Yup. Like in Jerusalem. They want control over the Watchers—these ancient god-beings that were sent by *big* God Yahweh to govern tribes of people here on earth. Got corrupt, corrupted the humans into worshipping them instead of Creator-god, got imprisoned for all of time under the earth."

He nodded to indulge her. "So your operating system is: that's all true."

"Well, I've seen it tear buildings and people to shreds right in front of me, so I think I operate like that, yeah."

"What would old Greek myths have to do with any of that biblical story stuff?"

So now *he's curious.*

She didn't know what to believe, so she gave him instead what Booker believed.

"Mythical heroes, gods, super-powered legends—all these things exist across the world in all ancient cultures, right? Giants and demi-gods. Maybe they *were* all real, just versions of the same thing. The Watchers were like the old Greek titans. The Greek gods and demigods were like...second gen. Demons: nephilim. Maybe."

It was hard to tell in the darkness whether he was looking at her with fascination or derision.

"I don't know," she finally muttered. "I just chase the things and fight the other things."

"And what do you do with the things you chase after you get 'em?"

"That's classified."

He looked back to the glowing pool. "Okay. You think it's all worth Jimmy Aslani being tortured?"

She had no words.

Ridley lay in the plush bed that night, her mind riled.

You overshared.

It doesn't matter.

Your mission integrity always matters.

He's on my mission!

He's not on that part. You idiot.

This was that moment. She felt it on every mission: the calm before the storm. She had to draw her brain away from the whirlpool before it cost her that much-needed rest.

Ridley pulled out her phone and drew up the music library. Nick Cave & the Bad Seeds' *O Children* carried her to sleep.

She dreamt of a cemetery, of statues reaching for her as something terrible chased after her...of not being able to keep up with Jimmy and Nas and Gabe ahead of her...of a huge owl screeching down from the sky...

And of a dark figure standing at the top of the stairs, with snakes for hair.

CHAPTER FORTY-TWO

CAPRI, ITALY

In any criminal territory, Ridley wanted to be the first one awake. Today, she was not.

Phoebe was already stalking around the pool on her phone, linen pants flowing, her voice slicing through the morning quiet.

Ruining the perfect Mediterranean sunrise.

By the time the others emerged, Ridley had downed a cappuccino and wolfed a cornetto stuffed with apricot jam. She tried to not rush Nas and Gabe through their breakfasts, but what was all the dawdling about?

Ivy was the last to appear. She wore navy capris and a blue-and-white striped blouse, as if she'd just stepped out of a Cary Grant movie in the French Riviera. Except for the Beretta tucked into the small of her back.

"The boat's ready," she announced with an odd level of cheerfulness. "Let's go."

We turned down a State Department detail only to get stuck with the mafia.

"Let's go, then," said Ridley, hoisting the relics backpack onto her shoulder.

"Your arsenal is onboard already," said Ivy.

Their weapons bag had been confiscated by the Camorra goons for "safekeeping" while they were at the villa. It was routine to return them.

A chauffeur drove them down to the marina. Cesare and Gianluca followed in a car behind them.

Capri was just starting to brim with the morning's tourist activity. The sun had risen like a diva, putting on a display with every fabulous bit of the island that people came here for, with its shining white cliffs and twinkling azure sea.

A motorboat ferried them out to a gleaming seventy-foot catamaran. Ivy led them onboard and introduced them to the three Filipino crew members.

Another two Italians greeted them on the lower deck. Though they were decently dressed for the hot summer day, they were clearly the muscle. One had a stutter. The other looked like Nic Cage.

Four scagnozzos, so they outnumber us.

The steward offered them each bellinis, but everyone declined.

"An hour to Napoli," Ivy told them as she sprawled onto a pristine couch outside on the lower deck. "Feel free to move about, explore the place, do what you like."

But neither Ridley, Gabe, or Nas left each other's sight.

As glorious as the journey was under a crystal blue sky, Ridley couldn't shake an ominous feeling. It only grew as the mainland came into view.

Ivy had been delightful enough company—for a mafia

queen—but no amount of charming smiles or contagious laughter from her could overwhelm the edge of menace.

As they caught sight of the port, Gabe muttered to Ridley, "That's hideous."

It wasn't exactly the seaside Italian city of dreams. The entire coastline looked hard, square, and industrial. The only allure to it was the sweeping rise of Mount Vesuvius on the skyline.

"Pompeii is nearby," said Nas, joining him and Ridley at the bow.

She had been mostly quiet during the trip.

"We're almost there. Almost the last piece," she said, as if to encourage herself.

NAPOLI, ITALY

They drove west in two Range Rovers. It was less than an hour along the Italian coast to reach Lake Avernus, where they parked in a small dirt lot on the northwestern edge.

Ridley carried the backpack and Gabe clutched the heavy duffel as they made their way down to the shore.

The lake was nearly a perfect circle, small and still.

"Avernus comes from an old Greek word—it means 'without birds,'" said Nas as she squinted out. "I just learned that."

"Now I'm learning Greek from *you*," said Ridley. "That was quick."

They stood in the middle of the walking path that ringed the lake. Bikers and pedestrians slid by them, miffed at the oblivious space-hogging.

"That smell is appalling" said Ivy, her expression crunching.

Her four men hovered about, not even attempting to blend in.

"Sulfur from the volcano," said Nas. "That's why the Greeks thought it was the entrance to Hades, because it would steam. They thought it was smoke."

The water came right up to the edge of the walkway.

"So, you're going to hell?" said Ivy.

"I hope not. Are you?"

The Englishwoman gave a shrug that went all the way through her eyebrows. "I've sent enough people there. You think I'd know the way."

Ridley remembered hearing about an incident shortly after their paths crossed in Amsterdam. A rival gang had been threatening some of the business owners under the protection of the Simons.

It didn't last long.

The remains of the young, vicious gang leader were found tied to a pillar in an abandoned parking garage. He looked like a mannequin made of ash and coal. A tire had been placed around his neck, doused in gasoline, and set alight.

Ivy's favorite first-greeting-of-the-day was, "I love the smell of burnt rubber in the morning!"

Nas and Gabe don't even know who they're dealing with.

Gabe was scanning the pedestrians coming from each side. Nas certainly was not in the clear. She wouldn't be for the rest of her life. As long as the Islamic Republic stood.

She pulled out a wad of papers she'd scrawled on.

"You know the poet Virgil? He wrote the Aeneid. He wrote that Aeneas comes to this lake to descend into Hades, but *also* about 'the dread cavern Sibyl,' where he had to go consult the oracle before going down to the underworld. That cave is where we have to go."

"So why aren't we there?" asked Ridley.

"The stele says we have to start here—" she shuffled the papers around in her hand like any overwhelmed professor. "It says to pass through the earth, from the lake to the Cave of the Sibyl. There's a tunnel only a kilometer from here."

"And there's a tunnel." said Gabe.

"Of course there's a tunnel," said Nas with a smile.

Ivy was eyeing the three of them, calculating.

"Cesare, Gianluca, come with me. You," she said, pointing to Stutter and Nic Cage, "stay on this side."

She won't be trapped in a tunnel without at least one end being secure.

Ridley touched Nas on the arm. "Let's go."

The entrance to the tunnel was only fifty feet from the lake-front. It was half-hidden in a thicket of tall grass. It was gated and chained.

"Ah shit, here we go again," said Gabe, dropping the equipment duffel to the ground.

He pulled out a crowbar and went to work on the padlock. Ridley pulled out a flashlight for the two of them.

"They were going to reopen it to the public," said Nas, "but they found some bats living in these caverns that had to be protected."

Ridley could have sworn she saw Ivy blanch. It would have been a first.

"These are the caves you're searching in for this helmet?" said Ivy.

"No, they take us to Cumae. *There* we find the cave of the oracle."

The Englishwoman turned away, muttering something to Cesare in Neapolitan.

Ridley looked at Gabe, whose every sinew was straining as

he pulled at the crowbar. A fresh sheen of sweat was already glazing his forehead.

"Come on, man," she called. "Are you even trying?"

He grunted to let her known how unfunny she was.

Seconds later, the metal popped, and the chain slid to the ground. Gabe yanked open the gate.

"Ladies first," he said, gesturing to Ridley.

"You get a gold star."

She switched on her headlamp and stepped through.

CHAPTER FORTY-THREE

NAPOLI, ITALY

THIS TUNNEL WAS no rough-hewn cave of rocks. It was an arching, clean-cut passageway, big enough for an army truck to roll through.

"It was a military route," said Nas. "The Romans built a naval base at the mouth of the underworld."

"On the hellmouth?" said Gabe.

"But there was no Buffy and no Slayer," said Nas pleased to have caught the American TV reference.

They passed into an immense cavern which ballooned out the size of the tunnel. Glancing up, Ridley spotted dark shapes hanging from the ceiling.

"Nobody breathe in the bat shit," she said, then looked at the Italians. "I mean, you guys can. That Marburg virus has to go somewhere."

"Shut the fuck up," snapped Ivy, her voice taut.

Touchy. Maybe we found her weakness. Huge colonies of bats.

One of the shapes overhead shifted, which sent a flutter through the rest of them. The leathery flap of wings echoed in the cavern.

Ivy pulled her gun. She wouldn't take her eyes off the ceiling until they'd reached a smaller section of the tunnel again, without bats hanging overhead.

Minutes later, they saw daylight beaming at them—through another locked gate. Gabe dutifully busted open the rusted lock and they emerged into a small canyon.

A smooth cliff loomed eighty feet over their heads. A thick forest lay behind them, almost butting up to the rock face. The space in between, though, was too well manicured to be natural.

"If this is Cumae," said Nas, cranking her head back to stare up the cliff, "then the Temple of Apollo is right above us, and the Cave of the Sibyl—"

She trotted a few yards down the broad pathway. The cliffs above them were clearly carved. There were alcoves cut into them, high overhead, and walls that looked like ancient brick.

Nas stopped at the entrance of a tunnel.

"It's here," she said, her voice eerily calm.

Ahead of them stretched a long stone corridor. It had been carved into the shape of a trapezoid, with the walls slanting inward toward the narrow ceiling. It was also bright with daylight. Wooden beams that were clearly modern had been built in as scaffolding.

"Okay," said Ridley. "This seems a little...open."

"The oracle existed for an audience."

They started into the tunnel, Ivy and her Italians bringing up the rear.

Sun poured through the wide shafts cut into the outside

wall. Small antechambers lined the left side. Each one was empty.

"People came here to have their fortunes read?" said Gabe. "By some girl high on drugs?"

"Did you see that in a movie?" said Nas, busy scouring each of the niches they passed.

Before he could reply, Ivy cut in. "What are you looking for? Secret buttons?"

"I, uh—I don't know yet. The stele says to 'make flow the rivers of the underworld,' so we need to find the rivers."

Gabe gave a nod. "That are hidden."

"Now you're getting the fun," said Ridley.

They carried on until they reached the end of the tunnel, where a vaulted alcove arched above them.

"Is this where this oracle sat?" asked Ivy.

"No," said Nas. "Probably where a servant sat to keep the gate. The oracle would be in here."

She turned left, into another short tunnel where there were three shallow chambers at the twelve, three, and nine o'clock positions.

Ivy told her men to stay outside in the broad tunnel.

As Ridley stepped into the inner sanctum, she felt her backpack begin to vibrate.

It's here.

"We're in the right spot," Ridley said, her voice ringing off the stone walls as if they'd been shaped for acoustics.

She gave Nas and Gabe a knowing look. If Ivy saw their bag full of magical ancient artifacts made of precious metals, it would severely destabilize their mission.

Nas took a flashlight from Gabe's duffel bag and began scouring the walls.

"The oracle—the Sibyl—served Apollo," she said, "but it's the treasure of Hades that's buried here."

"And Athena who's the grande dame over all of it," added Ridley.

"God," muttered Ivy. "Arms trafficking is less complicated."

Gabe pointed up at the ceiling of one of the arches.

"That looks like something."

Nas beamed the flashlight up.

Carved into the rock was the faint image of some kind of animal head. It was too far up to tell what. Ridley took out her phone, zoomed in, and snapped a photo of it. Nas peered over her shoulder to look—and gasped.

"Cerberus!"

It was a dog's head, faded from millennia, but clearly snarling and enraged under a pair of wolfish ears.

"Didn't Cerberus have three heads?" said Gabe.

Ridley stepped into the next chamber over. Sure enough, on that ceiling was a faint carving—a dog's head.

"Here. And let me guess," she said, pointing a finger-gun at the third chamber. "Head number three."

Nas rushed in and looked up.

"Okay! Yes!" she exclaimed.

Ivy squinted up at the carvings. "And what do you do with three pictures of dogs' heads?"

"Cerberus was the guardian of the underworld," said Nas, "so we have to *pass* him somehow."

Gabe faced the wall. "Would be nice if we had some sort of device to unlock all this."

He shot a look back at Ridley.

Damnit.

She dropped the backpack to the ground and pulled it open.

Inside, the *kibisis* was trembling.

What the hell is a bag supposed to do here?

With a grinding reluctance, she took it out.

Ivy's gaze lit on the shimmering gray fabric.

"Mary fuckin' Poppins," she said. "What is that?"

"It's a bag," said Ridley. "It's old and it's pretty weird and I think it's magnetized or something to react to this helmet."

That sounded great, Samaras. Believably dull.

"Do you like your women gullible?" said Ivy.

"Okay, it's not magnetized. We're not sure what it is, but it *is* old and weird."

She handed the *kibisis* to Nas, who stared down at it, perplexed.

"Can you lift it up to each carving?" she asked.

Gabe, the tallest by two inches, took the bag from Nas and held it up under one of the dog heads.

Nothing happened.

But then as he stepped across the sanctum to the next ceiling carving, the bag rippled with force. He stopped.

Stepped back into the middle. It was nearly tearing out of his hand.

"Put it down," Nas breathed.

Gabe set the *kibisis* down in the very center of the floor.

It was vibrating with such intensity that the edges of the bag started to blur.

"Oh, my God," murmured Ivy, "what—"

She lost her words when a blast of heat exploded from the *kibisis*. They stumbled back.

Ridley looked up at the ceiling, where the dogshead carvings were glowing red. "Okay..."

The Italians had appeared in the doorway alarmed, but Ivy ordered them out.

On the ground, the shimmering gray of the *kibisis* now rippled with molten light. The chamber suddenly felt like a dry sauna.

Gabe squinted against the heatwaves. "What the hell now?"

Something always opens somewhere—what are you missing?

“Would be a nice time for those rivers to show!” said Nas in frustration.

“You lot are gonna bake,” said Ivy, taking a step back.

Then a deafening *crack* rocked the chamber—and the stone split beneath their feet.

CHAPTER FORTY-FOUR

NAPOLI, ITALY

It was an earthquake within the chamber.

Ridley, Nas, Gabe, and Ivy stumbled and flattened themselves against the walls. The floor ripped open, and the *kibisis* vanished into it.

I hate when it's the floor. Couldn't it have been a wall this time?

It only lasted for two whole seconds. What remained at the end was a jagged chasm yawning before them, nearly three feet wide.

Ridley peered into it.

Below, stone stairs zig-zagged into the darkness.

"The next step is obvious," she said, looking up at the others with a smirk. "Flashlight?"

Gabe handed her one from the duffel. "Should've gotten glowsticks."

Ivy glanced at each of them in astonishment. "Who pays you for this?"

"My country 'tis of thee," murmured Ridley.

She stepped down into the crevasse.

With a few sweeps of the flashlight, she realized it was alarmingly deep. The walls were rough rock, nearly twenty feet wide. The air was musty and dank. She felt like a very tall hobbit descending into Moria.

Nas followed her down. "I think this was all volcanic rock!"

Ivy came behind her, speechless at the sight.

From his place bringing up the rear, Gabe's voice rang through the cavern. "Is this supposed to be the underworld?"

Ridley's beam hit on a long row of diverging troughs on the floor below. The end of each one snaked through the far wall.

"Rivers of the underworld..." Nas murmured.

"Dry rivers."

They reached the bottom of the stairs, nearly thirty feet from the surface chamber. Gabe pulled out his own flashlight.

Ridley spotted the *kibisis* where it had fallen. It had lost the molten shimmer. The gray fabric looked normal again. She picked it up—*cool to the touch*—stuffed it in her bag, and turned back to survey the cavern.

An iron bar arched over the spot where all the empty troughs began. Along it were five stone cubes the size of basketballs, pierced through by the metal. Ridley and Nas stepped up to them.

Each cube had five faces, and on each face was written a different word.

"Is that your Linear B?" asked Ridley, pointing to the written characters that were starting to look familiar.

"Yes, this is it!" said Nas, scanning down the row. "These are the names of the rivers of the underworld."

"Let 'em flow?"

Ivy interrupted. "What's that, then?"

She pointed to the far wall, where something was visible in the dim glow. Ridley and Gabe beamed their lights at it.

Above each of the troughs where they entered the wall was a section of mural. The work was richly colored, with dynamic figures of people and animals that looked almost like stylized cartoons.

It took a few seconds to realize what they were looking at.

"Underworld art," said Gabe.

"Bloody hell," muttered Ivy.

Literally.

The scenes showed agony, torment, sorrow, and anguish—pain and terror and punishment. Each panel seemed to contain its own variation on a theme.

Nas took them in. A shadow passed through her gaze.

It took Ridley a second to realize what that flitting darkness was.

Torture.

She sees her dad. Her older brother. Her friends. Her country.

"Okay," said Ridley to distract Nas' attention, stepping up to the iron bar with the row of stone cubes on it. "So these things must move—"

She gripped one of them top and bottom, and hauled.

It rotated with a faint grinding sound—but so did two of the other cubes.

Gabe laughed. "It's a Rubik's cube."

"Can we line them all up to match?" said Ridley, who pointed. "Turn that one."

He rotated one down the row—and one of the other cubes went with it.

Ivy stepped up and turned another. She was studying them intently as the multiple blocks moved again. Taking mental notes.

Ridley had almost forgotten that Ivy Simon was even more brilliant than she was bloodthirsty.

"Okay, bring it on, let's go," said Ridley, going to rotate another.

Nas' voice broke their focus. "I don't think it's supposed to match."

The other three looked at her. She took Gabe's flashlight from his hand and beamed it at the far wall again.

"These are all different," she said. "Each river is different. Each of the rivers has its own meaning. They're not just waterways."

Ridley squinted at the wall. "Can you tell them apart?"

"The river Styx is the one everybody knows about. The main river with the ferry to take you to the underworld. It was the river of hate. *That's* where Cerberus was."

She beamed the light at one of the panels. In it, the monstrous three-headed guard dog snarled over a young man who was cowering on a ferry barge.

"So that cube should say 'Styx,'" said Ridley, looking down at the corresponding trough that led into the wall under it.

"And that one—" said Nas, pointing the light at the next panel, "that's probably...Kokytos."

The painting showed several men and women on their knees, their posture nearly melting, their hands upraised.

"The river of lamentation."

"Okay," said Ridley, getting charged up. "Come read these for us, you wizardess. We've got a Rubik's cube to solve."

One by one, Nas studied the rest of the painted panels. She named them.

Lethe: the river of forgetfulness.

Acheron: the river of woe.

Phlegethon: the river of fire and punishment.

She searched for the right name on each cube. Then the four

of them began to rotate, remind, call out, switch, and argue as they tried to align the ever-shifting pieces.

Ivy synced right in like one of them, but she was clearly accustomed to being the boss. That did not quite take with the other three, though Nas still needlessly apologized to her several times.

The mafia queen was a whiz, though, directing them each on when and how many times to move their cubes. Like she was conducting a symphonic math equation.

"Do you practice with a Rubik's cube?" Gabe finally asked.

"Once you've got it down, it's just a kid's toy," she said.

He did as told.

And then Nas.

And then Ivy went.

"One turn," she said to Ridley.

Ridley was running blind. She couldn't keep up with Ivy's brain, but she could recognize when someone knew what they were doing.

She turned her cube once.

The action turned another cube twice.

There was a deep *thunk* beneath their feet. They all leapt back as if the floor might split open again.

Instead, stone gates at the head of each trough slid up, and a dam released itself. Water sloshed and raced down the channels.

Ridley whooped.

Somehow, getting this one felt different. Somehow, they needed to do what Jimmy had nearly died trying to accomplish.

Gabe had started to say, "Where's the thing—"

—when the painted wall began to crumble.

He pulled Nas back instinctively, but the cavern held fast. Only the far wall collapsed, as if in a controlled demolition, to reveal a small alcove behind it. Ridley aimed her flashlight at it.

There on a shelf of rock sat a helmet.

It looked like an ancient Corinthian helm without the mohawk plume. It was so black that it seemed to swallow even a straight beam of light.

Out of the corner of her eye, Ridley saw Ivy smile.

That's not good for us.

Ridley seized on the moment first, scampering her big frame over the flowing troughs. As she approached the alcove, she felt her backpack begin to shake, as if every item in it had come alive.

Ridley picked up the helmet with both hands.

It was sleek as a viper's hood, with almond-shaped eyes and a swooping slit for the mouth. Otherwise, it seemed as unremarkable as the sandals had been.

"You're not invisible," yelled Gabe.

"Thanks, captain," she called back.

She climbed back to the others.

"What's this about invisible?" said Ivy.

"It's just a joke about Greek myths," said Nas.

Ivy looked around at the cavern in all of its strangeness. "Oh, really?" Then she looked at Ridley. "Put it on then."

"I'm not gonna play with it like it's a toy," scoffed Ridley, handing it to Nas. "It's an ancient artifact that's gonna end up behind museum glass."

That was the wrong thing to have done.

Ivy looked at Nas, and her voice was alarmingly cold. "You put it on."

Nas tried to laugh it off, but Ivy had pulled the Beretta from her back before Ridley or Gabe had even considered needing a weapon.

You idiot let her make the first move—she's always *dangerous—*

Ivy kept it pointed low, but it was ready.

Nas knew the look and sound of someone who was full of

real violence. She slowly lifted the large helmet, slid it down over her wild mane of hair—

And vanished in front of their eyes.

Gabe's mouth fell open.

Ivy's gun hand sagged.

They heard the excited voice of Nas. "Am I invisible?"

"Yep," said Gabe.

"But *I* can see my own hands."

Ridley reached out for where she thought Nas' would be—and her hand clapped against a shoulder she couldn't see.

"Don't let anyone run into you," said Ridley.

Ivy stared at Ridley. "You knew about this?"

"No, I didn't *know*."

"It's *'worthless.'* You were fucking with us."

Ridley's world teemed with dangerous people. She was hard to scare and even harder to intimidate.

But there had always been something in Ivy Simon that chilled her. It was starting to glitter now, as if there was some basilisk in her gaze. Ridley had little doubt she would put a bullet in every one of them right there if she thought it would benefit her.

"Tell me what that thing really is," said Ivy, looking back at where Nas had last been standing.

The disembodied voice that answered her came from somewhere else. She had moved.

Clever girl.

"It really is the helmet of Hades," said Nas, "but he didn't make it. It was given to him by the Cyclopes when the gods of Olympus were going to war against the Titans. He let Athena borrow it during the Trojan War when she helped the Greeks."

Nas was moving around the cavern seemingly at random, her voice shifting and echoing around them. Ivy kept turning, trying to get a read on the invisible archaeologist's position.

"But it's most famous because Perseus wore it to slay Medusa."

Ridley watched the mafia queen who dealt in blood and coin try to process the meaning of that.

"Take that off, please," said Ivy, keeping her Beretta hovering low.

"*Nas,*" said Gabe, his voice hard with urgent concern.

Don't take it off, Nas...

Ivy heard his warning, too. She pointed the barrel of her gun at Gabe.

"This shouldn't be a difficult choice," she said. "Take it off."

"Don't!" yelled Nas.

It was just the attention-draw that Ridley needed. In one smooth flash, she pulled her own Glock and leveled it at Ivy.

"This shouldn't be a difficult choice," said Ridley.

A smile tugged at Ivy's lips. "I haven't been in a standoff in years! Imagine—I've survived every one."

"Because you're smart."

"Aren't I, though."

Gabe, unruffled by looking down the barrel of a Beretta, called to Nas again. "Don't take it off, Nas. Don't let her see you."

"Hey," said Ridley, "let's just all get out of this goddamn cavern, aright?"

The chime of a phone broke through the tension.

Ivy's.

Her gun never wavered as she pulled the phone from her pocket to answer.

They could just barely hear the voice on the other end. It was loud, urgent—panicked. Ivy's face went slack. Her eyes widened as she looked at Ridley, then Gabe.

"Sto vennèno."

She hung up.

"Something is happening in the lake," she said.

CHAPTER FORTY-FIVE

NAPOLI, ITALY

"In the lake?" came Nas' disembodied voice.

Ridley's gun still pointed at Ivy.

Ivy's gun still pointed at Gabe.

"We have to go!" said Nas.

She appeared suddenly at the bottom of the stairs, holding the black helmet in both hands. Her eyes were blazing.

"You know anything about *this*?" demanded Ivy.

"I don't know," said Nas. "I don't!"

Ivy looked at Ridley, who inclined her head to say, *Truce.*

They both let their guns dip.

Gabe moved immediately to block Ivy's path to Nas.

"Come on," called Nas as she nearly ran up the stone stairs.

Ridley gestured to Ivy. "You first."

"Chivalry?"

"So your boys don't shoot me."

They each holstered their weapons. Ivy went ahead of her.

Cesare and Gianluca rejoined them. Their boss explained nothing to them, but the urgency and possible danger that had sent their colleagues into a panic at the lake seemed enough.

Gabe took the helmet of Hades from Nas and stuffed it into the backpack that Ridley was wearing. It was so full that he could barely zipper it shut.

"All of the items are together," said Nas under her breath. "That's why the lake—it has to be."

"Wasn't it a volcanic crater?" said Gabe as they started back through the oracle's complex.

"And, or, the mouth of Hades?" said Ridley, clutching the straps of her pack.

"The stele said nothing about what would happen..."

Their hurry became a rush, became a jog and then a run. Gabe clutched the equipment duffel to his chest. Ivy and the Italians brought up the rear.

They were racing through the cavernous tunnels when Ivy's phone rang again. She picked it up.

This time they could hear only shouting. And then screams.

Ivy kept yelling into the phone, trying to get her guy to answer.

"Ivy," called Ridley over her shoulder, "what's happening?"

"I don't know—he said something came out of the lake!"

They ran.

It seemed an eternity. Ridley and Gabe began to outpace Nas, and had to slow back down for her. The Italian goons started to lag, their smokers' lungs huffing and puffing with the strain. Ivy snapped at them several times in Neapolitan to keep up.

They heard the commotion before they could even glimpse daylight.

Faint cries were punctuated by screams. Quiet—then another surge of distress.

Ridley pulled the Glock from her holster.

Gabe slowed just enough to pull the FN SCAR rifle from the duffel. He flipped open the barrel stock and sprinted with Ridley to the end of the tunnel, despite Nas' pleas for them to wait.

There was no clear line of sight from the mouth of the tunnel to the rest of the waterfront. The brush was too thick and high. But they could hear the fearful cries echoing toward them.

Ridley and Gabe swept out of the tunnel, weapons raised. The others followed closely. Ivy and her men had their own guns in hand.

They were nearing the edge of the brush when Gabe slid by a lumpen statue. Ridley glanced over at it—and her whole body tightened.

"Stop!"

It caught Gabe in his tracks.

She stared at the statue.

Nas followed her eyes, rounded the misshapen rock herself, and froze.

It was shaped like a man. He was dressed in modern clothes. He held a gun in his hand. He looked like Nic Cage.

And he was cowering away from something, terror petrified in his expression.

Nas looked at Ridley and Gabe, her face riven with fear.

Oh. Shit.

Ivy's voice was filled with alarm. "What is it? What's—"

She stepped around the statue to see what they were looking at. When she realized...her face contorted.

"What the fuck is happening here?" Her voice was more frantic than Ridley had ever heard it before.

"I think..." started Nas.

"He turned into a fucking statue?!"

Ridley looked at Nas, who met her eyes.

Then she said in a low voice, "Gorgons."

Ivy laughed, "Medusa, gorgons?"

"Medusa is dead," said Nas. "It's her sisters."

Gabe shook his head. The whole thing was wildly insane for him.

"And they do *this*—" Ivy gestured to the statue, "if they look at you?"

"If *you* look at *them*," said Nas.

Ivy gaped at her, but then said something to Cesare and Gianluca in Neapolitan.

Ridley looked at Gabe. "We gotta go."

Nas came up between them and said under her breath, "Whatever is happening out there, do not look directly at them. *Do not look at them.*"

Gabe started to move forward when Ridley exclaimed, "Pull out your phones! Use the cameras."

She grabbed hers from her own pocket. The others followed suit.

No way the 'turning-to-stone' thing works through a lens. No way. Probably.

She and Gabe led the way as they stepped out of the brush.

CHAPTER FORTY-SIX

NAPOLI, ITALY

THEY EMERGED ONLY thirty feet from the waterfront.

Cries echoed from across the lake as pedestrians scrambled madly. They were ducking around and hiding behind the human statues that now littered the path.

Ridley spotted movement in the corner of her camera screen. She swung the phone over, keeping it close to her face, desperately trying to not glance around it for the real sight.

The middle of the lake was roiling. Surging, gargling bubbles.

And above it, suspended thirty feet in the air, were two monsters.

Leathery wings—mottled green and gray—stretched across the sky. Spanning at least twenty feet, water dripped from them. Their legs were thick as trees, shapely as a woman's, dangling in the sunlight.

On their heads, snakes writhed and hissed.

Nas breathed something in Farsi.

Gabe stared at them through the phone camera, slack-jawed.

"Fucking *what?*" exclaimed Ridley.

"Oh, my God," cried Ivy.

Cesare and Gianluca burst into a stream of mixed English and Neapolitan curses.

Keep your eyes on the screen, Samaras. Do not look around it!

Gianluca couldn't help but glance up—and with a gargle of death, he froze.

Cesare bellowed as he watched his partner's skin turn ashen and then petrify. Gianluca's eyes went gray, then dulled, then became no more than rock.

"Don't look!" yelled Nas.

A hundred yards away, the monsters turned.

Ridley zoomed in on her phone to see one clearly.

Cold fear spilled through her gut. The face in closeup on her screen was the most hideous thing she had ever looked upon.

Its face looked semi-human, barely like a woman's. Fangs curled out of its mouth like tusks, and a forked tongue lolled down over green lips. Its skin was scaly—the color of rotting meat. Hands were the size of a suitcase, bristling with claws. Crocodile eyes blazed a bright blue.

But it was only because of its head that Ridley knew—*gorgons.* Its hair was a slithering nest of green vipers...darting, wriggling, snapping.

And this gorgon was looking directly into Ridley's camera.

She hit *RECORD.*

"What do they want?!" Gabe yelled to Nas.

"I don't know! Do they want the items?"

Ridley shucked off her backpack, but still held it in one hand almost possessively. She couldn't let go of it. Not after all they'd been through.

Not after Jimmy's sacrifice.

She frantically zoomed out to view both gorgons—in time to see the second one turn toward the camera.

The snakes writing on this one's head were black. The moment she saw this group of humans in the distance, her face contorted. Her lips snarled back from her fangs, and her orange crocodile eyes burned.

Ridley had never seen such hatred on a face.

The black-headed gorgon surged forward—

Gabe shot his arm out to pull Nas behind him.

Ivy and Cesare lunged back into the brush.

Ridley's stomach dropped—but she held out the bag, ready to throw it as a diversion—

When the green-headed gorgon *screamed.*

The sound felt like it was exploding inside their heads. The echo blasted across the lake, folding tourists down to their knees.

Ridley struggled to refocus the phone camera—

The black one had stopped, as if her sister's ear-splitting shriek was a command. Then the green one wailed again.

This time, it was not filled with fury, but anguish.

Nas murmured, "Medusa. I'm sorry."

Their sister was killed...and you're holding the murder weapon.

"Nas," said Ridley, not taking her eyes off her screen. "I'm gonna give you the helmet. Put it on."

She reached into the bag and pulled out the black helm of Hades.

When the gorgons saw it, rage rippled through their massive figures. Their wings beat the air—

Ridley shoved it at Nas. "*Put it on NOW* and drop flat to the ground!"

The gorgons surged forward.

Nas yanked the helmet down over her hair, and disappeared.

The creatures were coming straight for the shoreline.

No chance.

So Ridley hurled the backpack as far as she could.

The black-headed gorgon shot after it. The bag hit the water only a second before she did, diving like a peregrine falcon after its prey.

Gabe had no time to pull out the rifle. He and Ridley both drew their pistols in one fluid motion. They aimed at the green gorgon who hovered a hundred feet off.

"Hold..." said Gabe.

They still had to stare at their camera screens. It was making Ridley ache with paranoia that there might be something she couldn't see. She could feel every sinew in her forearm taut as piano wire as she gripped the gun.

And then the black one burst out of the water with a violent cry.

Ridley jolted the phone down to see the monster rising, dripping, howling—and unleashed a hail of bullets at it.

"Shit!" yelled Gabe, but then he had to do the same.

He unleashed a barrage at the green-headed gorgon.

It was a bad idea.

She screeched, and plunged toward them.

Ridley heard Nas scream somewhere behind them. The shrieking of the gorgon, the flap of leathery wings filled their ears as the massive creature blotted out the sun—

—and crashed down onto them.

Both Ridley and Gabe stumbled, flailing to keep their phones held tightly in front of their eyes—

But the gorgon smashed Gabe to the ground. His phone went skittering into the brush. He could only clamp his eyes shut and curl up in defense.

The monster had him.

The sound of its screams nearly split Ridley's skull. She scrambled backward, desperately clutching the phone in front of her face.

"Keep your eyes shut!" she yelled. "Keep your eyes shut!"

The black-headed gorgon rose above the shoreline, snarling as she looked on—

—as her sister snatched up Gabe in her clawed hands, and launched herself into the sky.

CHAPTER FORTY-SEVEN

NAPOLI, ITALY

THE AIR VANISHED from Ridley's lungs.

From nearby in the brush, Nas cried out. She appeared suddenly, holding the black helmet in both hands. She had dropped her phone and could not look up.

"Where are they going?!"

Ridley watched on her screen as the two enormous creatures vanished into the distance with Gabe.

She lowered the phone. Hit *stop* on her video recording.

It was all lost. Everything but the helmet of Hades, gone with Gabe.

Nas came alongside her. Stricken.

"Why did they take him..."

Ridley could say nothing. She stared at the sky, at the lake, at the waterfront in the distance.

Why? What are you gonna do now?

Kerik. Jimmy. Gabe.

And you have nothing but a stupid helmet.

"Why did they take him?" Ridley echoed back to Nas.

Nas put a hand on her arm. "We need to leave here."

Don't stand so long at the mouth of Hades.

Ridley picked up the equipment bag that Gabe had dropped. They hurried along the waterfront to the parking lot.

Both moved in a daze as they passed statue after statue. Women and children and men, frozen forever in stone terror.

Ivy's car was gone.

They trudged to the road to hail a car, trying to keep their eyes down in case the beasts appeared above. Finally a truck driver took pity and welcomed them aboard.

It was a long and terrible ride back to the city.

The CIA had safehouses in nearly every major city in the world.

All Ridley ever needed to do was dial a specific number, give her code name, and receive a call back with an address.

She preferred to memorize the addresses ahead of time, before any hour of need.

The safehouse in Napoli was a small apartment on a narrow street not far from the port. There was no one there when Ridley and Nas arrived, so she punched in the long code for the front door. She took the small signal magnet from the front hall table and snapped it onto the outside handle.

Officer inside seeking shelter.

They settled into the creaky third story guest space. They wouldn't see anyone for the rest of the night.

Nas seemed spent. Senses and emotions blasted, she said little. When she did, they were often half-thoughts that trailed off. She wanted to take a shower but realized she had no fresh clothes. Everything they had, they'd left in Ivy Simon's vehicles.

Ridley took a seat on the edge of the bed.

It was time to call her boss. She held her phone in dread hesitation.

If he knew she had lost it all, would he pull her from the assignment? Abort the mission altogether?

If she told him that Gabe had been snatched away by a monster from the underworld, the State Department would smash the whole thing up. They'd deploy an entire Special Operations team to storm the castle.

What castle...

So she decided—she would not call Booker. Not yet.

He doesn't know more than you about what's going on. Step up and figure it out, Samaras. This is what you do. This is what you're damn good at.

Nas emerged from the bathroom, drying her face. She collapsed into an armchair.

"I'm not an expert in Greek mythology," she said. "I'm just an archaeologist. I liked the myths, but I *loved* the history. I spent my life studying it, searching for it so I could *touch* it under my fingertips. I didn't see any of this coming."

"It isn't your fault."

Her eyes became glassy and her hand went to her mouth.

"Do you think he's alive?"

"Yeah," said Ridley, battling herself to believe it. "I don't know, but I think."

Nas nodded. She gazed out the window.

"My father will be tortured if I don't return to Iran."

Ridley sat up. "You can't go back."

She gave a bitter laugh. "They wouldn't stop torturing him if I showed up at the Ayatollah's doorstep. They would just torture us both."

"But...they didn't torture your siblings...very much, right?"

"My brothers and sister did not leave Iran. They weren't dissidents. They didn't condemn the rulers of the regime or fight for the oppressed. It's people like my father who have to be made into an example because *he did the right thing.* He was brave and he loves his country."

Ridley remembered the plane ride to Morocco sitting next to Jimmy. How that father had radiated pride.

She didn't even know what her own father thought of her cover story "job," being an interpreter for an American diplomat.

What would he think if he knew what I've really done? Would he *be proud?*

But she knew that she'd never hear from her father what Jimmy had said about his own daughter.

"He thought you were the bravest person he ever knew," said Ridley. "He said you had the lion of Persia in you. Like your mom."

Nas looked up at her in surprise. Tears slipped suddenly from her eyes.

"You know when I came to America," she said, "the most beautiful sound in the world was *everywhere*—women *singing.* You can hear it everywhere! You can hear Kelly Clarkson every day. In Iran, we could not hear Googoosh any day.

"One day I got on the subway in New York City and I sat down next to a man. I almost froze because I had never in my life been just *sitting* next to a man in public.

"But you know...I walked into a stadium—into the United Center to see the Chicago Bulls play. And I was allowed to be there and there were women everywhere around me and then the anthem of the United States of America began to play...and I cried. I cried. You don't know how beautiful that moment was unless you had seen an oppressive Islamic theocracy."

She wiped at her cheeks.

"Maybe I am in danger, but I'm *free.* The women still in my home country are really the heroes. They stand in public with all their bravery to say to the ayatollahs, 'We're here, unveiled. Where are *you?*' I cannot be braver than that."

This woman had rendered Ridley mute more times than she could count. She didn't know what to say to it all. She never knew what to say to Nas.

This will not be for nothing. You didn't lose Jimmy to torture for nothing. Kerik didn't die for nothing. Gabe wasn't ripped away by monsters for nothing. You won't let this happen.

"We're going to get this one back," she said. "We have to find out where those creatures were going and then...we'll know *something.*"

Nas leaned forward onto her knees and shook her great mane of hair. "I don't know. I don't know. I'm not an expert. I have no idea what they were doing waiting there!"

"We *find* an expert."

She laughed. "What shall we tell them?"

"Don't worry," said Ridley. "I'm good at the lying part."

"Oh!" said Nas, straightening up. "I know who. You're gonna have to be a *very* good liar."

CHAPTER FORTY-EIGHT

NAPOLI, ITALY

Yannis Kimoulis would not fly the nine-and-a-half hours from Serifos to Napoli.

The Senior Archaeologist at Greece's Ephorate of Antiquities within the Hellenic Ministry of Culture and Sports had far more important demands on his time, like overseeing the dig site on Serifos where Nas and Jimmy had discovered King Polydectes' palace.

But he would do a video conference.

Ridley and Nas split a Neapolitan pizza—delivered and left at the door—while they waited for his call that evening.

As she finished a slice and wiped her fingers, Ridley scrolled through local news stories.

There were accounts of a terrible outbreak at Lake Avernus.

The only living witnesses to it had no explanation for seeing the people around them suddenly freeze and turn to stone. Almost all of the survivors had been inside at the time. They'd heard screams and seen running, though the mayhem quickly turned to silence as one person after another petrified.

Every imaginable theory played out in the commentary.

Outbreak of a skin disease...the curse of Lot's wife in the Bible...a bioweapon being tested on civilians...an alien landing...

Of course, it had not escaped the all-seeing eyes of the agency.

It had not escaped the specialists at Osprey.

Ridley's phone had rung an hour ago. *Booker.*

She had not picked it up. Instead, she sent an encrypted message back.

Give me two hours

He would have been furious to find out from the news. Then worried that her silence meant she was dead, and then furious again to hear she was not.

Had better be good

Ridley had winced at the phone.

I have a good excuse because it was a terrible thing that happened.

She just needed something else—a lead, an opinion, a next destination—*something* before she debriefed him.

She was putting the weight of the world on Yannis Kimoulis, and he had no idea what he was about to get pulled into.

By the time the senior archaeologist appeared on the screen of Nas' phone, she and Ridley had agreed on their story.

"Nasrin," said Yannis, looking like something between Tarzan and a pirate on the cover of a romance novel. "You miss the dig already?"

"My father and I both," she said.

There would be no mention of where Jimmy really was. Unless Yannis was scanning Iranian news outlets, he likely wouldn't know the truth.

"Your Greek friend is there?" he asked.

Nas swiveled the phone to Ridley, who raised a hand and smiled.

IN GREEK: *"Thank you for helping us! She said you were the only one to talk to."*

Yannis tried to play down his grin.

Get those men right *in the ego...*

"She's a very good archaeologist herself, so she must know," he said. "What do you need from me now?"

Nas faced the phone.

"Yannis, you love the myths, right? Not just the history and the archaeology."

"Yes. Of course. You can't know an ancient culture if you don't know the stories they told each other, about themselves, the whole universe."

"I know, I know I need to study them more. Just following this strange trail, I've learned I need to. But I'm trying to...*piece together* a story right now and I don't have the answers or the ending."

He took a sip of his coffee, still only half-invested. "Okay, tell me."

Nas drew a breath. "This is a tale about the gorgons, as you know from when we found the stele. The other sisters though—what happened to them after Medusa was killed? Are there any more stories?"

"No. No stories. When Perseus killed Medusa, they chased him, screaming in a rage. That was the last mention of them in any of the writings. One was more angry, though, and one was more grieving."

"Which was which?" asked Ridley.

Yannis seemed surprised by her question. "Stheno was violence and rage. The most fierce of all the sisters."

The black-headed one.

"Euryale screamed in grief. A terrifying sound."

The green one.

"What would they want?" asked Nas. "If Perseus was dead, what would they want? They must be angry...would be angry."

Yannis laughed. "What kind of puzzle is this?"

"I just want to think through everything. It's fun."

"Eh...well, I guess they would be angry at the gods who gave weapons to Perseus."

Of course. Damn.

"Athena, Hermes, Hades and Hera," said Nas.

"Yeah. Hermes gave him two pieces, so maybe they would be more angry with him."

Ridley glanced at Nas, who was chewing over the possibilities. It didn't seem to fit for her. Also, the realm of *Hades* was where the gorgons had been hiding for how many thousands of years...

"But," said Nas, her voice lifting, "it was Athena who turned them into monsters to start. Athena who took Medusa's head and put it on the front of her shield to carry into battle. Oh, my God, they would be so angry at her."

He nodded, still bewildered as to what they were really even talking about.

"Yeah. Sure. They would be furious. So what, though? They're just immortal monsters. She's a goddess. Doesn't matter how angry—they wouldn't be able to do anything to her."

"Even if they had the weapons of Perseus," said Ridley.

Yannis laughed. "Yeah, obviously. Goddess."

It wasn't a question, asshole.

"Okay," said Nas, "so if they were trying to go after Athena and they had nothing to lose—obviously they're immortal but she can do other terrible things to them like eternal torment—what would they do..."

"Run to their monster mommy and daddy."

Gods of the sea.

"Not more powerful than Athena," said Nas. "That wouldn't work."

"Power in numbers," said Yannis.

She shook her head, her expression scrunched in thought. Then something lit on her face. "No—power in *power.*"

He was starting to get annoyed at the way she was resisting his ideas.

"There isn't a 'right answer,'" he said. "What are you trying to find out?"

Nas scooted up closer to the phone, practically vibrating with excitement.

"No, it can't just be other gods!" she said. "It has to be the only thing that ever defeated the gods!"

And then Yannis' annoyance melted away as he realized—

"Typhon," he said.

"The monster," said Ridley, recalling Jimmy and Nas telling her the story of the gods' war with the Titans. "The big bad."

"The biggest baddest," said Nas. "The last son of the earth mother, Gaia, who she created just to destroy the gods after the other Titans—all her other children—had been defeated."

"And he scared the shit out of everyone."

"Yes! And it worked—kind of. He invaded Mount Olympus and drove them all out. The gods scattered. Only Athena, and then Hermes, returned to help Zeus beat him."

Yannis gave a bemused wobble of his head. "So *now* you know mythology?"

Ridley ignored his snark. "Didn't you say he was thrown into Tartarus, under Mount Etna? How—in actual hell—would they get him out?"

Nas raised her hands in a frozen shrug.

"I don't know but doesn't it make sense?" she said. "They

want revenge on Athena. There's only one thing she was ever afraid of, that made her run away from her home, that almost destroyed all the gods."

"What does Jimmy think?" asked Yannis.

Nas stiffened but didn't lose a beat. "I'll tell him all of it when he gets back with our pastries."

"Now you have the 'right answer' to a metaphorical myth *hypothetical*—you feel better?"

"I feel better."

"Good. Now when are you coming back to Serifos? Unless you want me to give up the dig to somebody else. I know my second choice—"

"No, Yannis! Give me a few more days. I need to follow one more puzzle. Please. I can't let go of this part of our discovery. I have to complete the trail."

He waved a dismissive hand, irked but acquiescing.

"Tell me by the end of the week, Nasrin. I need a real time."

"I will. Promise. And Yannis, thank you."

They bid goodbye and hung up.

Nas stared across the room at the Helm of Darkness, at the black that seemed to eat light.

"It has to be that," she said. "I'm right. Athena. Typhon. The sisters want revenge and there's only one being who can help them get it."

And there Ridley had it. Something to tell Booker.

Gods and monsters and a mountain full of lava.

Nas turned to Ridley. "I think I know why they took Gabe."

CHAPTER FORTY-NINE

PALERMO, SICILY

It was only a one-hour plane ride from Napoli to Palermo.

Ridley had to leave her Glock and the FN SCAR behind at the safe house. Airlines didn't love them.

She and Nas stepped out of the small airport into a rolling heatwave.

"Do you know who—" started Nas, but cut herself off when she saw a man pop out of the passenger side of a gray SUV.

He was a full seven inches shorter than Ridley, with a baby face and a clean cut that looked like something between a faux hawk and a pompadour. His suit was tailored, open at the collar, and he brimmed with affable confidence.

"I'm Bass," he said, touching his chest. "Welcome to Sicily. I'll be your host. Could I grab your bag?"

Ridley carried a small duffel with the Helm of Darkness in it.

"No, thanks," she said. "Could you tell us what we should see while we're here?"

"The spotted mongoose."

Code phrases I love.

"You good?" he asked.

"Let's go."

"Would you guys like to get some...clothes, anything? Before we head to the house?"

"After, please," said Nas.

"Okay," Bass grinned, opening the back door for her. "Let's go. Driver's name is Hank!"

Neither Ridley nor Nas was up for much conversation, and thankfully their host could read the room.

Ridley's brain felt like a heaving tsunami, and her conversation with Booker the night before had only added to the violent volume.

She had been pacing the hardwood floor of the hallway, back and forth across the doorway to the bedroom where Nas was watching the news.

Ridley had sent him the video first. There was nothing else that could adequately explain what had happened that day at the lake.

Booker watched the footage. Then he called.

Her boss was rarely at a loss for words. He'd seen more unexplainable beings, visions, and horrors than she could even imagine. But this one, he stumbled over.

"Okay," he started. "So this is what happened in Naples... how there got to be statues of *people*."

"Yeah."

"I can't—that was incredibly quick-thinking to use your phone, Rid."

"We got away with it."

Barely. You could have been stone. Dead. A stupid statue forever.

"I have to tell State," said Booker, his voice filled with apprehension.

"You're not gonna show Rhodes the video—"

"I'm the shield, Ridley. No one else alive has done what I've done to protect Osprey. You do your job. You better trust me to do mine."

"Yes, sir."

It was only stress, she told herself, that had her questioning Booker Douglas. He had never hung his operatives out to dry, even when called on the carpet by the Director of the FBI himself.

"I know how to complicate things long enough to buy some time," he said, "but a missing and probably dead State agent abroad is bad news that I can't cover up, and neither can you."

"Yeah, I understand. This clock ticks."

As she paced past the doorway, Ridley glanced in to see Nas pressing a hand against her mouth, watching a news anchor drone on.

"What now?" asked Booker.

"Sicily. We think we know...it's all a long shot, but we think these beasties are taking Gabe there, and yeah, we think he may actually still be alive."

As long as he didn't open his eyes...

"What do you need?"

"I'm not sure. You know I'll tell you when I do. We're gonna go see about a volcanologist tomorrow."

"Oh, my God," he muttered. "Why—"

"It's just a precaution," she lied. "When in Sicily."

"Are you running with gear?"

Weapons.

"I'll send you my Christmas list," said Ridley.

"I'll send you an escort. Not the kind you'd ask for for Christmas."

"I was gonna ask, 'man or woman?'"

"And I *don't* ask."

Things had loosened. It felt better.

"We still have the Helm of Darkness," said Ridley. "Nas was wearing it when the gorgons started their attack. It's the only piece they don't have."

"Think that makes a difference? The whole set?"

Ridley stepped around a creaking spot in the floorboards.

"We really like the theory. Really suits us right now," she said.

"But you still don't know who actually did the hiding of all these items."

"No."

It bothered her. It had been bothering her the whole way, but there was nothing to do about it now. They hadn't found a single clue as to who had set them off on this treasure hunt.

If it doesn't matter to save Gabe, then don't think about it now. You'll think about that later.

"Well, send me your list," said Booker. "Check in tomorrow. I'll tell you as soon as I've crossed paths with State."

"Yeah, I will."

"Go to bed, Rid. Sleep is a superpower."

"Yep, check in tomorrow."

They hung up just as Ridley stepped back into the bedroom—

And stopped short.

On the TV was a video feed of Mount Etna. The chyron at the bottom of the screen read, *"SEISMIC ACTIVITY AT MT. ETNA."*

Nas murmured something in Farsi. Ridley raked a hand through her long thick hair.

And neither slept well before their short plane ride out of Napoli.

By the time they arrived at the safehouse the next day with

Bass and Hank, Ridley was feeling those zombie vibrations—the state of being sleep-deprived but somehow also wired at high voltage. Time felt like a tightening coil, and she couldn't let up now for even a moment.

Mount Etna wouldn't wait for them.

CHAPTER FIFTY

CATANIA, SICILY

The University of Catania was the best place in the world for a young volcanologist, and Lucilla Marchio never let her students forget it.

This morning, she walked the few blocks from her apartment to the school square. Despite the sun being set to "bake," she stopped for a hot cappuccino, sipping it on the way like it was both fuel and the nectar of the gods.

By the time she reached the enormous square and saw the bone-white building in all its Baroque glory, she was ready to talk about the thing she loved most in the world.

The headquarters of INGV, the National Institute of Geophysics and Volcanology, were in Rome, but Lucilla worked mostly in Sicily, heading up their department in Catania and lecturing often at the university.

She never tired of seeing a student's eyes light up the first time they hiked up to a crater, or watched an eruption right in front of them, or witnessed a cloud of dark ash billowing up into the sky.

From the dead legacy of Vesuvius to the volatile grumblings of Stromboli and Etna, from the dormant Vulcano to the underwater clusters, Sicily was unmatched. It was where the science came surging to life.

Lucilla had loved these terrible, awesome phenomena since she was a child, and had watched from her schoolyard as Mount Etna spewed lava in the distant darkness. All her life, she would never forget how it glowed in the night.

From that moment, there was only one profession for her.

The young Sicilian practically drowned herself in studies at university. Geology and biology and physics, geochemistry and geophysics and mathematics. As she earned a PhD, she added statistics, computer science, and remote sensing.

Her renown grew as it became clear that the brightest young mind in the field was also the hardest-working. By the time she was thirty years old, she was regarded as one of the leading experts in the entire world of volcanology.

She'd earned it, both in the lab and in the field. She had been to every great volcano in the world, dormant and active, some of them multiple times over. She'd stood in places that looked like the mouth of hell, sweated through Indonesian jungles, climbed to desolate Hawaiian mountains, and taken rickety boats to remote islands.

Today, she was going back to the one that had first enchanted her.

Lucilla had just emerged into the palm-shaded courtyard when she heard someone call her name.

"Lucilla Marchio?"

She turned to see a woman pushing off the stone rail by the stairs.

In another lifetime, this stranger could have been a

Mediterranean gladiatrix. She wore a faded blue V-neck, gray canvas pants despite the heat, and had braided her dark hair back in a way that seemed more practical than fashionable. She wasn't quite young enough to be a student, though.

"Yes?"

The woman approached Lucilla and offered her hand with a modest smile.

"I'm Ridley."

No, this volcanology professor didn't have a few minutes to talk.

Would she have a few minutes if the American government needed her expertise?

Well, that was different.

Ridley saw her straighten just a touch, puffed up by the notion that the United States needed her expertise for anything. The woman glanced at her watch.

"I have a class in one hour," she said. "We can talk in my office."

Ridley beckoned to someone behind her. From under a palm tree emerged a lion-haired woman with enormous brown eyes.

"This is my associate, Nasrin. We'll take any time you're willing to give us."

Minutes later, Lucilla sat at the desk in her small office, where the ceiling paint was cracking and folders were stacked high on almost every surface.

Across from her, Nas was leaning forward on one crossed leg, anxious to learn whatever she could. Ridley sat like a pharaoh on a throne, her long arms draped along the wooden arms of the chair.

"I heard that you are the world's expert on Mount Etna," she said.

"Yes, I am."

Lucilla Marchio could have passed for Prime Minister Georgia Meloni's older sister, with her blonde hair and eerily intense blue eyes. She lacked nothing in self-esteem, either.

"Someone has to be," the Italian woman went on, "and I worked hard to become that."

"No argument—"

"But what does the American government care about that? It isn't unusual that Etna erupts. It rarely hurts anyone."

Ridley ignored her question. "It's been rumbling for a day now?"

"Earthquake swarms started yesterday."

"That means it *will* erupt?"

"Sooner or later."

Nas spoke up, "Will you be able to tell, when it's about to happen?"

She laughed. "Not yet, but gradually it gets closer and we can see a window."

"Could you tell—"

"Have you felt the earthquake swarms?"

They shook their heads.

"You will. We measure harmonic tremors."

Ridley leaned forward. "What—"

"Sensors pick up the vibration from the movement of magma. The ground also shifts and we measure that. Gas emissions change as it all rises to the surface. We have more instruments on Etna than almost any other volcano in the world. I know this volcano's *heartbeat.*"

Ridley smiled. "Well that's why we're here in *your* office. What's the worst explosion ever on Mount Etna?"

"Eruption," she said with a mildly annoyed look. "It erupted in March 1669, and lava flowed down into the towns until July. Nobody died—*miracolo*—but people had to run from their homes. Many thought it was a punishment from God, but really it was a flank eruption."

"It erupted through the side of the mountain?"

"Those are the *most* destructive. Like your Mount St. Helen's in America. It was one of the worst ever in history. All of that force—" she gestured with her hands, "going *straight out* at the land instead of up toward the sky. Obviously, too, they happen at lower altitude, closer to a population."

"Is that the only time it went sideways?" asked Nas.

"No," said Lucilla. "It happens all the time with fissures that open on the sides, but not usually very bad. In 1928, a whole town was destroyed. Nobody died, but we have film of it, old black-and-white. 2001 and 2002 had eruptions that damaged a lot. That's when we started to put up new barriers for tourists around the worst areas, but people have gotten much stupider since they all have cameras on their helmets now."

She rolled her eyes.

"Have you ever been up at the top when the volcano is almost erupting?" asked Ridley.

"No," she said with a frown, "not when it is *almost erupting*, but volcanologists are often out in the field. We hike to the craters. We take measurements in person and see these things with our own eyes, but only a fool would stand at the crater when it's about to erupt."

"Do you consult on evacuation plans for the nearby populations?"

Lucilla glanced at the clock.

"What is this about? Is this some American secret operation on a volcano? Are you James Bond and there's a secret villain lair in the crater?" she laughed.

Ridley gave her a light smile, shaking her head as if she realized how absurd it all sounded.

"That would be fun—"

—because in a movie it would be guaranteed that James Bond would win and save the day—

"But I think the Brits would want to take that one."

"So, what then?" asked Lucilla.

Ridley hesitated. The balance of a lie was so delicate.

Bring her into the importance, make her think she's essential in a dire, confidential situation. Never tell the full truth.

"Look, I can't tell you everything, but I'm going to tell you this in trust—we're concerned about a hostage situation that may be developing...on the volcano."

Lucilla's face went slack. She looked at Nas and then back to Ridley.

"Where? At the crater?"

Ridley nodded.

"Why would anyone...?!"

"These are things I can't share, but you can imagine now, why I need to know everything that's about to happen on that mountain."

Something flooded the woman's gaze. A mesmerized horror.

"It's going to be terrible."

CHAPTER FIFTY-ONE

CATANIA, SICILY

Lucilla Marchio left the office for her lecture.

Ridley and Nas stepped back out into the blaze of morning heat. They'd be back in touch with her in a few hours.

It was all just beginning.

"Gabe won't survive up there," said Nas, wrapping her arms around her chest.

No, he won't.

"That's why I'm going to get him," said Ridley.

Her eyes roamed the dozens of students hurrying through the courtyard to make it to their classes. Anyone who passed close to Nas got a full scan.

This woman lived in the valley of the shadow of death. Ridley knew extreme danger, knew about seeing the whites of death's eyes, but she couldn't imagine an entire life without a true moment of relief.

The lioness...

They made their way back to the gray SUV, where they found Hank bopping along to a K-pop song. When he offered to turn it off, Ridley laughed.

"No. Teach us the lyrics."

He knew seven of them, and for a few minutes, they were an entertaining distraction.

When they arrived back at the safehouse, Ridley punched in the code to the front door. She swung it open for Nas to step in first.

But Nas stopped so abruptly that Ridley bumped into her. She was looking at the parlor room.

Ridley's hand seized toward the gun at her back as she pushed in front of the other woman to spot what she was looking at.

Perched on the edge of the sofa, playing with a deck of cards, was the Division Chief of Overseas Operations for the State Department, Joe Lasch.

He glanced up.

"Cool it, Jason Bourne."

Lasch nodded at the hand behind her back. She relaxed, but just barely. It was not good news to see him again.

"Chief Lasch. What are you doing here?"

His laugh was harsh. "Oh, you hadn't heard? An agent of mine is missing. You two were the last to see him. You shouldn't actually be surprised to see me."

Well, he's pissed.

Ridley glanced around for Bass.

"Who let you in?"

"You didn't know?"

As if on cue, the sound of heavy footsteps in the kitchen drew closer. Ridley tensed again—

The broad frame of Booker Douglas appeared in the doorway. He was wiping his hands on a small towel.

If he didn't tell me he was coming...this cannot be a good development.

She still felt relief that her own boss was there. Whatever Lasch wanted to get from her, at least she'd have someone to back her up.

Surely.

"Ridley," Booker's voice boomed. "Dr. Aslani."

"Sir," said Ridley.

Nas nodded at him. "Hi again, Director Booker."

"Let's all talk in the kitchen," he said, nodding to Lasch.

The CIA man got up and followed them into the bright tiled kitchen.

Booker preferred to have conversations while in motion, but if he couldn't get that, then at least he wanted to stand. He felt that giving people the space to move helped with difficult or uncomfortable exchanges.

Lasch leaned his weight forward on the wood-block island. Booker folded his thick arms across his chest. Ridley leaned back against the edge of a counter as Nas took up the space next to her.

"Director Douglas here," said Lasch, "told me that Gabe Tolkin was kidnapped in Naples."

Ridley gave a tight nod.

"By who?"

"We believe they're individuals who are interested in the same items that the Aslanis have been tracking down."

"Right." Lasch glanced at Booker. "You're the goddamn CIA and that's all the information you have?"

"They're not affiliated with any organized crime that we know of. They're not interested in a ransom. We believe...that they want him alive and they want to perform some kind of bizarre ritual involving him." She looked Lasch straight in the eye. "And that's what we're doing here."

She couldn't tell him. He would never believe it, and then he would laugh them out of the room. Then probably sound the alarm on Booker's mental health.

Lasch glared at Booker. "This is it? I have the goddamn clearance, Douglas. If you've ordered your ops to keep this from me, you'll have a subpoena in your hand tomorrow and a dozen senators calling for your ass in that chair."

Booker's expression turned dark. "You know nothing about the level of clearance involved here. You won't have my people on any political chopping block to satisfy your own interests. We're conducting a rescue operation for *your* agent right now, who *you* sanctioned to continue on this mission."

Ridley couldn't remember having seen him this angry.

"You won't run this," he said to Lasch. "You won't interfere. You'll listen to the intelligence being brought by an operative who knows what the hell she's talkin' about."

Lasch seemed caught out by the force of his words, as if James Earl Jones had just scolded him.

"I'm here for exactly that," said Lasch in a low, cutting voice. "I need her intelligence."

Booker placed his hands flat on the island counter.

"*You're* on a need-to-know level. And you don't need to know."

What the hell got into this *Booker?*

Nas looked between the men, watching the power play burning in front of her. Ridley leaned forward.

"Director Lasch. I need your help."

"What?" he said.

"This ritual thing...it's gonna be on Mount Etna."

"The volcano that's about to erupt."

"Yeah. So I need to get up there before it does, and I need the Italian government to let me, because I need the support of the National Institute of Volcanology."

Lasch stared at her, then at Booker.

"What the *hell* is it that you guys do?"

"Today, we save your agent," said Ridley. "From a volcano."

The director scoffed and shook his head. "Some goddamn chutzpah, Douglas."

"We work in the shadows, Lasch," said Booker. "You're the American State Department. You go ahead and ask in broad daylight."

Lasch's expression tightened. "If I pull this, you'll be giving me a full debrief or I *will* have your ass sat in front of Congress. Both of you."

Ridley reached out and offered her hand. He was surprised by the gesture, but shook it.

She could feel Booker glowering at her. She knew it wasn't her deal to make, but she'd worry about that later.

A fucking volcano is about to erupt.

And she'd never had to stop a volcano before.

CHAPTER FIFTY-TWO

CATANIA, SICILY

There would be no State Department business with the local authorities of Catania without the permission of the national government.

For Booker and Ridley, such politics were sometimes necessary, but always a drag. They were a clandestine unit of an espionage agency. It was painful for them to show their work to outsiders.

For the Division Chief of Overseas Operations, it was the water he swam in. Coordinating with friendly local authorities whenever possible was the grease he carried at all times, ready for any wheels he needed to roll smoothly.

Behind closed doors, Joe Lasch was direct and demanding.

In politics, he was collaborative and cooperative, always persuading the other party to his aims.

So it was when he spoke with the Undersecretary to the Prime Minister.

Ridley could practically see the Italian on the other end of the phone gesturing wildly as he spoke to his American counterpart.

What did the United States government have, to make them care about Italian volcanoes?

What are you trying to do?

What are you asking for?

What is that agent doing on the mountain?

Lasch walked him through the most basic redacted version. They needed to recover an agent who was thought to be in peril on Mount Etna. They needed the assistance of their National Institute of Volcanology.

It was one of the weirder requests he'd ever gotten.

The Italian Undersecretary had laughed. "Go on! But don't let any of your Americans die on our mountain."

It was a lot easier to get permission than any of them had been expecting.

When Lasch hung up with the Undersecretary, he looked across the safehouse kitchen to Booker and Ridley.

"Whatever you need to do, move now."

It was midday when Ridley, carrying a bulky backpack, reached the Etna observatory office of the INGV with Nas and Booker and Lasch.

The building looked like a grand villa, laden with thick ivy and ringed by giant palms. It was big enough to house a hundred and fifty employees, all keeping watch over the deadliest rumblings of the earth.

Lucilla Marchio met them at the entrance. She seemed especially impressed to meet a division chief of the CIA, as though it was her who personally warranted his presence.

There was an excited agitation in her eyes, though. It didn't take long to find out why.

"The activity level has been increasing so quickly...I've never seen it accelerate this fast," she said, leading them down the hallway, past bright cluttered offices and conference rooms lined with books. "And we monitor her every breath. Every day, every minute."

"Do you have a time estimate yet for eruption?" asked Ridley.

"It doesn't *work* like that. I can't give you a time. We know the progress—the rate—and maybe can say a percentage chance for a *window* of time, but we need data over time."

She stopped at a wall of tinted glass.

"We evacuated tourists at noon. We're watching for airspace, if we need to shut that down. If you're really so much determined to get to the craters, you don't have a lot of time," she said.

Lucilla rounded the glass door into the operations room.

Two technicians sat behind computers, at adjacent desks that faced an entire wall of screens. It was a tower of monitors, live video feeds, maps, and satellite imaging.

The techs looked up to greet Lucilla, who introduced her guests in English.

Nas was "an archaeologist."

Ridley and Booker were "from an American agency."

Smart, discreet woman.

"Here we work twenty-four hours a day," said Lucilla. "Here we can see all the data in live time, from across our whole network, over two hundred stations. It covers a huge area in this region of the world. But now—"

She pointed to a number of the monitors that were squiggling above baseline.

"Now we are watching Etna."

"Tell me what I need to know to get up there," said Ridley.

Out of the corner of her eye, she could see the two technicians exchange a glance.

Lucilla shook her head, still in disbelief.

"Which crater are you thinking of?" she asked.

More than one crater?

Unlike most of her preparation work studying city maps whenever she traveled, Ridley hadn't thought of a volcano as requiring a map...mostly just "go up."

Lucilla raised five fingers. She walked up to one of the screens and pointed.

"Right now, pressure in the Southeast crater is building. Its structure is weak and could collapse at any moment. That and Bocca Nuova—"

New Mouth—

"They sit above the favorite pathway of the magma, so they *wake up* first."

Ridley stepped closer to see the screen. On a thermal camera, she could see a bright glow near the edge of a crater.

"The rock is starting to heat up in the central crater, by Bocca Nuova and Voragine," said Lucilla, "but when Voragine wakes up...then we get very nervous."

Voragine.

The Abyss.

A sudden cold rippled through Ridley. That had to be the place.

"*That* crater will erupt?" she asked.

The volcanologist shrugged, but her shoulders were tight.

"It's not the most common, but it's a deep collapse crater. When it erupts, it's very violent. We don't like to see it."

How the hell am I gonna be able to tell one from the other when I'm up there?

"Okay," said Ridley, nodding. "That one does lava geysers then?"

"Yes, but—" Lucilla cocked her head at Ridley as though the American had skipped an entire chapter in the textbook, "lava eruptions from the summit craters are not what you have to be the most worried about."

Booker blinked as if he didn't know there *was* another chapter.

"It's the flanks. There are hundreds of fissures all over the mountain. They don't look as dramatic as lava exploding out of the top of a mountain, but they're much more dangerous. So, at least the pyroclastic flows are not common with Etna."

Ridley had done *some* homework on basic volcanic activity. While the lava was the showstopper, the much more dangerous threat was the cloud.

Pyroclastic flow. The scorching avalanche of rock and ash of a thousand degrees Fahrenheit that roars down the slopes at four hundred miles per hour—obliterating everything in its path.

Ridley scanned the wall of monitors. She understood little of what she was looking at, but could see the lights, the squiggles, the numbers rising, and the techs behind her speaking to each other in low voices.

"Tell me," she repeated, "what I need to know to go up there."

Lucilla looked at her for a moment.

"You have no idea how bad it's going to be up there," she said. "You're not going alone."

CHAPTER FIFTY-THREE

CATANIA, SICILY

The equipment room looked like something between an astronaut's locker and a hazmat biolab.

What are you getting into, Samaras...

Lucilla gestured to a man standing in the middle, assembling rows of gear on a bench.

"This is Sandro Leoni," she said. "He's going to go up the mountain with you because he is crazy and likes to do things like that."

The man looked up, tossing floppy black hair out of his eyes. He was in his mid-twenties, with a broad mouth and thick eyebrows that seemed to dash across his face.

"Welcome to the best place to work in the world," he said in a thick Italian accent.

He stepped forward to shake their hands, then looked at Ridley. "It's you?"

She readjusted the backpack straps on her shoulder and

raised her hand. "It's me. I'm Ridley Samaras."

He looked her up and down. She was at least two inches taller, though he was built like an outdoorsman. Meaty hands and thick forearms from rock climbing, a broad back, and below his cargo shorts, the calves of a baby rhinoceros.

"*I'm* going, too," said Nas.

They all turned to her.

Ridley snorted. "No."

"I'm the reason for all of this."

Sandro laughed. "Lady, if you can make a volcano erupt, I think we'll have a job for you."

Ridley exchanged a look with Booker.

"You're not goin'," she said again.

Nas' defiance flared. "*You* don't know what you're doing. You have no more experience on a volcano than me."

Lucilla crossed her arms, muttering something to herself in Italian.

But then Booker's voice boomed through. "Dr. Aslani, you're not going. You don't have the permission of the Italian government. And they won't give it to you."

Nas clenched her mouth shut. She was fuming.

"Okay, so this is great," said Sandro, "but now, I need to give you a two year education in twenty minutes."

Lucilla looked at Sandro. "It's Voragine."

His face went still.

"Voragine? Well, fuck. Have you had your last meal?" he said to Ridley.

"We're both coming back down that mountain," she said.

That's the spirit. As if you know.

"Sure! Yeah, let me show you your death shroud," he said, going back to the gear.

"Why are *you* going up then?"

Lucilla responded. "I told you, he's crazy. He climbed

Everest and K2 and El Capitan and base jumps and eats scorpions."

"Only in China," he said. "At home, just scorpion peppers. And now, volcanic ash."

They were interrupted by an urgent alert sound from Lucilla's phone. She pulled it out to look—and froze.

"Earthquake swarms are moving to the southeast flank. The gas ratios..." she trailed off. "It's time to send official alerts."

She strode out of the equipment room as she dialed someone.

Booker asked Sandro, "Alerts to whom?"

"Mayors. Mayors first. If it gets worse, the police, the president of Sicily, and the Protezione Civile. They're in Rome. If we have to call them?" he said, pushing a hazard suit at Ridley. "Red alert."

"They'll evacuate?" asked Nas.

"Yeah. Shut down the airport if there's ash, coordinate the evacuation of the areas in danger. Everyone has protocols, but our institute can't command anything to happen. We just give them the bad news and recommend what everyone *should* do."

He looked at Nas and Booker, suddenly serious.

"I think maybe you should both go to the café. Or back to the operations room."

Both seemed surprised. Nas looked at Ridley, still angry, still hurt, not wanting to leave her to this.

"Get some coffee," Ridley said, and grinned. "Drink at least one cup for me. Latte."

"Get your kit on," said Booker. "We'll be back in a few minutes. Lasch should be arriving soon anyhow."

Once they'd left, Sandro turned to Ridley and sighed.

"They didn't tell me why you want to go up there, but you know *nobody* does this. Except for YouTube daredevils."

"Really think we'll get Pompeii'ed?"

"Voragine doesn't just send lava." He held up a full-face respirator mask. "The gas will kill you. You'll breathe in ash and die."

"Okay."

"There are patches of rock that get warm and they can create landslides, a pyroclastic flow of hot rock and ash. Kill you. Lava bombs crashing down from the sky. Kill you."

"Lava *bombs?*"

He gesticulated the process. "Lava blobs get blown into the air. They cool instantly, become rocks, and rain down. It's hard to see them coming."

"Have you ever gone up a volcano when it's getting active?"

Sandro laughed. "Yeah, many times. I've stood right next to lava flows. But I don't go when it's having *this* much activity. This is...not a good idea."

He went through the rest of the equipment with her, rattling off some of the most deathly warnings she'd ever heard.

"Your shoes would melt so we wear special boots..."

"Helmets, because hot rocks on your skull feel bad..."

"Leg gaiters. Neck gaiters. You'll sweat but you don't want the hot ash on your skin..."

"Respirator, but it will clog with ash so you have to carry your own filter and change it out fast, without taking off the mask..."

"Climbing harness and rope and gloves..."

"Headlamps...whistle...medical kit...a GPS but also a compass... radio because phones sometimes don't work...and gas monitors.*"*

Ridley's mind spun like an overloaded washing machine. Every single thing he was laying out and every detail of its use would be life or death up there.

"What about those silver spaceman suits I've seen on National Geographic videos?" she asked.

"Aluminized suits? No," he laughed, shaking his head. "Those are only to get so close to the rim, like thirty meters or less. If it's hot enough to need one at Voragine, it's already too late. No one stands at the rim of of the Abyss when it's waking up. Death wish."

My God, what he's gonna think when he sees what's up there this time...

When Sandro was done with his emphatic demo, she nodded, then pointed to every item and rattled off the purpose and requirements back to him.

"I'm gonna need eyes up there," she said. "You have drones?"

He stood back and regarded her with a curious frown. "Who *are* you?"

IN ITALIAN: *"Maybe I'm crazier than you."*

Sandro laughed in astonishment. "You speak my language?!"

"They respect your food orders here more when you ask in Italian."

"Yeah, we have drones. It may become clogged with ash and die, but we probably have the budget for more."

He looked at his sport watch.

"Time to get dressed. Just the lower half. We'll drive and put on the rest up there. If we wait much longer, I won't get to my nephew's birthday party next week! But then I wouldn't have to get him a gift..." Sandro shrugged as if weighing it out. "If you've got anyone to say goodbye to...I'm only half kidding."

Ridley's gaze locked on the gas monitor. That hand-sized yellow block—her lifeline.

Who would you really call?

No partner. If her dog Maddie could understand, she'd call her.

Alexios? She realized it would be more for his sake than for hers. For all the distance they'd drifted to as adults, he would be destroyed if he never got to say goodbye to his younger sister... probably.

Her father—

In that moment, she *wished* that she wanted to hear his voice before the end.

But she didn't.

He wasn't Jimmy. She wasn't Nas. That dream was over years ago.

The wish dissolved as she lifted her eyes to meet Sandro's.

"I don't need to call." She picked up a pair of Nomex-blend pants and inspected the tag. "These'll fit."

Blue light flashed through the equipment room. She spotted the alarm bulb by the door, pulsing neon.

"No," said Sandro, "shit, not yet!"

"What is that?"

"The office has contacted Civil Protection because of the danger. She's going very fast."

Ridley slid the backpack off her shoulders.

"*I* have something—" she said, opening the bag, "that both of us are gonna need."

She pulled out a massive military helmet.

The attached visor was immense, tinted almost black, with a row of tiny cameras above it.

"What..." he said, staring.

"It's an Integrated Visual Augmentation System. IVAS. Specialized gear straight from the American military."

"Why are you bringing it up a volcano?"

She ignored the question.

"When I tell you to put this on up there, I need you to do it without question, without hesitation. No, I can't explain to you why right now. You'll understand when you see."

"When *I* see?" His brows rose. "You don't even know what a volcano looks like inside the crater."

"It's not for looking at the volcano."

CHAPTER FIFTY-FOUR

CATANIA, SICILY

THE SKIES that afternoon were a hazy blue. An island breeze swept away the heaviest of the summer heat. In the distance, the Mediterranean was a platter of sapphires.

But the air...smelled of hell.

Standing in the office parking lot, Ridley turned from the ocean to look inland.

On the horizon, the great beast was awakening.

Mount Etna loomed over the towns below like a slouched behemoth. A small plume of ash puffed up from its peak.

Sandro loaded the last Pelican case into the back of the Land Rover. On the side of the blue vehicle was emblazoned the INGV name alongside: *SULLA TERRA, PER LA TERRA.*

On the earth, for the earth.

"Thirty minutes' drive to the lower slopes," said Sandro. "After that, we'll drive up as high as we can get."

"Let's go," said Ridley.

She tucked the giant hiking pack she'd assembled into the trunk, shut it, and climbed in the passenger seat.

Sandro got behind the wheel, crossed himself, and started the engine.

In Lucilla's office, Joe Lasch paced, muttering down at his phone as he texted on a secure app. His State Department assistant, a skittish woman in her thirties, lingered nearby.

Outside the office, Lasch's security detail, a trim, hound-faced man in his forties, kept glancing casually down the hallways.

Booker stepped in with an expectant look.

Lasch spoke without looking up from his phone. "The prefect is sending two ambulances. They'll be waiting at the base of the mountain with burn unit specialists."

"We're lookin' at a few hours," said Booker. "I'll let you know when they start the climb."

He thudded a hand against the doorframe as he left. Instead of going back to the operations room, though, he went to the men's bathroom.

He checked that it was empty.

Then Booker pulled out his own phone and dialed.

Sandro and Ridley finally reached Piazzale Rifugio Sapienza.

It was a little motel and restaurant with a rental shop for hiking gear. It was also a station for the cable car that tourists could use to ascend the first leg of the mountain. That had stopped running an hour ago.

The lot was empty but for a few cars. A police vehicle was parked at a jagged angle by the entrance. Standing nearby, a male officer in a bright vest waved them down.

Ridley and Sandro got out, and he called to the policeman.

IN ITALIAN: *"They haven't evacuated?"*

The officer threw up his hands in frustration.

IN ITALIAN: *"My partner is getting the last of them. Stubborn Bulgarians."*

IN ITALIAN: *"Is everyone else off the mountain?"*

The man squinted up toward the peak.

IN ITALIAN: *"Yes, except the observatory. That's yours."*

Sandro nodded.

IN ITALIAN: *"Get off the mountain,"* he told the officer. *"Move fast."*

Only the INGV were authorized to go up the mountain now.

Sandro pulled out the radio and called back to the office.

"Catania, this is VT-3."

It was Lucilla who replied to him on the other end.

"Go ahead, Sandro."

"I'm going to talk in English so the Americans can understand. We're at Rifugio Sapienza. We're going to do our last logistics check and turn on the gas monitors before we ascend."

"Copy. The tremor amplitude is rising. I'll keep you informed."

"Copy."

He went to the trunk, opened one of the equipment cases, and pulled out the yellow gas monitors. Turning both on, he let them run the self-check—audible alarms, lights, and sensor readings.

"You have to keep it high on your chest," he said, clipping one to his collar. "Not more than nine inches from your face. All you care about is your breathing zone."

She took the other monitor from him and clipped it to the collar of her light blue windbreaker.

They got back in the car and kept driving—up the snaking narrow road. Green scrub gave way to gray volcanic gravel.

Ridley couldn't take her eyes off the plumes of ash ahead of them as they billowed into the air.

What the hell do you think you're gonna do to that, Samaras?

And she wondered if Gabe was even up there at all.

Lucilla stood with her hands propped on her hips, scanning the wall of screens in front of her.

The operations room had grown crowded.

The essential team members were there monitoring every shudder and breath and angry snort from Etna.

The seismology tech lead, Enrico.

The thermal-optical surveillance lead, Lara.

The operations assistant, Ciro, who ran communications and alerts.

Nas and Booker, who stood quiet and tense at the back of the room.

And then there was the liaison for the Protezione Civile, Lt. Col. Matteo Morelli.

He was a scruffy, dark-haired, imposing man in his late forties who had arrived only moments ago. As the connecting line between the INGV and the the agency responsible for national emergencies, he operated under the prime minister's office and would give the official orders for any evacuation procedures.

The American State Department chief was pacing the hall, frequently on his phone.

IN ITALIAN: *"The tiltmeter,"* said Enrico. *"Sudden deflection."*

Lucilla picked up the radio from the desk beside her.

IN ITALIAN: *"VT-3, we have a buildup on the flanks. Extreme caution advised. And* hurry."

Booker leaned toward Lucilla. "What was that?"

"There might be an eruption on the flanks," she murmured, "and we do not want that."

Nas shook her head and turned away.

"I need a restroom," she muttered, and walked out of the operations room.

By the time Sandro pulled to a stop on a small plateau, the plumes were billowing overhead in the winds. The late afternoon sun was nothing more than a dull shining disc behind the ashen clouds.

Ridley glanced at the altimeter on the dashboard.

2,400 meters.

"We go the rest of it on foot," said Sandro, shutting off the engine.

"We don't have time to do it all on foot."

"We have to go on foot *now*. If a slide starts, we'll lose the car and our way to get down the mountain fast. If it sinks...it would be like *The Neverending Story*."

"Why the hell did you have to bring up Artax?" said Ridley.

Sandro gave a half-cocked grin and picked up the radio.

"Catania, I confirm we're at the vehicle ceiling."

"Copy that," came Ciro's voice. *"What's your altitude?"*

"Two thousand, four hundred. Conditions are pretty bad."

"Copy. Infrared shows shallow magma in the Southeast crater."

"She always wants to go first," said Sandro. "Okay, we're going on foot."

He checked his gas monitor, then grabbed the half-face respirators from the back seat. He handed one to Ridley.

She pulled it over her head and secured the straps, sealing it around her face. She tugged on a light blue helmet. Adjusted her neck gaiter. Adjusted the gaiters around her boots, and stepped out of the vehicle.

She immediately felt the rumbling through the soles of her feet.

As Lucilla watched the screens, a dread chill crept up on her.

It was becoming more and more clear in both her gut and on the monitors—this was going to be an eruption for the history books.

Then she saw the gas readings.

IN ITALIAN: *"SO2 and CO are spiking together,"* said Ciro. *"Pressure breach."*

Lucilla was the lead volcanologist. This was all her call. If she raised the alert level to red, it was an automatic recommendation to evacuate the towns below the endangered flank.

She drew in a steadying breath and looked at Lt. Col. Morelli.

IN ITALIAN: *"I'm recommending you raise the alert,"* she said.

He lifted a brow.

IN ITALIAN: *"Already?"*

IN ITALIAN: *"It's going to erupt, Lieutenant Colonel Morelli, and from the signals it's giving us, this will be big."*

IN ITALIAN: *"I need a lava path confirmation. A projection,* something."

IN ITALIAN: *"I'm telling you, from all my years watching this mountain—you need to do it now."*

He straightened up, trying to hide his shock within a professional demeanor. Lt. Col. Morelli took out his mobile and dialed the National Operations Room in Rome.

"What is it?" said Booker, a steely urgency in his deep voice.

Lucilla looked back at him.

"Stand by for evacuations."

He stared at the wall of screens, between the video feed of Etna's peak to the satellite imagery.

And tried to imagine how Ridley would ever get off that mountain.

CHAPTER FIFTY-FIVE

CATANIA, SICILY

The backpacks they carried were stuffed, though Ridley couldn't tell Sandro why hers in particular was so heavy.

Just a Helm of Darkness crafted by the Greek god Hades.

Makes you invisible. No big deal. Just thought I might need it on top of a volcano.

But she was a professional at keeping secrets, and an athlete after all.

Only nine hundred meters with a respirator on.

"We try to stay away from Bocca Nuova," said Sandro, his voice distorted through the mask.

"Why?"

"It's too loud and distracting. The gas signals will distort our reading of Voragine."

They started to hike.

Sandro insisted on going in front of her. She chafed.

"Can you recognize pockets of superheated gas?" he asked,

waggling an infrared thermometer that looked like a hot glue gun. "Just follow me."

The gravel crunched beneath their feet. Every few moments, she felt the ground shudder. The pulse would vibrate up her legs.

She heard the loud crackle of the radio.

"Seismic tremor amplitude is up twenty percent in the last ten minutes," came Enrico's voice.

"Copy," said Sandro.

He said nothing to Ridley, but suddenly they were climbing faster.

"Are the drones ready to go?" Lucilla asked one of the techs at the back of the room.

The young man nodded slowly, his eyes riveted to the computer screen as he raced to post up the drones.

Seconds later, a new feed appeared on the wall of screens—a live drone.

It stayed wide of the massive plume of ash, soaring low around the flanks.

Booker's eyes lit up. He pulled out his phone, sent a discreet text, then fixed intently on the live feed.

"Anyone see them?" said Lucilla. "Put it on the bigger screen."

The drone tech transferred the feed to the biggest monitor on the wall.

Everything was hazy and smeared with gray—but then they spotted dots of color on the dark slopes.

"Yes," said Lucilla, moving toward the screen. "Move in."

Lt. Col. Morelli shook his head and muttered something in Italian.

The camera zoomed downward, pulling up at a hundred feet over the heads of the two hikers. They were moving *fast.*

"VT-3," Lucilla called over the radio, "we have eyes in the sky. We see you."

A moment passed, then Sandro's voice came over the line. He was barely even short of breath.

"Copy!"

"What's your altitude?"

"Twenty-eight hundred."

"Copy." Lucilla lowered the radio and said to the drone tech, "Show me the peak."

The camera tilted up, and they looked upon the mountain that was growing into a nightmare.

With every step, Ridley's feet sank through a layer of ash. It was whipping around them now, as fine as flour. Their clothes and packs were coated with a thin layer of dust.

The mountain rumbled. The low roar around them was growing louder.

It feels alive.

Like an angry god.

A hissing blast exploded beside only feet from them.

Sandro stumbled back as steam poured from the black earth.

"Steam vents," he said, his voice tensing. "The pressure inside is breaking open the mountain."

"Will that mean lava?"

"If the crack becomes a fissure, if it goes deep enough, yes."

Just as he was about to put the burners on his pace, something down the slope caught his eye.

IN ITALIAN: *"Oh, my God, what—"*

Ridley turned around.

A blue INGV Land Rover was speeding up the mountain toward them.

Sandro waved frantically, crossing his arms overhead in an 'X.'

The small SUV began to skid and stall, its wheels grinding—sinking into the layer of ash and gravel.

"STOP!" he bellowed.

We're way above the vehicle safety limit...what the hell is INGV doing?

Finally the Rover could go no further. Forty yards from Ridley and Sandro.

It was beginning to slide when the driver's door flew open and someone jumped out.

Nas.

The monitors that lined the wall were climbing, spiking, lighting up. The techs and scientist leads were speaking to each other in Italian, their voices tense.

Booker couldn't understand what they were saying, but the tone was evident with each new announcement.

This was all going very fast, and in a bad direction.

Lt. Col. Morelli was on the phone, coordinating with the Protezione Civile. Emergency procedures were tight and well-known. To live in the shadow of one of the most active volcanoes on earth meant that every step had to be drilled to perfection.

The airport had closed immediately. Every inbound flight was diverted. Highway patrols were in place. Every provincial emergency committee was on standby. Both police and Carabinieri were in preliminary evacuation postures.

Turning away from all the activity, Booker glanced around the room for Nasrin.

There had been so much going on in the operations room that he'd only just realized—she had been gone for a very long time.

He frowned and sent her a questioning text. He waited for a moment to see any sign of response, but there was nothing.

He stepped up to Lucilla.

"How soon do you think..."

She shook her head, not taking her eyes off the monitors.

"I have never in my life sent someone up a mountain like this," she murmured. "It won't be long. God help them."

"Nas!" Ridley yelled, but it was muffled through her mask.

The archaeologist had already put on the full-face respirator, pulled back her hair, and fitted a helmet over it.

She hauled a backpack out of the truck and started scrambling up the slope toward them.

"What is she doing?!" exclaimed Sandro.

Damnit, Nas. How could you—

Ridley and Sandro scampered and slid down to meet her.

"I'm not going back down this mountain alone!" she said.

Ridley grabbed both of her shoulders with a furious shake. "You're an *idiot!*"

The eyes looking back at her through the face shield were terrified, but not of Ridley.

"You can yell at me later," said Nas, adjusting the straps of her backpack. "I'm with you now."

"You don't even have a gas monitor!" said Sandro.

He yanked an extra from his own pack and fixed it to Nas' collar.

"Follow exactly in my footsteps!" he ordered, stabbing a finger at her. "Watch the ground in front of you and listen to everything I say *immediately!*"

"I will."

Ridley's face contorted into a fuming, helpless scowl.

There were dozens of things wrong and enraging about what this woman had just done.

But damn if I don't respect every cell in her body.

The lioness would not be left behind.

CHAPTER FIFTY-SIX

CATANIA, SICILY

Enrico leaned forward in his chair. "Harmonic tremor frequency shifting upward. The conduit might be clearing."

Lucilla gave a tight nod and said to Booker, "If a conduit is clear, that means there is no obstacle anymore to the magma. Gas or lava now have a clear path to the surface."

He wasn't a praying man, but Booker Douglas wasn't above a plea to a higher power right now.

"*Catania,*" Sandro's voice came crackling through the radio, *"we have an addition to our party—"*

"What?!" exclaimed Lucilla.

"—Nasrin Aslani."

Booker did a double take, his gaze sweeping the room once more. Lucilla turned back to stare at the CIA man.

"VT-3," she said, "you have the archaeologist *with you* on Etna?"

"Yes. She's wearing equipment, but we can't send her down alone safely."

Lucilla clutched her hands to her head. For several seconds, she did not respond. The room hardly breathed, every moment feeling heavier and longer than the last...

"VT-3, proceed upward."

"Copy."

Lucilla faced Booker with a scathing glare.

He shook his head in protest. "No, this was not part of our plan. She was forbidden."

Lt. Col. Morelli stepped in. "*Who* is that up there?"

"She's an archaeologist," said Booker. "An American citizen."

The Italian's dark eyes nearly bulged.

"I understand you are some authority from some American agency—I know my government gave you permission to send someone up there, but this is not tourism! What is an *archaeologist* doing?!"

"Lieutenant Colonel," said Booker in the basso tone that could command a foreign army, "she is rogue. We have nothing to do except wait and watch and support them with every means you have here at INGV. If you want to arrest her when she comes off that mountain—"

"*If she comes off* that mountain!"

"—we'll have words then."

Booker's tone was unmistakably final. The Italian liaison turned away in frustration.

Then the CIA division director spotted Lasch.

He was standing in the doorway of the operations room only feet away. His jaw was slack with shock, and he was staring at Booker.

The State Department had just lost all control of their own mission.

. . .

Thin white plumes steamed from the vast, desolate ground. The ash was growing thicker around the trio. The air was darkening.

Nas was hauling herself up as fast as she could go, but the pace of Sandro was nearly impossible for any untrained person. Occasionally she would slip, her knees and hands scraping the basalt. A few times, Ridley caught and righted her. Each time, Nas apologized as if ashamed.

Ridley felt the vibrations in her chest now. She could taste the sulfur in her mouth. The dull roar from within the mountain was growing louder.

You can't make it in time.

He's not even up there.

You'll die before you see the crater.

You can't defeat a gorgon.

You can't stop a volcano from erupting.

You can't keep a goddamn Titan contained.

Shut up, Samaras. Just get there first. Four hundred meters to go.

Then she realized—

She had only two of the IVAS helmets.

One of them would end up looking straight at the gorgons.

In the operations room, a dread confusion was beginning to ripple.

Lara, the thermal-optical surveillance lead, straightened slowly in her chair.

"The thermal cameras are—I thought it was just a heat reflection from the summit," she said, her voice rising, "but it's not. It's a separate thing."

She pointed to one screen, glowing white-hot.

"The summit."

Then to another.

"The south-eastern flank."

A bloom of heat was seeping through the darkness of the slope. Lara looked up at Lucilla, stricken.

"It's a decoupling."

Lucilla's expression went utterly still.

From beside her, Enrico exclaimed, "We've got a swarm at twenty-two thousand meters."

"What is this?" demanded Lt. Col. Morelli.

Lasch jumped in, his blood pressure rising. "Tell me what's happening here!"

Ciro spoke, his voice grave. "The mountain is splitting. There's so much pressure in it that it's finding new pathways for release."

Lucilla drew in a steadying breath. "Voragine will erupt, and somewhere else, a flank will open...into an uncontrolled lava path. Lieutenant Colonel Morelli, this is a red alert. Please move everyone in the lower towns to evacuate."

She picked up the radio.

"VT-3?"

A harsh wind blew sideways, pushing hot ashen air against the climbers' cheeks.

"VT-3?"

Sandro answered. "I'm here."

"The harmonic tremor is still focused at the summit, but we have a swarm—a thousand meters below your position," said Ciro over the line.

For the first time, Sandro stopped. He looked back down the mountain, scanning through the thick haze.

Until his eyes settled on a faint red glow on the slope, far below them.

Ridley and Nas followed his gaze.

"What is that?" said Ridley.

And every cell in Sandro's body went to war with itself. His face twitched and flexed as he stared at the glowing patch.

He croaked into the video. "Visible heat signature on the southern flank."

Ridley could see his expression, even under the face shield.

That is one of the worst looks I've ever seen on someone's face.

"The mountain will erupt in two places," he said over the low roar that engulfed them.

The breath left Nas' lungs. Ridley's mind raced through a scenario she had never envisioned.

How do we escape?

Or do we not.

It was Lucilla's voice they heard next.

"VT-3, you know—this situation requires immediate withdrawal. This is a catastrophic scenario."

Everything that Sandro knew about volcanoes, everything he knew about climbing, everything he knew about science was telling him to get off this mountain at triple speed.

To stay—to go up—was an act that violated every shred of self-preservation, even those of a daredevil.

He glanced at his companions—his charges.

He would be leading both of them into death.

But then he had seen enough of each of these women.

He knew that neither of them would turn back. If he left them here, now, they would still climb to the very mouth of the Abyss.

Himself, he would get to see his nephew turn nine next week. He would get to give him a video game and watch him eat cake and play football with his friends in the yard.

But he would never live without the nightmares of the two women he had stranded to their agonizing deaths on this mountain.

"Three hundred meters to the summit," he said. "We run."

Far below, in the shadow of the mountain, sirens wailed like air horns through the small towns.

In cafés and shops, in cars and on sidewalks and in offices, text alerts sounded in unison.

ATTENZIONE: Pericolo eruttivo. Seguire le indicazioni delle autorità.

Within minutes, municipal authorities would commandeer school buses from the lots where they sat quiet and hot during the summer. Elderly care facilities would be evacuated, their residents assisted out to safe zones by military units.

Ash as fine as flour would begin to settle on everything in sight.

On the highways, police would step out of their cars, lights flashing, and begin steering vehicles into contraflow lanes. Toll booths would open for free passage.

Tensions would flare as parents tried to gather their kids all over town. Farmers would be desperately trying to herd their livestock away, shouted at for clogging roads.

Tourists would try frantically to understand what was going on.

What's happening? Where are we supposed to go? Can we take public transportation?

But taxi drivers would be going straight home to gather

their own families, while buses would be used in evacuation zones.

And the skies over Mount Etna would grow dark.

CHAPTER FIFTY-SEVEN

CATANIA, SICILY

Ridley tasted metal in the air.

Her boots slid as she scampered through gravel. The plume of smoke had become so thick above them that it was blotting out the sun.

In front of her, Nas was huffing for air, fighting to keep up with every drop of adrenaline in her system.

The few moments that Ridley's feet rested on the ground, it felt as if she was standing on the engine of an eighteen-wheeler.

They were on the plateau now. The craters loomed above them.

But there was no sign of the gorgons. No sign of Gabe.

Three hundred meters...

Until you face the most terrifying Titan the world has ever seen—who struck fear into the gods.

Her gas monitor went off, beeping and flashing at her collar. The others did, too.

" CO2 spikes," yelled Sandro. "But we're okay!"

The roar was filling up her ears. Ridley was even more grateful for the bad ear, which muffled the sound of imminent catastrophe.

Nearby, another crack in the ground shot out steam like a water gun.

Nas jumped out of the way. Rocks skittered down the slope.

Two hundred meters...

The lip of the crater was so close. Ridley fixed her gaze to it. Just a mound of dirt over all of this—the worst of the fury of the earth.

What a place to bury a Titan.

She readjusted her helmet and wiped a layer of ash from her face shield.

"Aren't we close?" she yelled.

"Yes!" shouted Sandro.

Ridley pulled Nas back and spoke as close to her face as she could get.

"I need you to do something for me," she said to the Iranian woman. "You know the gorgons. You know what's going to be up there. I only have two headpieces, so I *need* you to function without your eyes here.

"Just look at the ground—*whatever happens,* do not lift your eyes. Do not look at them. Look at the ground. Look at the lava, I don't care. Only listen to me when I tell you to look away."

She swallowed, nodded. "Do you have the helmet?"

"In my bag."

"Give that to me."

Ridley shrugged off her backpack, dug into it, and pulled out the Helm of Darkness.

The black piece of armor seemed to be vibrating, as if it was alive to the pulsing power of the mountain.

Nas took it from her. "I'm going to wear it—when I need to. And you'll guide me," said Nas. "Every step? Be my eyes."

Ridley nodded.

We are so damned.

Then she called to Sandro. It was time.

The dynamic aerial footage began to crinkle and stutter.

"The ash is choking the drone," said the lead tech.

"Pull it back. Conditions are bad, visibility is poor anyway," said Lucilla.

The satellite feed, though, was not bad. The field team had disappeared under the ash cloud minutes before.

They were on the summit plateau now, nearing the craters of Bocca Nuova and Voragine.

"VT-3, what is your status?" asked Ciro on the radio.

Static shrieked on the other end.

"Starting our ascent to Voragine crater," came Sandro's voice.

Lucilla hugged her arms around her chest. Booker gripped the back of a chair until his knuckles paled. Lasch had his eyes closed, his jaw clenched.

They could do nothing but watch and wait.

The loose black sand gave way beneath their feet as they hauled themselves up the final slope of Mount Etna. The roar had become so intense that it felt like they were climbing into the engine of a 747.

Sandro and Ridley had shed their utility helmets, and now wore the massive IVAS systems over their heads. They attached clumsily to the face shields, but it was the best they could do.

The feed in their vision now was digital. It was an augmented, real-time, camera-fed view.

Gabe...please be here...

The rim of the crater loomed above. Sandro was scrambling up as fast as he could go—

And then they were there.

He pulled himself up first, then gave a hand back to help Nas. Ridley stepped up beside them.

They stood at the edge of Voragine.

It looked nothing like Ridley and Nas had imagined. There was no clean crater bowl.

This was a jagged pit nearly three hundred meters across. The steep walls dropped nearly fifteen meters to a slope of broken rocks, then flattened into a dark terrace.

Milky white vapors streamed up into a gray haze. The ash had become as fine as smoke on the air.

A veil of doom.

Below it all, the Abyss glowed orange.

Where is he? WHERE IS HE?!

Ridley scanned for any sign of life in the ragged, raging crater. The winds tore at them, hot and gusting, blurring their vision.

"VT-3!" came Lucilla's voice through the radio, though they could barely hear it over the noise. *"Where are you? Status?"*

Sandro answered. "We're at the rim. Medium visibility. Ash venting. There is incandescence."

"Confirm your gas readings."

He checked his monitor. "Sulfur peaking twenty-four... carbon elevated but below threshold."

"Do you see your target?"

"Not yet. Stand by."

"VT-3, you can't descend into the crater with those gas readings. You have minutes *up there."*

His expression was stony.

IN ITALIAN: *"I know, Lucilla."*

The mountain was seething.

"I don't see him!" said Ridley. "Wh—"

"There!" cried Nas. "I see him!"

She pointed down to the far end of the lower terrace.

Ridley's hand snapped up to her visor—zooming in on the tiny figure in the distance.

It was him.

Gabe, sitting on the ground, his knees drawn up as if to shield his face, arms draped over his legs. He was coated in ash and dirt.

"Is he alive?" said Nas, frantic.

"Probably," said Ridley, her throat tightening, "or he'd be slumped over."

How is he still alive?

Alarm volted through her.

Where are the gorgons?

But she saw nothing in the crater, on the rim, or in the skies.

Go get Gabe, you dawdling asshole!

She shucked her pack. Sandro did the same. They each pulled out their climbing harnesses, ropes, pickaxes...

"I don't know how to climb," said Nas, staring at them while they began to don their gear.

"You're not even supposed to be here," said Ridley, snapping on a carabiner.

She met Nas' eyes.

"It's time," said Ridley. "Take out the helmet."

The woman's expression filled with dread, but she didn't hesitate. She slid the bag from her back and pulled out the Helm of Darkness.

Sandro did a double-take. "What the hell is *that?*"

Ridley leveled him with a gaze that made his stomach lurch.

"Sandro, I'm sorry. You're gonna see some things that won't make any fucking sense. If I tell you to do something, *do it that second.* And whatever happens, make sure you're always looking through the visor of the IVAS."

He looked at her in bewilderment.

"What are we doing?" he exclaimed.

If he only knew—

YOU barely know!

"Just help me get my partner!"

She rushed to a nearby boulder, a remnant of a past eruption, and started to loop her rope around it. It was going to be ugly, but the rest of the ground was too unstable to hold her.

Sandro jumped in, helping her secure a line. He tied and double-checked the knot.

Ridley attached her harness and walked to the edge.

"Nas," she said, turning back to look at her. "Put it on. And shut your eyes. And *don't* open them until I come back and give you the clear."

"What?" said Sandro, looking between them.

"Don't worry," Ridley told him. "She's gonna disappear for a few minutes, but she can still hear you. I'll be back."

He shook his head in disbelief—the whole situation growing weirder and worse by the second.

Ridley turned her back to the ragged pit, and gripped the rope.

"Ready."

CHAPTER FIFTY-EIGHT

CATANIA, SICILY

Rocks skittered, tumbling beneath Ridley as she bounded and slid down the wall of the crater.

The heat was smothering.

Her head ached with the weight of the IVAS on top of her respirator.

It's a volcano.

Not an ancient superbeast.

It erupts all the time.

But not like this...

She reached the floor of the broad terrace, stumbling down the final slope of gravel. She unclipped herself and turned to face the crater.

Gabe.

He hadn't moved.

Twenty meters from her. She started to run, leaping from valleys of black sand onto patches of sharp volcanic rocks.

"Gabe!" she yelled.

He didn't respond.

Ten meters...

She tripped, landing hard on one knee. The hot slice of pain told her it was cut, but she refused to look.

She stumbled back to her feet and ran.

"GABE!"

Nothing.

Five meters...why isn't he moving?!

Then she was upon him.

He was slouched forward over his knees, head hanging, hair slick and dirty. He was smeared with ash, a thin layer of dust on his skin turning to sludge with his sweat.

And he was dressed in a short tunic that was clasped over one shoulder. The Harpe sword hung from a leather belt. The polished shield lay beside him. The *kibisis* was fastened to his belt. On his feet were the winged sandals of Hermes.

They made him out to be Perseus.

But his wrists and ankles were bound with rancid rope.

Ridley glanced up into the darkened sky—

Where are you bitches?

She dropped into a crouch beside him.

"Gabe—"

He moved. Lifted his head slowly, his eyes shut.

"Ridley."

It was a half-croak, half-whisper through peeling lips. She could barely hear it over the din that sounded like a freight train.

She gave a breathless laugh of relief. "I'm here."

"Are they here?"

She'd never heard that fear in his voice before.

"I don't see them."

He burst out, "Keep your eyes shut!"

A fit of coughing seized him.

"It's okay," she said, pulling a karambit from her belt. "I've got something for that."

Ridley started to saw through his ankle bindings.

"I need water..." he groaned.

"We need to get you up—out of here *now.*"

His eyes cracked open, red-rimmed and watering.

"Am I in hell?"

"In a few minutes, it will be," she said, pulling his wrists closer.

He blinked around. "A *volcano?!*"

She cut the ropes and tossed them away.

"They told me to put these on," he said as she began to help him up, "but I couldn't even see..."

The entire bowl was thrumming around them.

"They want her to come back for Perseus."

"'Her' is Athena, right?"

"Yeah. You know?"

He winced as she put an arm around his ribs. He coughed again.

"I didn't know gorgons could talk instead of just screaming," she said.

Gabe mumbled, "But I don't think it will work. I don't have all the items."

Ridley froze.

She looked up at the rim where she had left Nas and Sandro.

"We do," she breathed.

"*We*...Nas?! No! You didn't bring her!"

"I didn't bring her—she followed us!"

Gabe squinted up at the whirl of steam and ash.

"*She's* coming."

She.

Ridley looked up.

"If she's coming, that means the gorgons are coming."

Then Typhon is coming—

"When I tell you to shut your eyes—"

"My eyes have been shut for days," he said. "I know."

Ridley pulled a Beretta from the small of her back.

"You're leaving this place alive," she said. "And the world won't see that son of a bitch Titan. Not today."

And then, the air changed.

The roar of the crater faded into a dull hum. The wind drifted to a lull...and from the thickest plume of ash emerged a glow.

It wasn't the orange light of the lava which boiled below. It was something completely separate. Silver, luminescent shards scattering upward in the darkness.

"Electrical storm?" murmured Gabe.

Ridley could only shake her head as the shards began to collect, merging into a column nearly thirty feet high. "That's her."

The visage of a goddess half-formed.

The light that made her was all strings and slices, as though a constellation was coming to life, spun by quicksilver.

She spoke—but it wasn't a sound in Ridley's ears. It was in her chest, in her head, like someone had installed a speaker system on the inside.

YOU RETURN MY GIFTS

Gabe gawked.

"Yes!" he yelled before Ridley could stop him.

"NO!" she bellowed. "You don't return a gift to the ancient Greeks! It's a slap in the face, a—"

BROTHER, IS THIS YOU

Oh, my God.

None of them had thought it. No one had realized—this whole time.

Zeus, the serial philanderer. Zeus, whose children numbered in the hundreds. Zeus, the father of both gods and mortals.

Zeus, the father of Athena, and also of Perseus.

Ridley's thoughts were sprinting through her mind—

Can we fool a goddess? For how long? At what price?

Tell her about the gorgons? Let them fight, distracted so we can escape?

At the end of these was always one above all others: Typhon.

Nothing mattered if the most powerful of all the Titans was finally able to escape the boiling prison in which he'd been chained for millennia.

Gabe had just been the bait.

And so Ridley yelled at Athena as loudly as she could through her mask, "It's a trap!"

The face, a half-finished mosaic of light shards, *tightened.*

WHAT HAVE YOU DONE

"No, it wasn't us!" Gabe shouted.

"Gabe," said Ridley, "close your eyes. Close your eyes!"

She had barely finished the words when a dark shape burst through the cloud of ash above Athena.

A giant pair of leathery wings flapped—smoke flaring outward.

"GORGON!" yelled Ridley.

And she was looking right at it.

The hissing, writhing green snakes on her head, the tusk-like fangs that coiled from her mouth, and the blazing blue eyes—

Euryale.

Her mouth gaped wide, and a scream of unearthly fury blasted through the crater.

The sound was like an axe splitting open Ridley's head, crushing what was left of her eardrums.

She buckled. Gabe bent over, his face screwed up in agony.

Athena's enormous head snapped up.

Suddenly there was a spear shimmering in her hand. With her other, she raised a shield—

With the head of Medusa mounted on it.

Euryale's scream blistered with anguish.

Athena's spear blazed toward the gorgon—

The goddess didn't see the other sister coming.

Ridley spotted a flash over the western rim—and time seemed to slow.

Those monstrous wings folded like a peregrine falcon...the snakes black and alive all over her head...orange crocodile eyes fixed on her target...

Eighty feet away.

Ridley raised her gun.

FIRED—

AGAIN AND AGAIN AND AGAIN—

As the rage of Stheno exploded over the mountain.

CHAPTER FIFTY-NINE

CATANIA, SICILY

One of the bullets tore through the thick mottled wing of the gorgon and buried itself in her side.

Stheno pulled up short. Her shriek was as much of shock as of pain.

"You got her?" cried Gabe, spinning around, his eyes clamped shut.

"Yes—shit—"

The creature's eyes blazed like lava as they fixed on the masked human far below—

And dove.

Ridley staggered back, hauling Gabe with her. He stumbled, cutting the top of his foot on a rock.

She shoved him behind a boulder as the gorgon's hideous snarl zoomed toward them.

Ridley ducked behind the rock just as a whoosh of air swept over them.

Stheno veered upward—

Ridley stepped out and unleashed a volley—

Stupid pistol—

But the gorgon soared wide, climbing through the air, and sped toward the back of Athena. Ridley grabbed the extra magazine from beneath her windbreaker and reloaded.

She saw the quicksilver spear of the giant goddess burst through the ash cloud. It barely missed the legs of Euryale, who swooped away just in time.

But Athena was bound to no place.

Suddenly, it was as if all the shimmering pieces of her reappeared somewhere else.

Stheno had been about to ambush the goddess from behind, but then she simply wasn't there.

Euryale screeched into sight, tearing at the back of Athena's neck—

The goddess pulled her off and hurled the gorgon down into the crater—

But Euryale pulled up like a hawk before she struck ground.

The wind blew a gust of ash across the crater floor.

Ridley lost sight of the battle in the sky. Gabe seized with coughs. His eyes were leaking tears. The sulfur was seeping past his closed lids...

It's poisoning him.

She couldn't send him to climb the crater wall without his sight.

She couldn't leave with him as long as this preternatural battle hung in the balance.

How am I supposed to stop a Titan from exploding out of this mountain?!

Ridley realized that she had simply expected the answer would somehow come to her. She had always found the solution in the final moments, always plugged the dike before a surge of water could obliterate the town.

But here you are in a damned volcano looking at monsters and a goddess and you can't do a thing to stop a world-destroying being from bursting out of a mountain.

You can't stop this.

You have no power here.

Her entire body tensed—froze—

And then she looked at Gabe.

"Stay here. Don't look."

"No, what?!"

Ridley snatched the Harpe sword from his belt.

She got to her feet.

You have twenty rounds.

Kill the monsters.

Clutching the Beretta in her other hand, she walked out into the open.

The din of the volcano was like a freight train inside her skull. The furious screams of the gorgons ripped through it.

She clambered over the field of strewn, calcified lava bombs —toward the pit that glowed and howled—toward the colossus of light—toward the monsters that raged and soared through the sky.

She felt the heat swelling, as if it was trying to push the air back into her lungs.

All you need is one.

As if a goddess needs any more help than that.

She stopped and looked up to see the green and gray wings of Stheno slicing overhead.

As the gorgon sped back toward Athena, Ridley raised her gun and unloaded a hail of bullets.

This time, she was close enough.

Three of the rounds tore into the gorgon's leathery flesh.

Stheno turned to her in a rage—

Even at a forty foot distance, Ridley had never seen so much hatred in a face. It boiled from her crocodile eyes.

The gorgon flew straight at her.

The speed was shocking—Ridley hardly had time to react—

She dropped to the ground, rolling on her side, shooting upward as one of the claws nicked her shoulder—

Her ribs slammed against the sharp edge of a rock. Ridley barked in pain.

She scrambled back to her feet—

Stheno was swooping down again—

Ridley couldn't lift the gun in time to get any target...she stumbled and dove to the ground, just slipping the savage talons of the gorgon.

Stheno came around again.

Ridley ducked and bolted away. She fired a volley.

Two hit.

But the bullets weren't doing enough damage.

Out of the corner of her eye, she could see the quicksilver flashes above...

Twenty feet behind her was the edge of the magma pit.

The monster was driving her toward it.

She felt like the heat was melting the skin from her bones.

Stheno circled again, folded her wings, and shot down from the sky—a falcon on her prey.

Ridley raised the gun—firing—unflinching as the gorgon hurtled toward her—

Hold—hold—HOLD—

Until the monster was nearly face-to-face with her—

She let go of the gun.

Dropped to one knee.

And clasping the sword with both hands, she dipped her head low, held the point of the blade aloft, and braced herself.

The Harpe sword.

The gift of Hermes.

The sharpest weapon ever crafted.

Its curving blade ripped Stheno open.

The force of the impact blasted Ridley off her feet—

She skidded on her back, the scalding gravel tearing at her clothes.

The scream of the gorgon this time was pure pain.

From the darkness above, Ridley saw something plummeting toward the crater—

Euryale.

The tattered body of the other gorgon fell from the sky into the pit.

Ridley leapt to her feet.

Stheno had crashed only ten feet from the edge. She clutched at her chest, her gut...it looked like a seam had burst down her torso.

Blood the color of oil spilled from it.

Ridley picked up her gun.

Four rounds.

She leveled it at the face of the gorgon.

The expression there—beyond the tusk-like fangs, the burning eyes, the writhing nest of black snakes, the scaly skin—was frantic, enraged, and so full of anguish that Ridley's breath caught in her chest.

Her sisters.

And then she pulled the trigger.

Four times.

Stheno crumpled backward, and she fell.

She couldn't be this close and not see it.

Don't do it—

But Ridley couldn't help herself.

She stepped up to the edge and looked down into the

mouth of hell.

Sixty feet below her was a molten, seething floor.

A black crust of rock rippled along the top. Through its cracks glowed a sea of incandescent magma. The earth was roiling, surging, spitting up in bursts.

On one side of the pit, a patch on the surface flamed.

Ridley could make out a massive pair of wings—incinerated—and a flaming body.

The charred lake of magma began to bubble. Fountains, surging and collapsing.

The liquid fire was mesmerizing.

Ridley was baking alive yet frozen in place, barely able to look at it but unable to look away. It was the living molten sun, a glowing cascade, the most furious and primal thing she'd ever laid eyes on.

TYPHON.

But you can do nothing more.

You'll die here.

Seconds passed before she even reacted to her own thoughts.

A *boom* thundered up from the pit. The earth shook under her feet, as though she was standing on a stadium subwoofer.

Ridley tore her gaze away from the fiery lake and began to run.

She felt like she was suffocating on her own breath. With every step, pain scorched her ribs. The crater seemed like it had doubled in width.

As she passed the place where she had first found Gabe, she lunged down to grab the bronze shield.

The shield of Athena.

The voice boomed again in Ridley's head.

HERO

She looked up.

The towering goddess was clearer now, as if the silver webs and shards of light had begun to connect. She was terrifying in her magnificence.

I WILL GRANT YOU ONE THING

Ridley had to shake her head clear—*one thing?!*

"Stop Typhon from escaping!" she shouted, wondering how she could even be heard over the rumble of the mountain.

THAT IS FOR ME AND MY FAMILY

YOU WILL HAVE ONE THING

TELL ME WHAT

Ridley paused, a crowd of thoughts barreling through her mind. And then one shone over all others.

"Destroy the ayatollahs. Free their captives."

Through the darkness and the shimmer, Ridley couldn't see any expression on the face of the goddess.

But Athena nodded once.

NOW GO

Ridley bolted, sword and shield in hand. As she neared the boulder, she yelled to Gabe.

"Open your eyes! We have to get out!"

She saw him get to his feet, eyes cracking open like a newborn.

"Go!" she bellowed.

He looked behind her. The orange glow was blooming brighter.

"Come to me!" he called.

She reached him.

He grabbed her around the waist and clamped his hands together.

What—

And launched them into the air.

CHAPTER SIXTY

CATANIA, SICILY

THE SANDALS on Gabe's feet were searing bright, like they were vibrating so fast that they were generating their own light.

Ridley's stomach lurched as they soared up and up, above the crater rim, into the dark ashen sky.

They came down too fast, crashing hard against the top of the slope. Both buckled, rolled, and slid to a messy halt in the gravel.

They hauled themselves roughly to their feet.

Ridley could hear muffled shouts. She turned to see Nas racing toward them, clutching the black helmet of Hades.

The archaeologist nearly collided with Gabe, her hands hovering as if she was afraid a hug might break him.

"You're okay! You're okay?" she cried.

"Okay," he could barely cough.

Nas tore off her own respirator and put it to his face.

Sandro came jogging over to them. The expression on his face was one degree away from catatonic shock.

"Go, *now!*" he yelled, arms flailing.

Ridley ripped the heavy IVAS from her head. She looked at Gabe.

He was sweaty, smeared with dirt, scraped, his eyes red and watering, his lips chapped and flaking, golden hair greasy. And yet he'd never looked more like a Greek god.

"Take her down," Ridley said to him.

He gave a weary half-nod. She handed him the shield. Grabbed his belt to slide the sword back into its loop.

Gabe looked at Nas.

"Hug onto me as tight as you can."

Her eyes filled with glassy awe. She stepped into him, wrapped her arms around his lean torso, and pressed her head against his chest. He gripped his hands around her back and shot away.

Insane, this is so surreal I—

Sandro could only stare after the shrinking shapes in the sky. Then he looked at Ridley. Beneath the respirator shield, his face had gone utterly slack.

"It's going to erupt," he said in a flat voice.

She grabbed his collar, knocking off his gas monitor. It didn't matter now.

"We're going!"

She nearly hurled him down the slope in order to snap him out of his stupor—but then she looked back.

Rising above the rim, glimmering in the darkness, was the colossal figure of Athena. She was looking down into the crater, her quicksilver spear and shield raised.

Oh SHIT.

Ridley turned and hurtled down the mountain.

She and Sandro slid and stumbled, fell and rolled and scampered back to their feet. They leapt past bursting vents. Felt the ground beneath them heaving and rumbling.

He hollered once into the radio to alert the INGV of their sprint-evacuation.

How was it that Gabe and Nas were already clear? They asked.

Explain later.

The pressure in the operations room was so intense that Lucilla thought every person in it might burst from it.

On one screen, the thermal imaging flared.

"The southern flank is pressurizing!" said Lara.

"Infrasound spike at Voragine," said Enrico.

On another screen, they could see columns of ash pulsing from the crater.

"It's happening," said Lucilla under her breath. "Compound eruption."

Ciro cued the radio. "VT-3, there's a fissure opening on the southern flank. Avoid the ridge! You need to find another way down."

For a moment, there was no response. Then Sandro's voice came over the comms, out of breath.

"*Copy!*"

Lt. Col. Morelli's face had turned to stone.

Lasch was rubbing his forehead, unable to look at the screens of doom.

Booker felt like he might bite through his own jaw.

"Take the drone back up," said Lucilla. "Find them on the slopes."

The drone tech nodded and went to work.

. . .

Ridley and Sandro hurtled downward. The mountain beneath them was swelling, its seams beginning to burst.

Ash was falling over them like a mist. They could just make out their vehicle, still hundreds of feet away.

Then they heard it—a shot like a cannon.

BOOM

Ridley knew she shouldn't, but she slowed down and glanced over her shoulder.

At the peak of the mountain, a geyser of liquid fire erupted into the sky.

Hundreds of meters high. A blazing cascade against the darkness.

Sandro looked up to the summit.

"Lava bombs!" he yelled.

Then she saw them—glowing blobs spewing from the crater, raining down on the slopes.

Oh, shit.

They ran for their lives.

It was on the thermal feed that the INGV first saw it.

The thin fissure on the southern flank had ripped open.

A flood of red and orange burst across the screen.

It was as if the mountain had unzipped itself, and hell was streaming out.

Lucilla grabbed the radio.

"VT-3! If you're above twenty-two hundred meters, do not move down!"

Sandro's radio crackled just above the roar of the mountain.

"Move lateral! The flank opened!"

He grabbed Ridley's arm and jolted to a stop. Checked his altimeter.

"Twenty-three hundred meters!" he called back.

"Copy. The fissure is erupting—you need to move east! To your right!"

"Copy!"

Ridley didn't need to hear it again. She began to sprint, Sandro close behind her.

The ground crunched and slid beneath. Their lungs burned. Ash covered their face shields as they tried to paw it away.

Lava bombs the size of basketballs were crashing around them—fragments rolling downhill—

One the size of a car slammed into the ground between them, missing Sandro by only feet.

He shouted, skidded, and slipped down into an old channel of basalt.

"Sandro!"

Ridley turned back. She could hardly see. It was like being in a gray snowstorm inside of an oven.

"I'm okay!" he yelled, clambering to his feet.

But then a deep, ferocious ripping sound tore through their eardrums. Seconds later, a pressure wave slammed into them, knocking both to the ground.

Ridley's teeth rattled. She could taste blood.

"Fuck!"

She could hear Sandro bellow.

They climbed back to their feet.

And ran.

"I'm ordering the ambulances to evacuate," said Lt. Col. Morelli, dialing on his mobile.

Booker flinched, but there was nothing more he could ask.

The paramedics couldn't be expected to stay there as the full hellish power of a volcano raced toward them.

They couldn't be expected to wait for two people who may never get off the mountain.

He watched the lieutenant colonel speak gravely into the phone. Then the Italian's expression lifted in surprise.

IN ITALIAN: *"You have them? Who?"*

Lt. Col. Morelli looked at Lasch and Booker.

"They have two of yours. The man needs a hospital. They're taking him to the closest one that's open now."

Booker blew out a breath of relief, but the rest of him was a Gordian knot of tension.

"I'll take the address," said Lasch, nearly melting with relief.

His agent and his charge were alive, nearing safety. His job here was done.

Booker looked back at the screens.

His was not.

Ridley and Sandro barreled out of the thickest part of the ash cloud, and realized they had been sloping downward as well as sideways.

They scanned frantically for the car.

There is no way to outrun this volcano on foot.

IN ITALIAN: *"Yes!"* shouted Sandro, pointing. *"There it is!"*

She couldn't even see it at first, but galloped after him, careening down the slope.

Two hundred feet...

Something punched her in the back.

She didn't slow, but in only seconds, realized that the scorch she was feeling was her bag.

Ridley stumbled, ripping and shucking it off—

A glob of lava, half hardened, half rippling like an ember, had just ignited the cloth.

She bolted.

One hundred feet...

Sandro reached it first, going so fast he nearly slammed into the side of the Land Rover. He swiped the layer of ash from the windshield, tore off his backpack, and leapt behind the wheel, desperately reciting prayers in Italian.

Ridley jumped into the passenger seat as he snapped out the key and turned the ignition...

It sputtered—

Sandro howled like a man on the rim of madness.

He turned the key again—

And the engine growled to life.

As he threw the SUV into gear, Ridley looked up the mountain.

The wind had parted the ash cloud, and for a moment, she could see the summit.

Lava was spouting to the sky, a jet of molten orange that would have toppled the highest building in the world. The ash cloud swept around it like a glowing cyclone. Streams of lava flowed down the slopes of Mount Etna.

The plume far above it, though, was ink-black.

And in it, she could see jagged white flashes crackling to life.

Volcanic lightning.

The ash particles were colliding so violently, and the turbulence was creating so much speed that it sparked, like electrical veins pulsing in the sky.

That, or...

It was two seconds. Only two seconds.

Ridley saw something she would never forget. She would run her mind over it later a thousand times, as if trying to smooth a jagged stone.

There, against the darkness and the chaos, was a fractal pillar of light.

Moving.

A spear—

Lightning bolts exploded, jagged and blinding, so violent it seemed as if they were being hurled from above by a god—

Down into the crater.

Something flashed through the murky ash—

The same way Gabe had sped through the sky with his winged sandals.

Athena's words echoed through her head:

"THAT IS FOR ME AND MY FAMILY"

The Land Rover spun out of the gravel as Sandro yanked the wheel and stomped on the gas.

It was time to outrun an erupting volcano.

CHAPTER SIXTY-ONE

CATANIA, SICILY

Sandro Leoni would never win F1, but no one had ever driven a more perfect race than he did that day.

The Rover careened through the gravel, skidding over steppes of loose rock, speeding down old hardened lava flows, and hurtling over plateaus.

The pyroclastic flow was now unleashed behind them, a searing avalanche of hot ash and rock tearing down the slopes.

The flank eruption had ripped a gash in the side of the mountain. Geysers of lava spewed from the jagged wound, bleeding toward the city below.

Sandro raced wide of it—

To a thousand meters....

To five hundred...

To a hundred...

They hit the city limit as a veil of ash swept behind them.

He did not stop. He did not slow until they had reached the

edge of the evacuation zone, until the cloud of gray streamed and slowed behind them.

Ridley tore off her respirator mask and gasped for clean air.

Sandro radioed back to the operations room. He could hear the cheering over the line. Even the buttoned-up Lucilla Marchio sounded like she was melting in relief.

It only lasted a moment.

The violence of this eruption of the earth only miles away from their office had every one of the INGV staff at the very edge of their nerves. It was the volcanic event of a century. Only a handful of volcanologists in history would have ever seen anything like it.

The Protezione Civile had orchestrated an evacuation that they never thought they'd actually have to execute. The towns that lay in the shadow of the mountain had become ghostly.

A lightning storm raged in the blackened clouds above Etna. The lava poured down it in snaking trails of light.

Over the radio, Ridley asked where Nas and Gabe were.

Ciro told them, *"Ospedale Cannizzaro."*

"Is Director Douglas there?" she said into the radio.

Seconds later, that booming rich voice came over the radio.

"I'm here."

"Sir...we're okay. I'm okay."

She could almost hear him smile through the line.

"What I've been waitin' to hear. But you get yourself to that hospital right now."

"Is Director Lasch there?"

"He's already gone to the hospital. I'll meet you there."

"Copy that."

She set her head back against the seat and let out an exhausted sigh. Then she looked to her guide and companion.

"Sandro," she said.

"Yeah."

He kept his eyes on the road, but she knew that look well enough even in profile.

Shell shock.

PTSD.

Stunned disbelief—what you thought you understood about the world being blown to pieces.

"I know you saw things you didn't think could be seen," she said to him. "*Not real. Delusions. Hallucinations.* Whatever you're gonna be saying to yourself for the next few months. Go easy on yourself."

He stared straight ahead for a moment, then said, "Maybe it was the fumes."

She gave him a weary, lopsided grin.

"Yeah. I know that feeling.

Thirty minutes later, Ridley and Sandro staggered into the hospital.

The lobby was full and most of it was coughing. Patients with glassy red eyes were wheezing and clutching at their chests. Inhaling ash from a volcano was a different beast than catching a mouthful at a bonfire.

Despite the pain shrieking in her ribs and the general sense of her lungs being hollowed out, Ridley's only interest was in finding her boss.

And getting to see Nas and Gabe.

She spotted Booker's linebacker frame posted by the door of the care units. He was on his phone, but the moment his eyes landed on Ridley, he dismissed the caller at the other end and hung up.

He parted the crowd as he walked to meet them, and pulled Ridley into a bear hug.

It startled her. She winced at the pain in her ribs but didn't pull back.

Booker never tried to be a father figure to any of his operatives. While he had a fondness for some more than others, it was not his way to show any distinct affection, nevertheless an actual *hug*.

But today, with Ridley Samaras, he had never been so relieved to see one of them alive. The bottom of his stomach had dropped out when that volcano erupted.

"You *crazy*..." he muttered as he squeezed her into his embrace and felt her hug him back. "You..."

He pulled back to look at her. The dark hair at her temples was shot through with ash. The respirator had left red marks on her face. In those amber-brown eyes was a near-metaphysical exhaustion.

"Are they okay?" she asked.

He nodded. "Lasch and his team are back there. Do you need medical?"

"No." She glanced back at Sandro. "Can we give this Italian warrior a medal?"

Booker looked at the young volcanologist, whose face was stuck on 'stun mode.'

"You," said the CIA director, extending his hand. "You have the gratitude of the United States of America. I can hardly believe what you did today, young man. Thank you."

Sandro shook his hand, nodding.

"I...have some questions?"

Booker gave him a sober, sympathetic look. "Before we leave Sicily, we'll talk. I promise." Then he turned to Ridley and spoke in a low tone. "Where are the items?"

"With Gabe. Nas has one." She pulled off her neck gaiter, starting to feel claustrophobic. "Let's go back."

"I'll stay here," said Sandro. "I just need some water."

Back in the unit, Ridley and Booker found Gabe lying on a patient bed, looking terribly out of place in a faded hospital gown. A nurse was adding a solution to his IV bag.

Nas sat nearby wearing her own shabby gown.

That woman would not have stayed in her own bed for all the doctor's orders in this hospital.

When she saw Ridley, her expression flooded with tears. She leapt up and threw her arms around the operative.

"Oh, my God—oh, my God...I cannot believe it..."

Ridley tried to hide her wince as she hugged back.

"It was Sandro," she said as they pulled apart. "I never would have gotten off that mountain."

She looked at Gabe. Though his arms, legs, and neck were smeared with ash, his face had been wiped mostly clean. Those Paul Newman blue eyes were rimmed with red but seemed brighter than ever. Even his hair somehow shone golden under the dusting of gray.

"They gave you chapstick?" said Ridley with a grin.

"Nurses wanted me pucker-ready, for some reason," he replied in a cracked voice.

"Injuries?"

"Just what you can see," he said, holding up his hands and wagging his feet.

His wrists and ankles had been rubbed raw by the bindings. His foot had been bandaged.

The nurse spoke up in a thick Italian accent. "And severe dehydration."

"Would you give us a minute?" Gabe asked her.

She agreed, and stepped out to other duties.

"So," he said in a low voice when she'd pulled the curtain shut, "what...what happened up there at the end?"

"Did you stop Typhon?" asked Nas. "They say the mountain is still erupting."

"*I* couldn't stop shit," said Ridley, "but I took out one of the gorgons. The hyper vicious one. And Athena seemed to appreciate that."

She glanced at Nas.

The memory of that goddess reverberated in her head again.

"YOU WILL HAVE ONE THING...TELL ME WHAT..."

Making a request of a giant pillar of fragmented light that seemed to talk inside of her head wasn't quite a sure bet.

"Destroy the ayatollahs. Free their captives."

She couldn't tell Nas. She couldn't get her hopes up—these wild, supernatural requests.

Who grants that?

"She said her 'family' would deal with it," said Ridley.

"Her *family*," repeated Booker.

Ridley hesitated, then said, "I saw them. On top of the mountain, as we were escaping."

She could feel the intensity of each of them—staring at her, their breath tightening.

"Yeah, I saw them. I think those thunderbolts...that Titan is never getting out. Olympus wins again."

"But the eruption—" started Nas.

Booker spoke. "Mount Etna erupts all the time. It doesn't mean *escape*, just a whole lotta effort. This was the biggest in a century."

Gabe shook his head like it was all a fever dream and they were the mad ones.

"They could evacuate though, right?" asked Nas.

"Thanks to some very wise people in that INGV office," said Booker. "They saw it comin' early."

Ridley looked at Nas. “Where’s the helmet?”

“What? Oh—it’s with the other pieces. We couldn’t keep them in here. Mr. Lasch took them.”

Booker looked at Ridley. He pulled out his phone, heavy brow furrowing as he stepped outside the curtain.

The State Department has no use for those items...

Still, Ridley felt something prickling in her gut.

“They need to check you out,” said Nas, looking at her with concern. “And Sandro—where is he?”

“He needed some water,” said Ridley. “I’ve got no medical emergency.”

With every breath she felt a stab in her ribs, though. All over her body she began to feel stinging. She looked down and realized her clothes were ripped and bloody in half a dozen places.

Just a flesh wound.

She turned to Gabe. “What did you tell Lasch all those things were? Must have thought they were kinda weird...?”

It was only a flicker, but she saw it there—unmistakable—in those tropical blue eyes.

He’s about to lie to me.

“Just a bunch of old archaeology pieces. Ancient Greece stuff,” he said.

Why is he lying to me?!

“Yeah? Where’s he takin’ em? Kinda important to me, you know.”

He put up his hands. “I don’t know. I wasn’t worried about it. Just call him. We’re on the same side. I didn’t almost die for all this for nothing.”

Nas frowned, speaking quietly to Ridley. “Why are you worried?”

“We’re not on the same team,” she muttered. “We had different objectives.”

He got his. Where the hell is mine?

She stepped out looking for Booker, and found him with a heavy scowl, punching out a text on his phone.

"He's unavailable! Says the assistant. He'll get back to me. Says the assistant."

She gritted her teeth for a moment before saying, "I think Gabe is lying to me."

He looked up in alarm. "Why? About what?"

"About giving the items to Lasch. I'm tryin' to...I don't know."

An older man in a wheelchair parked nearby was watching something on his tablet. Ridley glanced at it to see a live news feed of Mount Etna.

The snaking river of lava.

Dark clouds bloomed from the summit and fire was still sloshing out of the crater.

But there was no more lightning.

Did they do it?

As she pulled out her own phone, still somehow intact in its industrial case, Ridley heard Athena's voice in her head again.

YOU WILL HAVE ONE THING...TELL ME WHAT

She dialed Ted back at the Osprey office.

It was time to find out about Special Agent Gabe Tolkin.

CHAPTER SIXTY-TWO

CATANIA, SICILY

Mount Etna would erupt for the next fourteen hours, though with every passing hour, its fury diminished.

The pyroclastic flow blew through the fringes of the nearest towns, and lava oozed down into some of the streets at the foot of the volcano.

Yet the cataclysmic event that had been brewing somehow never materialized. Amidst public grumbling, the INGV would maintain that every signal off the mountain had warranted the evacuations.

Nas was discharged from the hospital within hours. She was met by two new agents from the State Department who escorted her back to the hotel.

Gabe would be kept overnight for observation.

Ridley found Sandro in the lobby, guzzling water and chomping through his second bag of peanut butter pretzels.

She went up to him, cupped the back of his head, and looked into his shell-shocked eyes.

IN ITALIAN: *"You saved my life."*

He gave a nervy laugh.

IN ITALIAN: *"But now I'm crazy,"* he said.

IN ITALIAN: *"You're only crazy because you walked up to the crater of a volcano that was about to erupt. Everything you saw..."* she leaned close to whisper, *"we all saw."*

She kissed him on both cheeks, and left.

Booker and Ridley climbed into a car sent by the consulate. They were headed back to the hotel when he finally got the call he'd be waiting for.

"Joe," he answered in a clipped voice.

"What can I do for you, Douglas?" came Lasch's voice through the other end.

"You took some items from the hospital, I understand."

"Yeah, some ancient collectibles?"

"Seems like some mistake was made," said Booker. "Those are ours."

"Yours?" A beat. "Agent Tolkin sent those with us. They're already on their way back to D.C. Tolkin said that Secretary Rhodes specifically requested them."

Booker exchanged a stunned look with Ridley.

"*Rhodes* requested this?"

"I wasn't aware of any conflict of interest there. You can take it up with him."

They hung up.

"What the hell is going on," said Booker darkly.

Gabe said he didn't know where they were going.

He lied.

He's sending them to the Secretary of State.

. . .

When they reached the hotel, Booker took off to his room in a driven fury. He was rolling up his sleeves for a jurisdictional fight.

God help the State Department.

Ridley went back to her room and showered. The water circling the drain grew thick with gray sludge. Every cut and scrape stung in the hot streams from the showerhead. Still, she thought no shower had ever felt so good.

Her mind was a gyroscope—

The roar of that mountain—

The seething lava, like looking at the sun—

A GODDAMN GODDESS?

Her offer—

The bolts of lightning ripping through dark clouds—

Sandro's scream as he tried to start the car—

Fear thudding through her ribcage—

Gabe's eyes as he lied to her.

It drained the last of her reserves.

Ridley crashed into bed before the sun had even set over the smoking island.

She woke in a blinding pool of light that poured in through the window. She breathed in, slow and bleary, but then the searing pain in her ribs yanked her fully awake.

Rolling over, she reached for her cell phone charging on the side table. The screen was cluttered with news notifications.

ISLAMIC REPUBLIC HAS FALLEN

AYATOLLAHS DEAD

SERIES OF EXPLOSIONS ROCK MULTIPLE PRISONS

Ridley shot up in bed.

She ran barefoot to Nas' room.

The Iranian woman opened the door—she was on the phone, rattling off in Farsi, half-crying, half-howling with excitement.

Within a few seconds, she hung up and threw her arms around Ridley.

"They're gone! They're dead! Those killers—the whole thing, just overnight! My country..."

Ridley had never heard someone sob so hard with joy. Nas pulled back and wiped her cheeks, starting to laugh.

"And they're free! *My people!*"

"What happened?!"

"A massive earthquake last night, but it was like someone ripped open the earth to swallow evil. There's a death toll, but it killed the Supreme Leader and most of the Assembly of Experts and half of the *IRGC senior command!* Thousands of the bases of the Basij...the killers are dead, and the rest—something terrified the rest of them so badly that they've defected. They're done."

She ran to turn on the television. The news was streaming endless footage from Tehran. The streets were flooded with people celebrating, shouting, hugging, leaping atop cars and waving the flag of the Lion and the Sun.

Another sob burst from Nas as she covered her face.

"My father is free."

A surge of tears flooded through Ridley. It came up so fast that she had to shake her head clear.

"He's going to my brother's house—they will call me. And Mehrab Jalali is free! He walked into his mother's house this morning, starving and beaten and *alive! And Elnaz*—my beloved friend!

"But it's crazy—" said Nas, whipping around. "Ten of the prisons in Iran—they all hold political prisoners—they were bombed or struck with something last night. All the countries deny doing it—they don't know, but all the prisoners have escaped. They're free."

Ridley looked to the television. She crossed her arms to try to keep in the tide of emotions.

I killed a gorgon. She killed the ayatollahs.

The people of Iran had shed enough blood and pain to have earned this moment themselves. Whatever happened, they would have to take it from here.

Nas looked at Ridley, and began to weep.

"I can go home."

Ridley's throat became thick with tears.

"You can go home," she said.

CHAPTER SIXTY-THREE

CATANIA, SICILY

THE STATE DEPARTMENT became a whirlwind in this new global upheaval. The United States and Israel denied having played any part in the strikes on the prisons in Iran, but outrage flared from other Middle Eastern states, worried that they'd be next.

Booker knew that Rhodes would now be impossible to reach, even for a CIA division director. He'd have to confront the Secretary in person.

He booked first class tickets home for himself and Ridley that afternoon.

She was back in her hotel room packing an overnight bag when she got a call from Ted back in the Osprey office.

"You are now the biggest psycho in this little division of ours," he said to her. "We're gonna make you a plaque. A medal. A trophy."

She chuckled. "No names on that one."

"No names. Policy."

"You have somethin'?"

"You really asked me to hack up a personnel file of a State Department employee," he said. "Number one: you have to calm down. Number two: I started with the non-classified, non-flammable path. Social medias and financials."

"Okay..."

"There isn't much here, but then—since I don't even know what I'm really looking for—maybe it's all just going over my head."

"Did you—"

"*But.* There's just one thing here that doesn't fit. Agent Tolkin's been on assignment with you the whole time, right?"

"Yeah. We teamed up in D.C."

"Well, two days into your mission, he won a payout on a bet down at Keeneland—the race track in Kentucky? Horse racing. But it looks from his social media that he's never even been to a horse race before. He isn't really into sports at all."

She frowned. "So he was just gambling on his phone?"

"No. It *was* digital, but it was from a different phone, another line registered to him."

"I'm not reading you, Ted. Get there faster."

"Okay, okay. One of the horses in that race belongs to Neal Rhodes. Is that coincidence enough for you?"

"No coincidences," she said, yanking her bag closed. "Anything more?"

"No, but it's only been eighteen hours since you asked. Give me another day, yeah?"

"What about Rhodes?"

Ted paused.

"What *about* him?" he asked.

"What about looking into Rhodes?"

"Ridley...he's the Secretary of State. I'm not hacking into his stuff."

“Then find me someone who will,” she said. “Get me one of the outside guys, the muckrakers who love all that dark web stuff.”

She could hear him sigh on the other end, and pictured him shaking his sandy red hair.

“I’ll run it through the gutter.”

“Thanks, Ted. Owe you.”

Ridley hung up with him and dialed Gabe—no answer.

She called the hospital—he’d been discharged hours ago.

She knocked at his hotel room down the hall—no answer.

She rang down to the front desk—he’d checked out.

They’d been had.

ALEXANDRIA, VIRGINIA

Late summer on the Potomac was hot, hazy, and run through with tourists.

All the same, Ridley was happy to be back home. Moreso than usual, for some reason.

She picked up Maddie at her neighbor’s apartment. The little mutt nearly wiggled out of her skin, then went to fetch her favorite lamb toy and came running back with pride.

“You look even worse than the last time I saw you,” said Ana, eyeing the scrapes below the line of Ridley’s shorts, and the stiffness of her torso. “Tough translations?”

She winked.

If anyone knows you’re full of shit, Samaras, she *knows.*

“You wouldn’t believe it,” said Ridley, picking up Maddie who tried to wrestle up to her face with licks.

“She got gelato this time!” said Ana.

"Furry with fine taste, this one."

"I know you like to decompress on your own, but come on over for dinner this week. I'll make Italian."

Ridley had to suppress a laugh. "Let me buy the groceries, at least—and don't argue with that!"

She went back to her place, flopped on the couch, and fell asleep that afternoon watching reruns of *The Office*. Maddie snuggled onto her shoulder and dozed, head tucked beneath Ridley's chin.

The human's dreams were filled with smoke and fire and a shrieking fanged face from hell.

The next day Ridley was determined to be normal. Her after-action report wasn't due for another week anyhow.

She slept late and made herself shakshuka for breakfast. She rented a kayak and took Maddie out on the river. The little dog loved to stand at alert on the bow as if declaring her vessel to the world.

Ridley stopped by her favorite bar for a game of darts, where it was all hearty greetings and trash talk with the locals.

One guy asked for her number. She was not up for it. Later, a girl asked for her number. She wasn't up for that, either. Decompressing took its own time, and every mission required something different afterward.

That night, she sat on her couch watching the news, absent-mindedly stroking Maddie who was snuggled against her leg.

The scenes of Tehran were still jubilant. It was as though a dam of fear and suffering had burst through into a land of milk and honey and some chaos. It didn't matter that there were buildings to repair from the earthquake or that factions had begun to squabble for power or that getting fresh water was a struggle...they had fought for this moment for so long, and now their bloodied dreams had come true.

Somewhere across the world, Nas would be watching this, her heart brimming over.

Ridley saw grandmothers weeping with joy. She watched men hoist others onto their shoulders, holding flags aloft. She watched young women burning their hijabs and dancing in the streets. She heard singing.

Somewhere in there, in all of the wild celebrations, was Jimmy.

Free.

Ridley began to cry.

CHAPTER SIXTY-FOUR

ALEXANDRIA, VIRGINIA

The next day, Ridley's mind veered back to Sicily.

Gabe had lied to cover up some side gig with Rhodes, stealing the CIA's assets to pass them through the State Department.

Why does Rhodes want them?

She couldn't get it out of her head as she hauled her way through muscle-ups and pumped out clean and jerks at her Crossfit session. She couldn't get it out of her head as she tied a green belt over her gi that evening and hurled her drilling partners to the mat with furious *osoto garis.*

She was so consumed with the question that she burned the pancakes she was making that night. Maddie took care of the damaged goods.

Late that night, Ridley's wild wonderings snagged on something.

She got out her burner laptop. She ran the retinal scan and

punched in the access codes, then pulled up her file on Andreas Colby.

The billionaire's life was hardly shadowy. He wasn't a fame hound, but he never shied from a camera. He gave the occasional interview to fairly boring business outlets, and even weighed in every now and then on politics.

Most tellingly, he had not been involved in the Marc Pearson scandal, the revelations of the sex trafficking of minors that had destroyed so many businessmen and celebrities not long ago. Countries around the world opened investigations, arrested their own royal family members, and prosecuted their political leaders.

Except for the United States, where the gatekeepers and enforcers of the law saw their duty more as consiglieres of a mafia, tasked with "fixing" the problem rather than investigating it. Politicians at the very highest levels skated right through the most horrifying public evidence of their guilt. Yet Colby had never been accused of anything.

Ridley couldn't have imagined that when she unleashed it all into the public eye, but there was nothing else she could do.

Sometimes, she wished she could tell another soul that that had been her doing, but what would be the point? She couldn't tell another soul about *any* of her work. It was just one of those lonely jobs where you save the world and nobody ever knows.

She had combed through everything of Colby's in the last year. She knew his kids' birthdays and what he liked to eat at each of the Michelin-starred restaurants he frequented.

Why had it taken her so long to recall that—among his myriad of hobbies—he was into horse racing?

She had just begun sifting through her digital file collection when she got an encrypted message from Ted's outsourced hacker.

She accepted an invite link and he dialed her up on a blacked-out video call.

"You wanted something financial," said the hacker. "Only one thing so far. There are rumors about his horses. That he's been working with some other owners to rig races. So I went down that rabbit hole. He's definitely doing it. Whole cabal thing they've got goin'."

"In a way that's illegal?"

"You get kicked outta racing for it."

She dropped her head in relief.

Got him.

"I'll send you the files," said the hacker, "and the bill."

They hung up.

Ridley phoned Booker. He picked up.

"Rid," came that basso voice. "This is late."

She figured he was probably in his favorite leather chair reading some ancient history book, sipping on a bourbon.

"Gotta get you somethin' other than Bulleit, sir."

He kept a bottle of it in his office, though she'd never seen him drink it there and never so much as smelled it on his breath.

"Does me fine. What's goin' on?"

"Have you gotten to Rhodes?" she asked.

"Not with all that's happening in the Middle East right now...and *about* that—you know anything?"

She laughed. "I wasn't anywhere near it."

"No, but, uh...the INGV sent up a drone that day, you know that? Followed you part way up the mountain. Had to pull back again, but I thought there might be somethin' else that would happen at that crater. I had Ted hack into the stream to get their footage. Not much visibility up there and it wouldn't look like anything to someone who wasn't lookin' for it, but to me, it looked an awful lot like you found yourself talkin' to something. Somethin' made of light."

Ridley didn't reply for a moment.

"I gotta sort my thoughts out, sir. I'll be sure to have it all in my report. But I was calling about something else. Rhodes is dirty."

"What?"

"Not politically—not that I know of—but he's running some kinda gambling race-fixing racket."

"What does this have to do with anything?" he said, almost irritated. "You want me to blackmail the Secretary of State?"

"No, sir. I mean, probably not, unless you want to. But in my opinion, we're never getting those artifacts back."

"I don't accept that. What are you talking about."

"He's Order of Raphael."

Even before running through Neal Rhodes' entire stable and every race his horses had run in, she was certain.

Andreas Colby had been at seven of them.

Ridley couldn't find any background connection for the two of them. Colby and Rhodes had gone to schools that were hundreds of miles apart. They had different hobbies and played different sports when they were growing up. They didn't seem to have any friends or organizations in common.

But Colby was always there when Rhodes' horses won.

Rhodes had never been a collector of any antiques or ancient weaponry, but he was willing to cheat the CIA to get a hold of a previously unknown set of artifacts belonging to a guy that nobody believed was real.

It was just the kind of thing that the Order of Raphael lived for.

For an eight-hundred-year-old organization, they were

astonishing at keeping secrets—even the secret of their very existence.

They were also good at finding members, both true believers bent on gaining righteous power, and assets who were devoted to just the "power network" part.

It seemed that they had eyes and ears around the world.

And they were very into supernatural relics.

Billionaire Colby, and now the Secretary of State of the United States of America, Neal Rhodes.

She was certain.

CHAPTER SIXTY-FIVE

LEXINGTON, KENTUCKY

THE MOMENT she walked out of the Louisville Airport, Ridley felt like she'd made a terrible mistake.

The late afternoon air wrapped her up like a hot soaking blanket. Heat, she liked. Cold, she liked. Humidity made her want to climb out of her own skin. She wore a pair of sand-colored shorts, but the periwinkle button-down of thin cotton gauze may have been too much.

She gnashed her teeth at the air, slid on her shades, and went to find her KIA rental.

She hadn't told Booker where she was going or why, but what was there to lose now? Secretary Rhodes had taken just a couple days off since working like a madman over the last week, trying to soothe the fragility or Iran and work with partners in the Middle East to ensure stability. So of course, he went back to his old Kentucky home to recharge.

And that's where Ridley would find him.

The Secretary of State was the highest ranking member of the cabinet. He was fourth in line to succeed the presidency. One could not simply walk into his office in Washington, D.C. and confront him about being a member of the most influential secret society in the world.

Freemasons and Templars were just kids on a playground compared to Raphaels.

She drove east, passing Bourbon Trail party vans along the highway. She reminded herself to get a bottle of classic Booker's *for* Booker before she left.

So what if Rhodes actually confesses to being in the Order, Samaras? What then? As if that changes anything or gets you anywhere?

Tom Waits yowled over the radio. The smell of the distilleries—like funky bread dough—wafted over the roads.

Because you're sick of chasing shadows and names. Stand there and look him in the face, flesh and blood.

Before long, she could see rolling green fields sprawl in every direction. Dark fencing stretched for miles, hemming in pastures and grand mansions. Horses roamed and grazed and galloped in the distance.

You're just announcing yourself as an enemy...stupid—idiot move...

Her thoughts battled each other until she pulled off the main stretch.

The light was slanting now across the bluegrass pastures. She slowed the car as she approached an impossibly long driveway.

A stately plaque on one of the pillars said, "ARIEL FARMS Est. 1881"

There were cameras atop the grand stone wall, but the gate itself was open.

It felt almost too inviting, but Ridley knew the farm hosted regular tours throughout the week. The entrance wouldn't be Fort Knox. The residence would be.

She pulled down the gravel drive. Thick, leafy trees formed an honor guard along each side, casting mangled shadows on the lawn.

It took nearly a minute before she reached the main office, but the small parking lot was empty. She let the KIA idle as she tried to figure out which road through the fields she should take next.

Then she saw a woman two dozen yards off, walking along the pasture toward her. On the other side of the fence, a dark bay horse loped alongside the woman.

Ridley put down her window.

"You're lost or you're late," said the woman in a smoky voice, "or you're breaking the law."

She smiled as she approached, and then Ridley recognized her.

Julie Rhodes.

The wife of the Secretary of State had dark, nearly black hair, pulled back into a casual bun. Despite her barn boots and jeans and white T-shirt streaked with dirt, she looked somehow elegant. It was her full cheekbones, soft blue eyes, and mischievous smile that gave the impression that she'd been sculpted by some Renaissance master. She was in her fifties, with crinkling lines around her eyes and mouth which seemed to add some mystique.

Ridley stepped out of the car.

"I'm from D.C.," she said with a smile half-charming and half-apologetic, "which I guess makes me look lost all the time."

"Ah, one of those. D.C. would find my husband in a salt mine."

Julie unwrapped a peppermint and reached back over the

fence. The gangly horse pranced in excitement as he gobbled it off her palm.

"He's up at the house," said Julie, wiping her hand on her jeans.

"Which way...?"

"If you don't mind the smell, give me a lift?"

"No problem with me," Ridley grinned, climbing back behind the wheel. "Come on then."

Julie stomped her boots off before getting in the passenger side.

"I'm Julie," she said, "but I won't offer you my hand. Farm life. You can put a girl on an island but you can't take it out of her!"

"I understand that—and I'm Ridley."

"*Ridley*. What a pleasure to meet you. Do you ride?"

"On occasion."

"That boy there—" she pointed to the dark bay who was now rollicking by himself in the pasture, "he's eighteen months, just started ground work, breaking him in with a saddle. His name is Salem and he's going to be a *terror* on the track. Sired by The Spartan—his dam is Viennese Waltz. He got his father's stride but his *mother's* ferocious will to win. That's true genetics. Some buyers get so excited about the stud fee—they think the male is the only half that matters."

Ridley chuckled politely. "Some buyers are suckers, then. Am I interrupting plans for you and your husband...?"

"Depends on what you're here to do. Are you bringing him a pen or a sword? Go left here."

Ridley steered left, up a short hill.

"I'm not able to share that, but I shouldn't be long."

"Neal will probably invite you to stay for a drink. He's managed to keep those Kentucky manners despite all his time in Washington. There's a friend joining us later for dinner, but I'm sure you'll be able to say whatever you need to before then."

They wound under a canopy of poplar trees and reached the top of the hill.

There was the house.

A lush lawn and impeccable hedge led straight to a gleaming white home with colonnades, an open porch, and dark green shutters.

They parked in the circle and got out.

"Is this an old place?" asked Ridley.

"Yeah. This one was built in 1883, rebuilt in 1901 after a fire, and then built up again in the '50s. All Neal's family. His security detail stays in the cottage around the side. Come on in."

Julie trotted up the steps. Ridley eyed the place discreetly.

Looks like the damn White House.

She knew there had to be a layer of security here that was completely invisible, able to lock down within seconds.

The wife of the Secretary of the State wouldn't be so nonchalant with a total stranger unless she knew she had an intense level of protection just under the surface.

Hopefully...?

Julie opened the door with a passcode and went inside. Ridley stepped in behind her.

"Rhodey!"

It amused Ridley that this chic-looking woman called her husband by the same name as his drinking buddies from college.

"Oh, I think he wants to grill tonight," said Julie. "He'll be out back. That grill is such shit and he just won't buy another one..."

She led through the front rotunda, through a colonial-style kitchen with sleek appliances, and past a stately dining room.

Julie opened the glass door at the back of the house and stepped down onto a huge brick patio.

There stood Neal Rhodes, grill brush in one hand, grimy towel in the other, his forehead glistening.

"Neal," said Julie, propping one hand on her hip with a grin, "you have a visitor named Ridley. She came from Washington. I'm gonna go wash up, though. You enjoy your chat."

Rhodes squinted through his sweat, holding up both hands as if bewildered.

"Ridley? Okay, hi. I wasn't expectin' you. Have you got some ID? And who did you say you were with?"

"I'm with CIA, sir. I work with Director Douglas."

The blanket friendliness evaporated. "Oh, really? I don't need the ID. No one would claim that and show up here expectin' anything."

He set down the brush and wiped his hands clean.

Not many people *towered* over all of Ridley's five feet and eleven inches, but Neal Rhodes was a big man, nearly six-foot-five.

"I'm 'bout to make dinner here, Ms. Ridley, in my *home*. What is it you want? Other than to collect a package of items I swear to God is the least important thing on my mind right now."

"Oh, I'm here because that's not true."

A beat.

Their eyes locked, and his gentle face hardened.

He spoke slowly. "You have somethin' to declare to me?"

"Yeah, I do. You assigned Agent Tolkin to the Aslanis' protection detail not because of his skills—which actually need some work—but because you'd given him a side mission. Right? You needed to make sure you got your hands on all our discoveries before Booker could safeguard them. You sent him in with an ulterior motive and *guess what*—he fucked up so badly that he lost half his protection assignment!"

She was stunned to find herself trembling with fury.

Rhodes barely cocked his head. "You feel better gettin' that off your chest?"

"No—you're the the goddamn Secretary of State and you belong to a *cult?*"

"Ohh, see this is where you're gettin' wrong," said Rhodes, his voice so gentle that it was dangerous. "I don't belong to a cult."

"No one ever thinks it's a cult when they're in it!"

He chuckled. "No, I mean, really—whatever you think it is —I'm not in it. But if you think you can come here with some political scandal threat or *whatever*, you have fun with your monologue. Political scandals are nothin' anymore, hadn't you noticed? Scandals used to be about revelations, but everything is out in the open all the time now. People get outraged, but that burns out within a few days. And a scandal only works if the person in it feels shame, or pressure from their voters. But no one cares anymore. Let the cycle run for a couple days and the public will be on to somethin' else. I'm not about to lose any actual support for bein' part of *anything*. The president doesn't care. The people don't care." He spread his hands wide. "But I do appreciate your spirit."

Ridley burned.

"I know about the race-fixing," she said.

At that, a storm cloud rippled across his face.

Got you.

His voice went very quiet. "I believe you just blew up your whole career, Ms. Ridley, makin' an accusation like that."

"So *that's* unbearable, being found out as a racing cheat and banned from the sport hurts, but being part of some monstrous cult won't hurt you politically? With all your angel worship and weird-as-shit relic hunting—"

A man's voice cut through.

"Relic hunting?"

Ridley turned to see Andreas Colby standing in the doorway.

CHAPTER SIXTY-SIX

LEXINGTON, KENTUCKY

The billionaire real estate man, the thrice-married patron of the arts, the father of four grown tabloid-material kids, the owner of multiple sports teams—the man that Ridley had been following for what seemed like an age—stepped out onto the patio. He carried a lowball glass of bourbon neat in each hand. His expression was surprisingly friendly.

This is not how I pictured finally meeting this man.

"I guess I know who you are," he said. "And I'm sure you know who I am."

Even at sixty-one, he still looked like a runner. Six feet tall with a diamond jaw, shaved head, and dark, low brows that gave his icy eyes a permanent intensity. Even wearing a trim polo shirt, linen slacks, and boat shoes, he looked industrious. The kind of businessman who never stopped moving.

"Yeah," she said, "I know who you are."

He handed Rhodes one of the glasses.

"So," said the Secretary of State, "Andreas, Ridley."

"You know, I'd hire you," Andreas said to her. "You've actually been fun to watch. You fight pretty hard."

Of course he knows who you are, Samaras.

How did they know she was coming—she hadn't told anyone. How did they know who she was at all?

So much for that ultra-secure heavily encrypted black site laptop, piece of shit.

"I know if we killed you," he continued, "Douglas would have another operative pick up the work. You're probably *my* personal favorite of the division, though. So we let it go this time."

"Bullshit," she said. "You 'let it go' because you took everything we found and think you won."

Rhodes finally tossed aside the towel. He crossed his arms across his chest and suddenly looked like the bouncer you never wanted to cross.

Ridley fought back a surge of discomfort.

You just faced down a titanic volcano and a giant goddess and these guys are making you feel small? Get a grip.

Andreas cocked his head at her. "You don't make much money, do you?"

"Who cares?" she snapped. "I make enough for my hobbies and my dog, and my travel is on the house."

"You speak all these languages. You know all these cultures. You date but never tell a partner the truth. You've got few vices. Little family. Healthy hobbies. Your Navy record is outstanding. Major emotional trauma but that wasn't your fault. And you're braver in a fight than most soldiers."

"I *was* a soldier."

Andreas ignored her. "You think after what happened in Jerusalem that we wouldn't have a file on you?"

"You think you can recruit me just because you know things about my life? Obviously you don't know enough."

Andreas took a sip of his bourbon.

"Oh, you want one?" he asked. "It's George T. Stagg. Or some tequila? I know bourbon's not quite your favorite."

"You're offering *my* George T.?" said Rhodes. "The 2002?"

Andreas gave him a shrug and a squint like it was all okay.

"Actually, yeah," said Ridley. "Would you pour me one of those?"

He looked at her for a few seconds, then chuckled. He put his down on the wooden table and slid it toward her.

Audacity of a billionaire—

She grabbed it and tossed back the entire pour. It burned out through her nostrils.

Rhodes' eyes bulged at how she'd just wasted his precious liquid.

Ridley lifted her chin. "I'm not working for you. I'll never work for you, and all of your minions can go to hell. I'll even schedule their departure date."

"I'm sure you mean that," said Andreas. "If you won't take a job that will put two million dollars into your account every time you go out and risk your life—on a fuckin' *volcano?*—then take this advice. If you see us? Run. You don't think this order lasted eight hundred years across the globe but is gonna be stopped by a half-deaf washout."

Her stomach surged with hot and angry bile. She clapped the glass upside-down on the table.

"You can tell Gabe Tolkin that treachery is the deepest circle of hell. Give him a medal for getting there. Your boss—" she glanced at Rhodes, "really knows how to pick 'em."

Andreas looked genuinely surprised.

"Oh, you think *he's* my boss?" he laughed. "I'm just here to visit a friend. Rhodes isn't a member of the Order."

And...she believed him.

And it sent the ground spinning beneath her.

She tried to not let her confusion show.

"But don't worry, my superior is hearing this," said Andreas.

To hear a man of his stature and success admit that he had a superior...was disorienting. Truthfully, she had no idea how far up the chain of command went or what the structure was like —if it was a hierarchy leading to a pope-type figure or if it was like a hundred ayatollahs working in assembly.

Then she noticed a small camera above the doorframe.

Listening and *watching.*

Andreas pointed at her. "Tell *your* boss to let this one go. The artifacts you dug up? Consider them gone. You've lost. The racing blackmail you're trying to leverage against the Secretary of State? Not if you want to continue at the CIA. Now...you can walk out of here with your life."

He stepped back to free her path to the door.

Time to go, Samaras. Walk out of here before you say something that will get you sniped on the driveway.

As she walked back toward the house, she shot one more glare at Rhodes.

"I'm *never* voting for you."

She stormed into the kitchen, where Julie was assembling a tray of expensive charcuterie. She paused what she was watching on her tablet on the counter.

"Would you like to—" then she noted Ridley's body language. "Oh."

"Thanks for the hospitality," said Ridley.

Julie propped a hand on her hip. She'd cleaned up and changed into a lilac sundress, and looked every inch the country version of a politician's wife.

"Well, nice to meet you, Ridley. I hope you said whatever you needed to say."

"Yep. Have a good night."

Ridley strode through the rest of the house and out the front door.

She climbed into the KIA, knowing the cameras were seeing it all.

You failed—you lost the items forever—

But now they're basically useless.

Waste of time—

But you got face to face with Andreas Colby.

Because he's been tracking you, dumbshit—

Now you have another piece: there's a boss above him.

But you know nothing else!

She steered the KIA out of the front circle. It felt like a failure. It felt like an embarrassment.

How could Rhodes *not* be a member of the Order? It was so *certain*. Could he really not be? Why would they even bother to lie about that?

She had to shake herself from the squalling thoughts.

She hadn't failed all of this. The Titan did *not* escape the depths of the earth to wage a war of total destruction.

Nas was alive. Jimmy was alive. Even Gabe—*traitor*—was alive.

And an entire country was free from the brutal regime that had been brutalizing it.

Move on, Samaras. This one isn't personal.

She turned down the long drive to the entrance and spotted the same dark bay stallion in the pasture.

He was grazing, his tail fluttering in the warm breeze. When Ridley's car approached, he lifted his head.

Salem.

She stomped on the brake.

SALEM. Short for Jerusalem.

"You think after what happened in Jerusalem that we wouldn't

have a file on you?"

Ridley stared at the horse. Julie's words came rushing back.

Salem, son of Spartan—Greek, me—

and Viennese Waltz—Vienna—

Memories of her last mission in Vienna roared at her...the snow, the red flares, the blood on white...

would find him in a salt mine—running through the tunnels of the Wieliczka salt mines in Poland—

you can put a girl on an island—my childhood, Paros—

are you bringing him a sword?—the golden saber of the jinn—

"They might think the male is the only half that matters."

Ridley's jaw went slack.

She jammed the car into park.

Gripped the wheel.

Julie watching a tablet in the kitchen—

Andreas' voice—"don't worry, my superior's hearing this"—

It was not the Secretary of State who commanded the Order of Raphael.

It was his wife.

Ridley sat there as the engine idled.

She locked eyes with the young horse.

A bloody godmother.

She shifted the car into gear and rolled down the gravel drive, under the leafy rows of poplars, past the iron gate.

Julie Rhodes would have to be for another day.

Ridley pulled out onto the long Kentucky road.

ACKNOWLEDGMENTS

To everyone I've thanked in a previous book, you are all here as well.

To Claire, my long-distance, long-traveling, faithful friend. Few people in the world can make me laugh as hard.

To Emily and Breet, my daily copers. Don't know how I'd do it without you. Here's to drinks in Lima.

To Laura, partner-in-some-crimes. I may not be ready to burn down the world, but I'll be your uke.

To Jeff G., from jiu-jitsu to bourbon to being there for anything, you are the best Batman.

To Gina, adventure after adventure with the warmest of holiday celebrations. You are truly a friend for every season.

To Paul A., an unflagging source of support, encouragement, and cheerful creativity.

To Eden, whose generosity and support in all moments has been a blessing. Your resilience and up-for-anything attitude have been rejuvenating.

To Marie and Evan. Thank you for letting me be part of your lives in such a difficult moment. I treasured every visit.

To Jeff Circle, one of the most generous supporters of authors that I know.

To Christine Palmer, whose friendship and knowledge I've been privileged to enjoy over these many years. From a dinner table in Jordan to the (virtual) islands of Greece, thank you for sharing your wisdom, your company, and your family with me.

To Deborah Levison, whose writing has touched me profoundly and whose compassion has been a light out there in the darkness. Because of you, somewhere in Israel there grows a very young tree...

To Paul, the first person I ever reach out to when stuck in a quandary of my own creative making.

To Karen and Sarah for helping me bring all of this to the page.

To all of the readers. Writers live in their heads all day with these characters, in these places, feeling their emotions. It's a marvelous honor to release it all into the world and know that it now comes to life in the minds of other people.

Most importantly, for the women and men of Iran who have fought and sacrificed so much for freedom.

ABOUT THE AUTHOR

Ox Devere grew up in the Boston area. After earning a bachelor's degree in film, she moved to Los Angeles for work. There, she spent years in the film and television industry, developing a love of writing for the screen.

Shortly after the pandemic in 2020, she decided to transition from writing screenplays to writing books. Her debut novel, *Rage of the Jinn*, was published in 2023.

She now lives in the surrounding Boston area, where she collects books and bourbon. She avidly supports FC Barcelona, Manchester City, and any team that Messi is playing on.

www.ingramcontent.com/pod-product-compliance
Lightning Source LLC
LaVergne TN
LVHW091247150826
845673LV00006B/1342

* 9 7 9 8 9 8 9 5 4 2 4 4 4 *